Women sc   Dante
calmly caught   urtled
toward him. H̶e̶ ̶h̶a̶d̶ ̶t̶o̶ ̶t̶a̶k̶e̶ ̶a̶ ̶s̶t̶e̶p̶ backward to
absorb the blow as she landed in his arms, but he
managed easily enough. She weighed no more than
his tourney saddle. It was the color of her garments
that made him frown, the same bloodred color as
the steward's. He had already noticed the odd
groupings of colors in the hall, how all the knights
and their wives wore the same shade of green. It
seemed logical that the steward's wife would follow suit, but why would she be spying from the
gallery?

The girl remained strangely silent even after
he recovered his balance, as if she didn't realize
the danger of her fall and had expected someone
to catch her. Perhaps the fright had robbed her
of speech. The cloud of blond hair and a gauzy
red veil made it impossible to read her expression.
Deep blue eyes flecked with gold were all he could
see of her face. Her wide-eyed gaze reflected surprise and, amazingly, an intense light of curiosity,
as if she found something fascinating about his
face. As if she recognized him.

The sudden knowledge of her identity came without warning, an unexpected and unwelcome revelation. She was not the steward's wife. This was his
victim.

BY ELIZABETH ELLIOTT

The Warlord
Scoundrel
Betrothed
The Dark Knight

THE DARK KNIGHT

Elizabeth Elliott

BANTAM BOOKS
NEW YORK

A Bantam Books Mass Market Original

Copyright © 2012 by Linda Kay Crippes
Excerpt from Book Two copyright © 2012 by Linda Kay Crippes

Published in the United States by Bantam Books, an imprint of The Random House Publishing Group, a division of Random House, Inc., New York.

BANTAM BOOKS and the rooster colophon are registered trademarks of Random House, Inc.

ISBN 978-0-553-57567-5
ebook ISBN 978-0-345-53467-5

This book contains an excerpt from the forthcoming Book Two by Elizabeth Elliott. This excerpt has been set for this edition only and may not reflect the final content of the forthcoming edition.

Cover design: Lynn Andreozzi
Cover illustration: Craig White

Printed in the United States of America

www.bantamdell.com

9 8 7 6 5 4 3 2 1

Bantam Books mass market edition: July 2012

*This book is dedicated to
Saint Gina, My Lady of Perpetual Patience*

*"Thank You" says so little. . . .
In my heart it means so much.*

1

❦

LONDON, 1293

> ### The Magician
>
> *Here lies the start of the journey, both a beginning and an end. The Magician reaches to the heavens for guidance and points toward the paths of greatest potential. From his hand accept the power to shape destiny and the will that manifests great change.*

The Tower of London housed many royal secrets. The chamber above the dungeons held a carefully guarded one.

A narrow shaft of sunlight streamed in through an arrow loop in one wall, creating more shadows than light in the cavernous room. There, in a place few men entered willingly, a man dressed in long, dark robes stood before a row of dusty shelves. Searching for something, he moved into the light. The brightness made his blond hair appear an angelic halo of curls, a disarming contrast to the inky darkness of his robes that shifted and flowed around him like a living thing; at once bloodred, then black, then the deep blue color of midnight. He leaned closer to the cluttered shelves, pushed aside a dried frog and a stack of parchment scrolls to lift a tarnished metal chest.

"The signs are favorable, Sefu," Mordecai told the black cat who sat staring at him from the sun-warmed flagstones. He walked toward a scarred wooden table with the chest cradled in the crook of his arm, polishing the lid with the wide cuff of his sleeve. Beneath thick layers of grime and tarnish, the metal began to gleam the color of bright silver and he caught the faint scent of cedar. His fingers traced intricate etchings of moons and stars. "Fate may be my master, but I shall soon wield the power of destiny. Our visitor will arrive by nightfall. He will prove the truth of my words."

"Your visitor has already arrived."

The soft, lethal voice startled Mordecai and the box clattered onto the table. He glanced first at the cat, then toward the deepest shadows of the room where the figure of a gray-clad man emerged like smoke from mist. There was only one man who could catch him so off guard, so unaware of another's presence.

Recovering his composure, he picked up the box to make sure it wasn't damaged, then greeted his visitor with a genuine smile. "You will forgive my clumsiness, I trust? I did not expect to see a creature of night before the sun set."

The shadowy figure continued toward him. "I am what you have made of me, Mordecai; a creature of nightmares."

There was no arguing with the truth and Mordecai inclined his head to acknowledge as much. Many men would consider this the worst sort of nightmare, coming face-to-face with a man most often referred to simply as "The Assassin." Few lived to tell of such a meeting, but Mordecai was not afraid. If anything, he felt a certain measure of pride in his creation.

The man who stood before him bore little resemblance to the angry, frightened boy who had appeared on his doorstep all those years ago. Even then, Dante Chiavari had claimed only one purpose in life: to destroy the man who had murdered his parents and stolen his birthright.

It was Mordecai who had decided that the best way to serve justice to one monster was to create another.

Dante had proven himself an apt pupil. He had learned how to study his prey, how to memorize every habit and routine to find the weakness that would prove fatal. Moreover, he had honed an expert's knowledge of every substance that could kill or debilitate, along with the precise formulas required to accomplish either goal. But poisons were not the only way to kill. Long hours of practice had turned Dante's natural talent with blades into another deadly skill. He had earned the right to be feared.

Even more effective than Dante's sudden, silent arrival at the Tower was his appearance. The color of his garments blended well with the shadows, but not well enough to conceal their unusual style. He wore the garb of a Muslim warrior, an infidel transported from the Holy Lands to the cold shores of England.

Although it was an odd choice of garments for an Italian nobleman, for a man of his profession it was practical. The loose, flowing djellaba concealed many weapons of his trade, with only the ebony handle of a dagger revealed above the sash around his waist. The length of fabric drawn down from his headdress was fashioned to protect a desert dweller from the sun and sands, but served equally well as a disguise. All Mordecai could see of his face were eyes the color of emeralds; a cold, glittering color that reflected nothing of his soul.

A card appeared in The Assassin's hand, made of stiff parchment and illuminated with a painting that depicted a magician in long robes with one hand reaching toward the heavens and the other resting on a scarred wooden table. The face of the magician was an unmistakable portrait of Mordecai.

"I am curious to know why you have summoned me

to your lair," Dante said, as he tossed the card onto the table. "We were not to meet again until I returned from Venice. Are there new developments?"

Mordecai bit back a hasty retort. He reminded himself that Dante was unlike any other mercenary in King Edward's hire or any apprentice he had trained before or since. He remained silent while Dante drew the scarf away from his face.

There was a rumor at court that only dead men had laid eyes on The Assassin's face. An exaggeration, of course, since there were a few at court who were familiar with the Italian exile named Dante Chiavari, but only a handful of people knew that the exile and The Assassin were one and the same. Even in his guise as an exile, people tended to avoid him. When Dante turned his full attention on someone, there was a dark intensity to his character, an almost visible force that made people nervous. Still, he had long ago mastered the art of disguising his true nature as well as his face. Few would believe how easily he could blend into a crowd when he put his mind to it, especially since most people would say his face was one that they would remember.

Dark stubble covered the line of his jaw while deep brackets framed a hard, unyielding mouth. The profile of his face followed Roman lines more than his Venetian ancestry, and he had the look of a man who never laughed and rarely smiled. The business of death was hardly a laughing matter, so the lack of humor in such a man was no surprise. Judged separately there was nothing remarkable about his features, yet somehow they combined with those unusual green eyes to create a darkly handsome face.

More unsettling was the look in his eyes as his gaze slid away to survey the chamber. A predator was always wary of his surroundings, watching for unexpected dangers, constantly calculating distances and defenses. And like all predators, there were no ghostly shadows lurking in his hooded eyes, no demons of guilt. He was exactly what Mordecai had set out to make all those years ago: a killer without regrets, one who killed simply to survive in his world. What stood before him exceeded all of Mordecai's expectations.

"Everything is in readiness for your trip to Venice?" he ventured.

"Do you really have to ask?" Dante moved to one of the arrow slits cut through the thick walls and glanced out at the sky, then turned to face Mordecai again. He leaned his shoulder against the wall and looked deceptively relaxed now that he did not have to watch his back. "Everything is proceeding as planned and we leave on the morning tide, as I am sure you already know."

"Then nothing has changed to affect your plans in Venice," Mordecai said. "Your petitions will be held until the Council completes an investigation into the murders, but they will revisit the issue soon enough. Once everyone is free of Lorenzo's blackmail, the restoration of your name and birthright will be in everyone's best interests. Still, once you return to England, it will take months for the Doge to recall you from exile, months in which you must be seen in public here to dispel the notion that you have set foot in Venice anytime in the last decade. Have you given thought to what you will do in the months you are waiting for the Council's ruling?"

"I have given thought to what I will not do." Dante folded his arms across his chest, a clear sign that he suspected what was coming and didn't plan to go along with it. "There is nothing the king could offer that would tempt me. I am done with that life."

"That life is not quite done with you." Mordecai held up one hand. "Nay, do not argue just yet. There is good reason that you should listen to what I have to say."

He opened the silver box and removed the cards that lay inside, their backs identical to the one on the table, their faces as unique as the people they represented. The Tarot was an old art, one little known in this country and even less understood. Even his stoic protégé's expression betrayed a touch of curiosity when Mordecai began to arrange the cards facedown on the table.

"King Edward relies upon my skills to reveal the future," Mordecai said at last. "Men who practice dangerous politics know the risks they take and you were the consequence. For many years you have enforced the king's judgments without question or hesitation. Blind justice. You involved yourself in the affairs of men whose politics meant naught to you, whose deaths were nothing more than a means to an end."

"If you are trying to tell me that I have made enemies, I am well aware of the fact," Dante said. "'Tis the reason I have safeguarded my identity all these years, so they would not use my sister or anyone else whose life I value against me."

Mordecai turned over one of the cards, knowing it would be the one that Dante had just returned, the card that showed his own image on its face. "Your fate and the king's have become intertwined over the years. The fate of one woman in particular will affect you both in equal measure, but she is a scale that cannot balance. The weight will fall on either one side or the other."

Dante said nothing for a time, and then he released a deep sigh. "How could one woman be equally important to an assassin and a king?"

"The ties were so faint that I missed them at first." Mordecai traced the edge of one card, then turned it over. The card depicted a soldier stealing seven swords. "Seven of Edward's ten earls hold Marcher lands in Wales, and there is another rebellion brewing there. The taxes and soldiers Edward demands for the fight in France will soon push the native Welsh beyond the limits of their patience. The king must be careful not to alienate his Marcher lords or they will also turn against him and join the Welsh natives rather than fight them, and then he will lose Wales altogether. This I have known all along. What I did not see until recently was your involvement."

Mordecai continued to turn the cards over as he arranged them into a pattern, each stiff parchment card making a soft snapping sound against the table as he released the corner. Soon the colorful pictures covered the table, portraits of knights and queens, common soldiers and maidens, as well as cryptic symbols and sinister-looking creatures. Mordecai knew exactly what each figure represented. He laid down the picture of a long-dead Welsh prince, the last great ruler of Wales and the last line of its royal family. "Llewellyn's heirs prove the most troublesome in their bid to stir a rebellion and regain his crown, although his direct line is now all but extinct. Even his distant relatives have been quiet of late, but now one of Edward's Marcher lords has discovered an heir that Edward overlooked: a girl who is Llewellyn's great-granddaughter through her mother's side.

"Avalene de Forshay is her name," he said, as his finger traced the picture of a blond-haired queen dressed all in red. "As a female she would be irrelevant except that her father is Baron Weston, an English Marcher lord who controls key lands between those lords who remain steadfastly loyal to Edward and those whose loyalty wavers. If she marries another Marcher lord, Baron Weston would prove a powerful English ally to her husband while her Welsh blood will rally the natives to her side. Any son she bears will have the strongest blood claim to the Welsh throne. She is the perfect bride for any of the Marcher families, and the most ambitious one has found her out."

Mordecai flipped over a card that showed a forbidding tower set atop a rocky outcropping. "The Segrave family has vast holdings in Wales, and the king is negotiating for a marriage that will give the Segraves a rich English bride, more English lands, and another English title. Unfortunately, the potential groom is not a man given to sit idle while his future is decided for him. Faulke Segrave wants a break with England and knows a bride with noble Welsh blood is his best weapon to rally the native rebels to his cause. Add to that the benefit of an alliance with Baron Weston, and the balance of power would tip in the Segraves' favor. Faulke will try to seize Weston's daughter and force a marriage. You will make certain that does not happen."

"'Tis obvious Avalene de Forshay poses a problem for King Edward if she weds into the family of any Marcher lord," Dante mused, "but I still do not understand how this affects me."

"That was the mystery." Mordecai's finger tapped one of the cards that showed a mounted knight holding a gold chalice. The face barely showed from beneath the elaborate helmet, but on closer examination the knight's green eyes and profile matched Dante's exactly. "You should not be here, yet to remove you changes the entire outcome. As you say, the effect on the king is obvious. If Faulke Segrave weds Avalene de Forshay, the Segraves will convince the other Marcher lords to side with them against the king and Wales will be lost.

"There are others who could be sent in your stead whose skills would also ensure this marriage never happens. However, only your presence will somehow guarantee Faulke's marriage to an English bride. This matter is as important to the king as your business in Venice, and he will stop at nothing to ensure events play out in his favor."

"I believe you are dangerously close to insulting me," Dante drawled.

Startled, Mordecai looked up to find Dante's eyes had narrowed. "I assure you, there is no insult in this matter."

Dante shook his head. "I said that I wanted nothing more to do with the king's intrigues and I meant it. Yet do you really think I have so little loyalty that I would need some coercion to do this last job for Edward? Especially now that I know all of Wales is at stake?"

Mordecai's brows furrowed. "What are you talking about?"

"I can only assume that Edward intends to make some dire threat to make certain I carry out this assignment. I find it insulting that you or he would think I needed persuasion."

"Ah, yes, I can see how you might misunderstand the situation." Mordecai waved his hand toward Dante, subconsciously dismissing those concerns as he turned his attention again to the cards. It really was amazing how they fell into such similar patterns each time. "Your involvement has nothing to do with persuasion and everything to do with self-preservation. If this girl weds Faulke Segrave or if she dies by the hand of another assassin, you will never leave England alive. That is how your fate is connected."

Dante said nothing for a time, then he cleared his throat. "I should have known there was more to the story. Still, I am curious. How or why should I die if I never meet these people?"

"How or why does the sun rise each morning?" Mordecai snapped, his patience worn thin. "How or why does the sun warm the earth without touching it? Everything in this life affects everything that lives. Everything is connected."

"My apologies," Dante said stiffly.

"Of course, I could be lying," Mordecai taunted, as his lips curved in a sly smile. "Perhaps that is the coercion you suspect, my knowledge that you will believe your life depends upon doing this job just because I tell you it is so."

"You have taught me to lie, but you have never lied to me," Dante said quietly. "If this woman's death will avert a war in Wales and the loss of hundreds or even thousands of lives, then I will make certain she dies. If Faulke Segrave must marry an Englishwoman to put an end to his treason, then I will convince him he must do so. I would do this even if my own life did not depend upon it."

Mordecai rolled his eyes. "You have no need to convince me. I never doubted your loyalty. However, you may want to contain your enthusiasm until you hear the whole of it." He again tapped the picture of the girl. "Avalene de Forshay's death will solve nothing. Quite the contrary, it is imperative she remain alive until you convince Faulke Segrave to choose the English bride. Your own fate does not change until that time. Only then will you have a choice of what to do with the girl."

"A choice?" Dante echoed.

"Faulke Segrave must remain alive," Mordecai said. "The role he will play in convincing the Marcher lords to remain loyal to King Edward is just as critical as the role he would play in convincing them to rebel. Avalene does not have to die either, but she cannot remain in England and she cannot remain marriageable."

"Fine. If she causes no trouble over the matter, I will offer her sanctuary in a convent."

Mordecai nodded, then gazed upward and affected a thoughtful expression. "The king would feel better if she were wed to a man who has no ambitions in England or Wales. A man who lives far from England, one who will have few reasons to allow his wife to return here."

"Absolutely not." Dante held up both of his hands outward, as if pushing away from the idea. "I will take Avalene de Forshay to some faraway convent in the Adriatic, but I will not take an English wife. My wife will be a Venetian, a woman with an old and powerful family whose members will protect my wife and children should something happen to me."

Mordecai smiled. "I thought that would be your reaction."

"An Englishwoman, especially a troublesome one who is half Welsh?" He shook his head. "That's the last woman I would choose for a bride."

"Aye, that is what I told Edward," Mordecai said agreeably. "He even offered to provide a handsome dowry, but I told him you would not be swayed. No matter. Marriage or murder, mistress or nun, the girl is yours to do with as you wish once Segrave is convinced his marriage prospects lie elsewhere. The only condition is that you must make certain she never falls into the hands of anyone who could use her to further their ambitions in Wales."

"You have my word that she will cause no trouble in Wales or anywhere else," Dante murmured, with a bow so slight that it was little more than an arrogant tilt of his head. "If she proves troublesome, she will not live long. If she proves reasonable, she will disappear into a convent where none but I will know of her existence. Regardless of her fate, she will not return to England."

"Excellent." Mordecai rubbed his hands together, as much to warm them against the cold as to congratulate himself on a job well done. Still, he could not resist one last prod. "Be aware that this woman is not what you expect. The weights that balance her fate are like none other where you are concerned. Remember that she is innocent of any treason, as innocent as you once were when the Council exiled you from Venice. Can your conscience bear the burden if you must kill her?"

"Whether she plots treason or is merely the tool to bring about a rebellion, her death or disappearance will avert a war where countless lives will be lost. My conscience can bear that burden." A life was dismissed with the shrug of one shoulder.

Utterly ruthless, Mordecai decided, and utterly perfect for his plans—*the power to shape destiny*. Aye, it was a heady force to control. "On your return from Venice, can you and your men make port in Liverpool instead of London?"

"Aye, 'tis actually closer to the ship's home port at Montague." Dante's gaze grew suspicious as Mordecai struggled to contain his excitement. "Something tells me the girl will not be easy to seize and even less inclined to cooperate. Tell me how I can remove this thorn from Edward's side, and I will make it so."

Mordecai polished the silver box with his sleeve, appearing to give thought to the matter, when in truth he could recite the facts like a tutored child. The situation was a masterpiece, the most fantastic plan of his life, and this man could bring everything within his reach. History would soon rewrite itself.

He rubbed his mouth to hide a smile, then turned away and walked to a set of shelves. He removed a tightly rolled scroll, then returned and placed it on the table. "Soon after your return from Venice a messenger is due to arrive at Coleway Castle near Chester where Avalene lives with her aunt. A knight named Sir Percival will carry a message from Baron Weston that instructs the aunt to turn Avalene over to the knight, who will then escort her back to her father's fortress. 'Tis a ploy. Faulke Segrave will meet Sir Percival and 'abduct' Avalene from the road while her father can pretend he had no part in the Segraves' plot. 'Tis illegal for Baron Weston to contract a marriage for his daughter or for Faulke Segrave to contract his own marriage without the king's approval, but a marriage made by force is still binding. Once done, such marriages take years to annul and the damage will be long done, especially once a child is involved.

"Unfortunately for their plans, you will arrive at Coleway Castle three days before Sir Percival. You will claim to be the messenger of that name and deliver a slightly different version of the message."

Mordecai handed Dante the scroll and waited while he unrolled the parchment and read the contents. At last Dante nodded. "Will three days at Coleway be enough time?"

"Aye, they will not doubt your sincerity. Still, to make certain of your timing, you must leave for Coleway as soon as you make port in Liverpool. Waste no time." Mordecai took the scroll and then picked up a candle, tilting it to drip thick wax onto the center of the roll to seal it shut. "Keep in mind that Segrave will also be watching the road from Wales, and he will begin moving closer to Coleway when he sees the real Sir Percival approach. There are other dangers you will face, but none you cannot overcome."

"What of this disguise as Sir Percival?" he asked.

"Sir Percival came to Wales less than a year ago from Weston's holdings in Normandy. Those who greet you at Coleway have never seen him and will accept you as Sir Percival." Mordecai replaced the candle in its holder, then pressed his thumb into the wax seal. "Do not tarry at Coleway regardless of any decisions you make about the girl. The combined forces of Segrave and her family will work against you if you linger too long near the castle. Return to London where you can both remain safe. Remember, the guise of Sir Percival must be maintained until you leave Coleway."

Mordecai allowed a smile to play across his face. "I have little doubt this ploy will try your patience. You must present Sir Percival as a gallant knight well-versed in chivalry and a favored champion in the tourneys. Perhaps a bit of poetry would be in order as well."

Dante rolled his eyes and sighed. "I shall be the very picture of chivalrous drivel."

"That's the spirit." Mordecai handed the scroll back to Dante and saw him glance at the wax seal. It was an exact replica of the seal made by Baron Weston's signet ring, but Dante did not question how it came to be on the scroll. The parchment disappeared into the gray folds of Dante's djellaba. Satisfied with that part of the plan, Mordecai began to gather up the cards and stack them neatly on the table. "Take heart, Dante. You will have these matters in Venice and Coleway handled in short order and be back in London before you know it."

"What about Faulke Segrave?" Dante asked. "Where and when am I to meet him? Do I greet him as Sir Percival, or as myself?"

"I cannot provide every answer," he said. "Much will depend upon the forces at work when the future becomes the present." Mordecai straightened and placed his hands in his sleeves, an old habit from the Order. He nodded toward the stacked cards. "Choose the card that will guide you on the next steps of your journey."

Dante eyed the cards and made a small sound of impatience. "You expect me to risk my life on a game of chance?"

"Fate will guide your hand. The card you choose now will be the right card for your future, just as the Magician's card was the sign that guided you here."

Dante hesitated for a moment, then he fanned the deck across the table and chose a card seemingly at random. He turned it faceup on the table with an insolent flick of his wrist. "*Now* will you tell me how the steps of my journey will unfold?"

Mordecai ignored the sarcastic demand and instead studied the card's symbols: an aging king holding the staff of life. "This is the first sign. This is always the first sign: the card of deception and the sign of a tyrant. Carry it with you on your journey and its meaning will become clear when the time is right."

"The first sign?" Dante asked, his voice deceptively quiet. "How many times do you intend to play this game? And how am I supposed to decipher its meaning on my own?"

"Our lives are bound by the Fates and we can but interpret the signs as they appear. This is the first sign of many, and only the paths you choose can determine their number." Mordecai closed his eyes and concentrated intently on the image of the tyrant. Although he did not move, his robes eddied around him, moving dust across the floor, the fabric changing and absorbing the light. "Look again at the other side of the card."

Dante turned the card over. Handwritten words now filled the space between the borders, a neat, compact script that had not been there when he chose the card. He was a man whose life depended on rigid self-control, but he could not conceal the look of surprise that flickered like lightning across his face.

Mordecai smiled. "As I said, the meaning will become clear when the time is right. Today, I can tell you nothing more of the matter."

A dangerous light gleamed in Dante's eyes. "Mark my words well, Mordecai. This is the last time. My debt to the king is settled. Indeed, he will soon be in my debt."

"Your mind is so stubbornly set on the matter of debts and repayment that you do not see the truth. There are debts, and then there is balance." Mordecai opened the silver box and carefully placed the cards inside. "We will meet again when you return to London and before you leave again for Venice. I daresay you will have found your balance by that time."

2

VENICE

The Tyrant

Enter Caesar, a ruthless tyrant born of prejudice. Intolerance and decisions made of cold logic are the marks of this King of Wands. Expect no mercy. The key to his overthrow is the ability to remain unmoved by his lies.

Waiting in the darkness was the hardest part. It took practiced patience and willpower to remain motionless for hours on end, to stand so still that a mouse squeaked in surprise when it encountered a warm hand on the ledge that ran the length of the secret room. Dante did not flinch. He was long accustomed to being the thing that frightened others in the dark. The mouse scurried away as Dante tilted his head from one side to the other, stretching the cramped muscles of his neck and shoulders. There was no way of knowing how much longer he would have to wait. Time had lost its meaning hours ago.

A faint sound made him go still again. Eventually he recognized the sounds of footsteps in the hallway. He heard the door to the master bedchamber open, and then a narrow strip of light shined through the wall. He stepped forward to look through the opening.

Two servants entered the bedchamber. The first was a short, middle-aged man with a grizzled beard and shoulder-length gray hair that was in need of a comb. Still, the quality of his garments marked him a man of consequence in the household, likely the chamberlain. The flame of the oil lantern he held in one hand flickered as he walked into the room; he set aside the wooden bucket he carried in the other hand so he could cup the flame. Next he began to walk around the room to light oil lamps that hung from brackets set into the walls. The chamber grew brighter and brighter and soon the room was ablaze with light.

The second servant was a dark-haired boy of no more than eight or nine years of age. He carried a tray that looked far too big for his painfully thin size to handle and he walked with exaggerated care to keep everything balanced. The tray held a decanter of wine and two goblets, along with a large platter covered with a linen cloth. He tried to place the tray carefully on a table that stood in the center of the chamber but the tray banged against the edge. He managed to get the tray onto the table and proved surprisingly quick as he lurched forward, steadying the decanter of wine just before it would have overturned. The chamberlain gave the boy a casual cuff to the back of the head that nearly sent both the boy and the decanter flying.

"Clumsy beggar! That wine is worth more than you are. Have a care!" The chamberlain pointed to the wooden bucket. "Put the warmed bricks at the foot of the bed, then put a brick under the platter to keep the *cicchetti* warm."

Dante eased his way slowly toward the hidden door, then silently drew his dagger and sword from their scabbards. He knew there was nothing in the bedchamber to betray him, and everything in the secret room spoke of neglect and disuse when he had entered the chamber that morning. The section of paneling that hid the lever had a thick layer of beeswax in the grooves that looked undisturbed, and the hinges had creaked and protested when he slid aside the panel that was actually the hidden door. The hinges were now oiled and the door would once again move silently. He doubted the servants were even aware of its existence.

The long, narrow room behind the door was built generations ago by placing a false wall in front of the wall between the bedchamber and the solar, supposedly as a hiding place for the women and children of the family should the palace come under attack. Every generation since then had laughed at the possibility of any palace in Venice falling prey to invaders. Nations fell prey to Venice, not the other way around.

Although the room's original purpose had always been something of a jest, every member of the family solemnly swore they would never reveal its existence to any outsiders, not even the servants. Folly or not, everyone realized that secrecy made the room even more secure than the household treasury. At one time the shelves had held everything from rare jewels to the relics of saints, treasures collected by merchant princes over the course of more than three hundred years.

This morning Dante had found the room mostly empty, coated with dust, and the remaining contents just as he and his brother, Roberto, had left them more than ten years ago. Most were boxes made of rosewood, emptied of their contents then cast aside, deemed too bulky to carry away in the sacks they had stuffed with anything of value. A few of the larger pieces still remained, including a massive altarpiece made of solid gold, a prize from the long-ago war with Constantinople that depicted scenes of the Crucifixion. Dante figured the altarpiece along with a tempting number of jewel-encrusted plates and chalices would be gone by now if the room had been discovered since his last visit. Still, he had not lived this long by making foolish assumptions.

He stood near the door and kept a careful eye on the servants. The peephole was actually a long slit that ran the length of the wall, cleverly concealed as part of the paneling in the bedchamber. Each piece of trim was cut in half lengthwise to give the deliberate appearance of a gap between each section of paneling. Every piece of trim on the paneled wall was cut the same, but only the strip that ran at eye level concealed a peephole and he could see everything that took place in the bedchamber. Neither the boy nor the chamberlain so much as glanced his way.

The chamberlain finished his tasks by arranging the platter and cups just so, while the boy placed cloth-wrapped bricks beneath the covers at the foot of the bed. When the boy returned to stand next to the table, Dante noted a small metal cup and spoon that hung from a chain attached to an iron collar around the child's neck. The collar marked him a slave, while the cup and spoon meant he was also the family's taster.

"Go on then," the chamberlain said, as he lifted the linen cover from the platter.

The scent of cinnamon and nutmeg reached Dante and he knew tonight's *cicchetti* included spice cakes. That type of food was useless for his purposes, but the wine held possibilities, especially wine that had already been tasted. He watched as the boy shoveled food into his mouth at an astonishing rate, although he had scarce eaten more than a few mouthfuls when the chamberlain cuffed him again to knock him away from the platter.

"Now the wine."

The boy gave the platter one last, covetous look until the food was once again covered, then he held up his

cup while the steward poured from the decanter. The
wine was gone in one quick gulp.

"Get to your place," the chamberlain ordered, one
hand on the boy's shoulder to push him forward. "The
master is in no mood for your whining tonight. One
sound before dawn, and the next beating will be twice
as bad as the last."

The two reached the door just as Dante realized the
purpose for the chain he had found bolted to the wall
outside the bedchamber. He also knew the reason why
the boy was so thin.

Poison revealed itself more quickly in a child's body
than in a man's; thus nobles in need of the services of a
taster preferred children. Tatar and Circassian children
were readily available from the slave ships, and both peoples were regarded as barbaric heathens by both Chris-
tians and Muslims, and therefore more expendable. Most
were allowed no more food than the small portions they
tasted from their master's table, and constant hunger
meant they would perform their duty with enthusiasm.
This household had found one more use for the unfortunate creature. The boy was kept chained like a dog to
guard the door to the master's bedchamber at night. It
was a complication Dante did not need, but one that was
not insurmountable.

Once he was certain the bedchamber was empty, he
slipped the sword and dagger back into their sheaths.
He could hear the chamberlain talking to the boy in the
hallway, but the servant might return at any moment to
await his master's arrival. Dante reached for the handle
and breathed a sigh of relief when the door slid open
without a sound. A small glass vial was in his hand and
uncorked by the time he reached the table, then the
contents quickly dumped into the decanter. He swirled
the decanter until he was sure the wine and poison were

mixed. A moment later he was back in his hiding place.

As it turned out, there had been no need to rush. More than half an hour passed before the chamber door opened again. This time the chamberlain ushered in a middle-aged couple. Dante recognized them immediately as Lorenzo Mira and his longtime mistress, Donna Maria.

Dante realized with a sense of satisfaction that Lorenzo had not aged well. His hair had turned completely gray, there were dark circles around his eyes and many more lines on his face, and his odd, limping gait from a long-ago riding accident had become more pronounced. He looked almost haggard.

Donna Maria had changed as well, although she had made more obvious efforts to stem the tide of time. Her hair was blonder than it once was and the skin of her face looked taut and shiny, both changes the likely result of using lemons and other caustic acids to lighten her hair and peel away wrinkles. In his opinion, she had changed from a handsome woman to a well-preserved one.

"The boy has already tasted the *cicchetti* and wine," the chamberlain said, with forced cheerfulness and a smile that didn't quite reach his eyes. "Would you like me to pour the wine, my lord?"

Lorenzo merely waved one hand toward the door and the servant bowed his way out of the room. Both occupants watched the door for a few moments, obviously waiting until the chamberlain was well away from overhearing anything they might say.

Lorenzo finally broke the silence. "The Council meetings did not go in my favor. There is still a good possibility that I can sway more members before a vote is taken, but we must make plans in the event the Council accepts

Chiavari's petitions. I will not stand trial like a common criminal."

Donna Maria made a sound of impatience. "I thought your friends on the Council said you had no reason for concern."

"I have no friends on the Council," he corrected, his voice clipped and precise. "They are men who owe me favors or fear the consequences of my displeasure, or both. All have sufficient motivation to reject the petitions out of hand, but Chiavari has involved not only the Pope in his cause, but England's sovereign as well. One or the other might be dismissed, but together their words are hard to set aside without raising more suspicion." He folded his arms across his chest and gave her a hard look. "My spies say Chiavari has at least one witness who will swear they have firsthand knowledge that I planned my brother-in-law's murder to gain his fortune, and then falsely accused his wife of the deed." He slanted Donna Maria a meaningful look. "There is only one person still alive who could give such testimony."

Her hand went to her throat. "You cannot believe I would do such a thing! Lorenzo, I could not survive without you. My loyalty is yours until I die! When have I ever—"

He held up one hand to silence her. "You know me too well to betray me. 'Twas only a thought." He gave a nod that seemed to confirm his belief in her innocence. "So it seems Chiavari intends to produce false witnesses, which means it will be possible to buy a different story from their lips, else silence them altogether."

"He cannot possibly produce anyone who would tell the truth," she assured him, looking slightly more relaxed.

He went to the table and filled two goblets with wine, then handed one to Donna Maria. "We must still make preparations to move the children and enough wealth out of the city to survive in comfort, should we need to flee. You have a keener eye than I for such things, and a rare talent for knowing the cost of anything that crosses your path. Tomorrow I want you to go through the palace and the treasury. Make lists of everything of value that can be moved. I will have a ship ready to sail within three days. The estate in Dalmatia should be remote enough."

Donna Maria sat down hard on one of the stools next to the table. "You actually think Chiavari might succeed?"

"I think he is more determined than I anticipated, and has thus far proved impossible to kill." Lorenzo took a deep drink of wine, and then rubbed his forehead. "I sent countless men after him over the years, but only a handful returned. Their reports say he works as an assassin for England's king."

"I *told* you those 'harmless children' would one day prove troublesome."

Lorenzo held up his hands as if he had heard the complaint more often than he cared to. "There were enough questions about the deaths of their parents, and it wasn't as if we were murdering peasants. The Chiavari family is as old as Venice itself. Three more Chiavari murders within the city would have made it impossible for my 'friends' on the Council to vote me innocent in the matter." He lifted one shoulder. "I paid a fortune to make certain the Chiavari siblings never reached England alive. How was I to know they were clever enough to pay an equal fortune to ensure their own safety on the voyage? Even so, the girl was never a real threat, only the two brothers. Then Dante disappeared soon after Roberto's death and I thought him dead as well until a few years ago."

Donna Maria shook her head, as if having trouble accepting the truth of their situation. "All these years he has been biding his time, waiting until he was certain he could ruin you. Ruin us both!"

"'Tis no certainty I am bound for the gallows," he said, before taking another drink. "There are still those on the Council who are loyal to my cause, who must remain loyal to make certain their own secrets remain safe. Many of those same men branded Dante Chiavari a bastard and his mother a murderess. None of them will be in a hurry to admit such a grievous mistake.

"For the Council members I do not control, they are no more than sheep to be herded. The Chiavaris' fates were sealed the day I married Gian Chiavari's sister, and everything worked out just as I said it would. Chiavari is dead. The Council believes his English wife admitted under torture to poisoning him, as well as to having a lover that fathered her three children. She died before she could be brought to trial, and the children were named foreign bastards and exiled. As the only remaining Chiavari, my wife inherited everything. As her husband, I own everything that belonged to my wife. The Council ruled all of this in my favor. Their rulings still stand. Dante is no longer a Chiavari or even a Venetian in the eyes of the law, but he has ample reason to manufacture the evidence he brought forward. Unfortunately, he also has ample wealth and influence, but I will prevail in the end. Have faith that the Council will once again believe what I wish them to believe."

He took a seat on the stool next to hers and reached out to pat her hand. "No one will take what I have made my own, and Dante Chiavari will die no more than a day after he sets foot in Venice to testify before the Council about these charges. Once he is dead, there will be none left to support his claims. All will return to normal."

Lorenzo finished what was left in his goblet and set it down on the tray while Donna Maria took a smaller sip of wine and appeared to contemplate his words.

"We must proceed with caution," she said at last. "If Chiavari is as clever as you say, he will—" Donna Maria tilted her head to one side. "What is wrong with you?"

She scarcely had time to stand up before Dante was through the door and standing right behind her. He put one arm around her waist, then reached over her shoulder and drew his blade across her throat in one smooth motion. His gaze never left Lorenzo's wide-eyed stare as he lowered her gently to the floor until she lay at his feet. He bent to wipe his dagger on Donna Maria's skirts, and then smoothly stepped over the body to take her place at the table.

Lorenzo was still seated, a look of shock frozen on his face. He was trying to stand up but his body wasn't co-operating. At last he slumped forward until the upper part of his body lay sprawled across the table. His arms were spread wide, and one side of his face lay pressed to the polished mahogany surface. Dante moved his stool closer to Lorenzo's, then leaned over to look him in the eye. "Did you really think I would show myself in Venice while you were still alive?"

The muscles in Lorenzo's arms jerked of their own accord and his mouth moved wordlessly, a landed fish that was losing its fight.

"I had hoped you would be the one to drink the most poison," Dante went on, unconcerned by his prey's lack of response. He glanced over his shoulder at Donna Maria. "The one who drank the least had to die quickly, but you both have Chiavari blood on your hands so in the end it doesn't really matter who died first. I just wanted to see your face when you saw mine. I am told that I look exactly like my father, the same dark hair and tall build, the same green eyes. 'Tis said we even sound alike. How does it feel to face a ghost from your past?"

A small movement on the floor drew his attention. Donna Maria's leg twitched again, an involuntary movement that he'd witnessed before from those in the throes of death. There was no longer anything to worry about from that quarter, so he turned again to look at Lorenzo. "Did you know that your whore made sure the three children you had with my aunt were smothered within days of their births? Donna Maria made certain you would have no legitimate heirs with your wife so you would adopt the bastards she gave you and make them your heirs. Many believe she also poisoned my aunt to make certain she died in childbirth that last time. If the pair of you had your way, the next generation of Chiavari would not have a drop of Chiavari blood. How could you think I would allow this to happen?"

Dante continued without pausing. It was pointless to wait for a response from Lorenzo that would never come. "I would have preferred the public trial you had so dreaded. I wanted you both tried and publicly executed for what you did to my family. However, I no longer trust that justice will be served through the usual channels. You taught me that lesson well, *Uncle*. Indeed, I learned long ago that an honorable man cannot best you, so I have molded myself into the same sort of fiend that destroyed my family. How does it feel to know you have forged your own killer?"

Dante propped his arms on the table and rested his chin atop his folded hands. Lorenzo's mouth had stopped working up and down, but he could still smell wine on the faint puffs of his breath. He would not leave until he was absolutely certain this man would breathe no more.

It was an interesting experience to finally say anything he wished to say to Lorenzo Mira's face, knowing his enemy was helpless to do anything but listen.

"I saw my mother before she died," he went on, in a voice no more emotional than if he were speaking of the weather. "No matter how much torture was inflicted upon her, she would not confess. She knew she would die either way, and suffering days of torture gave her children time to escape from Venice, time to escape from you. A child's last memory of his mother's face should not look like mine. For that, I swore I would make you suffer every pain I know how to inflict in the hours before your death, and I assure you, my knowledge is considerable. You might be paralyzed, but I know you can feel everything as you lie here, helpless to stop me."

He leaned back and drew another small, thin-edged dagger, and then he sank the tip of the blade into the tender part of Lorenzo's armpit before quickly removing it. "I can see by your tears that it hurt. Imagine the hours it could take to inflict hundreds of those knife pricks all over your body. Is your heart beating faster in fear?"

Dante watched a few silent tears spill onto the table. "The harder your heart beats, the faster the poison spreads." He slid the flat of the blade along Lorenzo's face, leaving a smear of blood on his cheek. He kept his voice low and soothing. "Now can you imagine the fear you instilled in my mother before she died?"

Lorenzo's gaze remained fixed; not a muscle in his body moved. He would be dead within a few more minutes. If the poison in the wine did not finish him, the poison on the dagger's blade would. It was over at last and time to make good his escape, yet he could not resist the urge to taunt the man one last time.

"Your foul deeds have come to naught, Lorenzo. This palace along with all of my family's wealth and holdings will be mine. The Chiavaris have their revenge. You die with nothing."

Dante pushed away from the table, but stared long and hard at his handiwork before he returned to the secret room to retrieve a coil of rope. He closed the hidden door and used the cuff of his sleeve to wipe away his handprints from the wood, his movements calm and methodical as he moved across the bedchamber to the doors that led to the balcony. Once outside he took several long, deep breaths of fresh air to clear his head. The bedchamber reeked with the scent of Donna Maria's blood and death itself.

He tried to remember the last time he had stood on what had once been his parents' balcony. Scores of palaces lined the canals of Venice, homes of the city's prosperous merchant princes, but the largest and most impressive palaces surrounded him on this bend of the Grand Canal. Beyond the neighboring rooftops was the dome of St. Mark's, easily visible in the moonlight from his vantage point three stories above the water, but the canal itself was cloaked in mists that had rolled in from the sea at dusk. Dante gave a short whistle that was echoed a moment later by someone far below him in the fog. He uncoiled the rope and tied one end to the railing, then sent it over the edge. The rope suddenly went taut and Dante gave two quick tugs to signal that all was well. He returned to the bedchamber and dispassionately studied his enemy.

Lorenzo's face was the color of wax and his nail beds had turned a dark shade of blue. The breaths that had fogged the polished surface of the table near his mouth had disappeared. Dante sat down again to wait, unwilling to leave the chamber until he was certain he had accomplished his goal. At last a long, shuddering breath left Lorenzo's body and then a milky film began to cloud his eyes.

Lorenzo Mira was dead.

Dante silently repeated the fact several times, but it still didn't seem to take hold in his head. Bringing this man to justice had been the entire focus of his life since he was a boy. Lorenzo had now paid for his crimes. He looked at Donna Maria's body and felt the same hollowness at his core. She had murdered his cousins and possibly his aunt, thus she, too, had paid for her crimes. He felt no remorse.

Mordecai had trained him to never let emotions become involved in any assassination, but he had thought these deaths would somehow be different, that he would feel some great sense of satisfaction or at least a sense of relief. He should be glad that he had finally managed to carry out the sentence that should have been imposed upon them years ago. Instead he felt . . . nothing. In the end, he was simply an executioner doing his job.

A familiar sound brought him out of his thoughts, a metallic *clink* that came from the direction of the door, the sound of a small metal cup knocking against a metal spoon. Dante felt a chill go through him.

The child might have rolled over in his sleep, but the odds were just as good that he was awake and had overheard Dante talking to Lorenzo. Perhaps these deaths had affected him more than he realized. This was the first time he had been so careless.

He moved silently to the door, his ears straining for any other sounds from the opposite side. There was only silence.

He should have taken care of the boy the moment he was done with Donna Maria. Instead, his decision to taunt a dying man could have easily resulted in his own death. It still might.

Now he had a different decision to make.

He could well imagine the child's fate when the bodies were discovered in the morning. Likely the boy would be beaten until he gave a false confession and admitted that he allowed someone past him without raising an alarm. The chances of him surviving such a beating were remote. The chances of Dante freeing the boy before he made some sound of alarm that would get them both killed were just as remote. The best he could do was provide a quick, painless death for the child. Although a part of him rebelled that Lorenzo's life should cost the life of yet another innocent, he drew his dagger and opened the door.

The light spilled out from the bedchamber and he found a small face staring up at him, the expression seeming more curious than startled. The boy sat cross-legged on an old wool blanket, a sunken look about his eyes. Dante's view from the secret room had not revealed the extent of the child's starvation. His body was almost skeletal, his arms and legs little more than flesh-covered bones. After a long, tense moment, the child leaned sideways to look past Dante into the chamber where the bodies of Lorenzo and Donna Maria were clearly visible. His gaze moved next to the dagger in Dante's hand and he gave a long, shuddering sigh. It was the look of resignation in his eyes that awoke something in Dante that he had thought long-dead.

There was no way he could take a half-starved urchin on the journey that lay ahead. It was crazed to even consider the notion. Still, the decision was made. "What is your name?"

The boy hesitated, and then whispered in the same low tones as Dante, "My name is Rami."

"Well, Rami, if you remain silent and do exactly as I say, you may yet live through this night. If we are alive on the morrow, I will make certain your life changes for the better. Agreed?"

Dante kept his dagger at the ready while the boy stared back at him. He was beginning to wonder if the child was fluent enough in Italian to understand his meaning when Rami's eyes began to take on a light of hope and he gave a slow, uncertain nod.

"The collar will have to stay for now, but I'm going to use my dagger to pick the lock attached to this chain on the wall. If you make a sound, we are both dead. Do you understand?"

This time there was no hesitation. Rami nodded even as he cradled the metal cup and spoon so they would remain silent.

Dante made short work of the chain, then picked Rami up and carried him to the balcony, amazed at the lightness of his burden. He pointed over the railing toward the rope that disappeared into the fog.

"There is a boat at the end of this rope where two of my men await me. Are you strong enough to climb down by yourself or do I need to tie the rope around your waist and lower you?"

"I am strong, master." Rami lifted his arm to flex a pathetic little muscle, then gave a fierce nod. He shouldn't trust the child's strength, but there was something in Rami's eyes that made his claim believable. Whatever his ancestry, it was obviously warrior stock.

"My men are named Oliver and Armand, but do not speak to them unless spoken to. They will not harm you." He pulled up a length of the rope and made sure Rami had a firm grip. "Be quick about it, boy. I will follow in a few minutes."

Rami climbed over the railing and Dante watched him

until the child disappeared into the fog. There was no hesitation in Dante's steps as he returned to the bedchamber and checked the bodies again, just to make doubly certain his job was done. Next he went to the doorway and grabbed Rami's blanket. There was a growing pool of blood beneath Donna Maria's body, and he carefully blotted as much as he could onto the blanket without making its absence from the pool noticeable. The blanket was returned to Rami's place outside the door where he arranged it to look as if the boy had been killed there. With luck, they would think he had thrown the child's body into the canal.

He went again to the balcony and then he turned around for one long, last look at the carnage he had wrought, satisfied that justice at long last had been served. A moment later he disappeared over the railing.

3

❧

ENGLAND,
ONE MONTH LATER

The Thief

The Seven of Swords is the mark of a thief. Craft and cleverness are the thief's finest cloaks and the guides to his destiny. Choose the path well for success leads to failure, and failure leads to success.

Avalene de Forshay was in a foul mood. She was the kind of woman who expected others to perform their duties as well as she performed her own, and she thrived on order and routine. In a castle the size of Coleway there would always be unexpected problems, but she had learned to calmly work through them, one at a time, and soon everything would run smoothly again. Having three cooks, a pantler, and a baker fall ill on the same day qualified as the unexpected. To compound her problems, this was a feast day and the steward took great delight in reporting all manner of woes. One in particular had set her teeth on edge.

"The minstrels have arrived but they are not the troupe from Chester you requested," John had told her that morning as he brushed nonexistent wrinkles from his sleeve. At the same time, he had made little effort to hide a sly smile. "They are the troupe from Blackthorne you dismissed during the last Hocktide feast. I cannot imagine why they would come back to Coleway, espe-

cially after the scolding you gave them last year. If I recall correctly, you called them a third-rate troupe of
drunkards. Such a shame. Lady Margaret made particular mention that she was looking forward to hearing the
Chester minstrels perform. 'Tis too late to send for the
Chester troupe, of course, but perhaps the Blackthorne
troupe's skills have improved since we saw them last.
Shall I quarter them in the great hall?"

Under the circumstances, Avalene had little choice but
to grit her teeth and nod. Aside from his relation to the
lord of Coleway Castle, there was little to recommend
John to his post as steward. He had but one brilliant
ability, and that was to make himself look better in the
eyes of Lord Brunor and Lady Margaret by making
everyone else around him look worse. There was little
doubt that he was behind the mix-up with the minstrels.
He delighted in anything that would give him reason to
point out some failing or flaw in Avalene to her aunt and
uncle. If he could not find a genuine flaw, he manipulated the circumstances to create one.

It was little comfort that she was rarely his only victim. John routinely tormented those who were directly
accountable to Lord Brunor and Lady Margaret, and
made specific targets of anyone who appeared to be
gaining special favor with the lord and lady of Coleway
Castle.

Even more infuriating, no one had ever been able to
catch him in an outright lie or deceit. Complaints about
him were invariably rebuffed with one of his pitying
looks, as he claimed that attacks upon his honor were
festered by jealousy and his accuser's inability to live up
to the high standards and expectations set by their illustrious master and mistress. All of this nonsense was
carefully calculated to be spoken within earshot of said
master and mistress.

Aye, John knew every trick to ingratiate himself with the lord and lady of the castle and, to Avalene's great disgust, her aunt and uncle vainly lapped up his false charm like cream. Things would be very different in her own household, she vowed, as she took a deliberate route from the kitchens to the great hall.

The main course had just been sent out to the hall to be served, and she had stayed in the kitchens to make certain the final course would follow at an appropriate interval. With the most pressing crises taken care of in the kitchens, it was time to see if there were any disasters lurking in the great hall.

"Oh, good Lord."

The first thing she saw was a flaming torch fly through the air and land on one of the long dining tables that were set up on all four sides of the hall. Fortunately, nothing caught fire before the hapless juggler retrieved the torch, but everyone in his immediate vicinity looked nervous when he resumed the entertainment. Unfortunately, his was not the only blunder. Indeed, the entire troupe showed more ineptitude than talent and her hopes that they had improved in the past year faded fast.

There were almost a score of performers clustered together in groups and partnered according to their particular entertainment. To one side of the hall, four musicians provided a cacophony of discordant sounds from a psaltery, flute, and drums, while a buxom young woman sang loud and off-key about spring tulips. Near the high table where the lord and lady of Coleway were seated, half a dozen young men were attempting to form a human arch in which three men stood shoulder-to-shoulder to form the bottom row, two men would then stand on their shoulders, and then one would stand at the very top. The arch collapsed just as the men on the second row were in place, and she couldn't decide if it was determination or a complete disregard for their lack of talent that made them try the maneuver again with no more success. Three jesters moved around the long tables of diners to make fun of themselves and members of the audience in ways that should make the audience laugh. The looks on the faces around the jesters ranged from somber to annoyed.

She quickly glanced away from the jesters toward the group that worried her most. Four jugglers stood in the middle of the hall, paired together and facing each other to toss pairs of flaming torches back and forth. Already the hall smelled strongly of burnt rushes, and she carefully examined the floor for any telltale wisps of smoke. It was only a matter of time before a true disaster struck. Unfortunately, the strike came sooner than she anticipated and it came from behind her.

One moment she was debating the best way to apologize to her aunt and uncle for allowing this farce to take place. The next moment something struck her squarely in the back and propelled her forward. A boy's voice cried out in surprise as the pressure on her back pushed her to the floor, then she felt a body and something else fall on top of her, pressing her face into the rushes.

Nearly two hundred people were seated in the great hall for this feast. A hushed silence fell across the crowd, so sudden and so complete that Avalene was certain she could have heard a pin drop. She blinked twice from the shock of finding herself in such an undignified position, and then quickly pushed herself up until her weight rested on her knees. There were streaks of something wet and greasy on her skirts and a young page named Cedric suddenly appeared before her.

"My lady, are you hurt?"

She glanced over her shoulder and saw an empty tray

with a small roasted piglet on the floor beside it, the roast looking as if it had lain down in the rushes for a nap. The grease from the piglet was the source of the streaks on her gown and the now-distinct smell of roasted meat. Her gaze moved back to Cedric and she stared dumbly at his offered hand.

"I was watching the jugglers," Cedric said in a shaky voice. "I—I did not see you until it was too late. 'Tis my fault you fell. Are you hurt anywhere?"

She did a brief inventory. Everything seemed fine. "Nay, Cedric, nothing is injured but my pride."

Cedric held out his hand and helped Avalene to her feet. The conversations began again as if they had never been interrupted. Unfortunately, the performers went back to work as well.

"Pick up this mess and take it back to the kitchens," she told him. "Have one of the scullions wash off the piglet and it should be fine to serve again."

"Aye, my lady." Cedric bowed low, and then went about cleaning up the mess.

"Avalene!"

She turned to see Lady Margaret waving her forward, summoning her to pay attendance. Avalene sighed and prepared for the long walk to the head table.

Lady Margaret looked her best tonight in a deep blue gown that matched the color of her eyes. A crown-shaped barbette made of stiff white linen and topped with a short row of tightly bunched lace ruffles gave her a regal air. Its matching snood covered blond hair that now showed telltale streaks of gray, and the cloth wound tightly beneath her jaw effectively covered a chin that was beginning to sag. Avalene favored her aunt's coloring, although her own hair was more gold than flaxen and her eyes a much deeper shade of blue. Their features were dissimilar as well. Avalene towered a good head taller than her tiny aunt, and, according to Margaret, her feet were too large for a true lady, which likely contributed to her clumsiness. And there was no competition when it came to their faces. Margaret was considered one of the great beauties of her age. Avalene, on her best day, might be called pretty.

Her spirits sank lower when she realized Margaret was listening intently to something her husband and the steward were saying, and then Lord Brunor made a gesture in her general direction.

Lord Brunor was much closer in looks to his steward. Both men were of medium height with brown hair and hazel-colored eyes. Both had builds that were neither lean nor fat, but neither were they flabby nor muscular. "Nondescript" was the best way to describe their physical appearances. Only their positions of power at Coleway and their appreciation for fine clothing set them apart from more common men.

That, and Lord Brunor's failing eyesight, the result of an unfortunate accident at a tourney a few years ago. At his insistence, members of his household were only allowed to wear clothing of a certain color. Lady Margaret wore blue, his children wore yellow, other children of rank wore orange, John and Avalene wore red, knights and ladies of rank wore green, and so it went throughout the keep from the highest born to the lowest. Soldiers wore white tunics with gray pants. Servants wore their regular homespun clothing in shades of brown and gray, their position at the castle distinguished by the color of their head covering or hose or tunic or apron.

Many had initially balked at the change, Avalene most of all, as she had no wish to wear such a flamboyant color each day of her life. Eventually she had become accustomed to the new attire and even came to appreciate its unintended consequences. There were hundreds of people within the walls of the castle and the colors certainly made identification of a person and their duties a simple matter from almost any distance. Then there was a certain artistic touch to gatherings such as today's feast when the hall turned into an enormous palette of neatly grouped colors. However, the splash of red seated next to Lord Brunor put a considerable damper on her enjoyment of the scene.

"Where have you been?" Lady Margaret demanded. Her hand swept out to indicate the table and everything upon it. "The fish is salty, the beef is tough, and the bread is hard as a rock. You must speak with the cooks immediately."

Did her aunt truly think she'd been shirking her duties all this time? Leave it to John to give them that impression when she was not here to defend herself. "I just came from the kitchens, my lady. Remember, I told you that many of the kitchen staff were abed with bad stomachs?"

"Aye, but you told me about these illnesses early this morn. Surely you could have found servants to replace them who would not try to poison us." She nodded her head in the steward's direction. "There are just as many ill servants on John's staff, and yet the hall looks wonderful. Except for that awful Blackthorne troupe, but it is my understanding that you are also responsible for their offensive performances. Do have them stop before someone gets hurt or before I am driven mad by that horrible woman's shrieking. What she is subjecting us to is not called 'singing.'"

"I sent for the Chester troupe," Avalene insisted. Her gaze narrowed on John, but he pointedly ignored her and continued his conversation with Lord Brunor. "There was no reason for me to think—"

"Do not try to blame others for your mistakes," Margaret interrupted, her voice maddeningly calm and collected. "Learn to accept your shortcomings and work harder to improve them, and then perhaps you will not disappoint us so often. I shudder to think what shame you will bring upon your family if you marry into an illustrious family such as the Segraves. They are sure to think you were raised by wolves. Just look at your gown. A lady does not appear among her people wearing her dinner in her lap." She held up one hand when Avalene started to object. "Nay, do not try to make more excuses about how you soiled your gown. Really, Avalene, I begin to lose faith that you will ever be ready to become chatelaine of a great estate. I have told your father time and again that you have too much wild Welsh blood in you and we would all be better served if you would marry one of Lord Brunor's knights and remain at Coleway. At least we know what sort of trouble you would cause here."

Avalene felt her blood run cold. Life at Coleway was far from unbearable, but it would fast become so if she had to spend a lifetime running her aunt's household. She had always known her fostering at Coleway would come to an end when she married. She would be free of John's constant mischief, Lady Margaret's unending lectures, and Lord Brunor's whims that always resulted in more work for her. This was not the first she had heard of some scheme to keep her trapped at Coleway, and she could not help but wonder if John had a hand in it. His pranks had taken a vicious edge of late.

"My marriage to Faulke Segrave will be of far greater benefit to my father than marriage to one of your knights," she said. "Your concern is misplaced, my lady. You have taught me all I need to know to run an estate of any size. I shall make Faulke Segrave a very fine wife and my family will benefit greatly from the connection."

"Ah, well, we shall see what your father has to say on the subject." Lady Margaret waved away Avalene's concerns as if her entire future were some trivial matter. "I cannot tolerate any more of this sad excuse for entertainment or the shabbiness of your appearance. Perform your duties as I have asked before you return to the table to take your meal."

For the second time that day, Avalene gritted her teeth to trap angry words behind them. She bowed her head and sank into a low curtsy, and then turned and walked away with as much dignity as she could muster.

"You there," she called out to one of the tumblers. "Which one is your leader?"

He jerked his thumb toward one of the flame-throwers.

"Marvelous," she breathed. She took great care to approach the man in an obvious way, and then she waved one hand until he realized she wished to speak with him. Finally, his torches were secured and no longer flying through the air. "My lady bids your troupe cease the performances and take your leave of Coleway immediately."

His face, already red from the exertions of his performance, darkened a shade. "Our pay—"

She cut him off before he could start making demands. "There will be no coin. No matter what you have been told, you were not the troupe we sent for nor expected. The lord and lady are sorely disappointed and are not consoled by your performances. You have not earned your keep. However, I will have sacks of food sent to the gates that will be sufficient to feed your people at least this day and the next one as well. The guards will be told that you are not to receive the food until the last man has passed through the gates, and then the gates will be barred against you. Regardless of any summons you might receive in the future, know that it was not sent from anyone in a position of authority at this castle. Do not return here again."

Without waiting for a response or argument, she turned on her heel and headed toward the table occupied by a group of men wearing cream-colored tunics and brown hose. There was plenty of food to supply the troupe with the meals, as she had already accounted for the extra mouths to be fed until the troupe was originally due to take their leave. Holding their food until they reached the gate made it unlikely they would argue over payment and risk losing their meals as well. One problem solved.

"William, my apologies for interrupting your meal," she said to the oldest of the four men. "This troupe's minstrels have offended Lady Margaret's sensibilities and she feels the far superior skills of our own minstrels are her only remedy."

William had already pushed away from the table and the others were joining him. "Say no more, my lady. We shall be happy to oblige."

Avalene gave him a smile of gratitude, and then turned toward the kitchens. Two problems solved.

The kitchens were only slightly less chaotic than when last she left them, but she was glad to see that Maude, the sick head cook's wife, looked more comfortable in her temporary role as leader of this bedraggled band of servants. She watched Maude give firm direction to both the experienced kitchen workers as well as to those recruited to fill in for the day, and all hurried to carry out the orders.

"You see?" Avalene asked, as she gave Maude an approving nod. "I knew that anyone who produced twelve well-mannered and hardworking children would have no trouble at all with a staff this size."

"Well, it helps that six of the kitchen staff are my own," the heavyset woman admitted with a blush, "but you are very kind to think so highly of my skills, Lady Avalene."

Four of Maude's sons and two daughters were apprenticing under her husband, and Maude herself had first met her husband when she worked in the kitchens. It had not been a stretch for Avalene to know Maude would prove valuable here. "I have one more task I must assign. Lady Margaret bid me to dismiss the Blackthorne troupe and send them from the castle. They will not receive any coin, but I have promised to provide two sacks with enough provisions to feed their score of performers for two days." She then gave the woman her instructions for the gates.

Maude gave a brisk nod. "The provisions and your orders will be at the gates within the hour, my lady. Have no worries on that matter."

She patted Maude's shoulder. "I knew I could count on you. Have you received any word about your husband?"

"Aye, my Sally has been playing nursemaid and she says he and the others are all on the mend. Even if they are still too ill to work on the morrow we shall have fewer worries. We can serve much simpler fare after a feast day, thank the Lord."

"Aye, thank the Lord," Avalene echoed, with a heartfelt sigh. She plucked at her greasy skirts. "I must change my gown before I can return to the hall, but I will try to visit again when the feast ends to see if you need anything."

"Do not worry on my account," Maude insisted. "The hour grows late already and I doubt you have managed to find a moment to even feed yourself this day. Take the time you would spend here and do something indulgent, my lady. We shall be fine on our own."

"You shall spoil me," Avalene teased, but she felt confident enough in Maude's competence to appreciate those few extra moments she would now have to herself at the end of the day. "Send word if any problems should arise."

"Aye, my lady."

Three problems solved.

Avalene left the kitchens with a lighter spring to her step. She started up the stairs that led to the gallery, a covered wooden walkway that encircled the second story of the great hall. Here there were doorways cut into the stone walls of the hall that led to the towers. They were the only entrances to the towers, deliberately made this high so the wooden stairs could be quickly torn down to leave women and children safely above the fray. If attackers ever made it this far into the keep, they would have to work even harder to reach those who had retreated to the towers. The walkway had never been used for that purpose in Avalene's memory. These days the gallery was primarily a passageway to the towers, and even then, most people walked their route as quickly as possible while saying a few prayers.

There was a constant dampness in the great hall that torches and a single fireplace could not chase away, and Avalene had noticed the wood of the gallery was starting to rot and weaken in places. Just last month she had urged Lady Margaret and Lord Brunor to have the gallery refurbished or replaced, but John had assured them that one of the carpenters had assured *him* that the wood was still sound and such repairs would be wasteful.

She studied the wear patterns on the steps and men-

tally shook her head. Somewhere in Coleway an innocent carpenter would be punished when there was an
inevitable accident on the gallery. If there was any justice, the accident would involve John.

She made her way safely across two sides of the gallery and was just steps away from the doorway that led
to her tower chamber when a noise rose above the din of
the crowd and stopped her in her tracks. It was not the
noise of creaking wood that she always expected, but
the equally familiar sound of the chamberlain's iron-
tipped staff as it struck the hall's flagstones in three measured beats. Everyone immediately fell silent and Avalene
edged her way closer to the railing.

"My lord and lady," the chamberlain announced in
his most important voice, "a messenger from Baron
Weston has arrived and humbly begs your audience."

A messenger from her father! Avalene's gaze went to
Lord Brunor, who made an impatient gesture indicating
that he agreed to the audience. It occurred to her that
she had almost failed to witness the messenger's arrival.
Whatever news this man had, the most important of it
would be revealed in the next few moments.

She glanced down at her gown and was suddenly
thankful Lady Margaret had sent her from the great
hall. She could all too easily imagine the lectures from
Lady Margaret if her father's messenger had seen her
wearing a soiled gown at a feast. Worse, he would likely
report her slovenly condition to her father. Perhaps she
could rush to her chamber, change her gown, and return
before the man was admitted to the hall and began to
deliver his message. The idea was quickly dismissed.
There would be time after she heard the message to
change her clothing.

Despite her unease on the rickety gallery, she reasoned
the floor was likely stronger by the railing, where boards

that had started to bow in the middle of the gallery were more firmly attached to the frame of the structure. The boards definitely made fewer creaking noises there. She inched her way forward until she was directly above the head table. She was unable to see her aunt and uncle who were seated beneath this section of the gallery, but here she would have a good view of the man who spoke to them.

A trick of the vaulted ceilings also made the gallery an excellent place to eavesdrop on almost any conversation that took place at the head table and she intended to listen to every word. She had scarcely settled into a more comfortable position behind the tapestry when the chamberlain rapped his staff three more times. Every gaze turned toward the chamberlain and the massive doors that led to the great hall. His voice boomed out over the crowd one more time.

"Sir Percival of Weston!"

4

❧

Avalene reached between the balusters to widen a gap
between two of the tapestries that hung from the hand-
rail, certain no one would notice her hiding place since
every face was turned toward the entrance to the great
hall. She saw only the dark outline of a knight, silhou-
etted against the last fiery rays of the sun.

At last the knight stepped forward and her gaze was
drawn immediately to the silver griffin embroidered on
his deep blue surcoat that proclaimed his allegiance to
Baron Weston. His long, easy stride proved he was accustomed to the heavy chain-mail hauberk he wore beneath his surcoat, and one gauntleted hand rested on the
hilt of his broadsword, the unconscious habit of all
knights to keep the tip of the long weapon from striking
against the ground as he walked. Curiously enough, he
did not remove his helm, which meant she could see
nothing of his face.

Even if he were homely or scarred, he radiated the vi-
tality and danger of a warrior in his prime. Tall but not

towering, broad-shouldered yet lean in the waist, he was not the sort of man she had expected her father to send. In the past he had delegated this task to elderly or infirm knights and usually sent them in groups of two or three. She suspected it was simply a means to make them continue to feel useful.

There was nothing elderly or infirm about this man. Even if he had traveled all this way on his own, the sight of such a knight would make any thief or brigand hesitate to challenge such a formidable opponent. He appeared very capable of defending himself against any who might be foolish enough to cross him.

He came to a halt directly below her and no matter how she craned her neck, the most she could see was the top of his head when he removed the helmet and tucked it beneath one arm. Although his hair looked thick and dark, she couldn't be certain of its exact color in the dim light. Why she should feel any curiosity over the color of a man's hair was beyond her, but the curiosity was there all the same.

"I bring greetings from my liege lord, Baron Weston."

Avalene smiled, and then immediately frowned when she became aware of her silly reaction to such a simple greeting, especially since his words were not even directed at her. It was the sound of his voice, she decided. Not too deep, yet deeper than most, the smooth cadence was perfection itself. He had a voice that made people want to listen to what he had to say.

"The baron asked that I deliver the coins for his daughter's allowance into your keeping, along with a message." Sir Percival placed a leather purse on the table before Lord Brunor, then reached inside his surcoat and withdrew a rolled parchment scroll. "I can recite the baron's message, if you wish."

"Aye, proceed," said Lord Brunor.

Not that it mattered, but Avalene wondered if her father had warned Sir Percival of Brunor's failing eyesight or if the offer was simple courtesy. Her odd musings ended the moment Sir Percival broke open the wax seal and unrolled the parchment, then began to read aloud.

The baron's message opened with the usual flowery praise for the fine care and instruction his daughter received at Coleway, although Avalene wondered how he could be so certain that Lady Margaret guided her with a "firm but fair hand toward the ideal of English womanhood." As far as she knew, her father received news of her just two times each year from the messengers who delivered her allowance to Coleway. His own letters had never contained a word of praise or pride, or any sentiment that could mislead Avalene into thinking he might sometimes think of her with affection. Long ago she had accepted the fact that there was no longer any room in Baron Weston's heart for his only daughter. His new wife and sons filled that cherished place completely.

She released an impatient sigh when Sir Percival began a passage that related news of her stepmother and two half brothers. This part of the message would be long and glowing, and utterly boring as far as Avalene was concerned. According to her father, his sons were the cleverest boys ever created, while his baroness, Lady Anne, was the perfect wife and mother. It was hard to stir up sisterly affection for two brothers she had never met, born of a woman she secretly despised for taking her own mother's place in her father's heart.

While Sir Percival read through the baron's boasts of his sons' latest feats and accomplishments, Avalene began to mentally compose a glowing report of her own actions to send back with Sir Percival. Her father needed to know that she had learned—and mastered—the duties and responsibilities of a great household, and that she looked forward to the day she would become the wife of an important man who would prove a powerful ally to her family in Wales.

Or, perhaps she should be bolder and tell him that she would rather be roasted alive than marry one of Brunor's knights and be forced to remain little more than a servant at Coleway, burdened with all the duties of a chatelaine and more, but with none of the power that was owed only to the lady of a castle. She would not last more than another year before the lectures and torments at Coleway drove her mad. It was past time for her to marry and leave her family's home for that of her husband's. She said a silent prayer that it would happen very soon.

"Negotiations with the Segraves continue to move slowly," said Sir Percival.

Avalene leaned closer to the balcony railing, her own report suddenly forgotten.

"Lower your voice, Sir Percival," said Lord Brunor, motioning for him to move closer. "The servants have no need to hear this part of the baron's message."

Sir Percival stepped as close as he could to the table and leaned forward, then he continued the message in a much quieter voice. The others in the great hall tried to pretend indifference even whilst they whispered among themselves in tones loud enough to obscure even the smallest hints of Sir Percival's words. Only John, Lord Brunor, and Lady Margaret were close enough to hear the conversation.

Avalene scowled. She could hear nothing of the news that concerned her most. Did the negotiations move slowly because the baron feared for her safety? That thought seemed unlikely, since most fathers would leap at the chance to align their family with the powerful Segraves, no matter the rumors about Faulke. After all, daughters were expendable. The alliance made by her marriage would survive, even if she did not.

Doubts about her well-being should not be a concern, and yet what she knew of Faulke Segrave, along with the rumors she had heard of him, was hardly comforting. She would be his fourth wife, although that was not an unusual situation if a man were her father's age. Yet Faulke Segrave was just a few years older than Avalene and had managed to become a widower three times in less than a decade. The death of a wife in childbirth was not all that uncommon, and even the loss of two wives in such a manner within a short span of time would not be unheard of. But according to the most widely known and accepted facts, Faulke's first wife had died after a mysterious fall down a stone stairway, the second wife had died in childbirth, and the third wife had died from an odd fever that had not affected anyone else. Compounding the strange deaths was the fact that Faulke had married very young the first time, supposedly in a love match to a woman who brought little to the marriage, and then she conveniently died when a wealthy heiress caught his attention and later became his second wife. After her death he quickly married another heiress from an even more powerful family. Now there were rumors that the third wife had died when Faulke discovered there was a potential bride with strong blood ties to the last royal Welsh prince and hero, Llewellyn the Great.

No one at Coleway Castle knew of Avalene's relationship to Llewellyn, not even her aunt and uncle. Everyone was aware of her Welsh blood, of course, and the fact that her mother was a Welsh noblewoman. However, while people speculated upon her direct relationship to the Welsh prince, no one actually believed it. Her father had taught her to dismiss any claims as gossip and exaggeration.

John had convinced Lord Brunor and Lady Margaret that the facts of Avalene's lineage were fabrications since, in his words, *Every Welshman boasts of blood ties to Llewellyn whether they exist or not, and the Welsh are such good liars that they have all convinced themselves they are Llewellyn's long-lost sons and daughters.*

In truth, only the most foolish Welshmen boasted of such ties because everyone knew Llewellyn's descendants tended to live short lives. Those who were not killed in battle or executed for treason were imprisoned. All potential heirs to Llewellyn's throne were made wards of King Edward's most trusted noblemen, but all of those children died as mysteriously and suspiciously as Faulke Segrave's wives.

Fortunately, her grandmother had escaped her imprisonment in a convent and no one had kept a close eye on the female line until more recent years when the direct male line died out. By that time, Avalene's mother had been well cloaked in anonymity, having even kept the truth of her heritage from her husband until several years after their marriage. Avalene's father had quickly realized the wisdom of keeping the secret. By the time her mother died when Avalene was nine, she had been taught to recite her mother's family tree as easily as her name, but to never let anyone but her father hear the names of her ancestors.

Had the Segraves somehow learned her secret and another of Faulke's brides died because of it? It was a disturbing coincidence, but she felt certain her father would have discovered the truth of the situation before he agreed to a betrothal. He might have all but forgotten her since his new wife and family came along, but surely he would not tie her to a man who would murder her when a better prospect presented itself. His last missive indicated that he was favorable to the match, and so she had every expectation of becoming Faulke Segrave's next bride. Indeed, she looked forward to her marriage and felt certain the betrothal would be announced very soon . . . as long as Lady Margaret quit interfering in the situation.

Whatever her father's thoughts were on the matter of the Segraves, Avalene could hear none of them. The tapestry that concealed her hiding place also made it impossible to eavesdrop on the quiet conversation taking place below her. She braced her hands on the railing and rose to a half-crouch, and then turned her head sideways so her ear rested close to the top of the railing. The tapestries no longer muffled the sounds from the hall, but Sir Percival's words were still no more than indistinct murmurs. She lifted herself a few inches higher and leaned farther over the railing.

Dante Chiavari knew of the girl's presence on the gallery above him, likely a chambermaid who could not resist the opportunity to eavesdrop. He dismissed her from his thoughts as more nuisance than threat. What concerned him most at the moment was Lady Margaret's reaction to her brother's missive.

"This will not do," Margaret said. She had produced a handkerchief from her sleeve halfway through Dante's recitation of Baron Weston's plans for his daughter. The delicate scrap of fabric was well on its way to being shredded between Margaret's hands. "Tell him, John. Tell him why Avalene must not be allowed to leave Coleway."

Dante's gaze lingered a moment on Lord Brunor, who still appeared more concerned with his meal than the fate of his niece, then moved on to the man seated to Lord Brunor's right. John had already identified himself as the castle's steward and his oily smile made Dante take an immediate dislike to him. Aside from being garbed from head to foot in a rather startling shade of red, his features resembled those of Lord Brunor closely enough for Dante to assume they were kin of some sort. However, unlike Lord Brunor, there was a sharp, calculating look in John's eyes that immediately set Dante's instincts on alert. Very little would escape this man's notice. There was also the fact that the steward's opinions seemed to hold great sway over both the lord and lady. He could prove troublesome.

"The time for reason may be at an end," John said thoughtfully. "You have tried to warn your brother of Avalene's shortcomings, but he seems determined to move forward with arrangements for this match. I fear there is little more you can do to avert this tragedy."

"Tragedy?" Dante echoed.

"'Tis obvious Baron Weston told you little of Avalene's . . . character," Margaret answered. "The Segraves' holdings are vast compared to Coleway. The wife of Faulke Segrave will be expected to oversee several great households and hundreds of servants. Avalene can scarce manage a few simple duties here at Coleway without constant oversight by John. He is ever correcting her foolish mistakes. The girl is incapable of managing a household of any size, and we would all be best served if she were to remain at Coleway where John can keep an eye on her and we can all provide her the guidance she needs."

"The girl is not stupid," Brunor said at last, as if he'd read Dante's thoughts. "A bit lazy, perhaps, but no more so than most young women her age. The responsibilities of a husband and children will give her the maturity she needs, but I am in agreement with John and Lady Margaret. Despite their efforts to mold the girl into a responsible young woman, she will never master the duties required of a chatelaine. Such tasks are beyond Avalene's capabilities. I conveyed as much to Baron Weston in my last missive and suggested she remain at Coleway as wife to one of my knights. What says Weston to that suggestion?"

Dante had no idea. "The baron did not make me privy to such a suggestion or his opinions on the matter. My only instructions are to collect his daughter and return her safely to Weston. As the baron's message relays, I am also aware that he intends to move forward with her betrothal to Faulke Segrave, pending the king's approval of course."

"We should send a more strongly worded message to my brother," Lady Margaret said to her husband. "Oh! We should send John! He is sure to make Reynard see reason."

"My orders are clear," Dante said, in a voice that had all three of them looking up at him. "I am to leave Coleway within two days of my arrival, and Lady Avalene will accompany me."

"How dare you—"

"Be silent," Brunor told his wife. "He has his orders. I have stated our case to your brother, and he has made other plans. You must accept it. Avalene is Weston's daughter and he wants her returned to Wales. 'Tis our duty to make certain this man fulfills his orders."

Margaret leaned closer to Brunor and they began to exchange heated words, but Dante scarcely paid attention to them. A fine silt of wood dust drifted downward through the air, and then a few small bits of rotted wood brushed down his arm. He assessed the situation in an instant. The railing above him was about to give way. Unless the chambermaid had sense enough to immediately move back from the railing, she was about to land on the head table and perhaps injure Lord Brunor or Lady Margaret, and probably break her own neck in the process.

His readiness to protect the lord and lady would assure "Sir Percival's" acceptance at Coleway and play on the chivalry that Mordecai had urged him to exploit. He made his decision in a split second, just as the creak of rotted wood warned him of the impending disaster. He took a quick step sideways to position himself directly below the girl, and then he braced himself for the impact.

Women screamed, men shouted, and Dante calmly caught the bloodred bundle that hurtled toward him. He had to take a step backward to absorb the blow as she landed in his arms, but he managed easily enough. She weighed no more than his tourney saddle. It was the color of her garments that made him frown, the same bloodred color as the steward's. He had already noticed the odd groupings of colors in the hall, how all the knights and their wives wore the same shade of green. It seemed logical that the steward's wife would follow suit, but why would she be spying from the gallery?

The girl remained strangely silent even after he recovered his balance, as if she didn't realize the danger of her fall and had expected someone to catch her. Perhaps the fright had robbed her of speech. The cloud of blond hair and a gauzy red veil made it impossible to read her expression. Deep blue eyes flecked with gold were all he could see of her face. Her wide-eyed gaze reflected surprise, and amazingly, an intense light of curiosity, as if she found something fascinating about his face. As if she recognized him.

The sudden knowledge of her identity came without warning, an unexpected and unwelcome revelation. She was not the steward's wife. This was his victim.

"Oh, good Lord!" Lady Margaret rose from her seat only to turn and collapse against her husband's chest. "Lord Brunor! My goodness! Oh, my . . ."

Dante ignored Margaret's hysterics, his attention held by the hauntingly familiar eyes of the woman in his arms. Did she somehow recognize him as well? Did she know his true identity? Aside from his lingering worry that she would suddenly decide to denounce him for an imposter, he sensed intelligence and depth in her steady gaze. But there was something else about her, something in her eyes that held him captive.

Desire.

He couldn't recall the last time a woman had looked at him with such obvious longing, if ever. He terrified those who knew what he was and he avoided those who didn't. In the guise of "Sir Percival," this one gazed up at him as if he were indeed a noble knight, as if she had landed exactly where she wanted to be.

He drew a deep breath to clear his muddled senses, then another when he caught the trace of an odd scent. The girl smelled of . . . roasted meat.

Lady Margaret recovered her composure in short order and launched into a lecture that did not allow for explanations. She barely stopped to draw a breath. "You could have been killed, if not for Sir Percival's intervention. Nay, worse than that, you could have killed yourself *and* Sir Percival! And look at yourself, your gown dirty, your veil ruined. You will explain this . . . this outrage at once."

Avalene reached up to pull the tangled veil away from her face just as Dante realized he had held her for an unseemly amount of time. With a silent curse, he released her legs as if they had burned him and her feet hit the ground before her knees were ready to hold her upright. Both of his arms went around her shoulders and he ended up all but embracing her to make sure she did not fall. Even worse, the hair and veil came away from her face at the same moment. He had intended to ask if she had injured herself, but something in his chest seemed to shift to his throat, rendering him speechless.

Mordecai's card had given him a general idea of what she would look like. A simple painting that could never do the original justice. Beneath the crooked circlet and tangled mop of hair was a delicate, heart-shaped face that took his breath away. High cheekbones, a small nose, full, sensual lips, and eyes that invited him to her bed without speaking a word. He doubted she had any knowledge of the words. The look in her eyes was not that of a practiced courtesan, but the innocent adoration of a maid when she gazed upon her beloved.

His cold blood thawed so quickly that even his bones felt warmed. He wanted to shake some sense into her. Didn't she realize what that look of hers could do to a man?

He managed to tear his gaze from her face long enough to compose his senses, marshaling every thread of common sense to force himself to view her through safe, lifeless eyes. Rather than moon over the beauty of her face, he moved his gaze lower to gauge how easily her slender neck would fit between his hands. Soon he was fixated on the pulse point at the base of her neck that betrayed the rapid fluttering of her heart.

He was a man accustomed to making hearts beat with fear, yet when he looked at her face she appeared unafraid. She even wet her lips as her gaze moved slowly over him. It was nothing more than a nervous gesture, he told himself, even as he watched the tip of her tongue trace its path and wondered what other parts of her would be such a delightful shade of pink.

His gaze drifted lower again, but this time he couldn't

imagine his hands around her neck for any reason but to stroke the smooth, white column, to see if her skin was as soft as it looked. The gown's modest neckline revealed a tempting glimpse of even softer flesh, skin so luminescent that the color reminded him of pearls. She looked too warm and vibrant to be an Englishman's ideal of beauty, but even the barbaric English must recognize perfection when they saw it. He couldn't stop staring at her. Likely all men reacted in the same besotted fashion. This was what Mordecai had tried to warn him about.

"Sir Percival?" She reached out to lay her hand on his chest. Although he could not feel the pressure of her hand through the chain mail and padding, he was sure he felt the warmth of her touch. His chest began to burn. "You were not hurt?"

Hurt? He shook his head. He was not hurt. He was devastated. How else could he describe the force that rendered him both powerless and invincible at the same time? She stirred emotions that were little more than vague memories, so far removed from mere physical need and so long forgotten that he scarce recognized the feelings. Warmth seeped through him like a heady draught of mulled wine. Her lips parted again and his blood caught fire.

"Sir Percival?" A shadow of concern darkened her eyes. "Are you injured? I could not forgive myself, truly, did I injure you." She reached toward his face, hesitated, and then her hand curled back toward her chest as though she feared he would recoil from her touch.

Moving away from her was the last thing he would do. Everything about her drew him in, and yet, at the same time, everything about her warned him to stay away. His gaze went to the hand that still rested on his chest, so small and insignificant. The fingers were slender and well-shaped, the soft, white hand of a lady. He imagined her hand against his bare skin, even though he knew she would never knowingly touch anything so foul or corrupt.

Aye, he was injured in places she would never know. And he would wager a fortune that she had never known anything like him in her short, sheltered life. Beneath the disguise of a knight lay the true face of evil, a demon that lusted after innocence. And if he did not get these strange emotions under control, she would soon learn exactly what sort of monster she was gazing upon so adoringly. He shook his head again in an effort to clear his befuddled senses. *Gesù*. The girl was a witch.

"'Tis obvious your fall has rattled the poor man's wits, Avalene."

The shrewd undercurrent in the steward's voice *un*-rattled his wits in short order. He gave the man a curt glance. "Everything happened rather quickly. I needed but a moment to gather my thoughts."

"You are unsettled," John went on, his gaze focused sharply on Dante. "'Tis a common enough condition in Avalene's presence."

So, the steward was aware of his interest in the girl. A regrettable mistake, the kind he had not made in a very long time. In his world, truth was an illusion built upon lies, a place where one wrong word, one wrong gesture could cost his life. To argue against John's suspicions now would only confirm them. Instead he set Avalene an arm's length away from him, and then inclined his head in agreement with John. "I find it most unsettling when pretty maidens fall from the sky. Does this happen often here at Coleway?"

The corners of John's false smile tightened as a sprinkling of laughter moved through the crowd.

Dante turned toward Avalene and dropped to one

knee before the girl. He bowed his head, the very picture of a chivalrous knight. Mordecai would likely laugh aloud if he saw him now. "I hope you took no offense at my boldness. Pray forgive any impertinence, my lady?"

"Ah, I . . . you are forgiven," Avalene said. "That is, there is nothing *to* forgive. Please, there is no need to . . . I am entirely in your debt, Sir Percival. Please rise. Are you certain you were not injured?"

"Not in the least," he assured her as he stood up.

"Enough, enough," said Lord Brunor. "Sir Percival has delivered his message and rescued the maiden. 'Tis time for the poor man to enjoy the comforts of our home and hospitality, a just reward after his long journey. Sir Percival, the chamberlain will show you to quarters above the garrison. In the meantime, you are welcome to partake of our feast. Perhaps a bit of ale will restore your wits."

"Thank you, Lord Brunor. I appreciate—"

"There will be naught but a cold pallet in the garrison for Sir Percival," Margaret interrupted. "The comfort of a warm bed is the least we can offer the man to show our gratitude for his heroic rescue of our niece. The turret room near my solar should do nicely. Avalene, see that the room is prepared for Sir Percival and move what you will need to the solar. You nap often enough on the window cushions. They should make you an adequate bed for the next few nights."

Dante could tell by the way the other three looked at Margaret that something odd was afoot. He could scarce credit the notion, but it sounded as if Margaret meant to put him in Avalene's chamber and move the girl just a short distance down a hallway. It was unheard of to quarter a visiting knight anywhere near an unwed noblewoman. Surely he had misheard.

John was the first to find his voice. "My lady, this is most . . . unseemly. I feel certain Sir Percival would prefer the company of other knights and soldiers in the quarters above the garrison."

"Nonsense. There is nothing wrong with rewarding a man for noble deeds. Putting him in a room with a warm brazier and a soft bed is the least we can do." Margaret waved her hand to dismiss John's objection, although she gave her husband a sideways glance. "My mind is set upon the matter. Avalene, I will accompany you to make certain everything is prepared as I wish." She rose, then turned toward her husband. "My lord, if you will excuse us?"

"Aye, be off with you both," Brunor said, as he reached for a pitcher of ale, only to find it empty.

Avalene dropped into a curtsey before Dante. "Thank you again for your rescue, Sir Percival."

The proper response to her polite gesture was a gallant bow and then an offer of his hand to help her rise. Instead he found himself frozen in place by this alternate view of what he had so recently considered a modest neckline. Even the most banal response was beyond his ability. For the first time in his memory, he was dumbstruck. All he could do was stare in dazed admiration as she rose from her curtsey to follow her aunt to the stairway. He shook his head again, knowing the gown revealed far less of Avalene than the gowns of many other ladies in the great hall. Still, hers was the only gown he had peered down the front of. He sincerely hoped he was the only man who had ever enjoyed that view, because he had an insane urge to plant his fist in the face of any other male who had even imagined such a sight.

"John, there is a decided lack of refreshment," Brunor said, interrupting Dante's thoughts. "Find someone in the kitchens who can see that the pitchers are replenished, and then meet with the chamberlain to discuss the preparations that need be made to send Avalene off to Wales in two days. You will also speak with the carpenters about the repairs needed in the gallery. I will expect your report in the morning."

"Of course," John said, his oily smile firmly in place. "Avalene was supposed to— Ah, but that is of no consequence. I will see to the ale immediately. Perhaps I should meet with the chamberlain and carpenter after the feast so I can be here to serve you should anything else go awry."

Brunor gave John a pointed look. "I wish to speak with Sir Percival in private."

John looked as if he had bit into a green apple, but he set off to do as he was bid after muttering, "Aye, my lord."

"Have a seat, Sir Percival." Brunor indicated the chair that Margaret had recently vacated, then signaled to a servant. A fresh trencher piled high with slices of meat and fish soon appeared along with another pitcher of ale and a mug for Dante. Brunor waited until the servants had retreated before he spoke, and then in a tone only Dante could hear. "Is Reynard certain he wants to tie his daughter and his allegiance to the Segraves?"

Dante took out the small dagger he used for meals and then began to toy with the crumbling white meat of a fish fillet as he considered his answer. Telling as much of the truth as possible was always the easiest and most successful ploy. "The baron's mind is set on the matter. The Segraves will be a powerful ally on Weston's southern borders, and he wants this marriage to take place as soon as possible."

"Then you had best heed well this warning," Brunor said, as he leaned closer. "My wife intends to do everything within her power to put you in bed with Avalene."

5

❦

The Warning

The Hermit brings knowledge of good and evil, but not the ability to recognize the difference between the two. Accept his silent counsel of prudence and discretion. Act upon what can be changed and accept what cannot.

If Dante had lifted his knife a moment sooner, he would have choked on the first bite of his meal. Instead he managed to hold on to the food, and even forced down a small mouthful to hide his shock. He instinctively rolled the lump of fish over his tongue to search for any hidden taste of poison while his mind did much the same with this latest piece of astonishing news. What mischief were Margaret and Brunor about? Was this some ploy? More to the point, what could these two hope to gain from it?

The strange plan he had started out with all those weeks ago in London grew more bizarre by the moment. He set his knife aside. "You have me at a loss, Lord Brunor. Baron Weston sent me specifically because he knows I would never betray my liege lord or his daughter in such a vile manner. Why would your wife conceive of such a plan, much less assume I would cooperate?"

"My eyesight is not what it once was," Brunor said, "but I can still recognize when a man is besotted with a woman. Margaret and John recognized the signs as well. You do a poor job of disguising your emotions."

Dante wanted to laugh in his face, he, a master at disguising and controlling his emotions. Until today.

That Brunor had the right of it would indeed be laughable under different circumstances. *Gesù*. Even a near-blind man recognized that he acted like a lecherous goat. Avalene de Forshay had turned his head to sap. However, his brain still functioned well enough to wonder why they seemed determined to serve the girl up to him on a platter. "I meant no disrespect, Lord Brunor, but I had not been warned of her beauty. Indeed, I expected a maiden more plain than comely. I cannot explain what came over me, and can only apologize and swear that nothing will come of it."

"Ah, but you have yet to reckon with the force that is my wife," Brunor warned. "She has it in her head that Avalene should not leave Coleway, ever, and the only way to accomplish her goal is for Avalene to marry one of my men. She has pestered me endlessly with her schemes and plans. Now that she knows her brother has no intention of accommodating her wishes, her clever mind has latched upon the only other way to get what she wants. I believe she intends to make certain Avalene is compromised and discovered in bed with a lover. The man responsible will be immediately hung, of course, but not before Avalene's reputation is ruined. No decent man will want her as a bride after that. That is, no man her father would choose. Marriage to a lowly knight or a high-ranking servant will become the only path open to her. In you, I am certain Margaret sees a way to compromise the girl without losing one of our own men in the process."

Dante had long ago passed the point where anything he heard or saw could shock him. Still, it was highly strange for Brunor to confide so much in the man who was supposed to play the pawn. He stated the only response that seemed appropriate. "You astonish me, Lord Brunor."

"Oh, there is more," Brunor promised. "Margaret does not know this, but John has pestered me for years to petition Baron Weston on his behalf to contract a betrothal. When it became obvious I had no intention of making such a proposal to my brother-in-law, John began to work his wiles upon my wife to intercede. He is equally determined to keep Avalene at Coleway, and he intends to wed the girl himself."

Dante blinked once as he absorbed these new details. It was becoming clear that this would not be a simple matter of collecting the girl and riding out of the castle with a fare-thee-well. "Surely John realizes that Lady Avalene is above his station?"

Brunor made a sound of disgust. "John does not believe anyone is above his station. He has convinced Margaret that it is in everyone's best interests to keep Avalene at Coleway and thinks he has convinced me as well."

"You did voice your concern about Avalene's abilities to manage her duties as Segrave's wife," Dante reminded him.

"My objections to a match with the Segraves have more to do with politics than any doubts about Avalene's ability to manage a household," Brunor said. "'Tis obvious the Segraves mean to solidify their base of power in Wales, and there are many Marcher lords who have marriageable daughters. However, few of those lords would willingly tie their family to one so obviously intent on rebellion and treason. I was willing to entertain the notion of keeping Avalene at Coleway through marriage to one of my knights if Reynard wished to avoid ties to the Segraves, but it appears he has chosen the more dangerous path. That is his choice to make and I will abide by his wishes. However, my wife and steward will not be so easily swayed from their course."

Dante remained silent, waiting, certain he would learn more if he kept his mouth closed. His patience was soon rewarded.

"I will admit that I have allowed my wife and steward to cling to false hope longer than I should have," Brunor admitted, "but it seemed harmless until now. If what I suspect is true, this is no longer a harmless game and I will not have a knight lured to murder under my roof."

"I appreciate your concern," Dante said truthfully. "'Tis unexpected, to say the least, but much appreciated. Baron Weston would be aggrieved should his daughter wed a lowly steward, yet it could be argued that you would benefit from such a match. She has a large dowry and will obviously be sorely missed by those in your household. Such a situation could easily be turned to your advantage."

"'Tis a matter of honor," Brunor said in a flat voice. "I would not plot against one of my wards any more than I would tolerate another lord plotting against one of my own children in such a manner. My children will be sent to foster in the next few years and I plan to place them with some of the most powerful families in England. My wife does not seem to realize that our whole family would be tainted by such a scandal and our own children's futures would be affected as well. Strong alliances can be formed through fostering, and I value my alliances with other lords far more than I value the whims of my steward. The only way I would have considered Avalene marrying beneath her station and remaining at Coleway was with Reynard's blessing. I will not hold her here against her father's will."

It seemed Avalene was not the only person at Coleway who valued chivalry and honor, albeit Brunor's brand of honor was mostly self-serving. Dante nodded when Brunor lifted a pitcher of ale and offered to fill his mug.

"I will speak to my wife on the matter this eve," Brunor went on, "but I would suspect that John's thoughts will soon run along similar lines if they haven't already. He has an uncanny ability to bend people to his will without them realizing they are his pawns until it is time to assign blame. Know that your life is in the balance on this matter. You must be on your guard."

Wonderful, Dante thought, even as he gave Brunor a solemn nod. He could almost admire Margaret and John's machinations if they did not interfere so directly with his own. Already he regretted the promise he made to Mordecai that the girl would live until Segrave was convinced to take another bride. Life would be considerably easier if he could simply poison the girl, then make good his escape. Instead, all of this intrigue was bound to give him a headache by the time he left Coleway. "You have my most solemn promise that I will not be tricked into a compromising position with your niece, Lord Brunor. I shall also be on my guard at all times against any scurrilous tactics to compromise Lady Avalene's honor."

Brunor studied his face long and hard, then finally nodded. "My concerns could be misplaced, but I know all too well how my wife's mind works and John's as well. Do what you can to avoid being alone with Avalene while you are at Coleway, and I will send extra women on your journey back to Wales to make certain there are adequate chaperones. You should not lower your guard until you deliver Avalene safely to her father."

"You have my sworn word, Lord Brunor, that no one

will force Lady Avalene into marriage while I draw breath on this earth." Dante wanted to kick himself. The words sounded too self-assured, too possessive. "I have promised her father that I will bring her home safely and I would sooner die than break my word to Baron Weston."

"'Tis nice to see such loyalty," Brunor said, "but be advised that what I have told you goes no further. If Baron Weston inquires, I will deny this conversation ever took place. Do we understand each other?"

"Aye," Dante answered, "we understand each other very well indeed."

"Good, good, now let us speak of other things." Brunor filled his mug yet again before he settled back in his chair. "Tell me of your journey from Wales."

Rather than give Dante a chance to answer, he instead offered his own opinion.

"I journeyed there only once to fetch Avalene when she first came to live with us. Baron Weston's fortress is most impressive, but I have no great desire to return to such a troublesome wilderness. There are too few inns to sustain a traveler, and too many Welsh rebels in the forests. Now, the roads in England and France are a different matter altogether. A knight can journey to every tourney worth mention and sleep each eve in a soft bed."

Dante marveled at how easily the man could dismiss his wife's schemes and change the subject. "You have attended many tourneys, Lord Brunor?"

It was the right question to ask. Brunor launched into a long-winded tale that recounted every mud-splattered mile of his last journey through France, then a tale of a tournament at Crecy, which reminded Brunor a bit of the tournament at Chepstow. That naturally led to a complete accounting of the bloody combats and victorious revelries of every tournament that Brunor had participated in since boyhood.

Dante could hardly believe that the man who talked so inanely about meaningless tournaments was the same man who had shrewdly recognized and assessed a potentially dangerous situation in his household within mere moments and devised an effective strategy to deal with it. So far, nothing about Coleway or its inhabitants was what Dante expected and he was beginning to hope the night would end soon. There were only so many surprises he could tolerate in one day.

Mostly he was uncomfortable with his audience, as he was more or less on display in the great hall. The people of Coleway seemed convinced by his disguise, but they still saw him as a stranger, a curiosity to be stared at and whispered about. He could not recall the last time he had allowed anyone to study his face and features at such leisure. Although he tried to accept their stares, he kept his head lowered and avoided any direct gazes as he ate.

And then there was the great effort required to appear to eat with the enthusiasm of an Englishman while he actually consumed very little. Strong seasonings and spices were forbidden to a man who must move unnoticed through a crowd, or creep past a garrison of guards without betraying his presence. Most of the dishes before him were smothered with highly scented herbs and seasonings.

In this land of rain and water where nothing and no one ever managed to be clean, Dante made himself the exception. As a result he could smell an Englishman at fifty paces. Most reeked of onions and garlic, and their own stale sweat. Lord Brunor's scent revealed a fondness for ale.

"I vow my seams will burst if I eat another bite," he

lied to Lord Brunor. "My thanks for the bounty of your table."

"'Tis fair compensation," said Brunor. He drained yet another mug of ale, and then pushed away from the table. "I have little doubt that you wish for a respite after such arduous travels. Allow me to show you to your quarters, Sir Percival."

Brunor spoke in a purposeful tone that could be heard by any of the servants and soldiers at the nearest tables, a subterfuge so deliberate that Dante mentally rolled his eyes. Outwardly, he showed just the right degree of false pleasure. "I would appreciate your escort."

Avalene heard footsteps in the hallway and knew they belonged to Sir Percival when her pulse picked up. She took one last look around her chamber to make certain everything was in order.

The turret room was once a guard tower that recent expansions to the castle had rendered useless for that purpose, so Avalene had claimed the chamber as her own. Private quarters were a rarity in a castle, and the chamber offered more comforts than a soldier such as Sir Percival would expect. Most striking were the long, colorful banners that hung from pegs placed near the tall ceiling. In all, there were more than a score of banners that covered most of the circular stone walls of the turret, stretching from the ceiling to the floor. Half were made of blue samite with the de Forshay griffins stitched in white and silver. The others were solid black with a large, bloodred dragon emblazoned on the fabric, the standard of the Segraves. The banners were gifts for her father, and they gave her chamber a very noble air.

Elsewhere the furnishings were far simpler; several wooden chests were placed around the room, a stool's thick, burgundy-colored pad offered a soft seat near the brazier, and a basket filled with balls of thread was placed nearby. An ample-sized bed claimed a section of the curved wall across from the doorway; embroidered flowers of every color brightened the cream-colored bed curtains, along with the matching coverlet and pillows. An old, chipped ewer held a spray of wildflowers on top of a wooden trunk, and a half-dozen seashells were scattered next to the ewer.

Only a woman would fuss with such small details, arrangements meant to please no one but herself. She felt very much at home in this chamber, surrounded by her feminine comforts. Sir Percival did not belong here. Still, she could easily picture him in her bed. Why did that thought cause her cheeks to warm?

She had tried to explain away her strange reaction to the man as an unexpected result of her accident. Anyone would be shocked senseless by nearly falling to their death. Anyone would feel an overwhelming rush of warmth and gratitude toward the person who rescued them. The only flaws in her reasoning lay in the fact that she felt more warmth than gratitude, and she had not been shocked senseless. Quite the contrary, landing in Sir Percival's arms had set every one of her senses on fire.

First his scent had filled her head; leather and oiled armor, the crisp smell of the open countryside, and beneath it all, a faint, masculine scent that had made her want to lean closer to find its source. What stopped her was the piercing emerald color of his eyes that made all the colors in the hall seem suddenly pale. She'd had to work hard to pull her gaze away from his and she could scarce recall seeing anything but him. She could tell by the way he effortlessly caught and then held her that there was a hard, muscular body beneath his armor and she had actually stroked his arm and then his chest, trying to feel what was beneath the cloth and iron.

Later she admitted that it was her strange awareness of the man that had made her react in ways that were most unlike her, an immediate sense that she had landed exactly where she was meant to be, in the arms of a man who could hold her safe and secure against any threat. He was familiar to her in ways she could not fathom. She wanted to melt into him, to lose herself in his gaze, forget that anyone else existed. It was the singular most unique experience in her life.

The footsteps drew closer and she took a deep breath to steady herself and brushed the wrinkles from the skirt of her newly-donned scarlet gown, sparing a glance at her aunt next to her. Something fluttered in her stomach when Sir Percival finally entered her chamber and started toward her. Already she had forgotten how big he was and yet how gracefully he moved.

There were other things about him that seemed different from what she remembered of him in the great hall. His hair was not pure black, as she had thought. The candlelight in her chamber brushed waves of deep mahogany amidst the ebony, an unexpected flame in the depths of night. The same dark shadows defined his jaw, the sharp planes of his cheeks, the masculine lines around his mouth. Altogether, he had the face of a fallen angel; a dark, sensual vision of sin.

He watched her just as closely and his gaze drifted lower for a leisurely examination of every part of her. It was such a thorough inspection that she knew she should be offended. Later, she would be offended. For the moment, she basked in the rare warmth of a man's appreciative gaze.

The men at Coleway tended to avoid her for the most part, just as certain as she was that she would find some dreadful task for anyone who had time to gawk at or speak improperly to a maiden, especially one who had the power to make their life unpleasant. Flirting did not engender respect, and she tolerated none of it from her uncle's men.

There had been a few exceptions, of course, a few young men brave enough to offer their assistance in the gardens as she gathered herbs and flowers, or their escort when she joined the hunt, or to request her hand in a dance. Regardless of whether she found their company pleasant or tiresome, their attentions never lasted beyond one or two small signs of courtship before they began to ignore her or actively avoid her company.

John teased her mercilessly over her failures at even those most innocent of courtships, somehow aware of each rejection, slyly insinuating that they had found her personality as lacking as her beauty. She had tried to ignore John's venom, knowing he delighted in making everyone miserable, yet the poisonous words took root after a while. She felt clumsy and awkward around any man she found the least bit attractive. Knowing any encouragement would only end with her own hurt feelings, her deliberately cold, shrewish manner was always enough to keep them at arm's length. The ploy worked well on both sides. She could not recall the last man who had bestirred any interest.

Her father's knight was a different story entirely. He would be worth the risk just to see him smile at her again. He made her feel small and delicate, this man who had caught her so easily in his arms. Yet, for some reason, he also made her feel helpless and more than a little afraid that he could hurt her in ways she had never experienced.

Part of her awed reaction was due to his size and strength, she supposed, evident in every hard line of his body. But mostly there was something about the way he looked at her. Something . . . predatory. No man had ever looked at her that way.

She watched him as he followed her uncle into her chamber in a slow, unhurried pace and saw his gaze sweep across the room once, and then again, as if he were wary of some threat. Despite this awareness of his surroundings, she had no doubt that she was his prey. He ignored Lady Margaret and came to a halt directly in front of her.

"My lady," he murmured, as he made a slight bow. "Allow me to apologize for this intrusion. Your aunt's generous offer to lend me your quarters is a great honor, but Lord Brunor tells me you will be forced to sleep on a stone bench beneath the solar windows. 'Tis not right for a knight to enjoy his own comforts at the expense of a lady. I would sooner sleep on a bed of thorns." He didn't give Avalene a chance to respond to those astonishing statements before he turned to Lady Margaret. "I am well accustomed to hardship and discomfort, my lady. The window seat's cushions in the solar will provide a far finer pallet than any I had expected. I beseech you to grant me this boon as I find it a far more attractive reward."

"Nonsense," Margaret began. "You were promised—"

"'Tis a matter of honor," Brunor said, as he gave his wife a look of warning. "You must not force Sir Percival to accept something that would be at such sharp odds with a knight's code of honor."

Margaret pressed her lips together, but gave her husband a reluctant nod. "Very well, the reward was not meant to cause you distress, Sir Percival. Of course you may sleep in the solar whilst you are at Coleway. 'Tis only a few paces down the hallway, so that should work out equally well."

Brunor made an obvious sound as he cleared his throat.

"That is, I am certain you will be equally comfortable there," Margaret hurried to say. "The servants should have a brazier warming the room by now, and I ordered extra sleeping furs for Avalene that you can use. Aye, you will be quite comfortable. Did you happen to notice Avalene's fine needlework?"

There was a moment of silence as everyone absorbed Lady Margaret's abrupt change of subject, then each gaze slowly followed the direction of her hand to one of the dragon banners.

Sir Percival walked toward the banner to take a closer look. He touched the delicate needlework that outlined the dragon's claws and scales, and even the shadows she had achieved by dyeing many pieces of fabric slightly different shades of red.

"This beast is a work of art," he said. "Indeed, all of the banners are flawless. Such work requires long hours and an artist's eye. You have an exceptional talent, Lady Avalene."

"'Tis one of her more useful skills," Margaret said. "She cannot—"

Avalene broke in before Margaret could reveal some new flaw that Percival would report to her father. "Each year I send a set of banners to my father for the ramparts of Weston Castle. Perhaps you saw the ones I made last year? He requested the dragons specifically for this year's banners . . . as a gift for the Segraves. A betrothal gift, I suppose."

"I hope the Segraves will appreciate your abilities," he said, without answering her question. Impossibly green eyes stared at her with such intensity that it was almost a relief when his gaze left her face. "These banners are gifts fit for royalty."

"I . . ." She meant to thank him, but a different thought took shape in her mind as she looked up at him, a thought planted by her dealings with John and his cronies. "I think you jest, Sir Percival. They are simple banners, not works of art."

"I seldom jest," he said, "and never at the expense of a lady. The beauty of what I see in this chamber surpasses anything I have seen of the like. I am in awe of your talent."

She realized with a start that she believed him, believed with all her heart that he would never laugh at her, even behind her back as others had done in the past, usually at John's urging. She also wanted to pinch him, just to make certain he was real. In all her dreams and flights of fancy, she had never created a knight quite so perfect as Sir Percival of Weston.

She wasn't sure how long they stared at each other, but he was the first to look away. And still she stared. Brunor cleared his throat again, louder this time, and Sir Percival glanced at her. Their eyes met again only for an instant and his features betrayed nothing, yet within that flash of green was a warning so immediate and understandable that she instantly lowered her lashes.

"I believe a hunt is in order for the morrow to refill the larders," Brunor said abruptly. "We will have another feast the day after the hunt to give everyone a chance to say their farewells to Avalene, and then you can depart the morning after the feast. That should also give everyone ample time to prepare for the journey. What say you, Percival? Will that satisfy your schedule?"

"Aye," he said simply.

"Very well," Brunor said. "There are a few things I must discuss with my wife. Avalene, show Sir Percival to the solar."

"Aye, my lord." Avalene held out her hand toward the doorway. "If you will follow me, Sir Percival?"

He looked as if he meant to say something in response and then thought better of it. Instead he merely inclined his head in agreement, and then he fell into step behind her. The door from the turret led directly to the passageway from the great hall. Her nerves and awkwardness returned with a vengeance as she pointed out what she felt was necessary. "This hallway leads to the chapel and there is a garderobe through the doorway at the end of the passage."

He made no response and she quickened her step. Halfway down the dimly lit passageway she opened a door to reveal a room much larger than her own chamber. It was the main gathering place for the ladies of the castle to gossip and sew during the day. The row of wide, arched windows on the outer wall drenched the solar in bright, airy sunlight during the day and provided ample light for sewing, but there was a definite chill to the room in the evenings. In keeping with its mostly feminine uses, the room's plastered walls were painted robin's-egg blue and decorated with hundreds of painted vines and roses. Tonight the moonlight cast strange shadows through the mullioned panes, and the cheerful, painted patterns took on a more sinister appearance in shades of black and gray. Avalene was glad that Percival had insisted upon sleeping here, and heartily agreed that a knight should not force a lady from her own bed. He really was quite honorable.

"Lord Brunor must have had your baggage brought up as well," she mused, nodding toward the saddlebags by one of the window seats. His silence made her wonder if he had already reached the stage where he wished to ignore her. "There is a candle and flint near the brazier. Is there anything else you require, Sir Percival?"

Even though the question was a simple one, she again had that odd feeling that he was torn about his answer. At last he said, "Do you want to stay at Coleway, my lady?"

The question so startled her that she made an unlady-like sound in the back of her throat. "I can think of nothing—" She pressed her lips together before more churlish words could escape them. He would surely report every word of their conversations to her father. "That is, I am very grateful for all that my aunt has taught me and my uncle's many kindnesses over the years, but I look forward to the day I will be mistress of my own home. If my father can gain a valuable alliance through my marriage, all the better. Has someone told you that I do not wish to leave Coleway?"

"Not exactly."

She waited until it became obvious that was all he intended to say on the matter. Another fear took root, one that made her rethink her vow to be careful with her words. "Lady Margaret ofttimes thinks I am some great trial upon her patience, yet at other times she thinks I am all that keeps Coleway's household running smoothly. Indeed, I suspect she will do everything within her power to keep me from leaving. If she has suggested that I do not wish to leave Coleway, or that I am some-how not ready to become a wife, let me assure you that I do not share her opinions on the matter. Take me to my father, and I will run Weston's household until I have proven myself capable of managing a great estate. It will not take long before he realizes I will not embarrass our family. Or, has John told you some piece of gossip? You may not remain at Coleway long enough to realize, but the steward rarely has good things to say about anyone. He does not—"

Percival held up both hands. "You mistake the question, my lady. I simply wanted to be certain you were ready to leave what has become your home. Some ladies might become . . . sentimental on such an occasion."

Of course, she thought. He wondered if he would have a sobbing female on his hands when they departed. Instead she had given him ample reason to seek out John and Lady Margaret to find out why they did not think her ready to leave Coleway. What was it about this man that rattled her wits? She felt like kicking herself. It would be best for her to leave this chamber before she gave him any more bad ideas. "I look forward to the day we leave for Weston, Sir Percival. If you will excuse me, I'm certain my aunt and uncle will soon wonder what is keeping me."

She gave him a quick curtsey and all but fled from the room, keeping her gaze averted until she was in the passageway and the door had closed behind her. Still, she did not feel free of the invisible hold he seemed to have over her. He flustered her. There was no other word for it. He looked at her, and she could not think straight. She was fast losing count of the unexpected ways her body reacted to the smallest, strangest things such as the sound of his voice, or the scent that clung to his clothing. No other man had ever had such a disturbing effect on her. He was something entirely new to her world.

The girlish crushes in her past faded to insignificance, their pull nothing like this bone-deep awareness of a man. Whatever its causes, whatever her reactions, they had to stop. He was her father's knight and would soon be her guardian on the trip to Wales, and then nothing more. They would spend a few weeks in each other's company on this journey, perhaps she would see him on occasion at Castle Weston, and then she would go to the Segraves. Their acquaintance would last no more than a few months at most, and then it was unlikely she would ever see Sir Percival again. Mooning over a man she barely knew and would never know very well was as much a waste of her time as it was dangerous.

She reached the door to her chamber and stood with her hand on the latch as she contemplated the potential consequences of her unexpected attraction to Sir Percival. There were tales aplenty of disgraced maidens and adulterous wives. Until today, she had thought those women were either weak-willed or selfish. What honorable woman would risk disgracing herself and her family simply to be with a man who was not her husband or her betrothed?

Now she had a better appreciation for the lure of temptation. It would not be so hard to encourage a friendship between herself and Sir Percival on the journey to Wales. There were no rules against an innocent friendship or harmless flirtations between a knight and a lady. Knights pledged themselves all the time to ladies who were married or betrothed to other men, as a tribute to either their beauty or the warmth of their personality, or both. Countless knights had pledged themselves to Lady Margaret, and Lord Brunor actually took pride in their numbers. They walked with her in the gardens, carried her favor in tourneys, and composed countless poems and songs in tribute to her beauty that they performed with various degrees of success in the solar when Margaret held court with her ladies. Avalene had found it all rather nauseating at times, but the thought of Sir Percival being smitten with her enough to compose poetry made her heart skip a beat . . . until reality intruded once more.

His effect on her was undeniable, but she refused to hope that he felt the same way. His eyes were too worldly and his face too handsome to be instantly captivated by anyone so plain or ordinary. There must be a string of beautiful women who vied for his attentions at Weston. She was no more to him than a duty. That was the reason she had to—

"*Avalene will not leave Coleway in two days or two hundred.*"

The sound of her aunt's voice was muffled, but still loud enough to be heard clearly through the door. Avalene pulled her hand away from the latch and then leaned closer to the gap between the wooden door and the stone doorway. It was Lady Margaret's next words that caught her undivided attention and sent a chill down her spine.

"Aye, I am well aware that John wishes to marry her. 'Tis a small enough reward for all he has done for us and you should have petitioned my brother long before the Segraves became involved in her betrothal. Failing that, you could have helped me arrange her compromise with some traveling merchant or minstrel. Now the timing will appear suspicious."

Every drop of blood in Avalene's veins turned to ice. Her aunt and uncle, the very people charged to keep her safe, were plotting to ruin her.

It was not hard to piece together their plan. The man she despised more than any other had somehow convinced them to help trap her in a marriage that would shame both her and her father. The scandal was beyond her ability to imagine.

Numbed to the bone, she was helpless to do anything but listen as Margaret continued her argument.

"Still, you cannot fail to see my logic. If she is compromised by Sir Percival you can have him arrested. Even if you decide not to hang him, my brother could not argue our logic if we spare Percival's life and send him back to Weston Castle without Avalene. Reynard will still wish to marry her off quickly, and a steward who is cousin to a baron will be a fitting husband for a woman so disgraced."

Her aunt had to be standing very close to the doorway to be heard so clearly in the passageway because Avalene could not make out one word of her uncle's lengthy response. Despite pressing her ear as hard as she could to the crack between the wall and the door, the conversation in the chamber was impossible to follow until she heard Margaret's answer. "Aye, you are correct, my lord. I had not considered those possibilities. Perhaps we should both meet with John tomorrow to discuss your concerns. Surely he has thought of them as well and will have a solution, which is fine by me as long as the trap is sprung by tomorrow night. In any event, she could walk in upon us at any moment and this discussion is best saved for our own chamber. I will go see what is keeping her."

Avalene scrambled away from the door and schooled her expression into blank innocence. She pretended to still be walking down the passageway toward her chamber even as the door opened and she met Lady Margaret's startled expression with one of her own.

"Oh! How long have you been here?" Margaret demanded.

Avalene glanced over her shoulder to collect her wits, then turned and lied to her aunt's face. "I just returned from the solar. Sir Percival was kind enough to answer a few questions I had about my family at Weston."

That such questions had never occurred to Avalene while she was alone with Sir Percival caused a momentary pang of guilt, followed by a wave of relief. Margaret appeared to believe her. "Well, do not dawdle. We have all had a long day and your uncle is determined that the hunt begin at dawn on the morrow. 'Tis time for us all to be abed."

"Aye, my lady," Avalene murmured as she stepped to one side of the passageway. "I will bid you good eve."

"I sent word to the kitchens to let them know we will break our fast earlier than planned," Brunor told Avalene. He followed Margaret from the chamber and stepped into the passageway, then turned to give her a considering look. "You are welcome to join us on the hunt."

"Cook may not be well enough to return to his duties," she said. "'Tis best if I remain here to make certain the meat is properly dressed once it arrives." She wondered how they failed to notice the way her voice wavered, the way her hands trembled, even though she had them clenched behind her back. Their only concerns, as usual, involved their own comforts. Who would see to all these small details once she returned home to Weston? *If* she returned to Weston. "Will you be attending the hunt as well, my lady?"

"Of course," Margaret said, looking slightly perplexed. "You know well enough that I never miss a hunt."

"And Sir Percival? Will he go on the hunt as well?"

Brunor answered before Margaret had a chance. "Aye, why do you ask?"

"I need to plan a midday meal for the hunters," she said, thankful to have thought of such a plausible explanation so quickly. "I will have food sent to the huntsman's lodge at midday, and then the food carts can haul the game back to the castle to be dressed. I will also speak to the marshal about the carts I will need for the journey to Weston."

She breathed another small sigh of relief when Brunor nodded.

"Do what you must to prepare for your journey," he said. "Use your time wisely. Already the hour grows late and you have much to do on the morrow. We will bid you good eve, niece."

Somehow she managed to keep her expression politely blank as she bid her aunt and uncle good night. Her wobbly knees held steady as she watched them walk away until finally they turned the corner at the end of the passageway. She even felt a strange sense of calm as she stepped into her chamber and quietly closed the door behind her, and then she leaned her back against the door and slowly sank to the floor.

6

The Plan

*The dark holds comfort when
The World of light illuminates
the path to disaster. The teach-
ings and beliefs of the child
prove the source of reluctance
to leave all that is familiar.
Resistance to change makes the
jailer a prisoner, yet not all
prisons contain chains.*

Avalene awoke with a start, the sound of her own cry
echoing in her ears. The covers had tangled around her
feet and she struggled to sit up, desperate to free herself
from the last drugging effects of the nightmare, needing
to assure herself that she was well and truly awake. The
gasping sound of her ragged breathing completed the
transition from sleep to awareness.

She opened her eyes and discovered she was in her
chamber at Coleway . . . safe . . . for the time being.

"Foolish dreams," she said aloud. Given the plot
afoot to compromise her father's knight and force her
into a ruinous marriage, it was hardly a surprise that
she would have nightmares. What she found surprising
was that she had managed to nod off in the midst of her
worries.

"Foolish *nightmares*," she amended, although she still
trembled like a frightened mouse.

Moonlight streamed through the windows in her
chamber, so bright that she would scarce need a candle

if she decided to move about in the room. The position of the moon said the night was only half spent; it would be hours yet before the hunt began and she had still not decided what she would or could do to avoid her fate. She rubbed the sleep from her eyes and tried to clear her jumbled thoughts. Surely there would be a way to escape the castle during the hunt?

Perhaps she could say that she intended to ride out to the huntsman's lodge, and then make a break for her father's fortress in Wales. The problem with that plan was that none of the guards would let her set foot from Coleway without an escort, and she could never survive such a journey on her own. Women did not ride alone outside the walls of a city or fortress, no matter the excuse. Her best hope lay in convincing Sir Percival of the danger they both faced.

Ah, that was it! She sat up straighter in bed as the plan that had taken shape before she fell asleep came back to her in a rush.

She had intended to wait a few hours until everyone in the keep was asleep before she crept from her chamber and paid Sir Percival a visit in the solar, hopefully to talk him into helping her escape from Coleway. The last thing she remembered was thinking the dragons and griffins on her banners appeared particularly sinister in the moonlight, and then . . . nothing.

Her gaze moved along the tall rows of banners that hung still and motionless on the walls . . . or did they? A dragon banner near the door seemed to billow slightly, as if the beast were drawing a deep breath and preparing to release a blast from its fiery nostrils.

Avalene shuddered. The chamber could come alive with any number of creatures if she gave herself over to fanciful imaginings. Instead of dwelling on her fears, she forced her gaze upward to stare at the black void of the beamed ceiling as her thoughts turned to the conversation she must soon have with Sir Percival. She had practiced the words over and over before she fell asleep. Now she silently repeated them to refresh her memory.

Would he believe her accusations? What if he repeated their conversation to her aunt or uncle? If she could not convince him of the danger, they were both doomed.

For some reason, a fragment of her nightmare kept prodding the edge of her mind. She could remember nothing of the dream except her mother's voice and the urgent warning that had finally awakened her, ancient Welsh words that sounded familiar, yet their meaning eluded her.

She whispered the words aloud, *"Nid dieithryn fydd angau,"* and the meaning came to her even as she spoke the translation, "Death comes in disguise."

She heard a small rush of air in the darkened chamber, the almost imperceptible sound of a quickly drawn breath.

'Tis nothing but a draft, she told herself, even as her pulse quickened. Was the room suddenly colder? Her bedding lay in tangles at the bottom of the bed. She pulled her favorite quilt closer to her body and smoothed the sheets.

Another small noise made her hands still. A chill of certainty made her shudder. Someone—or some*thing*—was in the room with her.

She clutched the quilt to her chest like a shield as she listened for any other noise, any small sign that she was not alone. The silvery moonlight that streamed through windows made her plainly visible and vulnerable to any intruder while the recesses of the room remained in impenetrable night shadows. The room was silent but she had the distinct feeling that she was being watched.

She tried her best to sound firm and in control of the situation, bravely calling out, "Who goes there?"

In response, the dragon banner moved again, seeming to open its wings for flight. The figure of a man materialized, stepping from beneath the great beast's wings. The only sound she could manage was a small squeak of fright.

"Have no fear, my lady. 'Tis I." The man moved away from the banner into the moonlight and added, quite unnecessarily, "Sir Percival."

"Oh!" She laid a hand over her racing heart. "You scared me half to death."

She waited for him to explain his presence, but he remained still and silent. Too still and too silent for her peace of mind. Whatever garments he wore blended with the shadows so well that she could make out only the most basic of his features; the vague outline of his body, the shadowed planes of his face. More of him remained hidden than revealed. A flicker of some unknown emotion made her shiver, the same shiver that she experienced each time she saw him. Its source still remained a mystery. Excitement? Fear?

Danger.

The word popped into her head and refused to leave. She was alone with him, trapped in this chamber with a man she scarcely knew.

"You should not be here." She was pleased that she managed to sound calm. Her heart pounded so loudly in her ears that she was certain he must hear it, too.

The hard tone of his voice did nothing to reassure her. "Where are your guards?"

"My guards?" she echoed. Was he somehow part of the plot? Would the guards burst through the door at any moment to catch them together? She might somehow be able to explain away a trip to the solar, but his presence in her bedchamber in the middle of the night defied explanation. She would be ruined.

"Aye, your guards," he repeated, in the same dangerously quiet voice. "I heard your screams in the solar, which means a soldier on night watch should have heard your cries as well. Where are the guards who should be posted here?"

"W-what screams?"

He made a sound of impatience and took a step forward. She hugged her knees to her chest, instinctively trying to make herself as small as possible, feeling as if she were a mouse that had found itself in the path of a hungry cat.

He came to a sudden stop. "You fear me?"

She lifted her chin. "I do not."

"You are not a good liar," he said, and this time she definitely heard a brief note of amusement, the sound scratchy and raw as if his throat were unaccustomed to laughter. "I did not come here tonight to harm you, my lady."

He could be lying. John was an excellent liar. Perhaps Sir Percival shared that skill. Why else would he be in her chamber at this time of night if he was not part of the plot against her? "Why are you here?"

"Put yourself in my place, if you will." He spread his hands in a gesture of impatience, and the edge returned to his voice. "'Tis the dead of night and a young lady of the keep screams in terror, yet none of the soldiers or servants can bestir themselves to investigate this matter? Do the people of Coleway place so little value on your safety?"

"You are here because you thought I was in some sort of danger?" It took her a moment to comprehend that she had screamed loud enough in her sleep to awaken and alarm him. He was not here at John's direction, and his anger wasn't directed at her. She lowered her head to hide an inappropriate smile of relief and . . . something else. It wouldn't do to let him think that she was belittling his concerns when, in truth, she felt absurdly pleased by them. She looked up to find him standing directly in front of her and she let out a startled gasp. "However do you move so quietly?"

He ignored the pointless question and lifted his hand as if he meant to touch her face, but then his arm dropped back to his side. She could see much more of him now that he stood so close; the contrast between the moonlit marble of his face and the dark stubble on his cheeks, the square jaw, the outline of sensual lips. He did not look pleased.

She forced her gaze away from that dangerous territory and inspected his clothing instead. His shirt was a strange-looking garment with a cowl neckline, and he wore a pair of snug leather breeches; both garments not quite black but lighter, a shade of gray, she supposed. It was impossible to be sure in the moonlight.

"You are in danger when you are left vulnerable, Avalene." He made her name sound like an endearment, one that made her feel as if butterflies suddenly took flight in her stomach.

She tried to ignore the effect to concentrate on the problem at hand. "'Tis you who are vulnerable, Sir Percival. Do you know what would happen should someone discover you here? What would happen to us both?"

"I made certain no one was about before I came into your chamber," he said. "You are obviously in no danger, so it appears there was no need for concern."

"Oh, there is need for concern," she said in a rush. "We are both in danger, just not for the reasons you might think. Indeed, the truth is so scandalous and fantastical that I hesitate to share my worries lest you think them lies or exaggerations."

He did not answer for a long time. Instead he sat down next to her on the bed and seemed to mull over her words. He left enough space between them to be deemed proper in the daylight, perhaps in the solar, but he was much too close for a knight in the chamber of an unwed maiden in the middle of the night. His effect on her should be the last thing on her mind, but she also had to judge how much she could trust this man, this stranger who held her fate in his hands. She could see him much more clearly now, but his expression remained remote despite the intimacy of his words.

"You can tell me anything, my lady. 'Tis my duty to know everything about you: your likes and dislikes, your friends and enemies, your habits and routines. Even your concerns and secrets. How else can a knight protect his lady?"

"You are not my knight," she retorted. How on earth had they stumbled into *this* dangerous territory? Either her imagination was working overtime, or he was somehow declaring himself, pledging himself to her service. Impossible. She was not the sort of woman who inspired declarations, at least, not declarations free of scowls or muttered curses.

He lifted one brow. "Whose knight would I be, other than yours?"

"You are sworn to my father," she said simply.

"A knight can be sworn to his liege lord," he said, "and also be sworn to a lady."

She tried to ignore the way her pulse fluttered. This was not happening. Perhaps she was still asleep and this was another part of her dream. Her sense of self-preservation took over and her voice took on a frosty edge. "'Tis not my place to ask if you have sworn your heart to a lady, and this is hardly the time or place to pursue such a topic."

"Perhaps," he murmured, "but know that I will not brush aside anything you might tell me, or make light of anything that causes you concern. I am here for *you*, my lady. You can trust me."

She had an irrational urge to hug him. Instead she caught her lower lip between her teeth, torn between the instinct to keep her secrets to herself and the inevitable need to ask for his help. Her chances of escaping from Coleway without his cooperation were impossible. Her chances of reaching Weston without him were nonexistent. The decision was obvious. She had to trust him.

"There is a plot afoot to see us involved in a terrible scandal," she began. Her gaze went to the door. "My uncle's soldiers could burst into this chamber at any moment. John could not have asked for a better arrangement if he had planned this meeting between us himself. Indeed, your sudden appearance here seems very . . . suspicious, given what I know of Lady Margaret's plan. I have no doubt that John had a hand in shaping it."

"You are speaking of the steward?" he asked.

She gave a brisk nod, and then the words tumbled out in a rush. She told him what she'd overheard earlier between her aunt and uncle, and about John's involvement in the plot. "I know from experience that John is a master at getting what he wants. Mark my words; this will all come to pass unless we do something drastic."

"These are very serious charges," Percival said slowly, his brows drawn together in a frown. "You have accused your aunt and uncle as well as a high-ranking servant at Coleway of plotting a crime against my liege lord and his daughter. You find my sudden appearance suspicious, and yet I am in your chamber even now in response to your cry of distress. It was your signal that drew me here. I would be foolish not to wonder if you are working with the steward to engineer your own ruin so you can stay at Coleway. Perhaps you fancy yourself in love with Coleway's steward. Is that why you summoned me here?"

"I detest John, and I did not purposely summon you here," she hissed, and then she pressed her lips together to curb her sudden urge to call him thick-witted. He was actually putting together the pieces of the puzzle just as she would have done in his place. He had asked for her trust and she had practically accused him of plotting against her. It was hardly surprising that he did not quite trust her yet, either. "I had planned to sneak into the solar after everyone was asleep to tell you of this plot but I fell asleep. And then I had a nightmare. I have them quite often. At least, I have them often enough that no one thinks much of it when or if they hear me cry out in my sleep. The guards quit rushing to my chamber door years ago. So, that is the reason no one but you rushed to my side when I called out."

"As I said to you earlier in the solar," he began, "I would not think it unusual if you find yourself reluctant to leave Coleway. I'm sure your father would even understand if you fancied yourself in love with Lord Brunor's cousin, John, and wished to marry him. There is—"

"I want *nothing* to do with John," she whispered furiously, "and my fondest hope is to leave Coleway as quickly as possible. I am *not* plotting against you, Sir Percival. However, 'tis possible a spy has reported your presence here to John by now. We must devise a plan quickly. As it happens, I had many hours to think things through before I fell asleep. Would you like to hear what I have decided, or would you rather argue about the steward?"

"My pardon," he said stiffly. "I did not intend to start an argument. Please tell me what you have decided."

She gave a satisfied nod. "First, everything will work best if you make some excuse not to attend the hunt in the morning. I am already staying behind to see to the meals, but I can change my mind midmorning, or as soon as we are certain the hunting party is beyond sight of the castle. I know exactly where Lord Brunor will begin the hunt, and I can tell the castle guards that you will escort me and no other escort is necessary. They will not like it, but I will insist that no other soldiers be spared from the walls and they will not dare defy my orders. We can escape the castle and no one will know we are missing until the midday meal. Our absence might go unnoticed even longer if no one inquires about us until they return from the hunt." She folded her hands together in her lap and smiled, pleased with her logic and cleverness. "What think you of my plan?"

Percival remained silent so long that she was tempted to push against his shoulder to rattle some response from him. At last he said, "Those are, indeed, drastic actions you suggest."

She blinked once when it became apparent that was all he intended to say. Was he slow in the head? "I believe John will try to put some plan into action after the hunt tomorrow. Your arrival was expected, but not your orders to take me back to Weston. I doubt John has had much time to think through his plan or put the pieces in place. We must put our own plan in place first and be well away from the castle before John or my aunt and uncle realize what has happened. What say you, Sir Percival? Will you honor your duty to my father and take me away from Coleway tomorrow during the hunt, or, will you fail us both by refusing to act upon what I know to be true?"

He shook his head. "I scarce know what to say, my lady. Plots and counterplots, ploy and counterploy. You have my head spinning."

A sinking feeling began in the pit of Avalene's stomach as she watched him rub his forehead. If simply hearing the plan was too much for him, actually carrying it out would be beyond his capabilities. It was rare that she misjudged people, but apparently Sir Percival was not the man she had hoped or imagined. He would be useless to her cause. In fact, he could actually create many more problems than he would solve.

"Perhaps I have misjudged . . . the situation," she said carefully. "Aye, just hearing the accusations aloud makes me realize how crazed they sound. Perhaps you are right, Sir Percival. I am overwrought at the thought of leaving Coleway and my imagination is playing tricks on me. You must attend the hunt tomorrow as planned. Pray forget I made any of these awful accusations against my aunt and uncle or the steward. They have been all that is kind to me through the years and do not deserve to be slandered. Please, I am so ashamed of my outburst. I promise that I will not cause you any more trouble. Can you promise that you will say nothing to anyone else about our conversation tonight? Truly, they are no more than the hysterical ramblings of an emotional woman."

That last part was one of Lord Brunor's favorite responses whenever Lady Margaret used tears to try to win an argument. It might have been a bit much. The way Sir Percival remained so silent and watchful unnerved her. There was intelligence in his gaze, or, at least the impression of it that had not played out in their conversation thus far. She should not feel such keen disappointment that he was not the kind of man she had hoped he would be.

"Oh, you have my word that I will not repeat what you have told me," he said at last. He spoke with sudden surety and any confusion seemed completely erased from his mind. "As for the hunt, I had already planned to find an excuse to stay at Coleway should you not participate. My duty is to stay close to your side, Lady Avalene. Your father has heard disturbing rumors and has ordered me to take you away if need be. Your fears are well founded. I had to be certain you were really intent on leaving Coleway, or determine if you were part of the plot to keep you here. I am satisfied that you are not working with the steward."

"Why, you," she spluttered, "you could have—"

"I had to be certain," he said, as he reached out to give her hand a firm squeeze. "My plan is almost the same as yours. We will leave Coleway tomorrow much as you imagined, but we must be clever about what we do after our escape. The road to Wales will be the first place they will look for us. We must ride east toward London, and we must ride hard and fast. How are your skills on a horse?"

She looked down to where his hand still covered hers. Her eyes closed briefly against the spinning sensation that might be relief, or it might have something to do with how quickly he had changed from thickheaded minion to quick-witted leader of their small rebellion. There was that feeling again of danger mingled with something else.

He withdrew his hand and she was able to breathe again, which was all well and good except that then she caught his scent. Some devil seemed to whisper hints of what his skin would feel like beneath her hands if she were brave enough to reach out and take his hand again. The fact that she even entertained such a crazed idea finally shook her from her stupor. "I am an excellent rider, Sir Percival. You need not worry that I will slow our flight."

"Is there something else that is bothering you?" he asked. "Something I should know about?"

She plucked at a piece of thread that had worked its way loose on her quilt. "Tomorrow I will tell the biggest lie of my life to my aunt and uncle, and then I will flee the place I have called home and the people who have been my closest family for more than half of my life. After tomorrow my life will never again be the same. My entire future depends upon a man I have known for less than a day. My future depends upon you, Sir Percival." She studied his face, trying to reassure herself that she was doing the right thing in trusting him. "Tell me the truth. Do you think we will succeed?"

He answered without hesitation. "I have no doubt of my plan, so long as you remain cooperative."

"What makes you so certain?"

The corners of his mouth curved upward. "I was sent here to protect you and see to your safety, my lady, and I am very good at what I do."

A small sound of skepticism escaped her lips before she pressed them together.

"You have some doubts about my abilities?"

"I have doubts about anyone's ability to outwit John," she said. "There is also the fact that you arrived here scarce prepared to steal me away from Coleway. What if there were no hunt tomorrow? Or, what if I had not overheard my aunt and uncle discussing the plot and refused to help with my escape? Then there is the fact that you are alone, even though my father suspected some sort of trouble." She shook her head. "I am not brimming with confidence."

"Put your mind at ease, Avalene. I was sent alone because it would require an army to take you from Coleway by force, an army that would never be allowed through the gates. Even if I rode with a small troop of men, the odds of us getting away safely without raising an alarm were slim. But one man, alone? Our chances of escape are much better and we can move much less noticeably once we leave the fortress. 'Tis easy enough to track a group of ten or twenty soldiers, or learn news of their passage near villages, but two horses might escape notice."

"I had not thought of that," she admitted.

"There is also the element of surprise on our side, since I doubt they view a lone knight as much of a threat. However, I did not arrive here unprepared."

"You are unprepared right now," she pointed out, motioning toward the door. "What if soldiers came through that doorway right now to arrest you? What good would you be to me in the dungeons?"

"So you think me defenseless?" His mouth curved into a very predatory sort of smile.

"I think you are unarmed." Her gaze turned speculative as she eyed the broad set of his shoulders. At least he looked intimidating. "There is a difference between unarmed and defenseless."

He gave a short laugh. "Rest assured, my lady. I am neither."

"Mm-hm." The strange shirt he wore distracted her. On closer inspection, the loose neckline seemed to form a hood of some sort. "'Tis of little importance, since it appears John has not yet had a chance to put his plan into action."

"Ah, but danger could walk through your doorway at any moment." He made a quick gesture toward the door that was followed almost immediately by a soft *thunk*.

Her startled gaze flew to the doorway where she half expected to find the danger he had so accurately pre-

THE DARK KNIGHT 101

dicted. Instead a shaft of moonlight revealed the quivering blade of a dagger, its tip embedded in the very center of the wooden door. As she watched, two more daggers joined the first in almost impossibly quick succession. She looked at Sir Percival, then at the daggers, and then back again.

He stood up with leisurely grace and walked toward the door to retrieve the weapons. He fingered one of the blades, testing its edge, and she could have sworn he was looking at her neck.

"How did you do that?"

"'Tis a trick I learned as a child." He inclined his head in a mock bow. "Do not think I am incapable of defending you, Avalene. My talent for escaping dangerous situations is the reason I was chosen for this duty. There can be no guarantees that we will escape Coleway without incident, but our odds improve if I can be certain you will follow my orders without question."

"I am accustomed to taking orders from no one," she mused, "save the occasional edict from my aunt or uncle. You are my father's knight, and therefore you are sworn to serve everyone in my family. I easily outrank you."

"Have you escaped from many castles?" he asked. "Do you know how to elude mounted search parties? Do you even know which roads lead to Castle Weston?"

She pressed her lips together. "You know the answer to all of your questions."

"Aye, I do know the answers to those questions," he said. "What I need to know is if you will concede your rank until you are safely returned to your father. For the duration of this adventure you must treat me as your lord and master. You must not question my decisions or orders, no matter your own feelings or inclinations. You must trust that everything I do is with purpose, even though you might not be aware of the purpose or how it affects you. Your life and the lives of others will often depend upon your complete cooperation in this matter. Can you abide by those limitations?"

Everything within her rebelled at the idea of voluntarily giving up control of anything. Giving orders was second nature to her. Accepting them without question was not one of her strengths. "Would it matter if I said 'No'?"

His lips curved upward and he slowly shook his head. "You will make my life considerably easier if you say 'Aye' and mean it."

She caught her lower lip between her teeth and looked over his shoulder to the window behind him. The moon had moved noticeably across the sky since she awoke. As she watched, a stray cloud drifted across its surface and momentarily plunged her chamber into darkness. The castle was filled with sounds during the daytime. Now, all she could hear was Sir Percival's steady breathing and the uneven beat of her own heart. He was asking her to give over all that she was into his keeping, to trust his orders as much and as quickly as she would trust her own. There was little doubt that he was her best hope, likely her only hope to escape Coleway Castle.

The cloud moved away and she could see his face again. He had not looked away from her and she could see steely determination in his eyes. She knew almost nothing about him, but no matter the odds, there was no doubt in her mind that he would do whatever he felt was necessary to keep her safe. On that deep, elemental level, she already trusted him. Completely.

"Aye, Sir Percival. And I mean it."

7
❧

News traveled fast at Coleway Castle. The bailey was unusually crowded for midmorning, and the crowd it-self was unusual. It seemed that everyone in any posi-tion of leadership or authority who hadn't ridden off to the hunt had gathered around Avalene. They had lain in wait and accosted her the moment she set foot in the great hall that morning with endless questions about how things should and could be done once she left Cole-way for good.

Of course, they thought they had two more days to get their answers. She could not imagine their reaction if she told them her departure was much more imminent, and, in fact, would happen that morning. Already a cry of disagreement had gone up when she declared her in-tent to join the hunt. The tone of their ceaseless ques-tions had become a contest of shouts as people tried to wrest her attention from whoever held it from one mo-ment to the next.

All the while, Sir Percival stood stoically at her side

with one hand at her elbow to help guide her through the crowd, his expression utterly placid. Although he did not object to the delays in their departure nor did anything to help facilitate it, somehow he managed to get them from the hall and across the bailey toward the gates in little more than a quarter of an hour. Part of her distraction had to do with the pressure of his hand, how his thumb rubbed her arm in a seemingly random yet soothing pattern. She realized that he always managed to touch her more often than anyone else ever had, more than she had allowed any other man to touch her, whether it was his hand on her elbow, or at her waist when the crowd pressed in closer, or even holding her hand, as he had last night.

He had stayed in her chamber to plan their escape until just before dawn when they had both begun to worry that the morning guards would soon be patrolling the passageways. There was no longer any doubt in her mind that he was her best and likeliest means of getting away from Coleway before John could create some trap for them both. They had reviewed the plan over and over until there was no doubt about what part they would each play to avoid the hunting party's departure, and then to get their own horses prepared to supposedly join the hunting party as quickly after their departure as possible.

She had been surprised at how quickly they formed a conspiratorial bond, at how seamlessly their ideas meshed, and how quickly she considered him a friend as well as her protector. Somehow she had never considered the possibility that they would be friends, never considered that she would be the least bit appealing to him, but he seemed genuinely interested in everything she had to say.

It was a heady feeling to hold the interest of a man so

seemingly perfect as Sir Percival, but this morning all she could think about was their escape. All that stood between them and freedom were about a score of people who seemed intent on driving her mad with their questions.

She rubbed her forehead, trying to forestall a headache, no doubt brought on by the stress and turmoil. They had to leave, but the crowd seemed no thinner. "My lady!" the marshal shouted, as he waved one hand and stood on tiptoes to see over the massive shoulders of the blacksmith. "I must know how many baggage carts you intend to take with you to Wales. If they are to be ready in less than two days, I must start to assemble the train now. I also need to know how many soldiers and servants will accompany you. How many will be on horseback? How many will walk? I must—"

"You will all cease shouting at your lady," Sir Percival said at last, addressing the group at large. His voice was calm but firm. The crowd instantly fell silent, likely from the shock that he had finally deigned to speak to them, and awe that they were being addressed by a knight who was unknown to them, one who exuded power and authority. She had to admit that his chain-mail armor and surcoat looked impressive. If anyone thought it strange that he would dress in the same garments for a hunt as he had for his journey from Wales, armed to the teeth, they were too intimidated to remark upon it. "You will not begrudge Lady Avalene a few hours to enjoy herself at the hunt. Your questions can wait until her return. Until that time, prove her trust in your abilities and go about your business."

Not one person argued with him. Oh, a few grumbled, but the men sketched reluctant bows and the women grudgingly curtsied, and then the crowd began to disperse. Without thinking, Avalene started to hold up her hand to catch Maude's attention before the cook could lead her away, but Sir Percival's hand suddenly moved from her elbow to her wrist, stopping the motion. He leaned down so that only she could hear his words.

"Do not even think it."

"But I—"

"You are leaving for a few hours, remember? There is no call for heartfelt good-byes to set out on a hunt for the day."

He was right. She had meant to call Maude over to somehow say her farewells without giving away her secret, but Maude was clever enough that she would have guessed something was wrong. How on earth had Percival known her intent?

She watched the people she had grown to love walk away from her as they made their way back to the great hall or to their duties in other parts of the castle. There was little chance that she would ever see them again, or stand here again in the bailey at Coleway with the sun warming her face, surrounded by the everyday sights and smells of the place she called home; the massive gray stone walls, the earthy smell of dirt that had been packed down by hundreds of feet coming and going from the gates, the faint smell of a coal fire from the smithy and the much more immediate smells of the stables that were built along the curtain wall near the gates. Even as she said her silent good-byes to her home, her gaze was drawn to the two horses that were saddled and ready to take them on their journey.

Sir Percival's big bay horse let out a long, loud whinny and then tossed its head so violently that the stable boy who held the reins was lifted from the ground before the animal once more relinquished control to the boy. Ava-lene's horse, a black gelding named Bodkin, responded by shaking his head as if he were competing with the bay for attention. Bodkin and the bay were of a similar size, both large and muscular, both built to withstand long journeys. They would have little trouble outpacing the palfreys and delicate Arabian mounts that most of the hunting party favored. She was just surprised that the stable master had not questioned her more closely about the reasons she chose Bodkin for a hunt.

"Come, my lady, I will help you mount." Sir Percival kept a firm grip on her hand as he guided her to the horses. He lifted her easily into the saddle, hardly hesitating when he felt the small rucksack she had hidden beneath her cloak. He did not speak again until he had mounted the bay and they had both turned their horses toward the barbican. He kept his voice low and urgent. "If we are accosted by another horde at the gates, insist that you must join the hunt before it's over and promise that you will speak to them upon your return to the castle. We are fast running out of time to make good our escape."

"The captain of the guards already spoke to me this morning," she said, her voice just as low, "and you were right about his worries. He wanted to be certain I was determined to go on this hunt, and he did not think a woman should be outside the walls with less than three knights or soldiers. I reassured him that you would see me safely to the hunting party and made it clear that I do not take orders from him."

Percival gave her a hooded look, and then nodded toward the gates in an unspoken order to remain silent on the subject until they were outside the walls. The distance to freedom looked within reach, and yet impossibly far.

They started forward and the horses' hooves striking the ground sounded unnaturally loud yet felt impossibly slow, as if they were marking the steps to a disaster. Avalene kept her head down and stared at the reins in her hands, counting their horses' steps, wondering if she would have the courage to charge the gates if they were ordered to halt. Fortunately, the captain happened to be at the gates as they approached. He held up one hand to acknowledge them, and then waved to the gatekeepers to let them pass without question.

She finally released the breath she had been holding when the crisp clatter of their horses' hooves changed to muffled beats as they crossed the wooden bridge over the moat. The stiff set of her shoulders began to relax in slow degrees as they made their way through the village and started to pass the fields that surrounded the castle. Another mile along this road and then they would be out of sight from the guards on the walls. Once that happened, they could make their way through the forests until they reached the road to London.

"You did very well in the bailey," Percival said at last, in a normal tone of voice. There were a few peasants working in the fields and tending the flocks of sheep, but none were close enough to overhear them. However, they were still in plain sight so they rode side by side on the road at a deliberately easy pace, as if they were simply enjoying the warm morning sun and the vistas of the pastoral fields of sheep and ripening crops on their way to the hunt. "Do you think anyone suspects that something is amiss?"

"Nay, but I would have given away some hint had you not stopped me from calling cook's wife over to say good-bye." She looked into his face, and then couldn't look away. "How did you know?"

"I have been watching you all morning," he said, "waiting for you to betray your emotions in some way. You gave a little sigh just as you tried to raise your hand to call the woman back to your side. Otherwise, I am impressed. You have made this part of our escape easier than I had dared hope."

There was an odd feeling in her chest when she thought about Percival paying such close attention to her that he noticed something as insignificant as a sigh.

"We are not safe quite yet," she pointed out, with a glance over her shoulder. The walls of Coleway still towered behind them, and a group of soldiers loitered near the drawbridge. She shivered once, and then turned her attention forward again. "The path that leads to the hunting lodge is just over the crest of the hill. I took the path in the opposite direction only once and never rode very far, but I know it will eventually lead to the old Roman road to London. 'Tis about an hour's ride through the old Hamlet Forest, although I am not entirely certain I can find my way."

"I know the way," he said. "If you will recall, last night I mentioned that one of my men awaits us along the Roman road and two more will join us on the morrow. I hoped we would be leaving the fortress on our own and you know why I did not want to complicate matters by bringing my men within the walls of Coleway. We will not outnumber any search party. Still, I will feel better when we have a few more swords to protect our backs."

She had not forgotten those details. They were simply pushed to another part of her mind while she concentrated on the part of their escape that involved getting past scores of soldiers and avoiding the hunting party. Oddly enough, now that they were in the very midst of the most dangerous part of their plan, she felt only the smallest sense of urgency. Something about Sir Percival put her at ease, as if they truly were on their way to the hunt. It was a most unusual feeling, since she was accustomed to worrying about and managing everything and everyone around her. It occurred to her that she was now the one being managed. Not manipulated, as John had often tried to do, but managed, easily and efficiently. Sir Percival's calm manner assured her that he could handle any problems that arose.

He tilted his head to one side. "Why are you looking at me that way?"

"I am just thinking how remarkable my life has become in so short a time." She surprised herself by smiling in genuine delight, certain now that they were going to make it to freedom, unconcerned about what might await her tomorrow or the next day, as long as she had Sir Percival by her side. Already his presence felt familiar and safe, even though she scarcely knew the man. She had not slept at all after he left her chamber, but she did not feel the least bit tired. Her body felt tense and ready for flight, yet at the same time, forced into a false state of calm. She probably looked a fright from worry and lack of sleep. Sir Percival looked perfect, relaxed and well-rested, as if he were, indeed, off to participate in a hunt. "I still do not understand why you volunteered to come to my rescue."

His mouth tightened in what she was beginning to recognize as impatience. "Your father suspected that the announcement of your betrothal to Faulke Segrave would set acts in motion against you that would ruin his plans for an alliance. I have a talent for finding my way out of difficult situations, and I could not stand idly by while my liege lord's daughter was about to be endangered. Do you doubt my honor, or are you finding new reasons to doubt me?"

"Nay," she said quickly, "I would never cast doubt on a knight's honor. I just feel very strange, as if this is all some dream that I am watching from a safe distance while it happens to someone else. I suppose I should be frightened and anxious, or perhaps I should be teary-eyed and hysterical, as you feared I would be. Instead I feel numb. None of this seems real."

A strange expression crossed his face, and he seemed engaged in some private debate about whether or not to say something more on the subject. At last his mouth quirked downward and he released a brief sigh. "'Tis not uncommon to feel as you do when your life changes very quickly. I experienced similar emotions just after my parents died. Later I realized that I could not recall what had happened during the weeks right after their deaths, that I was missing entire days; I had gone through the motions of my daily life, and nothing all that traumatic happened during those particular days, but I still have no memory of what occurred."

"Oh, I am so sorry to hear about your parents," she murmured. And she truly was sorry for his loss. However, her situation hardly compared. No one had died, and she was actually relieved to be leaving Coleway, even under these circumstances. She felt as if a great burden had been lifted from her shoulders.

"It was long ago," he said, "and fortunately my brother took good care of me. Or, perhaps I let myself drift away because I knew my brother would take care of me. Either way, you can be assured that I will guard you just as diligently as my brother guarded me, my lady."

"I feel very fortunate that my father chose you to protect me," she said with sincerity. She was touched that he had shared a painful part of his past with her. "How old were you when your parents died? That is, if you do not mind my asking."

He tilted his head to look upward as he considered her question, as if he would find the answer in the sky. She found herself fascinated with the play of muscles in his neck, how just that part of him could look so masculine.

"I was nearly grown, thirteen or fourteen summers. I cannot recall for certain."

"Were you already fostered with a family to train for knighthood," she asked, "or did relatives take you in?"

He gave her an odd look, and then shook his head. "I was not fostered, nor were there relatives to turn to for help. Indeed, my situation was not entirely different from your own."

"Truly?"

"I did not have an aunt and uncle plotting to force me into a marriage," he said, "but there were a few similarities."

"How so?" she asked, too curious to care if he thought her rude.

He rode on a few paces before he answered, and then he spoke without pause, his words toneless. "An uncle by marriage seized everything that my father owned as soon as my parents died. My brother and sister and I were turned off our own lands within days. We were hard-pressed to survive those first few years until . . . until your father took us in. Now I can make certain my liege lord's daughter does not fall prey to another nefarious uncle and his henchman. I will do whatever is necessary to make certain you are free of John and Lord Brunor."

"I am grateful for your loyalty," she said quietly. Her words caused something to flare in his eyes, but he looked away before she could be certain of its meaning. Assuming he was uncomfortable with his reminiscence, she deliberately said nothing more about his painful childhood. "I have no doubts that you will defend me with your life. With any luck, we will not encounter any trouble on our journey and your willingness to defend me will not be put to the test. How long do you think the journey will take from here to London?"

She saw him take a deep breath and then release it. "The journey should take a week, no more than two," he answered. "It all depends upon the weather and the roads, as well as any detours we might take to avoid search parties."

Last night he had explained that they would be safest if they took a ship from London to Wales. Although such a route would be much longer, her father's castle stood along the Welsh coastline and there were fewer dangers in making the journey by ship rather than overland through the wilderness from Coleway with their small band. Few if any of the search parties would follow since they would assume Sir Percival would ride directly west toward Weston Castle. The odds of being caught would fall significantly once they put a few miles between themselves and Coleway.

"Have you been to London before?" she asked.

"Aye," he said slowly. "London is familiar to me. I am often there on business for your father."

"Is London really as large as they say?" she asked. Dozens of questions about their journey had come to mind since he had announced their destination last night. "Can you really not see from one end of London to the other, even from the highest tower in the city? Are there really as many people living in the city as there are in all the whole of England? Is it true you could live the whole of your life in London and not know everyone who lived there?"

"'Tis hard to know which question to answer first," he said with a chuckle. Her own spirits felt lighter now that his somber expression had disappeared. "London will be like nothing you have ever seen, on a scale you can scarcely imagine. It would be hard to find a tower or steeple within the heart of the city where you could see the whole of the city, but there is countryside beyond the walls. You definitely cannot see its ends by looking across the city from any of its gates. Perhaps one of the church bell towers would offer such a view, but I have not put the matter to the test. As to there being as many people living in London as there are in the rest of England, the crowded streets certainly give rise to that impression but it is just that; an impression. And I believe it would be entirely possible to live your life without meeting everyone who lives in London. There is no place for everyone to gather at one time as there is in a castle. There are tall houses in vast numbers, dozens of churches, guildhalls, and public squares. Then there are the palaces of the noblemen, which are like small cities within their own walls when their nobles are in residence. The king's palace within the Tower of London is the grandest palace of all. There are people within the Tower walls who never venture into the city."

"Have you been to the king's palace?" she asked. "Have you been to the Tower?"

He had, and proceeded to describe both places in quite satisfactory detail. Then he went on to tell her about the grand churches, the market streets, the docks, and dozens of other places that sounded strange and wonderful; theaters and zoos, pavilions and parks.

"I cannot wait to see the entire city!" she exclaimed. "Will we have time to explore London before we set sail for Wales? That reminds me. Have you ever been on a ship before? This will be my first voyage. I have heard that people sometimes become ill from the sway—"

Sir Percival held up one hand to halt her questions even as he reined in his horse. "We are beyond sight of the guards at Coleway."

She glanced over her shoulder and realized with a start that he was right; they had crested the hill and the walls of Coleway were no longer visible. She had been so fascinated with his stories of London that she had almost forgotten the precariousness of their situation. Almost, but not quite. She nodded toward the path that led to the Roman road. "The trail is not wide enough to ride side by side. Do you want me to lead or follow?"

"Lead," he said decisively. "I will be able to keep an eye on you and will have your back should anyone ride up behind us. In the unlikely chance that we encounter anyone from the hunt or anywhere else, simply tell them we were uncertain where to look for the group. Once they trust that nothing is amiss, I will deal with them. However, my man has been keeping an eye on this route from the Roman road. 'Tis unlikely we will encounter anyone."

She wanted to ask him more questions about London, but there would be plenty of time in the coming days to satisfy her curiosity. Instead she gave him a brisk nod, then turned her horse and set a fast pace. At last, she was on the road that would lead to her new life.

Avalene tilted her head back and closed her eyes as her horse entered a small clearing. The morning sun felt warm on her face, her horse held a comfortable gait, the pleasant smell of pine and moss filled the forest, birds chirped and squirrels chattered. This was not such a bad way to spend a day. Indeed, she was looking forward to the entire journey. London had been an intriguing mystery to her for as long as she could remember. The opportunity to see the great city was something she had never allowed herself to hope for. Now she began to daydream about what London would look like and all the wondrous sites she would see. Perhaps there would be a—

"My lady!"

Avalene's eyes popped open at the sound of Sir Percival's voice and she drew her horse to a halt. She glanced around her but saw nothing out of the ordinary, so she waited until he rode up next to her, marveling again that this perfect male was her escort, her protector. "What is wrong, Sir Percival?"

"We are almost to the road," he said, motioning toward a line of bushes ahead of them that stretched out on both sides of the path. It took her a moment to comprehend that the bushes marked the edges of the Roman road. Even as he spoke, she noticed a horse and rider emerge from the tall thickets near the crossroads. "'Tis my man, Oliver. There must not be any trouble ahead or he would have warned us by now."

She followed his lead as he rode toward Oliver, watching the newcomer as carefully as he watched her. The hood of his brown cloak obscured much of his face. Finally he tilted his head back and shook off the hood, revealing short-cropped dark hair and a hawkish profile. His face was weathered to a leathery brown and the creases around his blue eyes spoke of long exposure to the elements. Brawny and barrel-chested, he had the battle-hardened look of a professional soldier about him. When he finally turned his attention to Sir Percival, he offered little in the way of a greeting; no smile or nod of recognition. He simply bowed his head to the knight.

"My lord," he murmured.

"Do you bring any news?" asked Percival.

"Nay," Oliver said, as he straightened to cast suspicious glances at Avalene. "Everything is as you expected . . . Sir Percival."

"Excellent," Percival said. "And the others?"

"They are in position near Beversham."

"This is the Lady Avalene," Percival told him. "You

will accept her orders as you accept my own, and do whatever is necessary to keep her safe."

"Aye, my lord." Oliver seemed to receive some imperceptible order from Sir Percival, a lightning-fast exchange that made Avalene's brow furrow. She dismissed it a moment later as fancy when Oliver turned his horse toward London and waited for them to take the lead.

"Let us be on our way," Percival said, as he motioned for Avalene to ride next to him. "Oliver will bring up the rear, but the road is wide enough here for you to ride alongside me."

"*This* is the Roman road?" she asked as she urged her horse forward again. The road was indeed wider, but scarcely more discernible than the path they had just left. "I expected something grander than a trace. I thought Roman roads were paved with cobblestones."

"Some are," Percival said. "Most are as you see this road, marked only by disuse and countless grasses, bushes, and trees that have come and gone over the years. Only a few are still in use day to day, and those have been either built up or repaired."

She gave a small sniff, unimpressed with what she had thought would be one of the more interesting sights of their journey. She had always wondered about the long-dead Romans who had conquered England and she had heard many stories about their skills at building roads and walls. This road looked like little more than a beaten-down goat path, although she had to admit that it ran in an exceedingly straight line. She dismissed the disappointment of the road and turned her attention to another matter that had been troubling her. "Why do you have only three men with you, Sir Percival? That is, I know why you did not bring more with you into Coleway, but could my father not spare more than the four of you to see me safely returned to Wales?"

Percival gave her a sharp look and seemed to consider his answer before he spoke. "Fewer men mean we can move more quickly without worrying about rations and the other problems that arise when traveling with a larger group. We will try to go around most villages unnoticed, and avoid notice in general. That would not be possible with a full company of soldiers."

"Ah, I recall you mentioning that reasoning," she said. "Still, I assumed you would be more concerned about bandits than being noticed by local villagers. Some of the minstrels say there are bands of thirty or forty men who raid in the forests."

"Exaggerations," he said, looking unconcerned. "There haven't been large bands of thieves in this part of England since the days of King Richard. Minstrels are known to exaggerate tales to make them more exciting. Likely they heard of some small group of bandits in the area and embellished the story."

The minstrels that traveled from one great castle to the next were the main source of news from beyond a lord's borders. She had always paid close attention to any news related to Wales. Now that she had opened the subject of lawlessness, she decided to take it a step further. She lowered her gaze and pretended to adjust the fit of her riding gloves as she questioned him. "We heard rumors from several groups of minstrels that the king's taxes fall heavily upon the Welsh and our Marcher lords."

He made a noncommittal sound and lifted his shoulders, as if to say it was none of his concern.

"Some believe the most powerful families in the Marches may revolt," she said. "The king would be hard pressed to put down a rebellion if the Segrave, Bohun, Mortimer, and de Clare families rose against him at once. Some say my father might be favorable to the match between myself and Faulke Segrave because he intends to side with the Segraves against the king. Some say—"

"You must stop listening to 'Some say,'" he interrupted, his lips curving into a smile. "'Some say' this, 'Some say' that. These tales sound like more creations of minstrels' imaginations, containing some small grains of truth with many embellishments."

"Do you know which are embellishments and which are truth?"

He lifted his shoulders again. "'Tis true, the king's tax is not popular in Wales, but what royal tax has ever been popular anywhere? The Welsh natives are restless. Conquered peoples are always restless. And the Marcher lords always have an eye toward increasing their own power. A weak king alienates the Marcher lords at his peril. A shrewd king holds their respect. Edward knows how to handle the Marcher lords. They will not rise against him."

"What of the Segraves?" she asked in a low voice, encouraged that he would speak to her of politics. Most men would not. "Even the traveling merchants speak of Segrave soldiers being dissatisfied with their lot in Wales and how their lord and his son will soon set matters right with the king."

He gave her a considering look. "Most women concern themselves more with sewing and gardens than with serious issues such as loyalty and rebellion. Why do these things interest you?"

She made a concerted effort to keep from rolling her eyes. Why was it that most men thought women should remain ignorant of "serious" matters? "A good wife knows everything that could affect her husband, most especially his politics. If I am to be a Segrave, I would like to know where my loyalties should lie; with Wales or with England?"

"You speak to *me* of treason?" He gave her such an incredulous look that she wondered if he jested with her. Apparently he was serious. "There is no question where your loyalties should lie."

"Can you honestly tell me the notion has never crossed your mind, that you have never considered the possibility that my father would support a rebellion?" she asked. "Or considered the possibility that you would be forced to betray either your liege lord or your king? In all likelihood, that is the choice I will face as the wife of Faulke Segrave. If you can tell me this will never happen, I will be greatly relieved."

His lips were pressed together in a straight line. "A woman's loyalties must lie with the man charged with her protection," he said carefully, "whether it be her father or husband, or even the knight sent to rescue her. You must trust that the man charged with holding your life safe knows what he is about and will know what is best for you in all matters, including matters of politics. As I am currently your protector, you must trust me when I say the Segraves will not rebel against Edward. Therefore, you must set aside any thoughts of betraying your king."

He sounded very sure of himself. She wished she felt half so confident about the Segraves. "You are certain?"

One brow rose as he regarded her and she knew that she had somehow insulted him.

The knight sent to rescue her. She liked the sound of that. "Do you know the Segraves, then? Have you met Faulke Segrave?"

Whatever he saw in her face made him frown. He was annoyed with her, his patience stretched to the edges of politeness. "Nay, I have not met the man, so do not ask me if I know what he thinks of you or his plans to marry you. I have no idea and would not venture a guess."

"I had no intention of asking any such things," she lied.

He gave a slight nod toward the road ahead of them. The clearing they were riding through was about to end at a line of trees that marked the entrance into another forest. "The road narrows, my lady. It would be best if I took the lead so you will be protected between Oliver and me. I doubt the road will widen again for many miles."

Avalene found herself staring at his back as he rode out ahead of her, well aware that she and her questions had just been dismissed. So she had asked a few harmless questions. Why should that be such a great annoyance?

Actually, what seemed to irritate him most were her questions about Faulke Segrave. She pressed her lips together. Did he dislike the Segraves, or was it possible he felt . . . jealous?

Dislike, she decided. If even a few grains of the minstrels' tales were true, then it was no secret that the Segraves would rebel, given the chance. Sir Percival was a loyalist through and through. Even the mention of treasonous thoughts had affronted his senses. That was the source of his irritation.

It was only in her fevered imagination that he experienced jealousy. Just as it was only in her imagination that he viewed her as anything more than his liege lord's daughter. She was a duty and a responsibility. Nothing more.

8

The Witches' Sabbath

Enter the Knight of Cups, a champion without armor and a lover from a faraway place. Pursued by shadows and demons, this knight bears a message that will require a choice: Beware the consequence of decisions made in haste.

A full moon turned the forest into a strange world of stark light and impenetrable shadows, a world that seemed to reflect Sir Percival's grim mood. He had scarcely spoken since they made their way onto the Roman road, and they rode hard throughout the day and well into the night. All of her questions about her feelings and his had long since faded from her mind beneath a haze of exhaustion.

At last Percival paused at the crest of a hill where a flat outcropping of rock offered a moonlit view of the valley they had just crossed. The two men studied the terrain. Avalene looked out over the valley and wondered what they hoped to see in the darkness across so vast a distance. Up close her two companions were almost as plainly visible as if it were daytime, although it was eerie the way the moonlight leached all color from their faces. Their skin glowed chalky white while their eyes were coal black. She shivered and returned her attention to the valley that was cloaked in the shadows of countless trees. This was a foolish waste of time.

"No one would dare follow us through the forest at night," she told them, as she drew her cloak tighter against the damp chill in the air. Somewhere in the distance came the lonesome hoot of an owl. "That is, no one will follow us on this night."

Sir Percival turned toward her, his face stern yet starkly handsome in the moonlight. "Is there something special about this night, my lady?"

She gestured toward the sky. "'Tis the Witches' Sabbath."

"The Witches' Sabbath?" Oliver echoed. "I have never heard of such a thing."

"'Tis peasant folklore," Percival told him. "Some say that witches gather in their covens when the full moon rises on the eve before the true Sabbath."

"Witches are not the only creatures who gather under the full moon," she said in a hushed voice. "'Tis a night when evil spirits of all sort roam the countryside; demons who search out the souls of hapless innocents and cavort with the Devil's brides in unspeakable rituals."

"Saints preserve us," Oliver whispered, as he crossed himself against evil.

Percival's mouth curved into a smile and he began to chuckle. "Who filled your head with such nonsense?"

"My aunt," she answered primly, hurt that he would laugh at her. "I wondered why you insisted that we continue to ride rather than seek shelter in the village we passed at dusk. I know we are supposed to avoid villages, but surely this night could be an exception? Lord Brunor says the only men who venture abroad on a Witches' Sabbath have the heart of a lion or the head of a fool."

Percival rubbed his chin. "I take it you have cast me into the role of the fool?"

She bit her lower lip, wishing she'd said nothing at all

about fools and lions. Sir Percival saw nothing amiss with his plan to continue their journey. The two men seemed accustomed to traveling at night and Percival thought the Witches' Sabbath was just a silly old superstition. More complaints would only make her look hopelessly naïve in his eyes. Perhaps it was best to extend an olive branch.

"Forgive me, Sir Percival. I gave my word that I would not question your actions or comment upon them. I spoke rashly to defend what my family believes to be truth, and I was wrong to insult you."

The reassuring smile disappeared. "Never apologize for defending your family, Avalene."

He turned his horse abruptly and made his way back to the road, obviously expecting her to fall into line behind him. Somehow she had managed to insult him twice. No wonder he was growing tired of her. She looked at Oliver, but he simply nodded toward the road and indicated that she should follow Percival. She gave a frustrated sigh and fell into line.

They rode single file again. The sting of rejection occupied her thoughts for a time, but gradually the stillness of the forest began to press in on her. She knew she should feel safe with two strong, capable men to guard her, but swords offered little protection against the dangers that lurked in the darkness. Not that she gave complete credence to witches and spirits, but bears, lynx, wolves, badgers, and boars were much more genuine threats to their safety, along with the dangers from two-legged predators who might be hiding in the woods. Every small sound in the forest became a portent of approaching evil; the unnerving howl of a wolf, the rustle of a small animal in the underbrush, a sudden flapping sound in a tree.

'Tis nothing more sinister than a bat or an owl, she

told herself, even as she clutched one hand over her racing heart. And that was likely a hedgehog, she decided, when something stirred the branches of a large bush. A cowardly voice in her head argued that it was something much more sinister. Any number of sly creatures could follow them through the forest, watching, waiting to leap upon their prey without warning.

Sir Percival reined in his horse so abruptly that she nearly leaped from fright when her own mount brushed up against his. The knight gave her no more than a cursory glance as she gathered her wits along with her reins and pulled her horse to a stop. He motioned Oliver to his side.

"What is it, my lord?"

Percival pointed toward a long-dead tree that stood at a fork in the road. Its bark and most of the branches had been stripped away by weather and time, leaving a silvered trunk that gleamed like a skeleton in the moonlight. The two remaining branches resembled pale arms stretching toward the moon that hung directly above the tree; a grim, headless specter reaching for a cold orb of light. Avalene shuddered in fear even as she saw a glint of metal near the "chest" of the ghostly tree. A dagger, she realized, embedded into the heart of the dead wood.

"Stay with her," Percival told Oliver, as he gathered his reins. When she realized his intent, she placed her hand on his arm and he stilled immediately.

"'Tis something evil," she whispered. "A warning to turn back, or a lure to coax you into a trap."

Her concern seemed to startle him. His hand came to rest on hers, separated by the leather of their gloves, but his warmth still seeped into her. "'Tis nothing more than a dagger stuck into a dead tree, my lady. There is nothing to fear."

She studied his face and tried to decide what made her

so certain that he was lying. There was nothing in his expression or the soothing tone of his voice to betray him, but she watched as he looked at their hands touching, then at her shoulders, then a spot above her head. It finally dawned on her that he wouldn't look her in the eye and tell a lie. At any other time, she would have smiled over the revelation. But not now. Now she almost wished for ignorance, for blind faith in his word.

"'Tis evil," she insisted, tightening her grip on his arm.

He reached out and stroked her cheek with one gloved finger, and then his thumb brushed across her lower lip as if he could somehow mark her with his touch. The caress was so tender and unexpected that she drew a startled breath.

"I can hold my own against any evil," he said softly. "'Tis innocence and beauty that hold the power to ruin me."

His gaze lowered to her mouth, lingering there for a heartbeat, then his hand abruptly fell away and he loosened her hold on his arm. She was dazed, unable to move, unable to make even the smallest sound. What had just happened? He turned to speak over his shoulder even as he urged his horse forward. "Guard her, Oliver."

So many thoughts buzzed through her head that she could scarce concentrate on any one of them. Had he been talking about her? Did he truly think her beautiful? How could she ruin him? Was it possible he wanted to kiss her?

She watched in silence as he rode forward, certain she should do or say something to keep him away from that forbidding tree. Instead she touched the tips of her fingers to her lower lip, feeling for all the world as if he *had* just kissed her. Why had he touched her that way?

Sanity kicked in . . . a little reason, in small degrees. Perhaps he touched all women that way. Perhaps he knew his effect on them and used it to silence every woman who tried to argue with him. She should be angry that he dared take such liberties. Something inside her insisted that he had every right to touch her however he wanted, the same part of her that longed for him to touch her again.

The questions were forgotten when he reached out with both hands to remove the dagger and she realized that the knife held something pinned to the tree, which turned out to be a flat scrap of parchment. He stared at the parchment longer than she thought necessary, tilting it toward the moonlight several times to study both sides. She wondered what could possibly be so interesting on so small a page. Finally he slipped the dagger and the parchment into a leather sack that was tied to his saddle. When he rode back to rejoin them, his mouth was set in a grim line.

"'Tis an edict from the local sheriff," he said, "offering a reward for the capture of poachers in the area."

Another lie, she decided, and this one more obvious than the last. The moonlight was bright, but surely not enough to reveal writing on so small a surface. She looked at Oliver and saw him nod an acceptance, but she again had the impression that some silent message passed between the two men in that brief exchange. What were they hiding?

Sir Percival dismounted and handed his reins to Oliver. He said something beneath his breath that she doubted even Oliver could hear, and then he was gone. She saw him move away from the horses toward the brush, and then suddenly he disappeared into the shadows. She rubbed her eyes and told herself it was just a trick of moonlight that had made him appear to melt into the night.

She turned toward Oliver. "Where did he go?"

Oliver answered in a low voice. "To make certain we are alone, my lady."

She looked into the shadows and impenetrable darkness of the forest and decided she was very thankful to have two such brave men to accompany her. There was no way she would venture into those woods alone before daybreak.

Oliver moved his horse closer to hers and long, tense moments passed. Just then, Sir Percival appeared again in the clearing. It was the color of his clothes that made him seemingly appear before her eyes, she decided, marveling again at his talent for blending into the darkness. He was still hard to see in the shadows but his movements were unhurried, so she assumed there was no immediate danger.

"There are no signs that anyone else is in the area," he told Oliver, as he took his reins and remounted. He brought his horse next to Avalene's, and then held out his hand. "You will ride with me for the rest of the night. Oliver, take her reins and the lead."

She opened her mouth to protest, but the only sound that came out was an unladylike "umph," when his arm slid around her waist. She clung to his arm for dear life, even though she was reluctantly impressed at how easily he removed her from the saddle. Rather than position her behind him on the horse, he lifted her onto his lap. It didn't take long to regain her wits, if not her dignity. "Sir Percival! What are you doing?"

"I should think it obvious," he said, as he ignored her frantic efforts to rearrange her cloak and skirts. With a slight nod, he gave Oliver a silent order to ride ahead of them, and then he glanced down at her. "Put your head on my shoulder and rest while you can, my lady."

"I cannot.".

"Why not?"

"The reasons should be obvious." They were to her. His arms encircled her on every side, and their bodies were pressed together from shoulder to thigh. No man had ever held her in such an intimate embrace, and this man made her realize why maidens were trained to discourage this sort of impropriety. It was entirely too appealing. Rather than admit as much, she tried her best to appear scandalized. "'Tis indecent!"

"'Tis necessary," he countered, as he turned his horse toward the road. "We cannot stop to rest until we reach Beversham, and you cannot stay awake that long."

"I can," she insisted, without any real conviction.

In truth, fear was all that had kept her awake for much of the night. Now the forbidden feel of his hard, male body was fast affecting her senses. His heat warmed her as no fire ever could, but she still shivered as they rode past the dead tree.

After the initial shock wore off, her heartbeat began to slow down and her breathing evened out. Really, there was nothing to complain about except propriety, and who but them would ever know? She wanted nothing more than to do as he ordered, to curl up in his arms and allow the slow, rocking movement of the horse to lull her to sleep. There was just one question that bothered her. "What was on that parchment?"

"Go to sleep, Avalene."

She frowned and folded her arms together at her waist. "If I had a suspicious mind, I might think you were trying to distract me. There isn't a sheriff in England who would post an edict with a costly dagger. A nail or peg, perhaps, but never a dagger. And why in a place where so few would be able to decipher the message? 'Tis a rare man who can read, and most rely upon their priest to decipher any writing. 'Tis the reason notices are always posted near the village church at Coleway, where the priest—"

"Do you ever have a private thought?" he demanded, clearly exasperated.

"Oh, I have private thoughts aplenty," she assured him, "but sometimes I find it easier to reason through a problem aloud. By telling what little I know of sheriffs and their warrants, I hoped you would explain the flaw in my reasoning, or be persuaded to tell the truth about that scrap of parchment."

A muscle in his jaw tightened. "First I am a fool for laughing at a silly superstition, and now I am a liar? One can only wonder how low I will sink in your regard when you have known me an entire fortnight."

"I do not think you a fool," she said quietly, even though Oliver was too far ahead to overhear their conversation. This was the reason men disliked her. Somehow she always managed to insult them. She should be grateful that Sir Percival was too polite to yell at her. "And I think the only reason you would lie to me is to spare my feelings."

He narrowed his eyes. "If you truly believe that I would lie to spare your feelings, then why press for a truth that might frighten or hurt you?"

"You need not lie to protect me," she told him in her firmest voice. "I am in the midst of the wilderness on a night when all God-fearing souls should be close to hearth and home, and yet I would know the dangers I face rather than travel in ignorance. I am a woman full-grown, not a child to be cosseted, Sir Percival."

"On that score, we agree. You are most definitely a woman."

The look in his eyes made her suddenly aware of every inch of where their bodies touched. She lowered her gaze, knowing she wouldn't be able to hold a thought in her head if he continued to look at her that way. "Will you tell me what was on that parchment?"

"'Tis a message from . . . one of my men," he said. "One who awaits us in Beversham. He knew we would ride this way and wanted to warn me that there are, indeed, bandits about in the forests. So, it seems you were right in that regard. We should remain silent for the remainder of the night so we do not alert them to our presence."

She considered his words, then shook her head. "You are keeping something from me."

A stillness came over him, even though they continued to ride at the same pace. "Why are you so certain that I am not telling you the truth?"

"There is something in your tone, in the way you look at me," she said, as she lifted her shoulders. "I cannot explain it very well. You will laugh if I try."

"Oh, I will not laugh," he promised.

It didn't seem possible, but the moonlight made his eyes even more potent. He looked at her as if he could see every secret in her eyes. She spoke without thinking. "I feel as if we are somehow connected when we speak about almost anything, but I feel that connection break when you lie. 'Tis almost as if . . ." She shook her head again. "Nay, I cannot explain it. I just know when you are being less than truthful."

His eyes closed for a few moments, as if he were processing that information. When he opened them again the look he gave her was remote, guarded. "Those are frightening words to any man, my lady, but I am afraid they do not ring true. What I have told you is the truth."

He was still lying, she was certain of it. Except that

now he looked at her as if he found something unusual in his arms, something he found a bit alarming.

As neither of them looked away, his expression began to change. He looked at her in a way that was bolder and more intimate than any other man had ever dared. The intensity of his gaze both unnerved and excited her and the threads of their conversation began to slip from her fingers. The way he stared at her, the way his gaze lingered so often on her mouth . . . Was it possible her feelings were not so one-sided after all? That would be bad. No, that would be impossible.

They had been talking about something important, but she could recall none of it. The horse continued to move forward but it could have walked off a cliff and she wouldn't have known or cared much. He hadn't taken his eyes off her, their gazes still locked in their silent exchange. In that timeless moment she saw every reflection of her own feelings in his eyes: uncertainty, resistance, and an inexplicable, irresistible pull. The impossible. He wanted her. At long last, he had recognized her attraction to him and it had triggered a response.

A response that could prove dangerous.

The sensible side of her knew it was folly to consider any sort of dalliance with her father's knight. Staid, sensible Avalene de Forshay was a woman who held her honor sacred. She was immune to the illicit lures of carnal sin. She had never willingly allowed a man to hold her this close. Her pulse never fluttered over the way a man looked at her. She never stared into a man's eyes and wondered what it would feel like to kiss him. Until Sir Percival. Every thought in her head strayed into dangerous territory whenever she was near him, and now her girlish daydreams were about to stray into reality. It was time to turn away and put an end to this foolishness.

Instead some strange new beast inside of her took hold and lifted her chin, offering herself to him. The way he took the bait so easily sent a thrill of shock and feminine power through her. He lowered his head until their lips were only a breath apart and then he halted. She knew he was trying to defy the invisible force that drew them together, but she was already secure within its grasp. His breath felt warm against her mouth, small puffs of air that made her aware of how sensitive her lips were to his touch. The reasons for resisting what felt so right began to fade away.

The restraint she sensed in him would soon break, of that she was certain. She wondered if he would be gentle, or if he would claim her lips with all the rough, urgent passion that she had sometimes glimpsed between lovers. One could stumble upon couples engaged in illicit trysts in almost every corner of Coleway, and she had sometimes laughed at the way they seemed oblivious to everything and everyone around them. Now she was beginning to understand that madness.

"Avalene," he whispered, and her name sounded like a benediction. Their lips touched a moment later as his mouth brushed across hers in a caress that put scarcely more pressure on her parted lips than his breath. Once, twice, then again he stroked her lips, as if he could learn the shape of her mouth by touch alone.

Finally he fitted his lips to hers in a kiss so gentle, so filled with reverence that she felt tears come to her eyes. Like everything else about Sir Percival, his kiss was perfect. It was a kiss that a knight bestowed upon his lady-love, a kiss that spoke of the yearning he suffered for a lady who was forever beyond his reach. It was a kiss that sealed fates.

She kept her eyes closed; and something inside her changed in that moment. Something that had slumbered deep within her awakened and rose toward the light. If she had known that kissing could be this pleasurable she would have tried it long before now, but some instinct told her it would not be the same with any other man, the same instinct that told her she had just met her fate.

"Avalene?"

"Percival," she breathed, delighting in the taste of his name on her tongue. Her lashes fluttered open and she smiled.

He spoke a low yet fluent curse. "Do not look at me that way."

The quiet voice that knew this was madness became quieter. She tilted her head back, offering herself to him again, craving a deeper taste of desire. She watched him hesitate, but at last he lowered his head once more to kiss her.

The tip of his tongue traced the seam of her lips before she shuddered and opened up to him, reveling in both her surrender and his, secure in the knowledge that he was caught in the same sensual spell. His taste was intoxicating, an elixir that became suddenly vital while his kisses commanded her surrender. Gentleness gave way to need as his hand moved to the back of her neck and then to her head as he held her in place, her head tilted back, his mouth feeding upon hers. She pressed herself closer to his chest and at the same moment felt something in him change. He was suddenly very still.

"*Gesù*," he groaned, as he tore his mouth away from hers. His voice took on the hard edge of anger. "You must stop tempting me this way."

His gaze scarcely touched her face as he lifted his head, and his hands quickly returned to the reins. He stared straight ahead at the road. The haze of desire drifted into confusion as she realized that he was ignoring her. Indeed, he acted as if nothing momentous had just happened. His jaw was set but otherwise he looked unaffected, while her whole world had just come undone.

Or maybe it hadn't.

"You are . . ." She shook her head, certain she had to be mistaken in what she'd heard, yet just as certain that she was not. "You are blaming me for that kiss?"

"I must stay alert to any signs of trouble and be able to act upon a moment's notice," he said in a rough voice. He leaned away from her. "I cannot do that if you are intent upon seducing me at every turn."

"I am seducing you?" she sputtered. Was it possible? She had no experience in seduction, had no idea that she would have any talent at it. Apparently she did.

"Protest your innocence all you want," he said, "but you know exactly what I am talking about. You are a lady, Avalene. You had best remember how to act like one."

Her hand flashed out to slap him before the thought fully formed in her mind. At least, she tried to slap him. He caught her wrist before it came anywhere near his cheek, and forced it back to her side.

"You cannot tell me that I am the first victim of your charms," he said, a clear note of anger in his voice. "I suppose there was little harm in teasing and tempting the men at Coleway, but we are no longer safe within the walls of a castle and this is not a game. Our very survival could depend upon my ability to stay on guard, to sense danger around us."

She felt as if someone had just dumped a bucket of cold water over her head. Oh, how she longed to say something clever and biting. Unfortunately, humiliation robbed her wit. "Put me down."

"Stop *squirming*," he bit out. "You will stay exactly where you are. This is not the first or the last time we will be in close quarters on this journey. We must both accustom ourselves to the . . . inconvenience."

Oh, this was much worse than the other rejections. He had just reduced the most wonderful moments of her life to an *inconvenience*.

"I warned you at Coleway that you must be ready to follow my orders without question," he said. "You cannot ply me with kisses and then expect to control me with a crook of your finger. I am not some callow boy you can bend to your will. Nor am I a man as spineless as the steward, whose fixation with you will be the death of him yet. Whatever love games you played in the past to get your way with men will not work with me. And I said to cease that squirming!"

You deserve this, her staid, sensible voice said. The kisses that had meant everything to her meant nothing to him. Worse, they had made him angry. The pain of rejection washed through her along with irrational anger. She kept her tone as level as she could manage. "Put me down or I swear I will scream. I will kick your horse, I will—"

Percival reined in his horse, but he would not let her slide to the ground. His chest rose and fell as he took deep breaths, as if he had just exerted himself at some difficult task or was about to face one. That left little doubt in her mind that *she* was the difficult task.

"This is not the time to act like a child, Avalene. You have my apology if I hurt your feelings, but—"

"Enough!" she snapped. "I agreed to obey you without question, but I did not agree to sit silent while you all but accuse me of being the village whore. I am not some Delilah bent on seducing every male in my path. I have never played 'love games' in my life, and I do not bend men to my will by promising—" She took a cleansing breath, unwilling to even speak the foul words. "If you must know, you are the only man I have ever kissed. Now, you will unhand me at once, you odious man!"

He simply stared at her until she began to wriggle around again, trying to free herself from his grasp. His hold on her tightened. "You acted as if . . . That is, you seemed very knowledgeable. I am hard pressed to believe you are a complete innocent."

"Is that supposed to be an apology?"

"That was supposed to be an observation." He rubbed a hand across his face. "However, it seems I do owe you an apology."

"Fine," she snapped. "I will hear your apology when I am mounted again on my own horse."

He shook his head, even as he spurred his horse forward. "You must ride with me. This is one of the orders I would expect you to follow without question under different circumstances, but I have insulted you and I suppose you deserve an explanation."

"I deserve an apology and to be allowed on my own horse again."

He looked down at her and seemed to lose his train of thought. "Truly, you have never been kissed before?"

Should she be flattered that he thought her an experienced kisser, or insulted? Her thoughts felt as if they were drenched in syrup, struggling to make connections that should be obvious. Rather than stare at him in befuddled silence, she folded her arms across her chest and looked away. "I want my horse back."

He shook his head. "You are not hardened for a long ride the way Oliver and I are. You are angry now, but that will fade and you will start to lag behind. We need to keep moving, and we need to move as quickly as possible."

"We should have stopped in the last village," she said. "If we had stopped, I would not have had to ride with you and there would be no reason to blame me for anything."

He made a sound of impatience. "Your uncle's steward is so infatuated with you that I would not be surprised if he is searching for you even now."

"He is not infatuated with me," she argued, struggling to keep up with this turn in the conversation. Why was he so focused on Coleway's steward? John took delight in tormenting everyone, and cared for no one so much as himself. Infatuation was hardly the word she would use to describe their relationship. "The only reason he wants to marry me is to strengthen his ties to my aunt and uncle, and to gain my dowry. John's feelings for me do not extend beyond his ambitions."

"I know an obsessed man when I see one," he retorted. "He will not easily let go of all his schemes to win you. He will pursue us until there is no hope of recovering you, and a full moon will only aid their search. Eventually someone will find our trail, or someone who noticed that we took the path to the London road will give our direction to the search parties. We must plan for the worst case, that a search party is no more than an hour or two behind us. That means we keep riding."

She tightened her arms across her chest and looked away from him. He truly intended to ignore what had happened between them.

"When you are finished being stubborn you should try to rest," he said in a softer voice. "We will ride as hard the next four or five days as we rode today. My men will have extra horses so we can have fresh mounts and change horses as they tire, but we will not rest long in any one place."

"I am still waiting for your apology," she said. He had already dismissed their kisses as inconsequential and seemed content to pretend they hadn't happened. Her wisest course was to seal up the shame and anger in a distant part of her mind, and pretend the same. Why couldn't she let it go? "You have admitted that I am due an apology, but I have yet to hear it."

"Ah, yes," he said slowly. He pursed his lips. "I was wrong to think you were purposely trying to seduce me, or that you were a practiced seductress. Apparently I was also mistaken in my belief that you wanted me to kiss you. I do humbly apologize for taking any unwelcome liberties."

She *had* wanted him to kiss her. She had kissed him back. He was letting her know that he was well aware of those facts, which was almost as insulting as being accused of seducing him in the first place. It was one of the worst apologies she had ever heard.

"I agree that this is the wrong place and time for such indulgences," she said. "Indeed, there is no place or time that would be right for us to . . . to have any type of . . . romantic relationship. You are my father's knight. I am promised to another. We must not allow this to happen again."

He made a noncommittal sound and they rode on in silence. Well, that was that. Reason prevailed. She should not find it depressing that he found her logic so easy to follow.

"I suppose you are right," he said at last, sounding in better humor than she could muster. "These are unusual circumstances. We were both carried away. You have my word that I will do my best to resist such temptation in the future."

She studied his face, suspicious that he was making fun of her, but his expression remained stoic. Still, the humiliation of his rejection would not fade. "The task would be made much easier if you would allow me to keep my horse."

"I already answered that particular request several times," he said. "Accept the fact that you will never be beyond my sight before we reach London. Even then we will be in close quarters in the city and later on the ship. However, I feel certain we can control our baser urges if we put our minds to it."

Was he mocking her? She could not entirely dismiss the notion. Perhaps a dose of guilt would make him understand the seriousness of the situation. "My honor is as important to me as yours is to you, Sir Percival. 'Tis acceptable for a lady to give her favor to a knight, or even reward her knight with a chaste kiss for some heroic deed, but what we did was wrong. My father entrusted you with my care and I would not . . . I would not want to tempt you into breaking that trust. We both have our reputations to consider."

He gave her a pointed look. "Have you not yet realized that your honor is already lost?"

She blinked once, very slowly, stunned by the unexpected cruelty. Why would he say such a horrible thing? She shook her head, as much to deny the words as to stem a rising tide of dread. Unfortunately, he kept talking.

"You will be in my company for many weeks without the benefit of a chaperone. Most will assume we exchanged much more than a chaste kiss or two. We left your innocence at the gates of Coleway."

"We must hire a companion for me immediately!" How could she have overlooked such an obvious flaw in her plan? She had been so focused on escape that she hadn't thought about a chaperone, not once during their long ride. Instead her head had been filled with daydreams about the man who had ruined her. Now, when it was too late, she realized the full, awful truth of his words. The honor of any unmarried noblewoman who traveled in the company of men without a family member or respectable female companion would be questioned, no matter her protestations of innocence. Worse, the damage could never be completely undone. Innocent or not, she would be considered a fallen woman. "You must find someone and explain what has happened—and what has not happened, and then she can vouchsafe my reputation for the remainder of this journey."

"And where do you propose I find such a woman?" he asked. "What you are asking for is a woman who is willing to leave her home to go with strangers at a moment's notice, a woman who herself has a spotless reputation, a woman who knows how to handle a horse, which means she must be more than a mere servant. Even if we stumbled across such a paragon tomorrow, I doubt she would be willing to travel all the way to London at our pace, and then on to Wales. If two men and a woman rode up to Coleway as strangers and told our same story, would you allow any of the gentlewomen at Coleway to leave with us?"

"I would send a company of men with her," she said.

"Would you really?" he drawled. "You would donate a company of armed men and a gentlewoman of good repute to three strangers to make a journey that would last at least a month, by the time your people return from London? That would also assume that you believed the story being told by the three strangers." He shook his head. "'Tis much more likely your uncle would have all three thrown into the dungeon until he could send a messenger to wherever they came from to verify their story. What do you think would happen to us if we found ourselves in such a situation and a message were sent to Coleway?"

They both knew the answer. She would be returned to Coleway, and Sir Percival would be hung.

"You could remain as chaste as the most pious nun in England on this journey, and it will not matter. There will still be those who doubt your innocence." The certainty of his words made it clear that he had already thought through the problem and saw no solution. "You are ruined as completely as if your aunt's scheme had worked and we were found abed together at Coleway."

She had to remind herself that he was not trying to be cruel. He was simply stating facts. No matter how she tried to deny the truth, he was right. She was ruined, her honor destroyed. No one would look at her the same way ever again. And all she had to show for her disgrace were a handful of kisses. Kisses that he regretted.

It did not ease her guilt to know that she was the one who had taken the first steps toward sin, that she had somehow seduced him. Her behavior would justify anyone's doubts about her honor. Just two short days together and already she had kissed him. Two days! What would happen over the course of the many long weeks they would spend together?

The coming weeks stretched out in her mind, an agony of shameful longing and guilt. How long could she resist?

When they finally reached Wales, her father would have every right to doubt her honor. It was a fleeting thing.

"I had not thought this through," she admitted, feeling dazed. "I thought of the servants who would accompany us in the baggage train, but I did not think of what would happen when we left without chaperones. You are right. We will not find a suitable chaperone before we reach London. My honor has already been compromised." Another realization made her eyes widen with dread. "The Segraves! They can break the betrothal contract once this becomes known. My father will be furious."

"Your father knew your reputation would be ruined the moment you left Coleway without a chaperone."

Of course he knew. And he had sent Sir Percival on this mission anyway.

There were growing rumors of rebellion in Wales, and other men with ambitions who would overlook any stain on her honor. Ruined or not, the Segraves would be foolish to release their claim and risk her falling into the hands of their rivals. Between an alliance with her father and her Welsh heritage, Faulke had sufficient motivation to accept her as soiled goods despite the insult to his own honor. From what she had learned of him, Faulke's ambition far outweighed his ego. No, the marriage would go forward as intended, she decided.

And then what would happen to Sir Percival?

Regardless of his noble intent, regardless that he was here by his liege lord's order, Sir Percival would be held responsible for her ruined reputation even if he never touched her again.

"Faulke Segrave will challenge you," she whispered. A woman's husband or betrothed was obligated to challenge the man responsible for her ruin, and such challenges almost always resulted in a death. Given Segrave's ruthless reputation, she doubted it would be a fair fight. "My father must have known this when he sent you to Coleway."

"Aye, he was aware of the consequences," he said, "but once you are safe, I intend to leave Britain before Segrave can issue a challenge. I will not return."

The news shouldn't have come as a surprise, or cause an almost physical pain at her core. She had known since they met that it was unlikely she would ever see him again after her marriage. But there had always been that slim possibility. She hadn't realized how much she had clung to that faint thread of hope. A thread that had, in fact, never existed.

Once she was safely delivered to Weston, Percival would leave her. He would start a new life somewhere, likely with a large reward from her father, and she doubted he would ever think of her again. Rather than mourn his loss, she should be grateful that he would be safe from Faulke's challenge. Perhaps in time . . . At the moment, she felt only pain. "Where will you go?"

"'Tis best if you do not know."

Was it? She could not imagine living the rest of her life without knowing where he was, without knowing if he was safe. But what point would it serve to satisfy her curiosity? What point would there be to allow her heart to yearn for him more than it already did? No, he was right again. It would be best if he made a clean break from her life when the time came.

"We will have many weeks together before we part ways," he said, as if he knew her thoughts. "You must learn to live for the moment, Avalene. These next few weeks could be the greatest adventure of your life. You will see much of the English countryside, visit the great city of London, and take your first journey by ship. You must follow my orders to help us make a safe journey, but otherwise you are bound by few rules. Certainly fewer rules than you have been bound by in the past or will be in the future."

"There are always rules," she said, although her voice sounded uncertain.

He shook his head. "That is one of the few benefits of a ruined reputation. The worst has already happened. You can do as you please."

She studied the shadowed planes of his face in the

moonlight. "What, exactly, are you suggesting, Sir Percival?"

"Is it really so hard to guess?" he asked. "You must realize by now there is a certain . . . attraction between us. Once we are safe in London, what harm could there be in enjoying a few kisses on occasion?"

"They were wrong," she breathed. Did he think she needed any encouragement to contemplate sin? She tried to remind herself that the attraction he felt for her was nothing more than lust, a surprising turn of events to be sure, but she must stop deluding herself into thinking his feelings ran as deep as hers. He had already made it clear that the kisses they shared meant far less to him than they did to her. How much deeper would her feelings run if they shared more kisses? "*We* were wrong."

"Do you really think so?" he mused. He lifted one hand to indicate the darkened forest all around them. "As I said, this is not the time or place for a dalliance, but other opportunities will arise. We are already breaking most of the rules. What harm could there be in breaking a few more?"

What harm, indeed? Those were likely the words used on countless women as men led them to the edge of their downfall. She could almost see the vast emptiness below her, feel its pull. This is how women effected their own fall from grace; willingly, eagerly . . . stupidly.

"You know there is something between us," he said in a low voice, in that tone she found most irresistible. "Do you have no wish to indulge yourself just a little, to know what it is like to be kissed by a man who wants you regardless of your dowry, or family connections, or your marriage prospects? A man who wants *you* and nothing else?"

Oh, he was good. She pressed her lips together before

she could say something stupid. Her sluggish voice of reason finally stirred to life.

"I do not think any more kisses would be a good idea." Her voice held none of his smooth cadences. She sounded as if she had swallowed a frog. "In fact, I think it would be a good idea if I closed my eyes now and tried to get some sleep as you suggested."

His lips curved upward. "As you wish, my lady."

She pulled her hood up to give herself the illusion of privacy, even as she tried her best to think through everything he had said, everything he had implied, and everything he had proposed. It was almost too much to take in.

She was ruined. And all she could concentrate on was the fact that he had kissed her, and wanted to kiss her again. Amazing.

How different this journey would be if she had left Coleway with a full baggage train and a cadre of servants. It was unlikely they would have had occasion to speak more than once or twice a day, and the opportunity to kiss him never would have arisen. Their arrival at Weston would also be a far different homecoming than the one she had envisioned. What was her father thinking? Did he hope the Segraves would break the betrothal? Despite her conjecture, Faulke Segrave might not want her after he learned that she was traveling alone with a knight and his men for more than a month. If that happened . . . would her father allow her to wed the knight he had sent to ruin her?

The idea was as appealing as it was absurd. She quickly pushed it away. The impossible had already happened. Percival had admitted that he was attracted to her. He had kissed her. Lightning would not strike twice. Even with her ruined reputation, her father would never allow her to marry a poor, landless knight. If the thought of a marriage beneath her rank had ever crossed his mind, he would have left her at Coleway to marry the steward.

It was Percival's intent that confused her the most. He was perfect in so many ways, and yet there were things about him that she found surprising and a little disturbing. She had never expected him to speak to her so boldly, to suggest that there could be more between them than what had already happened. How easily he had set aside his honor. She had thought him so chivalrous. Even when he put an end to their kisses, she was certain he was trying to do the honorable thing, to follow his knight's code even as he accused her of seducing him. But then he suggested they break even more of the rules. Why would he suggest such a thing?

The answer came to her in a flash. His honor was ruined as surely as her own. He would be forced to leave England when this journey ended. Until then, he was as free of the rules of propriety as she was, and they would both exist in this strange, lawless world until they reached her father's fortress. She could kiss him as often as she wanted and it would make no difference to her reputation, or his. He could hold her as close as he wished, and everyone would assume he had done much worse. The price he would pay was exile.

She had been so caught up in trying to grasp the damage done to her reputation that she had not considered the damage done to his. His life would change even more than her own.

He had volunteered to rescue her, knowing the price to them both. She could not think of any other man who would have made such a sacrifice for a woman he had never met. He truly was the noblest man she had ever known.

Perhaps living in the moment was not such an outlandish idea after all. As he said, the damage was already done. If he wanted to kiss her again . . . she would let him.

Her head jerked up and she realized that she had nearly fallen asleep. There was so much to think over, so much to consider, but her thoughts kept scattering. Already his warmth was seeping into her, chasing off the dampness of the night air. As he predicted, the lack of sleep had caught up with her and she felt herself drift again toward slumber.

9
❧❧

The Merchants
of Venice

The Seven of Cups reveals a
time for visions of the future.
Many potentials become evident, but potentials require
choices. Dreams of the future
bring feelings of well-being and
security, yet the dreams are not
yet reality.

Avalene opened her eyes to shadowy shades of daylight, surprised to realize it was no longer nighttime and
she was no longer moving. Her gaze moved upward
through the canopy of a willow tree. Long, trailing willow branches formed a living tent of green and gold all
around her. The gently swaying switches carried the lingering scent of morning dew, but she remained dry and
warm in her sheltered haven. She didn't need to look
over her shoulder to know the identity of the man who
held her. Sir Percival's familiar warmth and scent envel-
oped her.

Sometime during the night or early morning, Percival
had managed to dismount without waking her and settled them both into this makeshift bed beneath the willow tree. They lay side by side, back to front, their
bodies fitted tightly together in a position even more intimate than when they rode together. Her "pillow" was
a solid male arm, and her blankets the soft wool of his
cloak and hers. His other arm lay draped over her waist

as if to make certain she stayed close to him, even in sleep. Oddly enough, she felt no sense of shock or maidenly modesty at waking in his arms.

Later she would be annoyed at his presumption. Later she would think about the kisses they had shared the night before and the way she responded so readily to his tempting offers, in thought if not in deed. There would be plenty of time to fret over all of those worries in the next few weeks. For now she wanted nothing more than to relax in the warmth and comfort of his arms, luxuriate in the illusion that the rest of the world and its worries were very far away.

She turned to look over her shoulder but her head was tucked beneath his chin and she could see no more than his arm. Moving slowly, careful not to wake him, she turned her whole body until she faced him. His head rested upon a leather saddlebag and the windblown branches cast moving shadows across his face, giving the illusion of shifting expressions: a stern look that melted into smooth, boyish innocence. Then the shadows caught the angled features of a devastatingly handsome man.

His eyes remained closed and she studied the crescent sweep of his lashes. There were so many mysteries to ponder about a man who should be almost dull with normalcy; a landless knight like so many at Coleway, men who offered protection from the lord's enemies in times of war, or an escort for the lord and his family when they traveled to fairs, shrines, or tournaments. Such a man would not be expected to make so many life-or-death decisions about the fate of his liege lord's daughter, and he would certainly not be so irreverent as Sir Percival was in her presence. He was unlike any other knight she had known, or even any other man she had known. Whatever this attraction was between them, the normal rules of chivalry and courtship did not apply.

Indeed, he made clear there were no rules. They were free to do as they wished. The world of convention and propriety was far away. For this brief moment in time, she was not bound by the rules that made a courtship between an unwed noblewoman and a landless knight impossible. She could do almost anything she wanted. She could smile and flirt with him, kiss him if she pleased. She could . . .

She blinked once, astonished at the lewd direction of her thoughts, and just as astonished that she did not recoil from the idea. In her mind she stepped closer to the place where rules were left behind, drawn to look over the edge and into the abyss. How would it feel to open her arms and throw caution to the wind, knowing it would be Sir Percival who caught her?

She didn't know why she felt so certain of him. He had pledged to protect her with his life, but there was an underlying emotion at work that was harder to define, even though it was just as important. It was the way he made her feel when she was in his company, as if she could do or say whatever came into her head and he would understand, that he knew how her mind worked and the meanings behind her words. It was the sort of connection she saw between people who had been friends for a very long time, or siblings who were especially close, or couples who were long wed. She and Percival barely knew each other, but she felt that same sort of bond with him, a sense of ease that was as comfortable as if she had known him all her life.

Her hand reached out seemingly of its own volition to rest against his chest. Warm stone was the first thought that went through her mind. He was so much bigger and harder than she, but there was a gentleness she sensed in him that made his strength intriguing rather than alarming. She suspected he was a man who had known little of gentleness in his own life, but every time he touched her he seemed to do so with great care, as if she were some sort of breakable treasure. Perhaps it was those small quirks that enticed her, that effortlessly drew her in.

He still hadn't stirred from the weight of her hand on his chest and she grew bolder, moving her hand upward until her palm rested lightly against his cheek. The warm, sandy texture of his face fascinated her. Her palm tickled where it rested against the dark stubble that shadowed his jaw.

He shifted in his sleep and she went still as he turned his head and rubbed his cheek against her hand. After releasing a deep sigh, he rolled onto his back and then his breathing returned to normal. Her thumb now rested near the corner of his mouth and then she watched it move across his lips. She knew this was madness, but the lure proved irresistible. He would never know. She could pretend for just a few moments that there was nothing wrong with touching him as if it were her right. Even in sleep his mouth looked hard and unyielding, but her fingertips encountered skin as soft as her own. She closed her eyes and let her thumb rub over his lower lip, remembering his kisses, wondering when he would kiss her again, wondering how many kisses they would share before this dream ended.

If they were captured and returned to Coleway, she would be forced to endure John as her husband. When they reached the safety of Weston, she would be given to Faulke Segrave with her honor in tatters regardless of her actions. From all accounts, Faulke was a handsome man, but she had known other handsome men at Coleway and they failed to stir any hint of the desire that Sir Percival could arouse just by looking at her. Percival was risking his life for her and had already forsaken his honor. Both their lives were at risk on this journey. Allowing him to introduce her to passion seemed a small price to pay. Indeed, it was a selfish price on her part. She had never wanted another man the way she wanted him, and there was a growing fear that she would never again want another man in the same way.

Suddenly his lips parted and a low, husky voice emerged. "You are playing with fire, Avalene."

She jerked her hand away halfway through that announcement and gaped up at him. The fire he had warned her about was in his eyes, banked for the moment in shades of mossy green, but warm enough to make her blush. She bit her lower lip, trying hard to think up a believable lie for her brazen behavior. "I—I did not think you would awaken . . . er, mind, if I . . ."

"You did not think you would be caught," he finished for her, in the same deceptively mild voice. His eyes narrowed when she began to chew her lower lip again. In one smooth movement, she found herself on her back with Sir Percival looming over her. There was a harsh edge to his features that she interpreted as anger. "Did you think your boldness would displease me?"

"I have no idea what will please or displease you." She blinked once, searching for the right answer. "You do not look very pleased."

"I do not look satisfied," he countered. His gaze fastened on her mouth as he rubbed his thumb over her lower lip, mimicking what she had done to him earlier. "Little girls who play with fire get burned."

She wanted to tell him that she was not a girl, remind him that she was a woman full-grown. She could not utter a word. He had burned her lips with his touch alone. His fingertips inflicted the same sweet punishment along the curve of her cheek and she shuddered, feeling a familiar tendril of liquid heat unfurl in her belly.

"Ah, *cara*," he breathed, as he gazed down at her. "The thoughts you put in my head."

Cara. The word sounded foreign to her, yet vaguely familiar. She had heard the word somewhere before, but not in tones so seductive or in a voice that made her breathless with anticipation. Would he kiss her again?

Her thoughts dissolved into swirls of emotion when his lips touched first one corner of her mouth and then the other. He moved lower to trail chaste kisses along the length of her jaw, and lower still to her throat, seemingly intent on exploring every inch of exposed skin. When he lingered near her ear she heard as well as felt him draw a deep breath, as if her scent intrigued him. He slowly released the breath and her whole body rose upward, drawn to him by some invisible force.

"Aye, impossible thoughts," he murmured, settling some of his weight until his hips rested lightly upon hers. Helplessly, she pressed upward again. His low groan turned into words of encouragement as his mouth trailed a path toward hers. "Kiss me, Avalene."

Her sensible voice argued that this was *wrong*. Then his hand cupped her cheek and all she could think was, *this is so right*. She obediently turned her head to kiss him. The instant their lips met she felt a tingling sensation begin . . . in her toes, of all places.

Impossible thoughts began to fill her head as well. Thoughts that maybe the fall would be worth it, that maybe she did deserve to indulge herself on this journey, to learn about lovemaking from a man who found her desirable, from a man of her choosing rather than a man chosen for her by others. This was not wrong.

Determined now to please him, she tried a more serious kiss like the ones he had taught her the night before.

He responded immediately, fitting his mouth to hers, but still letting her set the pace. Soon the chaste kisses were not enough to satisfy the craving that began to build inside her. A craving for what, she wasn't entirely certain, but each kiss whet her appetite for more. Unfortunately, he seemed in no hurry to ease her hunger.

A wicked thought entered her mind. Before she could think better of the idea, she darted her tongue between his lips in a tentative stroke. He made a sound deep in his chest that was part growl, part groan, and then he took control. He taught her exactly how to taste him, drawing her into his mouth, then gentling the pressure to stroke her with his tongue. The intimacy should've shocked her. Instead, she tangled her fingers through his hair to hold him closer, growing hungrier.

Somewhere in her drugged senses she realized that his hands were skimming over her waist and hips, and then working at the ties that fastened her surcoat to loosen the garment. His mouth moved away from hers and she tried to tell him all the amazing thoughts that were running through her head, every feeling, every wonderful new sensation that he brought to life within her. The only sounds she could make were small sighs, then soft little moans when his teeth nibbled painlessly along the sensitive curve of her shoulder.

Her eyes widened when he sat up just long enough to pull his shirt over his head and toss it aside. He tugged at her surcoat until that garment, too, lay in a heap. She had scarcely drawn a breath before he leaned over her again, his weight braced on his hands. "Touch me, Avalene. I want to feel your hands upon me."

Her gaze drifted across the vast expanse of his naked male chest, at muscles that stood out in rigid relief along his neck and shoulders, and even along the flat planes of his stomach. Before she could think to refuse his order, he made the decision for her and placed her palm against the center of his chest.

"Feel how my heart beats for you, *cara.*"

For a moment she could feel nothing but the hard warmth of his bare skin, the rough texture of the dark hair across his chest. Then she felt the steady rhythm of his heart, strong and vital, the very essence of his life force. Tears welled in her eyes when she realized what he had just done and all the implied meanings, intentional or not. He had just placed his heart in her hand.

"What is this?" he asked, as he brushed away a stray tear with his thumb.

She could hardly explain what she did not understand herself. Instead, she put both hands on his chest and marveled at the difference between her pale skin and his sun-bronzed flesh. "I like touching you."

She felt the vibrations of laughter beneath her palms.

"And here I worried that I had shocked your maidenly senses."

"I have shocked myself," she admitted, as she spread her fingers to feel more of him. Her hands drifted lower until they rested on the hard ridges of his stomach.

A deep shudder racked his body and her startled gaze flew to his face. His brows were drawn together, his mouth set in a grim line.

"Did I do something wrong?" she asked. "Are you hurt somewhere?"

"Aye," he answered hoarsely. He shook his head as if trying to clear his thoughts. "Nay, 'tis not pain, but frustration. This is not the time or place for love play."

Despite his words, one hand moved to the laces of her chemise as his gaze held hers captive. Instinctively, she tried to stop him. Panic set in when he effortlessly brushed her hands away. He began to untie her laces. She looked from one side to the other, searching for a gap in the branches that surrounded them. "We should not be doing this. Where is Oliver?"

"Asleep on the ridge above us," he said easily, as he loosened the gathered neckline of her chemise. He glanced over his shoulder toward a place where the ground began to rise. "My other man, Armand, is keeping watch, but he cannot see through the branches of this tree and neither would dare approach before calling out. We are alone." He turned back to her with a determined expression. "You are so beautiful; I just want to look at more of you. 'Twill go no further, I swear."

He parted her chemise before she could object and she felt a chill of cool air on her breasts. She crossed her arms over her chest to cover herself and closed her eyes as well, but he gently pushed her hands away.

"So beautiful," he murmured. His hand moved to her throat and he stroked the sensitive skin with the tips of his fingers. He traced a line down the center of her chest and her own breath caught in her throat, waiting to see what he would do next.

She had overheard enough gossip to know that a man often fondled a woman's breasts when he kissed her. Percival's intentions appeared obvious, but he surprised her by tracing the same innocent path back to her throat, his fingers lingering on a pulse point in her neck. She felt a painless ache in her breasts and *wanted* his touch there, but he lowered his head for another kiss and his fingers brushed along the line of her jaw.

Eventually his hand began to drift lower as if he couldn't help himself, at first stroking her shoulders, then moving to her breasts, tracing their shape, cupping her as if to gauge their weight. The ache intensified. He drew back far enough to look into her eyes and then he brushed his thumb across one of her nipples in the same kind of stroke that he had used on her lips. Her back arched and she gasped, overwhelmed by the shock of sensations that surged through her.

He seemed to know how to calm her, how to gentle the ragged burst of emotions. He cradled her face and made small hushing sounds near her ear as his lips pressed kisses into her shoulder. Her breathing had barely returned to normal when he shifted to settle more fully between her legs. Their lips touched at the same moment his chest touched hers, and the weight of his big body settled over her. They both gasped.

Nothing could have prepared her for the sensation of his bared skin against her own, at the unexpected shock of contact that passed between them. She wanted to ask him if that always happened, but he took her breath away with deep, drugging kisses and she soon forgot the question. She was in heaven . . . until his whole body suddenly stiffened and went still. He gathered her closer until it felt as if she were surrounded by him on every side.

The words he bit out were laced with such quiet venom that at first she thought it was emotion that made them incomprehensible. *"Rami, se veramente vuole morire, la accontento. Allora, lasciaci in pace! Capisce?"*

She was even more astonished when another voice answered, the voice of a child.

"Sì, mio padrone."

Avalene followed the direction of Percival's gaze and caught a glimpse of a foreign-looking boy with dark brown hair and honey-colored skin. Long willow branches lay over his shoulders like a woman's hair, as if he had just pushed through them. He wore strange garb and seemed very thin, and he held something in his hands that might have been a tray of food. He bowed and backed his way out of their sanctuary through the trailing canopy of willow branches. For a moment they both remained frozen in place.

"That boy saw me naked." She pushed against Percival's chest to get him off her so she could put her clothing to rights, and was grateful when he released her.

"He did not see you naked," Percival said, even as he rolled off her and picked up his shirt. Despite her agitation, she could not help but watch him. Powerful muscles stood out in hard lines along his shoulders and arms, flexing in fascinating ways as he put his shirt back on. "I suspect Rami got an eyeful, but I doubt it will cause him any lasting damage."

Her hands stilled on her laces. "You think my humiliation is cause for humor?"

"Nay, I think it fortunate that Rami interrupted us when he did." He looked at her over his shoulder and his lips curved upward in a grin, his expression so unexpected and so disarming that she felt her breath catch. "You are entirely too tempting in the morning, my lady."

She didn't know what to make of his lighthearted mood. "Are you . . . are you going to blame me again for those kisses?"

He shook his head. "I knew full well what I was about."

"I should say so," she grumbled.

That broadened his smile. "Still, I went further than intended. You have my apologies, my lady."

Percival rummaged through their saddlebags and found her rucksack as she tried to work a knot free in the laces of her surcoat. Rather than give the sack to her, he sat down and began to search through its contents.

"This is much less than I imagined you would try to bring along." He handed her a comb from the bag, and continued digging. "An extra chemise, stockings, a comb, hairpins, ribbons, needles, threads . . . what is this? Ah, never mind. 'Tis a clever little mirror."

She had never seen him so at ease in her company. Usually there was an underlying element of tension between them, as if he were constantly on guard. She almost hated to ruin his mood. "Why did you speak Italian to that boy?"

Percival stilled for a moment, then went back to his exploration of the rucksack. "He understands only Arabic and Italian. Where did you learn to speak Italian?"

"Merchants. Italian merchants," she clarified. "Where did you learn the language? And where did that boy come from?"

"Rami is newly arrived from Italy and does not yet speak more than a few words of French and English," he said. "Fortunately for Rami, I learned to speak Italian when I was a child, and there was an Italian knight in your father's service who helped polish my skills with the language. The men who are with me also know the language." His mouth turned downward as he continued to riffle through her belongings. "Where did you encounter Italian merchants, and how is it you were allowed in their company long enough to learn their language?"

Despite his casual tone, she felt certain he was focused entirely on her answer. She could understand his concern. All Italian men had a certain reputation when it came to women, an almost instinctive power to seduce them. Even the youngest apprentices had a way of focusing all of their attention on a female that made them hard to resist. "The merchants seek lodging at Coleway each year on their journey between the fairs at Shrewsbury and Chester. Their parties stay at Coleway for at least a fortnight."

One dark brow rose. "You were allowed to associate with these men?"

"Only in the great hall or common areas," she said, "and only when my aunt or Lord Brunor were present."

His curt nod indicated acceptance of her answer, but his continued silence encouraged an explanation.

"I spent little time with the merchants since I could ill afford their wares, but their apprentices often carried trinkets that they would barter for the veils I embroidered." She would not admit that she was just as flattered as every other woman at Coleway by the attentions of their intriguing visitors. She recognized early on that the Italians enjoyed all women and she was nothing special. "I learned a few words of Italian by bargaining with the apprentices."

"It seems you learned enough to understand what I said."

It was more question than comment and she dutifully answered. "I have a talent for learning languages, although I have not had much occasion to practice my Italian. Perhaps I can learn more from the boy, Rami. Who is he, by the way? A page? Your servant?"

"He was a slave, a recent acquisition of mine from a cruel master. I do not like to see children abused." He slid apart the two halves that protected the polished surface of her mirror, then tilted the metal disk this way and that as if he were intrigued by the way the light reflected off its surface. "An Italian merchant owned Rami, perhaps one of the very merchants who visited Coleway. Rami still looks painfully thin because his master was slowly starving him to death. In a moment of weakness I decided to purchase him. I have little use for the boy and offered him his freedom, but he refuses to leave. He tries hard to please. Ofttimes he tries too hard."

And that was how she learned Sir Percival was a true knight and hero. She couldn't name one knight at Coleway who would have bothered himself to save a heathen child in such straits. There was a soft heart beneath Percival's forbidding exterior, another unexpected surprise.

"That was very good of you to rescue the boy," she said. "'Tis little wonder he wants to please you."

He made a noncommittal sound and brushed her concern aside. "Our breakfast still awaits us, and then we must be on the road again. 'Tis already well past dawn."

The thought of leaving their lair made her feel suddenly awkward. They had been moments away from being entirely naked and spied upon by a little boy. In a field. With God only knew how many other people about. She was not acting like herself, but Percival had no way of knowing this was out of character for her.

"There is something I must tell you," she blurted out. The sudden intensity in his eyes was disturbing enough to make her grasp for words. "I do not—that is, I am not—I have never before been so free with my favors!"

The look in his eyes intensified, but he remained silent.

"Given my actions last night and this morn I would no longer blame you if you thought I was some sort of harlot. I do not know what came over me. I never act this way. Something is wrong with me."

The corners of his mouth turned up again. "Aye, there is definitely something wrong with you. Many things, as a matter of fact."

Many? She could guess at a few, but what more did he find wrong with her? Apparently the confusion showed in her expression.

"'Tis not such a mystery," he said in a kind voice. "You are fleeing from an unscrupulous steward who would force you into a dishonorable marriage with the help of your aunt. You are in the middle of the wilderness with a man you barely know and without a chaperone. We are both aware of the attraction between us and we both know this is perhaps the only situation in which we are not bound by any rules. Few young women ever find themselves in such a predicament. I would be worried if you felt perfectly yourself under these circumstances."

"I—I appreciate that you have treated me with honor," she said in a quiet voice. "Many other knights would not behave as nobly as you have."

He took her hands and pressed his thumbs into the centers of her palms in gentle, soothing motions that should have been calming, but instead felt incredibly wicked. "I have never wanted nor needed to force myself upon a woman to gain her favor. If you decide to find me repulsive, then you need not worry that I will take you against your will. If you continue to find our interludes as pleasant as I do, then I suspect you will lose your innocence before this journey ends. Normally I am a patient man. I would prefer to wait until we reach a soft bed with no worry of being overtaken by a search party, but our time is limited and I wish to enjoy every moment with you to its fullest. If you waken me the same way each morn, 'tis possible I may not wait until we reach London to make you mine."

Her cheeks warmed over the way he said *make you mine*. "What we are doing, what we will do is sinful."

"Is it?" he asked. "Our bodies recognize that we are well matched, even if our minds rebel against the idea. We are in a moment out of time. You are not pledged to any man but me and I am pledged to no other woman. Life is an uncertain thing, Avalene. Events in the future will likely separate us, but no man or woman knows if God will bless them with a future. Our path is uncertain. Today is all that is sure. We can live for just these moments as if we were pledged to each other. Indeed, we actually are pledged to each other in a sense. I am your knight. You are my lady. Time is all that can change those facts, but time is not yet our enemy."

His logic sounded so reasonable that she wondered if he had practiced the speech. It was certainly persuasive.

"This is all happening so quickly," she said. "I did not expect to find myself in such a position . . . ever. Suddenly I am supposed to disregard every tenet that I have lived by all my life?" She shook her head. "I should resist everything about you that I find irresistible. Just the touch of your hand upon mine is enough to make me forget myself. But then another voice inside me says this is wrong, the same voice that cannot believe I let you unlace my gown and chemise as if I were a common strumpet. I am not that kind of woman, and yet . . . somehow I am."

"I suspect you will discover many surprising things about yourself on this journey," he said. His gaze dropped to their joined hands and he released his hold on her as if he had been unaware of the contact. "For the first and perhaps the only time in your life, you are free to act upon impulse."

"I cannot bring myself to think it is right." She laid her hand upon his arm and it seemed a reflexive gesture when he covered her hand with his own. "At other times, there is nothing about this that feels wrong. Can you give me a little time to sort through my feelings? Truly, I am not so impulsive a person as I have acted since we met. I need time to come to terms with everything that has happened, and decide how to move forward."

"Are you asking for my permission, or do you seek permission from yourself?" His words were harsh, but the look in his eyes was gentle, understanding. "I will not blame you again for our intimacies, but you must admit that you have a hand in bringing them about. I am not a monk, my lady. If you tempt me, I will respond. If you hold yourself apart, I will respect the distance you put between us. However, I am not above plying temptations of my own. That is the best I can promise."

"'Tis a fair bargain." She forced herself to take her hand from his arm, and then released a small sigh. "I shall try my best not to tempt either of us until I can think clearly again and decide what is the best course."

"I trust you will let me know when that momentous decision comes about." He surprised her by catching her hand and turning it over to place a brief yet sensuous kiss in her palm. "Right now, I am famished and in need of sustenance. Let us break our fast, and then you will have all day to think over your decisions before we stop again for the night. Just be aware that I intend to sleep with you every night until we reach London." His smile grew wider. "For your protection, of course."

10

This was turning into a more interesting and enjoyable interlude than Dante could have possibly imagined. To think he had been opposed to the plan! Without it he would likely be sitting in the squalid heat of London to await his summons from the Council, bored and restless, his thoughts dwelling impotently upon what awaited him in Venice. Instead he had this last chance to enjoy the fresh air and sunshine of the English countryside, with the distraction of a beautiful woman on his arm. A beautiful, willing woman, he corrected, as his gaze slid over her.

Avalene was busy putting everything back into the rucksack that he had unpacked, her movements elegant and economical, her attention focused completely on the task. He had never encountered a woman so beautiful who was so completely unaware of her looks. Nothing in her manner indicated that she thought herself out of the ordinary, and yet she was stunning, a treasure that had awaited his discovery. Last night he had staked his claim on that treasure.

Although their kisses were meant to be a distraction from her chilling discovery that she could sense his lies, the distraction worked in ways he hadn't intended. One taste of her emptied every rational thought in his head. It was not until she called him "Percival" that he finally came to his senses and realized she had neatly turned the tables. His clever ruse to drive her away by insulting her with accusations of seduction and then crudely suggesting an affair were also miscalculated, but he had hardly been thinking straight. He wanted her, and at the same time, he wanted to keep her safe. How could he protect her from himself?

The question no longer mattered. He had made a decision during the long night as he held her in his arms and watched her sleep, the beast inside him always plotting, always planning.

"Please, do not let me keep you from your meal," she said, pulling him from his thoughts. Her fingers worked at the ribbon that bound her braid. "I would like to comb and replait my hair before I join the others, if you do not mind?"

Mind seeing her hair unbound? He wouldn't miss this for the world. "I will wait."

She pursed her lips, but did not argue. He stretched out again on their makeshift bed and propped his hands behind his head, content to linger. He had never watched a woman comb out her hair. He was soon fascinated by the way her slender fingers loosened the plaits, the graceful sweep of her comb through the long, golden strands. Such a simple pleasure, an intimacy he had never known before he met Avalene. Just watching her made him feel relaxed and at ease in a way that no one else had ever managed. He felt like a different man when he was with her.

His sister complained that he tended to brood too

much and view life too seriously, even though she was well aware of the reasons for his views. Brooding was the last thing on his mind when he was with Avalene. When she wasn't busy clouding his mind with lust she made him feel downright cheerful. He just couldn't quite pinpoint the reasons why.

"Let me plait your hair." Where had that idea come from?

She arched one brow. "Do you often plait ladies' hair?"

"Nay, but I would like to plait yours." He would like to feel the silky strands between his fingers, wrap it around his hands, let her hair—

"Another time, perhaps."

He couldn't believe she had refused him. What she saw in his face made her smile, the serene Madonna smile that always made him want to smile back at her.

"I can do this much faster than you can." She divided the locks into three strands, and then began to braid with practiced efficiency. "This is also the one thing I might be better at than you."

Why that innocent remark should send his thoughts in lewd directions was a mystery, but away they went. She was all softness and curves from the swell of her cheek to the shapely lines of her ankles. Her skin was so flaw-less and translucent that nearly every emotion could be gauged by her coloring; her moods ranged from wool white, to shell pink, to the deepest flush of scarlet. He was arrogant enough to be certain that he was the source of most of her blushes.

It was the tension between them that flustered her most and caused the most delightful reactions to even the smallest lures he sent her way. It didn't take him long to realize that she'd never been courted. Not in the in-nocent, acceptable ways that all young maidens were courted in every household the size of Coleway, and certainly not in more clandestine ways. Was that part or all of the reason she responded so readily to him now, because this was the first time she was made aware of a man's desire for her?

He felt a new emotion stir to life as his gaze moved over her. Possessiveness. Jealousy. Or a mixture of both. The feelings were so foreign to him that it was impossible to tell.

He watched her finish her braid and take the mirror out of her rucksack to examine her reflection. She looked up at him from beneath her sweep of lashes, found his gaze upon her, and blushed shell pink. No, those blushes belonged to him alone. She was his now, just as Mordecai had promised—his to do with as he pleased. The possibilities that came to mind were endless and all most pleasing. There were remarkable depths of passion locked beneath her cool exterior. He could not wait to wade deeper.

Mordecai had warned him of this lure, and perhaps the magician had even cast some love spell over them both to hurry along the inevitable. There was no longer any doubt in his mind that he would do just as Mordecai had suggested and take full advantage of this time with Avalene. He could pretend to be the gallant knight for a few more weeks. As long as she remained blind to the beast that lurked beneath his disguise, this could well be the most enjoyable journey of his lifetime. He only wished it could last a lifetime.

It was a childish wish, but a part of him yearned to be the man she thought him to be; she made him want to be worthy of her. Unfortunately, the die was set long ago and it was far too late to redeem himself. He was not an honorable knight. He was not worthy of her. When she learned the truth, this masquerade would be at an end.

He watched her bite her lower lip, stared helplessly as she let it slide out slowly from beneath her teeth, the thoughtful lip-bite rather than the nervous lip-bite, or the embarrassed lip-bite, or the *I'm not going to laugh aloud* lip-bite. He recognized the differences already.

It was just one of many small mannerisms that never failed to send a wave of desire through him. Sometimes it lapped at him like the warm, gentle pull of a tide. Other times it hit him with enough strength to take his breath away, like now. He had just kissed her. Could she still taste him on her lips?

"What is wrong with you?" she asked, worried by whatever she saw in his face.

"Nothing," he answered promptly. "What is wrong with the men at Coleway?"

She tilted her head to one side as if she were trying to listen to his thoughts, trying to read the meaning of his words in his eyes. "Pardon?"

"Why were you never courted?" It was a reasonable question. Nothing on earth would have stopped him from courting her had he been a respectable squire or knight at Coleway. Any male with a pulse had to feel the same. What force or threat had stopped them?

"I was courted!" she protested hotly, and then she bit her lower lip, mostly on the left side with her mouth twisted slightly to the right. It was the same lip-bite she had used on the day they left Coleway, the one he had noticed every time she told someone a lie about the reasons for their departure. Her expression turned defensive. "I had a few admirers."

"Yet I was the first to kiss you," he mused, trying to contain a smug smile. "Surely I am not the first who *wanted* to kiss you."

She mumbled something under her breath, and her face became almost as red as her gown. Interesting.

"I'm sorry, I could not hear what you said."

She looked up at him and he was surprised to see the threat of tears in her eyes, the shimmering surface of a blue lake. She spoke each word very carefully. "You are the first."

Did she think he did not believe her? Granted, she had a natural talent for kissing, but he had recognized her innocence soon enough. As soon as he had quashed the irrational jealousy that someone else *might* have kissed her first. He tried to keep his voice gentle. "I just said as much."

She twisted her hands in her lap and would not look at him. "No, I meant that you are the first to kiss me as well as the first who wanted to kiss me."

Gesù, she actually believed what she was saying. "You expect me to believe that no other man or boy ever tried to steal a kiss from you? Or lingered in your presence for the sheer pleasure of your company?"

"I am not trying to make you believe anything," she said, her voice curt now. "I am telling you the truth. Apparently I have a tendency to speak my mind too freely, and most men do not like to keep company with opinionated women."

"Who told you that nonsense?" He was already sure of the answer, but she actually had to consider the question for a few moments.

"John, I suppose." She lifted her shoulders and her lips turned upward at a forced angle, as if she were practicing how to laugh with people who made fun of her rather than let anyone know how much it hurt her to be laughed at. "My failed courtships were always a source of great amusement to him."

They were not a source of any amusement to Dante. He wondered if he would have time to return to Coleway before they set sail for Venice. He would very much like to show the steward *his* idea of amusement. "Did you ever consider that John was behind those failures, that he engineered them?"

She shook her head, offering a wry smile. "I have no one to blame but myself. I am hardly the type of simpering maid that most men seem to find . . . interesting."

The expression in her eyes was almost apologetic, and yet strangely hopeful at the same time. Was she hoping *he* found her interesting? Mission accomplished. Yet why should his interest be so unexpected?

The proof was before him, as unbelievable as he found it. Her no-nonsense modesty and complete lack of vanity made sudden sense. She didn't think she had anything to be vain about.

"John threatened them," he said, picturing it in his mind. "He used some threat that made each of them run away from you, and then he made you think their defection was somehow your fault, a ploy to undermine your confidence, to keep you from encouraging them."

She shook her head again, but it lacked confidence. "Why on earth would he do such a thing?"

"I told you he was obsessed. He wanted you all to himself with no rivals, even rivals who would be allowed no more than innocent flirtations." He didn't add that he probably would have done the same thing, had he been in John's shoes. The thought of any other man touching her, kissing her, made his fists clench. "Do you really have so little understanding of your appeal?"

She looked at him with guarded eyes and he could see that she did not. Her gaze had turned wary, as if waiting for him to spring some hidden trap. In that moment he could have cheerfully slit John's throat. Possessiveness he could understand. But to break her spirit? That, he would never understand. He was only thankful that

John had failed in that regard. She was bruised but unbroken.

Perhaps he could heal her.

The thought lodged in his head and refused to be silenced, even though it was an absurd notion with countless flaws. He was the monster that destroyed. No one would cast him in the role of a healer. Still, the idea intrigued him. He felt the most ridiculous need to make her happy, to keep her safe and protected. To truly make her his own. Not just for a few weeks, but for as long as she would have him.

He had never taken responsibility for anyone but himself. Even his sister had been left in the care of an uncle when they arrived in England. Granted, that had not turned out so well and he still carried a measure of guilt for abandoning her. Could he abandon Avalene as well, leave her fate in the hands of others? Then there was the bigger question: Would she want him to take responsibility for her?

His mind raced forward to the inevitable day when she learned he was not the gallant Sir Percival. That would be the day her smiles turned to tearful pleas, the day she would cringe whenever he touched her in the most innocent ways. Still, there was no reason she needed to learn of his deceit until they were on a ship bound for Venice. He had already intended to keep her sequestered in London and not reveal any portion of the truth until they were at sea. That part could proceed as planned. There was also a good possibility that she would never learn he was a notorious assassin. His men would not reveal the truth if he forbade it. He could tell her the king's reasons why she had to leave England for good. He could also tell her something close to the truth about the reasons he had abducted her; that he owed

Edward a favor, that he really had saved her life. Would that be enough to regain her trust?

Even if he managed to earn forgiveness, the next hurdle would be convincing her to live with him as his mistress. He was still determined to take an Italian wife to form a political alliance and secure his family's safety in Venice, although the idea was becoming less appealing with each day he spent with Avalene. Nevertheless, he would not give up all of his carefully laid plans because of an infatuation with a woman who did not even know his real name, whom he intended to make his mistress before she made that momentous discovery. Perhaps he would change his mind, but as things stood, he would be lucky if she did not simply run from him screaming.

She would never agree if she knew a convent was her alternative. Taking the veil was an acceptable occupation for a woman of her station. Living in sin with a man was not.

She need never know of the convent, the beast inside him whispered. Instead he would make her understand how well he would treat her, the comfortable, even lavish lifestyle she would lead. He would install her in some monstrous palazzo where she could make use of the chatelaine skills she so cherished. He could picture her there on a balcony overlooking the canal, smiling up at him. He could picture himself there as well, just as happy with his innocent, opinionated beauty.

No, he decided, she was far too precious to be locked away in a convent. Deceit was his specialty, and he would do whatever was necessary to keep her. He would lie to her for the rest of their lives if it meant she would stay with him willingly. She was his reward for all the years he had spent in the darkness of men's minds.

"Sir Percival?" She sounded nervous.

He smiled at her effortlessly, filled with new purpose.

"Avalene de Forshay, you are the most beautiful woman I have ever met."

She blinked twice, very slowly, as if she expected him to disappear each time she opened her eyes. She sat in frozen silence. He was fairly certain she had stopped breathing as well.

He had lied to her about almost everything else, but in this he would be completely honest. She would know his true feelings about her. This morn he had gone too far, allowed his lust to rule his senses when he bared her shoulders and breasts. That was a lapse of control that made him feel more delight than regret, but he would be more careful with her in the future. He would show her the respect she deserved. He would court her. It might be his only hope to outweigh the lies when the time came to reveal a few.

"'Tis true," he assured her. "Avalene, you could be the most opinionated woman in Christendom and I would have found a way to court you, had I been a knight at Coleway. I have wanted to kiss you from the moment we met."

Her mouth formed a delightful little O but no sound emerged. She really was irresistible.

He cupped her cheek and kissed first her lower lip, and then her top, and then both lips together when she recovered enough to kiss him in return. He drew back before she could lead him too far astray. There was a little V between her brows and she wouldn't meet his gaze. "What are you thinking?"

"I scarce know what to think," she murmured. Her lashes lifted and the wary look was back in her eyes. "Yesterday you did not want me. Today you do. I am . . . confused."

"Yesterday I was still trying to resist you." He stroked her cheek with the tips of his fingers and watched her eyes lose focus, and then she gave him an enchanting little shiver. "I should have known it was a pointless cause, me, trying to be noble."

She made a sound of disagreement, and then her teeth worried at her lower lip. Uncertainty. "Did I truly seduce you last night?"

"Aye." He couldn't help but smile. She was seducing him right now.

"That was not my intent," she admitted.

"I know," he said. "You do not have to try very hard. Actually, you do not have to try at all. God help me when you intentionally set out to seduce me. You will leave me in ashes."

Her lips curved upward. If she only knew the power she could wield over him. "I will try not to distract you again . . . when you do not wish to be distracted."

"Mm." Aye, she was more dangerous than she knew. It was time to move them both away from their bed before he weakened and decided to spend the day there. "Now is one of those times when I do not wish to be distracted. We need to eat and be on our way."

"Oh." She looked startled, as if she had forgotten where they were. "Of course. I will get my things."

"Just leave those," he said, when she began to gather up her cloak and saddlebag. He stood up and then held aside a handful of willow branches, indicating that she should precede him. "Rami will pack the horses while we eat. Let us refresh ourselves then find some food."

She caught her lower lip between her teeth and hesitated. One of her fainter blushes stained her cheeks and he guessed the problem easily enough.

"Do not tell me you lack the courage to face a boy?" he teased. "A woman who fled her home with no more than a rucksack and braved the night of the Witches' Sabbath in the wilderness is afraid to face a child?"

"I am not afraid of him," she said, as she lifted her chin. "I am simply embarrassed. You should be as well."

"I am a man. We do not get embarrassed over such matters." He placed his hand on her waist and ushered her out of their cozy lair. "Trust me, everything with Rami will be fine."

The view beyond the willow tree was nothing unexpected to him, but he allowed Avalene a few moments to get her bearings and let her eyes adjust from the shade to the bright sunlight. The tree they had slept under stood in the midst of a small clearing of deep green grass, spiked here and there with tall clumps of golden straw that had survived the winter in haphazard fashion. Behind them was a ridge where Oliver would be keeping a lookout. Ahead of them the grass grew gradually shorter then disappeared entirely, replaced by dark, mottled stone as the clearing gave way to a bluff. Armand sat cross-legged near the edge of the bluff with Rami seated next to him, both turned away from Dante as they studied the seemingly endless vista that encompassed a gently sloping valley and the lush forest.

The sight was breathtaking and the exact reason he had chosen this vantage point—to make certain they could see an enemy's approach from miles away and flee at the first sign of danger. He wondered if Avalene would realize his strategy and question him. A knight filled with pride and honor would stand and fight to protect those in his care, no matter the cost. He was not a man of honor. Those who ran lived to fight another day.

Armand glanced over his shoulder, nudged Rami, and they both rose to face them. Although Oliver and Armand were his two most trusted men, they were nothing alike in looks or temperament. Oliver had the rough, hard-bitten look of a common soldier while Armand had a very youthful, angelic-looking face that made women of all ages sigh. Ironically, Oliver had the softer heart of the two while Armand's ruthlessness often approached that of Dante's. He kept a close eye on Avalene to see how she would react to the handsome knight.

Surprisingly, she seemed to have eyes only for the boy, but her expression was one of confusion. He looked to Rami and realized something was definitely wrong. The boy's face had lost all color and he began backing away in a pace that matched their approach.

"'Tis the woman in red," Rami said in Italian, now holding up both hands as if that could halt Avalene's progress.

"Why is he looking at me that way?" Avalene asked.

"'Tis the same woman you just saw beneath the tree," Dante told him, also speaking Italian. "What is wrong with you?"

"I did not see her face," Rami breathed, as he began to back away from them. "Her face. 'Tis identical to the face on the card Oliver showed me." He began to back away faster as Avalene reached out to him. "Do not touch me, jinni!"

The words were scarcely spoken when Rami's heel caught on a rock and he began to tumble backward toward the edge of the bluff. Before Dante could reach the boy, Armand had his shoulder down and he rammed into Rami, knocking him sideways and sending him hard into the rocks. For a moment, no one moved, no one spoke.

"What on earth?" Avalene pressed her hands over her heart, and then rushed to the boy's side. Armand stood up and brushed gravel away from his knees as she knelt down next to Rami. The boy's head rolled back when she tried to lift him and it became obvious he had hit his head on the rock ledge and lost consciousness.

"There is no blood and he is still breathing," she said,

as she carefully turned his head to reveal a nasty lump that was already forming near his temple. "Do you have any cold cloths I could use to bind his wound?"

Dante just stared at her. Did she seriously think he had cold cloths sitting around, waiting for use on an injury? A single jerk of his head sent Armand to search out the supplies.

"That was the strangest thing," she said, as she patted the boy's hand. "It was almost as if he were afraid of me. I heard him call me 'the woman in red,' which is plainly obvious from my clothing, and then something about my face. What else did he say to you?"

"He is afraid of you," Dante said, frowning at the boy. He might as well tell her that much, since Rami was unlikely to be any fonder of her when he awoke. "You remind him of a picture he once saw of a *jinni,* an evil Arab spirit that sometimes masquerades as a beautiful woman."

"You must tell him I am not evil!" She looked from Dante to the boy. "I suppose he will be frightened all over again if he awakens to find me hovering." She stood up and moved to stand next to Dante. "You must see to his injury."

"There is nothing to 'see' to," he pointed out. "I will wrap his head when Armand returns, but there is little more to be done. 'Tis nothing more than a bump."

Avalene placed her hands on his side and actually tried to push him toward the boy. "You must sit with him until he awakens. Every injured child should have someone to sit with them."

He wanted to ask who had left her alone when she was ill. Instead he reached out and took hold of her wrists, pulling her away from his side and back toward Rami. "You are the woman. Tending children is not a man's job when there is a woman available. Rami will overcome his fear soon enough when he realizes you intend him no harm, and then you can dress his wound."

"*Ahgh.*" Rami began to stir. A moment later his eyes opened and then he tried to strike out at Avalene. Dante doubted Rami was even aware of his actions, but he had the boy's arms pinned to the ground before Avalene could draw a startled breath.

"*You will never raise your hand to this lady nor call her insulting names,*" Dante told him in Italian. "*Do you understand?*"

"*Ah-aye, my lord.*"

"*How do you feel?*"

Rami gave Avalene a look that said he would rather be in a viper pit than be this close to her, but to his credit he gave a sigh of resignation and then gingerly felt his head. "*The light hurts my eyes, and now there is a demon inside my head, beating upon my skull with a hammer.*"

"Is he all right?" asked Avalene. "Do you have a wineskin or something else he can drink?"

"Aye," Dante said. "There is a wineskin next to my saddle beneath the tree. Will you get it for him?"

Avalene nodded, and then she was off to fetch the wineskin.

Dante spoke quickly, running his words together in the hope that Avalene would not be able to translate their meaning even if she overheard them. "*She understands a little Italian. Be careful what you say in her presence. Saying nothing at all would be best. Understand?*"

"*I am sorry, master,*" Rami said in a low voice. He gave Avalene's retreating figure another worried look. "*Oliver showed me the cards and told me—*"

"*No harm was done except to yourself,*" Dante said. "*Still, you have insulted her. That will never happen again. To prove your remorse, you will let her care for you and act grateful."*

Another nod, this one tinged with a look of fear. *"I will not fail you again, my lord. Please, let me prove myself worthy."*

"Do not prove yourself a burden," Dante warned.

Armand returned about the same time as Avalene, holding what had once been a finely woven linen shirt that was now a neat stack of dripping wet bandages. He laid them on the grass near Rami, and then turned to Dante. "Should I help Oliver ready the horses?"

"Aye, we should have left at daybreak," Dante said.

"He cannot ride," Avalene countered. "Look at his eyes. There is something not yet right with him."

"He looks fine to me."

"He needs to rest."

"Absolutely not." He gave Rami's shoulder a gentle prodding and spoke again in Italian. *"Can you ride?"*

"Aye, my lord." Rami struggled to his feet, ignoring Avalene's outstretched hand. He wobbled back and forth in his efforts to steady himself, looking as if he were a drunken villager on May Day. He sank back down to the ground and knelt on the rock, breathing as hard as if he had just run a long race. *"I do not feel so good."*

Avalene had no need for the boy's words to be translated. They became unfortunately obvious to everyone a moment later when Rami leaned forward and lost his breakfast.

"On second thought," Dante said to Armand, "you might as well wait to get the horses ready."

An hour later, there was little more to be done for the boy. Avalene announced the injury would require a day or two of rest before the boy's nausea and dizziness would fade away. Armand had thrown sandy dirt over the spot where Rami had become ill to smother the smell. Avalene had dressed the boy's head and then gathered the necessary ingredients to make willow bark tea. Even now, Rami rested comfortably beneath the tree in the bed Dante had so recently vacated. All that remained was to wait for the swelling to go down.

Time was a precious commodity, but their vantage point would provide plenty of warning if they were being pursued. They could spare a day at most, Dante decided, as he eyed the midday sun. He would give the boy a day to recover and then they would continue the journey, one way or another.

In the meantime there was one chore he could do that would help set his mind at ease. He motioned for Armand to follow him up to the crest of the ridge where they found Oliver watching over the tethered horses and the valley to the east. It was his first real opportunity to speak to his men without Avalene underfoot and he assured them that all was going according to plan before he reviewed the specifics.

"There will be search parties set out by now from Coleway," he told them. "The real Sir Percival will soon arrive and they will realize I have no intention of taking Avalene to Weston Castle. Faulke Segrave would be close by as well, and it's possible he's descended upon Coleway to offer his services to the search party. We must assume that one or more of the parties has thought to set out on the road to London. Indeed, 'tis the route they will first suspect once they realize she is not in the hands of the real Sir Percival. I am going to backtrack to see who is behind us. Armand, you will stay close to Rami and Avalene. Oliver, if I have not returned before moonrise, come look for me."

"I had already started to prepare the horses for our

departure," Oliver said. "Your horse is saddled and ready, my lord."

"Excellent."

"My lord, there is another solution to this problem," Armand said, before Dante could stalk away from them. "The three of you could set out while I remain here with Rami. You could tell the lady that we will catch up with you in a day or two. If Rami does not recover quickly . . ." Armand lifted his shoulders in a way that left little doubt as to the boy's fate should his injury linger.

"If that were my intention, I could eliminate the boy by slipping poison into the willow bark tea," Dante told them. "He would simply appear to die of his head injury and Avalene would be none the wiser."

He shook his head and actually felt a bit sorry for the boy; Rami's luck had taken a decided turn for the worse. It was a matter of simple math; forfeit one life or five. Still, he had grown fond of Rami in the weeks since his rescue and he sensed that Avalene had a soft spot for the child as well. "Our press for time is not yet so urgent. I will give him today and this eve to recover himself, and then we will see where things stand. For now, Avalene seems to have taken an interest in the boy and that might prove useful."

"Aye, my lord."

"I will return early if I find a search party closer than I anticipate," Dante said. "Otherwise, I will see you again around moonrise."

11

Pursuit

*The Queen of Pentacles is
alone and seems safe, but this
is but an illusion of security.
Beware Nature's light in the
darkest hour, for there are
those who covet the thief's ill-
gotten gains and all may be
lost.*

"Are you hungry, my lady?"

Avalene looked up from her sewing to see Armand step through a gap in the willow branches. The smell of wood smoke came to her as if it had followed him. Her stomach rumbled in response. "Aye, a meal would be welcome, Armand. Thank you."

Armand opened his mouth as if he meant to say something more, but changed his mind at the last minute and let the branches fall back into place. Her gaze went to Rami as she heard Armand walk away.

The boy looked terrified, just as he had every time one of the men came anywhere near them. She could not understand why, unless they had somehow mistreated him. It was also possible he was afraid of all men, since his last master had most definitely mistreated him. However, she did not recall seeing any fear in Rami toward Armand before his fall and he now looked at her, the woman he had all but run from, as if she could answer all his prayers. The child was exceedingly strange.

Rami lay on her cloak with his bandaged head resting on her saddlebag. He had drowsed in and out of sleep all day, but now he was clear-eyed and alert. His brown eyes were almost black in the shade of their makeshift tent, narrowed now in an expression that was far too shrewd for a child of his age. He sat up slowly, as if he wanted to be sure Armand was gone before he drew any attention to himself. His gaze returned to her, an unwavering, penetrating stare that made her uncomfortable.

"You want more willow bark tea?" she asked. He nodded eagerly. She set aside her needle and thread as well as the stocking she was mending, and then reached behind one of the saddlebags to retrieve a wineskin that was now filled with the tea she had brewed earlier that day. Rami nodded and took a long drink from the skin.

"Are you hungry?" she asked. "*Ha fame?* I can ask Armand for an extra portion, if you like."

Rami's eyes grew round and frightened again at either the mention of Armand's name or the extra portion of food, she wasn't sure, but suspected the fear lay with Armand. He shook his head even as he winced, and then launched into a torrent of words spoken so quickly that Avalene could only understand a scant handful. Mercy. Repay. Stupid. Lord Dante.

"Who is Lord Dante?" she asked. All of the color left Rami's face. "Oh, is he your last master? The one who starved you?"

Rami squeaked in fright and scrambled backward when Armand suddenly appeared again, stepping through the trailing willow whips.

"My lady, there is fresh meat roasting on the fire if you would care to join me?" He did not wait for her answer, but turned to the boy. "*Ha fame*, Rami?"

Rami shook his head so hard that he had to have hurt himself. He lay back down and pulled the cloak up until just the top of his head was visible.

"He seems quite frightened of you," Avalene said, knowing the boy could not understand her words.

Armand ignored the remark and spoke again to Rami. "*Soggiorno tranquillo. Capisce?*"

"*Si, capisco,*" came the reply.

"He was not bothering me," Avalene protested. "He just needs some rest and then I am sure he will be himself again."

"I am sure you are right," Armand said agreeably. He extended his hand. "Shall we eat, my lady?"

Avalene gave her hand to Armand to help her rise. Beyond the willow tree the sun almost touched the hills to the west, a glowing red beacon framed by dark clouds that would surely bring rain before morning.

Armand had built a fire by the edge of the bluff with what looked like a rabbit roasting on a spit and an iron kettle nestled in the coals. The closer she got to the fire, the more her stomach rumbled at the enticing scents. She took a seat on a ledge as he indicated, and then took a moment to study her companion as he prepared a bowl of food for her.

Armand was, without doubt, the prettiest man she had ever laid eyes upon. Tall and broad-shouldered with blond hair and blue eyes, he fit every idealized description of the hero knights depicted in the troubadours' tales. Verily, he could have walked straight out of Camelot or a painting of the Rapture. All he lacked was a halo.

He handed her a spoon and bowl of food, and then began to fill his own bowl as he asked, "My lady, is something amiss?"

Avalene shook her head. "Do you think Sir Percival will return soon?"

"Aye, my lady."

She waited in vain for him to elaborate, or to make some other comment that might start a conversation. Several hours ago he had told her of Percival's departure to ride on patrol using the same terse tone he employed now. She had been disappointed in both Percival's absence as well as his failure to tell her himself that he was leaving. It was a foolish disappointment. She could not expect him to check with her each time he made a decision. And there might be benefits to his absence. Surely the men who rode with him knew him better than any other. "Have you known Sir Percival very long?"

"Aye, my lady."

"How long?" she asked, getting annoyed with his brusque answers.

"Many years."

It unnerved her the way he held her gaze with each question until she grew uncomfortable under the scrutiny and looked away. He might be pleasing to look upon, but there was something about Armand that she did not like, something aside from his nearly-rude conversational habits.

She concentrated on finishing her meal as she watched Armand refill his bowl.

"If I may have your leave, my lady, I will take a meal to Oliver."

Avalene nodded, and then went to the spring to rinse her hands and get a drink of sweet water. Next she found some bushes to see to more private matters. Armand had still not returned from the ridge by the time she went back to the bluff, so she sat down to keep watch over the valley. She had scarce found her seat when she saw a flash of color at the crest of a hill across the valley, barely distinguishable in the fading light, but there all the same.

Her heart lodged in her throat until she saw a shape that had to be Sir Percival mounted on his big bay horse emerge for a few more seconds before he disappeared again beneath the canopy of trees. She watched the road behind him, but it did not appear he was being followed. Just as she turned to see what was keeping Armand, she heard a series of short whistles and he appeared beside her.

"Go back to the willow tree, my lady." He took the spit that had held the rabbit and began to spread apart the embers in the fire. "Pack whatever you have and be prepared to ride by the time Sir Percival arrives here."

"What is wrong?" she demanded.

"Sir Percival would not return during the daylight unless he encountered a search party," Armand told her, even as he picked up her empty bowl and began to scoop sand and gravel over the ashes. "Pack your things and rouse Rami. Sick or not, he will have to ride."

She hurried to do as he said and found Rami already sitting up and looking anxious. "We must leave."

"*Che cosa ha ditto?*"

"We must go," she said, trying desperately to remember the word in Italian. The answer suddenly came to her. "*Andiamo!* You must not be sick again or I am certain Sir Percival will be very displeased. No matter what, if any of the men ask how you feel, tell them you feel fine. Do you understand? *Capisce?*"

"*Come?*"

Avalene rolled her eyes, knowing it was not the boy's fault that he couldn't understand her. It was her lack of skills at Italian and her haste to pack their belongings. "*Andiamo. Capisce?*"

"*Sì, andiamo.*" He rose from the makeshift bed and began to roll up the cloak. "*Dobbiamo lasciare.*"

"Well, I'm sure that means something close enough to what I was trying to say," she muttered.

She piled as much into her arms as possible and left a smaller pile for Rami to carry. As she made her way from the willow, she saw that Rami understood her intent and followed her with the rest of their belongings. The horses were at the top of the ridge and she trudged up the hill to find both Oliver and Armand saddling the horses. Armand went back to the willow to retrieve her saddle. Within scant minutes, the saddlebags were added and the horses stood tethered but ready. She turned to watch the clearing, waiting impatiently as Sir Percival rode up to the ridge and finally dismounted.

"Innaffi il cavallo," he said to Rami, as he handed the boy his reins. Avalene understood enough to know that the horse was to be watered, and Rami set off for the spring on unsteady feet to accomplish the task. Percival barely spared her a glance and turned instead to his men. "The alarm must have gone up soon after we left and they pressed hard in pursuit yesterday. There are close to thirty of them but they are burdened with more packhorses and gear. Still, they are only about four hours behind us."

"We could hide in the hills and let them ride past us," Armand suggested.

"I thought of that as well," Percival said, as he shook his head. "There is only the one road to London in this district and we will run the risk of either catching up with them or meeting them on the road should they decide to turn back. The odds are better that we can outrun them. All of our horses except mine are fresh and they are encumbered with more men and packhorses than we have, which means it will take them longer each day to set and break their camps. We can ride another twenty or thirty miles today and tonight if the moon holds, and gain at least as many more miles tomorrow."

"Did you see my uncle?" Avalene asked. Despite his failing eyesight, Lord Brunor was an excellent tracker.

Percival gave her a strange look, and then shook his head. "I was too far away to see their faces."

"The horses are ready to leave," Oliver told him. "If you don't mind switching mounts with Rami, the bay would hardly know the boy was on his back and you would have a fresh horse for the next leg of the ride. Or, would you rather I remove the packs from the Arabian and change the saddles?"

"I'll ride Rami's horse." Percival tilted his head to look past Armand. "Here he is now. Let us depart."

Oliver and Armand began to remove the tethers from the horses while Percival led Bodkin to Avalene and handed her the reins. He lifted her effortlessly into the saddle, his hands lingering only a moment on her waist.

"I take it Rami is well enough to ride or you would be complaining by now," Percival said, still looking up at her as she rearranged her skirts over the saddle.

"He rested most of the day and is well on his way to recovery," she said. "You were kind to allow him time to mend. I doubt his injury will slow us down."

"Excellent. Your curative powers must be exceptional." He glanced over his shoulder toward where his men were busy preparing the horses, and then looked back at her. "There is something that has been bothering me all day."

He crooked his finger, indicating she should come nearer. What had she done wrong to earn such a forbidding look? She leaned down and then almost lost her balance when he cupped the back of her head with one hand to bring her face closer to his.

"It has bothered me that I had to wait all day for another taste of your lips," he murmured. "Kiss me again, Avalene."

She did as he asked and immediately lost herself in its warmth and urgency. All too soon their lips broke apart when her horse shifted its weight. Percival rubbed his thumb across her lower lip as if to seal his kiss there, and then he turned away to mount his own horse. He glanced over his shoulder as they started forward and gave her a mischievous wink. And that gave her plenty to think about for the next few hours.

Oliver, Dante, and Armand stood at the edge of a small creek late the next morning. They watered the horses while Avalene and Rami wandered across the road in the opposite direction, Avalene to find a secluded place to relieve herself and Rami to stay close enough to make certain nothing happened to her.

"You are certain it was Faulke Segrave?" Oliver asked.

Dante wiped away the misty drizzle from his face, and then kept an eye on the brush where the pair had disappeared. This was the first opportunity he'd had to speak privately to his men since he had discovered they were being pursued. "I recognized the lead rider's standard from the banners in Avalene's chamber; the Segrave's bloodred dragon on a black field. Every one of the horsemen had the same device emblazoned on their surcoats and all looked well armed. If Segrave and his men manage to overtake us, 'tis doubtful we could hold out against ten-to-one odds. That they are almost within striking distance means Segrave picked up our trail immediately after Avalene and I left Coleway."

"Aye, so it would seem," Armand agreed.

"The man is determined. I fear he will not be easy to dissuade," Oliver added.

"Aye, I have yet to formulate a persuasive argument that does not involve the threat of death," Dante admitted. "'Tis a dilemma I have never faced before."

He had also not expected to find anyone pursuing them within a score of miles. His guard had been lowered by his own arrogance as well as by distracting thoughts of his captive. He had almost ridden right up to Segrave's party before the sounds of the horses and armor finally penetrated his dulled senses. He had managed to get off the road and make his way to a ridge where he could remain hidden yet still see Segrave's soldiers as they rode by. It had taken time to work his way through the woods and get ahead of their pursuers again. As a result, Segrave's party was uncomfortably close.

"I found another of Mordecai's cards this morning that warns of leaving Avalene alone in the moonlight," he told the men, and then he recited the magician's cryptic message. "I have thought about its meaning all morning and I feel certain that 'Nature's light in the darkest hour' must mean moonlight."

"Aye, that would make sense," Oliver said. "So that means she will be safe as long as she is not left alone at night, but does that also mean we will stay a step ahead of Segrave?"

"'Tis likely everything will proceed as planned so long as we make certain Avalene is never left alone while it is dark."

Dante actually looked forward to accomplishing that goal. Avalene had slept in his arms again last night, albeit far less comfortably than in their lair beneath the willow tree. Yesterday they had ridden the thirty miles he had been determined to put behind them before clouds finally obscured the moon and they had to stop or risk injuring the horses. They had barely dismounted and unsaddled the horses before the rain had started.

The massive oaks they camped beneath had offered only temporary protection from the rain and their clothes were soon soaked through to their skin.

The only pleasant part of the night had been the hours he had spent holding Avalene beneath his cloak, their bodies pressed tightly together for warmth. He still marveled at the way she turned to him for comfort, almost kittenish in the way she burrowed into his hold. Still, the rain was a miserable companion and certainly not conducive to what he had originally planned for the evening. Not one of the pleasures he had fantasized about since their interlude beneath the willow tree had materialized. Now with the Segraves close on their trail, the odds were becoming less favorable that they would enjoy any of their trysts, the innocent rites of courtship he had planned to carry out before they reached London. That was another strike against Segrave. He was beginning to heartily regret his promise to spare the man's life.

"If the weather improves we can be in London by the end of the week," Armand said. "Segrave will have a hard time finding us once we are swallowed up by the city and safely behind the palace walls."

"I studied the faces of the men who rode with him," Dante said. "None were familiar from Coleway and all of the men wore the Segrave standard rather than Coleway's."

"My lord," Oliver murmured, with a nod of his head toward Rami and Avalene.

Dante watched the bedraggled pair make their way toward them. Rami held Avalene's arm as if he were escorting his lady across a grand piazza instead of a muddy English road, chattering to her about God only knew what. He doubted Avalene understood more than every third word.

The boy acted fully recovered from his fall, although Dante suspected he still suffered from headaches. Still, Rami had turned out to be much more amiable with Avalene than Dante had hoped, given their troubled introduction. His original plan to send Rami to his sister to train as a squire no longer sounded so logical. Rami was not English and never would be. He was far more adept at the machinations and intrigues that took place within an Italian household. Rami had listened without question to the part he would play in the plan to abduct Lady Avalene, and then had the gall to make a few suggestions as to how best to deceive the lady. Some of what he suggested was rather clever. A child his age who was that well versed in deception belonged in Venice.

Avalene, on the other hand, made him think of the beautiful blond Madonna paintings that could be found in almost every church. There was something serene and yet commanding about her presence. Throughout their escape, not one of the situations he had put her into had ruffled her composure, and yet she blushed prettily whenever he spoke of his desire for her. Not once had she complained about the weather or the other discomforts of the journey, and yet he knew she suffered as much as or more than any of them. She took every hardship in stride and even managed to remain in good spirits. The way she smiled at him, like she was doing right now, made him feel as if he had just received an undeserved blessing.

"Are we still making good time?" she asked, as she came closer.

"Aye," he said. "If we can keep up this pace, we will stay ahead of the search party." He knew she meant to take her reins when she reached toward him. Instead, he took her hand and lifted it to his lips to kiss the back of her kid glove. As always, her blush pleased him. "Would you like to ride with me for a while? Perhaps you could sleep."

"I do not want to slow us down," she said, although she did not withdraw her hand from his.

He had been making a concerted effort to touch or hold her whenever the opportunity arose, as long as it did not interfere with their flight. Just a day ago she would have withdrawn her hand from his as quickly as possible. His small attentions during the day coupled with how intimately he held her each night were having their effect. That she now stood calmly within his hold was an encouraging sign. "We will make the best time if you ride your own horse, but tell me if you become too tired."

She murmured her agreement, and then walked to her horse and waited patiently for him to help her mount. He made sure his hands lingered on her waist and brushed intimately along her hip and thigh. He felt a measure of satisfaction when he saw her shiver, certain it had little to do with the weather. He intended to take every opportunity to learn the shape and feel of her, and make her more and more comfortable beneath his touch while he was about it. If the skies cleared they might even have a dry bed for the night. He had spent most of the long hours in the saddle thinking of the things he would do with her when they weren't riding. Not all involved kisses and caresses, but those played a major role. He did not want to take things too far while they were on the road, but he was determined to make the most of what little time they had alone together. She would be ready and willing to take him as her lover by the time they reached London, where they would have privacy as well as a comfortable bed. She would be his at last.

As he turned his horse toward the east, he allowed his imagination free rein over fantasies about how they would spend their first few days in London.

Unfortunately, the weather grew markedly worse rather than better, changing over from a light drizzle to a steady rain. Lightning flashed in the distance, followed by an ominous roll of thunder that made his horse toss its head and take an uneasy sidestep, as if they could somehow walk around the sound. They were crossing a wide meadow where the sights and sounds of the storm felt more intense than when they were beneath the canopy of the forest.

Dante's gaze went to Rami and then to Avalene, who both rode ahead of him. All of the horses were struggling with mud that sucked at their hooves. The horses were spaced farther apart as a result, but they were all within a dozen lengths of each other. Rami rode at point and was just passing beneath a large oak, the only tree in the meadow. Both Rami and Avalene looked pitiful with their hoods pulled low and their shoulders slumped. They had to be cold and soaked to the bone like the rest of them, but he and his men, and even Rami, were accustomed to these sorts of hardships. Avalene was hunched over so far in her saddle that she looked ready to fall off her horse if a good wind caught her. She would never hold up if this weather continued for another four days. Perhaps it was time to have her ride with him again.

A chill wind touched the back of his neck and he glanced over his shoulder. Armand rode behind him with Oliver and the packhorses bringing up the rear. Behind Oliver a towering bank of ominous black clouds marched steadily toward them and the wind suddenly began to gust even as the temperature became instantly cooler. The tall grass in the meadow turned choppy, as if the meadow had suddenly become the churning waters of a sea. The wind created green currents and waves that flattened huge sections of grass across the meadow, then shifted direction just as quickly to allow grass in the calmer areas to spring back to attention.

Even as he watched, the feeble daylight took on an eerie shade of yellow-green and a solid wall of gray rain moved toward them. The thunder became a constant rumble and the force of the rain pelting the forest sounded almost like the rolling beat of hundreds of drums. Dante's horse shied nervously when rain mixed with hail began to sting them with the ferocity of a swarm of angry bees.

He looked for Avalene but suddenly could not see beyond a few feet in front of his own horse. Still, he was almost certain she would stop under the tree where she would be safe and spared the sting of the hail. Rami was so determined to prove his injury would not slow them down that Dante was equally certain the boy would still be riding, which meant Avalene would be ... alone. Safe and alone.

A wave of panic rolled over him as quickly as the storm had come upon them. The signs became glaringly obvious even as he spurred his horse forward. *The Queen ... is alone and seems safe. ... Beware Nature's light in the darkest hour.* He had never known the sky to be darker during the daytime yet such a strange shade of green.

Those thoughts had no more than crossed his mind when the air around him suddenly changed, becoming utterly still and silent. Hail continued to fall from the sky, no longer driven by the winds but landing as if they were pebbles tossed carelessly from an open hand. Just as the last lumps of hail fell, the next sign appeared in an abrupt burst of blinding light, a bolt of lightning that shot straight into the heart of the oak that sheltered Avalene. The shaft of lightning that split the sky was as wide as a river and brighter than the sun. In an instant the entire top half of the tree burst into a cloud of red and gold flames.

The explosion of sound that immediately followed was nearly as spectacular, a force so powerful that the ground shook, the sound so loud that Dante's ears rang. His horse stopped dead in its tracks but Dante kept going. Half-blinded and mostly deaf, time seemed to slow down as he sailed through the air. He had a ridiculous thought that this was the first time in his adult life that he had been unseated from a horse.

The landing was harder than he anticipated. It knocked the thoughts from his head and the breath from his body. He rolled onto his back, gasping for air until he felt as much as heard his horse's hooves pounding dangerously close to where he lay. He curled into a ball and covered his head with one arm while he rubbed mud from his eyes with his free hand. The horse was probably blinded by the lightning as much as he was, and could trample him without knowing it.

His vision finally cleared and he could see that his horse had started to buck as if there were a demon on its back. Even as he struggled to his feet, the bucking turned into long leaps and then the animal bolted toward the forest, passing Armand at a dead run.

Armand had been thrown as well but had somehow managed to hold on to his horse's reins. He now had his hands full with a different problem. The long reins gave his horse plenty of room to rear up and Armand was doing his best to stay clear of the deadly hooves that slashed the air above him.

Dante turned toward the sound of more rapidly approaching hoofbeats and found himself directly in the path of Avalene's horse. Even as he made a diving leap to one side, he caught a glimpse of her ashen face and heard her strangled cry of "Help!" as the horse bolted past him. He was on his feet in an instant, but could only watch helplessly as her horse raced past Armand and Oliver, and then disappeared over the crest of the hill.

Oliver was still mounted, but the packhorses had entangled themselves in the tether lines along with Oliver's horse, and the animals could do little more than trot in nervous circles. God only knew Rami's fate. Dante wasted a few precious seconds venting the vilest curse that had ever passed his lips, and then he took off at a run toward Armand, who had his horse under control by the time Dante reached him.

"Both of us!" Dante shouted, pointing toward Armand's horse. Armand understood and swung into the saddle, then held out his hand so Dante could mount behind him.

They spied Dante's horse as soon as they reached the top of the hill. The reins trailed along the ground and the horse stepped on the lines and tripped itself twice before they were close enough to grab the bridle. An instant later, Dante was back on his own horse, thankful the reins that had hampered the animal's flight hadn't snapped. He held them to a slow but still dangerous canter, given the condition of the road. He scanned the road ahead and the surrounding brush. There was no sign of Avalene.

"There!" Armand shouted, over another boom of thunder. He pointed toward a spot in the road.

At last Dante saw long gashes amongst the puddles where a horse had lost its footing in the mud, but there was no sign that it had gone down. At least the horse was instinctively staying to the road.

They entered the forest again and found the road firmer, which made her trail easier to follow. The branches above them were too high to strike a rider, but she would be hard pressed to avoid low-hanging branches if the horse took her off the road. The farther they rode, the more he hoped for such an accident. Where was she?

Soon ancient oak, elm, and walnut trees rose high above the forest floor. Rain dripped from the canopy of leaves but no longer fell in torrents. The thick carpet of moss and decaying leaves muffled the sounds of the storm as well as their horses' hoofbeats.

They had ridden several miles when Dante reined in his horse before a bend in the road. He had a bad feeling about this forest. Armand pulled up beside him.

"Go find Rami and help Oliver gather the horses, and then take them into the woods near the edge of the forest," Dante said. "Make sure no one can see or hear you from the road. If I do not return by nightfall, search for me in this area."

"Aye, my lord."

Armand turned his horse and rode back toward the clearing. Dante left the road and led his horse to a thick clump of brush, where he dismounted. Satisfied that the animal was hidden from view, he made his way forward on foot. Over the years he had learned to trust his instincts and every one of them was on high alert.

His caution was soon rewarded when he found Avalene, but his relief at finding her unharmed was short lived. She was surrounded by more than a score of soldiers, and all wore the colors of Faulke Segrave.

Dante flattened his body against the mossy bark of the tree trunk and muttered under his breath, "And this makes the day perfect."

12

❀

Avalene recognized the dragon that was emblazoned on the chest of every man who surrounded her. At first her brain had trouble comprehending that she had stumbled across a band of Segrave soldiers in the middle of the wilderness. Her luck was astonishing.

Later there would be time to decide if it was good luck or bad. At the moment she was fully occupied trying to control her horse and recover from the fright of her life. One of the soldiers swiftly dismounted and took hold of the horse's bridle to make certain the animal wouldn't bolt again, but her hands were fisted in Bodkin's mane and she couldn't seem to let go. She could scarce absorb the fact that she was even alive. The man who held her bridle was saying something, but only two of the words he spoke penetrated her senses, two words that stood out as clearly in her mind as the crack of lightning:

"Lord Faulke."

Her horrified gaze went to the obvious leader of the soldiers as he maneuvered his horse to face hers. All she could do was stare at the dark-haired man. The man she was supposed to marry. Faulke Segrave.

She shook her head. This was wrong. They weren't supposed to meet this way. She wondered if her expression looked as appalled as his. This could not be happening.

How long had she dreamed of this moment, her heart filled with anticipation and excitement? Their first meeting was to take place in the great hall at Coleway where she would be dressed in her finest gown, ready to impress Faulke with her poise and grace. Instead she was soaking wet in the midst of a muddy forest and surely looked her worst. Even more humiliating, she was literally scared speechless.

Her stomach roiled and her relief at being rescued evaporated. For an awful moment she thought she was going to be sick. Faulke Segrave was not supposed to be here. Not yet. Their betrothal was not yet finalized. She was supposed to go to her father's fortress in Wales. She was supposed to spend the next few weeks with Sir Percival.

Sir Percival! She cast a wild look over her shoulder but the road behind her was empty. He was gone, vanished along with all of her foolish fantasies about him. Reality crashed down upon her, robbing her of breath. They would never again be together. She might never see him again. Her reputation was destroyed, and now she would never commit the crime that had ruined her. And Percival would be lucky to escape this forest with his life, if Faulke learned he was nearby.

Her heart pounded so hard that she was certain the others must have heard the terrible rhythm, and then an awful shudder wracked her body. Every part of her felt suddenly numb, her body frozen in place while her mind struggled uselessly to awaken from a nightmare. Except she was already awake and the truth refused to be silenced. She forced herself to take stock of the man who now held her future in his hands.

A strange calm settled over her as she studied Faulke Segrave. She felt an odd sense of detachment that allowed her to view him as if he were any stranger she would meet under unusual circumstances. She noticed that he had the natural air of a leader about him, a look of intelligence and confidence that would inspire men to follow him. The black wool hood of his cloak was pushed back to give her a clear view of his face, a face well matched to the minstrels' descriptions she had based her own imaginings upon. High cheekbones emphasized eyes that were a deep shade of blue, and a few days' growth of beard covered a strong, square jaw.

For a man rumored to have murdered at least two of his wives, he looked pleasant enough. Most would call him handsome. His voice was inoffensive as well. Not half as pleasing as Sir Percival's, she amended, but far from offensive.

Except that he was shouting at her.

Granted, her ears were still ringing from the blast of lightning, but she was not deaf. She stared at his mouth and tried to make sense of his words.

"Do you understand what I am asking, my lady?"

She had no idea what he had just asked. Perhaps he had inquired if she had suffered any injuries. That would be a sensible question to ask, considering the circumstances. "I shall be fine."

"I assumed that much." He spoke in the measured tones that most people reserved for the slow-witted. "However, I asked your name."

"Oh." That made sense. For the time it took to blink her eyes. Why would he ask her name? Who else did he expect to find on this road?

Something wasn't right. Her initial feeling that he shouldn't be here became a certainty. How had he learned of her escape from Coleway, and how could he have found them so quickly?

Her heart gave a painful stutter. Faulke had no idea that she was the woman he intended to marry. She was a stranger to them, a woman on a runaway horse who could be anyone. She could lie, a lie that would give Percival and his men time to find her or time to escape. If Percival came across them in pursuit of her, she would have to think of some way to warn him to go along with the lie.

"She is not right in the head," said the man closest to Segrave. "Look into her eyes, cousin. 'Tis madness I see."

Her gaze moved between the two men and she noticed a superficial resemblance, dark hair, blue eyes, but her attention returned to Faulke as he nudged his horse a few steps closer to hers and stared hard into her face.

"She is frightened," he said at last. "God alone knows what that animal did to her. Lady Avalene needs time to recover from her ordeal."

Her tattered heart gave a sickly flutter. So, they did know who she was. But why were they even looking for her? And what did he think her horse had done to her? Wasn't it obvious that she was unharmed?

It suddenly occurred to her that the animal in question wasn't her horse. He was referring to Sir Percival and the treatment she had received in his care. Somehow they knew that she had left Coleway with Sir Percival, and they thought he had taken advantage of the fact that they were not chaperoned.

Her mouth hung open until she realized the expression probably confirmed their notion that she was indeed lack-witted. How dare they call Percival an animal! She was the one who had seduced him, the one who had decided to sin. He had not forced her to do anything against her will.

Her anger turned to astonishment as she watched Faulke's eyes soften and fill with what looked like pity. "Can you tell us what happened, my lady? What threats did the cur make that convinced you to leave Coleway with him?"

Oh good Lord, this was worse than anything she had imagined. They truly thought Sir Percival was some sort of blackguard. "I . . . Uhm . . . I am fine."

The look the cousins exchanged was telling. Now they were certain she was an idiot. She honestly didn't know if that was a good thing or bad.

"She is lack-witted," the cousin declared. "Most likely she was lack-witted long before the King's Assassin had his way with her. Why else would her father hide her at Coleway all these years? 'Tis obvious he wanted to conceal her condition."

"You are too quick to judge, Richard." Faulke glanced at his cousin. "Did you not learn your lesson from the squire?"

"He told us all he knew," Richard argued, "and then he threatened to reveal the plot to her uncle unless we paid him double. He got what he deserved."

"The squire saw the assassin's face," Faulke pointed out. "We have not. There was no need to kill him."

"All of Coleway saw him," Richard said, and then he nodded toward Avalene. "I'll wager she saw much more than his face."

Faulke rubbed his jaw. "Did he . . . harm you, my lady?"

She was still stuck on Richard's casual mention of the King's Assassin to answer the question.

Until that moment, she had thought the King's Assassin was a legend; a preposterous tale of a ghostly infidel who floated through solid stone walls to find and execute traitors. Some versions of the tale said his victims died of fright, that he could materialize from thin air and disappear just as easily after his wicked deeds were done. Others said he cut the throats of his victims while they slept and then drank their blood. Most of the stories were exaggerations, but all agreed that anyone plotting against the king should not sleep easy at night.

Faulke and Richard spoke of the King's Assassin as if he were a real man. As if he were Sir Percival. And they thought *she* was lack-witted?

Sir Percival was a noble and chivalrous knight, as far removed from the evil creature reputed to be the King's Assassin as . . . Well, she could not think of two men who could possibly be more different. The idea that they were one and the same was so absurd that she felt a bubble of laughter build inside her. It was hysterical laughter; shrill, frantic sounds that were half laughter, half sobs. Good Lord, what was wrong with her?

Faulke and his men obviously wondered the same. They stared at her as if she had just lost whatever they thought was left of her mind. Their incredulous expressions only made her laugh harder.

It was just as obvious that they had no idea what to do with a hysterical and possibly unbalanced woman. Percival might roll his eyes at some of her antics, but he had never doubted her sanity. He would know that she needed him to put his arms around her right now. He would know how to make her feel safe and protected. But he would never hold her again.

The laughter dissolved away until there was nothing left except her sobs. She wanted Sir Percival. At the same time, she prayed to God to keep him far away from the Segraves. She feared the challenge over her honor would come much sooner than either she or Percival had ever anticipated, and Percival was clearly outnumbered. He and his men would be slaughtered.

She was aware of Faulke giving out orders during her hysterics, but she paid little heed until she realized a group of soldiers were preparing to search for Percival and his men. There would be no formal challenge, nor even the semblance of a fair fight. The Segraves would simply cut them down.

"Nay!" she cried out. The men who weren't already staring at her fell silent and turned expectantly. She needed to explain that Sir Percival was not the enemy, and they should not murder him before she could tell them why they had fled from the castle. An explanation might make a difference, but there were too many parts of the story to sort out, she was still shaking, taking gasping breaths, and there was no time to explain. She panicked and said the first thing that came into her head. "You will not find him on the road!"

Oh, good Lord. That was exactly where they would find him.

Faulke gave her a considering look, and then turned to his cousin. "Take half the men and search the road for tracks leading from the forest. Find out where she came from, then report back to me."

"Aye, my lord."

"Heed me well," Faulke warned Richard. "I want him alive. In fact, send a rider back to tell me where he is before you attempt to take him."

"Aye, cousin." Richard's reluctance to follow the order was evident in his tone.

Faulke waited until Richard and his men rode off, then he dismounted and began issuing orders to set up a temporary camp. Eventually his attention returned to Avalene. She remained frozen in place, watching helplessly as Richard and his men disappeared around a bend in the road.

Faulke held out his hand to her. "You can rest beneath the shelter until my cousin returns with word of the assassin."

It was not an offer. She glanced at her own hands and realized that she had loosened her hold on the reins sometime during her hysterics. After a few deep, steadying breaths, she managed to slide her leg over the saddle but her knees gave out the moment her feet touched the ground. Faulke caught her easily by the shoulders, and then he placed one arm behind her knees and swept her up against his chest.

Until a few days ago she had never been carried about by a man. It seemed only natural to make comparisons. Both times she felt gratitude, but with Sir Percival there had always been something more, an awareness of him as only a woman can be aware of a man, an awareness that made her feel breathless and giddy. Every time Percival touched her she felt a warm flush spread throughout her whole body.

With Faulke, she was simply grateful that he hadn't let her land in the mud and even more grateful when he set her down upon a soft, dry fur that one of the soldiers had placed beneath the shelter. Her clothes were soaked and she was chilled to the bone, but at least she was on solid ground again and out of the elements. Her muscles had been tensed for so long that they felt shaky and disjointed, as useless as broken bow strings.

She glanced up to find Faulke eyeing the furs as if he contemplated taking a seat next to her. In the end he simply folded his arms across his chest and watched her as if she were some strange creature that might yet prove dangerous. "Are you hungry?"

She shook her head.

"Where was he taking you?"

She tried to decide if it would be better to tell the truth or to lie, but found she couldn't focus her thoughts enough to make up anything believable. The truth it was. "First to London, and then to my father. Sir Percival did nothing wrong; he was simply following my father's orders." She watched as he almost imperceptibly shook his head. "Are there soldiers from Coleway searching for me? Perhaps the steward and Lord Brunor?"

"I know not." He clasped his hands behind his back, his gaze contemplative as he looked at the ground. "We had a spy at Coleway who came to me soon after you left the castle. We were on your trail before anyone at Coleway knew you were missing. Even so, they will probably send search parties to the west."

That explained what they were doing here, but not why they were at Coleway to begin with. And how had they missed stumbling across the search party from Coleway that Percival said was in pursuit? He gave her a look that she supposed was intended to impart something meaningful and knowing. Whatever it was went over her head.

"The only reason we rode east is because we already knew you were not with the real Sir Percival, and the man who took you would never escort you to Wales."

"What are you talking about?" What Faulke said made little sense. Did he still think Percival was the King's Assassin? Ridiculous. "I left Coleway with my father's knight, Sir Percival."

"You are mistaken," he said in a calm voice. "My spies in London sent word that the most trusted and feared agent of the king was sent to abduct you from Coleway—the King's Assassin. The logical escape route would be the road to London, which is exactly where we found you."

"Sir Percival is not an agent of the king. We were bound to London, but only because he had to rescue me from a plot to force me into marriage to Coleway's steward. 'Tis true!" she insisted, when Faulke gave her a skeptical look. "I overheard my aunt and uncle talking about a plan to catch Sir Percival alone with me to ruin my reputation and force me into a marriage with the steward before you or my father could intervene. My father knew something was amiss at Coleway and that was the reason he wanted me returned to Weston Castle before he made any announcements concerning my marriage."

"Then you know of our betrothal?"

That proclamation caught her off guard. She put one hand to her throat. "We are betrothed?"

"Aye, more or less," he said at last. "Our families have agreed to the terms but we are obliged to wait upon the king's approval before we can receive the church's blessing. However, considering the circumstances, no one will question my right to marry you immediately."

"Wh-what?"

"I have negotiated a betrothal in good faith with your father. 'Tis my responsibility as your betrothed to safeguard your life as well as your reputation." His gaze raked over her as if she were a prize mare up for inspection at a fair, a prize he found lacking. "The plan that Coleway's steward hatched to force you into marriage will now work to my benefit, although it will be our marriage that will restore your honor."

"You cannot marry me without the king's permission." It was the only argument she could think of, even as all the implications crystallized in her mind. Whatever doubts she had about the reasons Faulke Segrave wished to marry her were gone. If she were nothing more than the daughter of a Marcher baron, he would break the betrothal. That he intended to go forward with the marriage meant her Welsh heritage was far more important than her reputation. The Segraves were plotting civil war.

"Oh, I can indeed," he countered. "The betrothal is a mere formality. Even without this . . . complication, we would have been wed within a few months. I was under the impression that your father had sent word to Coleway about our impending betrothal to give you time to prepare yourself to leave your uncle's household."

"He did," she admitted, "but even his last missive said nothing was finalized."

"The missive delivered by the man masquerading as Sir Percival?" he asked, even as he shook his head. "I am certain the real Sir Percival carried a more informative letter on the matter. In any event, I have found you and that is all that matters. The king can no longer interfere."

She shook her head. "We must await the king's approval."

He studied her face again, and then spoke slowly and in a slightly louder voice than was necessary. "You fled Coleway to escape a marriage your father would never agree to. You were alone with a man who was masquerading as your father's knight. An immediate marriage is the only means of saving your reputation. We shall be wed as soon as we reach Wales." He gave her a pointed look. Suddenly he reached down and took her chin in his hand, tilting her face to one side and then the other. "Were you . . . mistreated in any way?"

"I am fine; just a little shaken." She understood what he was asking and she tried to think of something that would distract him from the subject. She pulled away from his offensive grasp, trying to make it seem a casual move. "I am curious about why you seem so certain that

Sir Percival is not . . . well, Sir Percival. He had a message bearing my father's seal. He wore my father's device on his surcoat. He knows things that only a knight in my father's household could know. What makes you think he is not who he says he is?"

"I do not think he lied about his identity," Faulke said. "I *know* he lied. The real Sir Percival was to contact me before he entered Coleway so we could review the plans to get you safely from the castle. I have been camped along the road from Wales to Coleway for a week, and Sir Percival had still not passed that way before our spy let us know that you were gone. The real Sir Percival never reached Coleway."

A low rumble of thunder emphasized his words and this time she did shudder. He glanced up at the canopy of leaves where the rain had started to fall harder, and then eyed the lean-to again.

"Do you mind if I join you?" he asked, indicating the furs.

She scooted over as far as the small shelter would allow and tucked her skirts closer when he took a seat next to her, sitting cross-legged, angled to face her. He suddenly seemed much larger.

He dragged a hand through his hair, pushing back the wet strands from his face, and then he calmly proceeded with his story. "You were deceived, my lady. The man you spent time with, the man you allowed to take you from Coleway? He is a cold-blooded killer. We were all surprised to find that you were still alive. Indeed, your good health is the only reason I have any doubts that he is the King's Assassin. He has never before been known to let one of his victims live, and you would be far less trouble to the king if you were dead. We thought certain he would . . . dispose of you soon after you left Coleway. My hope was to capture him or one of his men and discover where they had placed your body or other proof of their crime."

He spoke of her death in such a detached tone that the meaning of his words did not seem possible. She spoke her reasoning aloud, as much to reassure herself as to convince him of the truth. "Sir Percival had ample opportunity to kill me and make good an escape on his own. He is not the King's Assassin."

"Perhaps not," he allowed, "but my spies in London were quite certain the assignment was given to the King's Assassin, and I have never known them to be wrong. There is also the growing possibility that he was specifically ordered to bring you back to London alive. 'Tis the only explanation for your continued good health at his hands, no matter who he might be."

She tilted her head to one side. "I do not understand."

He eyed her expectantly for several moments, as if the answer should be obvious.

"Why would the king want me in London?" she asked. "Please, I am trying to understand, but nothing makes sense."

"Our fathers are at court even now to present our betrothal contract for the king's approval," he said at last. "The king's approval should be a mere formality. No Marcher baron or his heir has ever been denied the king's blessing to wed the bride of his choosing. If the king denies the contract, everyone will see the refusal for exactly what it is; another obvious effort by Edward to limit the powers of every Marcher baron in Wales. My father will take a refusal as an open invitation to incite rebellion among the other barons. Edward knows this as well as he knows that the results would be much the same if you were to conveniently die shortly before our betrothal. He has no choice but to agree to a contract that will put key fortresses under our control and make him vulnerable in Wales should we ever rebel.

"However, once Edward approves the contract, you and I are tied for life as surely as if we were wed. The king can say he had you fetched to London as a surprise for our betrothal, but come up with any number of excuses to keep you from me. Based upon your lineage and the fate of most Llewellyn descendants, my guess is that witnesses you have never met will suddenly appear and swear you spoke to them of a rebellion. You will likely be sent to the Tower on some trumped-up charge of treason. Edward is known to manufacture evidence when it suits his interests, and you are a mere woman. He can imprison you for the rest of your life without formal charges and our betrothal contract means I will never be allowed to wed another. I am my father's only heir, I have no sons, and you are the last of your mother's line. As long as we are both alive, betrothed and yet unwed, both our lines are extinguished."

Her heart rebelled at the idea of Faulke as her husband, of the intimacies she would be forced to endure. And yet those emotions paled next to the thought of spending the rest of her life imprisoned in the Tower. She had visited the dungeons at Coleway on occasion and the pitiful prisoners Sir Brunor kept there. They were mostly thieves and poachers who were released within a few months, but a great many sickened and died within the first weeks. Even those who survived were greatly changed from the people they were when they went into dungeons. She could not picture herself as one of those listless, walking skeletons.

Something of her horror must have shown in her expression. He leaned forward to brush his knuckles across her cheek and she drew away from him without thinking. He ignored her reaction and managed a reassuring smile. "Do not worry, my lady. I will protect you from the king and his henchman. If I am right, and I am most certain that I am, you are worth far more to everyone alive than you are dead. The king's agents will not harm you, and I will keep you safe."

She would feel better about his pledge to protect her if she wasn't so suspicious of his entire story. He was mistaken about Sir Percival. He was mistaken about the king. The man she knew could not be the villain that Faulke claimed. Her king would never knowingly imprison an innocent woman for a lifetime. Yet Faulke swore the real Sir Percival had never entered Coleway. And a great many of her mother's relatives, both the innocent and the guilty, had died in the Tower.

Once again she glanced around her before she realized she was looking for Sir Percival, hardly caring that the evidence was mounting against him. Surely Faulke was trying to frighten her into agreeing to his plan of a hasty marriage. Everything he said about Percival were lies or some vast misunderstanding. She could not be so completely mistaken in her judgment of the man. No matter Percival's true identity, she had never doubted his pledge to protect her. He would be looking for her. He would find this camp eventually, or Richard would find him and bring him back, and then everything would be explained to everyone's satisfaction. This was all a horrible mistake.

"Tell me, Lady Avalene, how did you escape?" Faulke asked.

She looked up at him and blinked once, caught off guard by the question. She did not view a near-death experience as an escape. "Lightning struck a tree just as I rode beneath it and my horse bolted. I would not have willingly left Sir Percival's company."

"Ah, just so," he mused. "You thought yourself safe."

"I knew myself safe," she countered, before she thought better of the retort.

Faulke's gaze turned speculative. "There are rumors that the King's Assassin often wears the garb of an infidel. Even though he is no heathen, many believe that he is a foreigner. Did the man you knew as Sir Percival wear any strange clothing or speak any foreign languages?"

She blinked one more time, and then she giggled. Horrified, she clapped a hand over her mouth but the muffled sounds kept coming out of her. Sir Percival, the King's Assassin. The idea of it truly boggled her mind.

At the same time, a silent voice asked how many more coincidences she could ignore. Faulke insisted that the man who arrived at Coleway could not possibly be Sir Percival. The man who claimed to be Sir Percival had worn gray, foreign-looking garments the night he had entered her chamber at Coleway. He moved almost silently and handled a knife exceedingly well. He and his men, and even the child in their company, all spoke Italian. Percival warned that a search party from Coleway was just hours behind them, and yet it was the Segraves who were behind them. Her mind struggled to wrap itself around the possibilities.

Faulke was back to staring at her as if she were crazed and possibly dangerous. The last of her laughter died away as the impossible became plausible.

The excuse to ride to London and then take a ship to Wales suddenly sounded preposterous. She had been a fool to believe they had to travel east to end their journey at a destination far to the west. No one traveled by ship if they could avoid it. Her father would not risk her life on such a foolish journey, and he would not send so few men to escort her. Everything Faulke told her rang of truth. Everything. He had not made a mistake. She had. In more ways than he could possibly realize.

The man she knew as Sir Percival was not her father's knight.

Faulke had told her as much several times now, but the words had never truly registered because the idea was too incredible to even consider. Now they registered. Indeed, they made perfect sense. Everything made sudden sense.

She should have recognized from the start that something was wrong with Sir Percival, or, more to the point, that everything was too right. If she prayed God to fashion a man for her, Percival would be the answer. Everything about him was perfect, from his looks to his manner to his character. Somehow he had known how to attract her interest, how to dazzle her with his worldly charm that, now that she thought about it, seemed oddly out of place for a humble household knight. A considerable amount of time spent at the royal court would account for that polish and sophistication. He had used all of his wiles to make her feel safe in his company, to cast himself as the knight errant sent to her rescue. He played the role flawlessly.

She felt sick.

Aye, his astonishing attraction to her was the next warning that went unheeded. Handsome men did not fall at her feet, besotted by her beauty, tempted beyond reason to steal kisses and intimate caresses. All he had to do was smile at her and she pushed aside her misgivings to bask in the warmth of his regard, thrilled that he wanted her, too, flattered that her perfect knight was equally smitten. Or so it seemed. Deep down there had been a lingering certainty that he would come to his senses and grow tired of her, that he would realize she was not as pretty or desirable as he made her feel, that her charm would fade as quickly as it had for every other man. And still she had opened her heart and allowed him in. The horror was not that she had fallen in love. It was that she had allowed herself to fall in love with a man who didn't exist.

"Are you unwell?" Faulke asked. He watched her changing expressions with alarm. "You look very pale."

"I'm fine," she lied. There was a dull roaring sound in her ears. Everything began to grow dark around the edges of her vision. Faulke looked as if he were reaching for her through a long tunnel. Her eyes drifted shut and she let the darkness take her.

13

❧

The Betrothal

Joy, contentment, and pleasure spill through the fingers like wine from an overturned cup. The outpouring from the Ace of Cups signals an end to the beginning. Prepare to embark upon a new journey to seek a new beginning.

The problem with fainting was that nothing got solved in the short amount of time you were unconscious. Avalene awoke beneath the lean-to just as heartsick and miserable as ever. The only good to come from the embarrassing episode was solitude. Faulke had apparently decided he had better things to do than sit with a woman who might keel over again at any moment. Actually, he had politely asked if she felt better, assured her that one of his men would fetch him if she felt ill again, and then excused himself. She was left to her own devices, although the weather kept her from venturing beyond the lean-to.

The rain had stopped more than an hour ago but she was still soaked through and freezing. Dusk fell early in the forest, along with the temperature. She would give almost anything for the oblivion of unconsciousness or the warmth of a fire. Instead she rubbed her arms, wriggled her legs, hugged herself and shivered, then started the routine all over again.

It was obvious that Faulke had ordered everyone to be ready to leave at a moment's notice. Most of the men had dismounted in the hours since Richard's departure, but none of the horses were unsaddled and only the packhorses were hobbled to graze. There were no fires, no more warm furs or dry cloaks. Other than an occasional stare of curiosity, the men left her alone with her thoughts. Faulke glanced in her direction every so often as well, but he, too, seemed satisfied to leave her be. Perhaps he thought she needed time to come to terms with this change in her circumstances. She doubted a lifetime would be enough to absorb it all.

She looked around the campsite at the men who surrounded her and realized again that this was the sort of escort she had expected from her father; more than a score of mounted soldiers plus Faulke and his cousin Richard. Had she really believed that her father would send a lone knight, two soldiers, and a child?

One of Percival's particularly appealing smiles flashed through her memory and the butterflies took flight again in her stomach, quickly followed by a dull thump of pain in her chest.

There was something seriously wrong with her. She had honed her instincts for survival when it came to men and Percival had effortlessly brushed aside her defenses as if they were nothing. She told herself over and over that what she felt for him had been nothing more than an infatuation. Granted, it was a particularly strong infatuation, but an infatuation nonetheless. She had deluded herself into thinking she loved him. Love was not based upon lies and betrayal, and there was no escaping the fact that her interpretation of love had been based upon both.

So why did her heart skip a beat each time she thought of him? Why did her breath catch in her throat each time she thought she heard Richard's return, her gaze searching for a glimpse of her faithless knight?

It occurred to her that, while her mind finally knew and accepted the truth, her heart still had trouble letting go of the illusion. She had to crush all of these treacherous feelings before anyone guessed the truth. If Richard brought Percival back as a prisoner, she would have to appear completely unaffected by his presence. She would have to behave as if he meant nothing to her. The task did not seem possible. It seemed every memory of him included a touch or caress that had made her feel warm and safe and . . . special. He had bewitched her. She was bewitched still, and she was very much afraid that everyone in camp would become aware of that fact if she had to face him.

Her gaze moved over the men and found Faulke again. Her intended husband was handsome, rich, and powerful. Yet she felt nothing at all for him. There were no butterflies in her stomach when she looked upon him, no quickened heartbeat, no feelings of breathlessness. There was a sureness in her, a certainty that went beyond questioning, that she would never experience those feelings with Faulke or any other man. She would never again allow a man to have that much power over her, to toy with her as if her feelings meant nothing, to twist her heart until her whole body ached.

In every way imaginable, it was for the best that the affair with Percival . . . or whatever his name might be, had ended before it began. She would forget him. Someday. Until then, she should be thankful that their trysts went no further than they did. She had allowed a handsome man to kiss her and caress her, but those were not unforgiveable sins. One day she might appreciate that her first and only taste of passion was with a man she had thought she loved.

She was so engrossed in her morbid thoughts that she barely noticed when Faulke began to walk toward her. There was a wary look in his eye.

"How are you feeling, my lady?"

She lifted her shoulders in a small shrug but remained silent. The more she observed him, the more she realized that there was something about Faulke that made her nervous, a feeling that his benevolence toward her was forced and his kindly demeanor false. However, she allowed for the possibility that she could be misjudging him. Her trust in all men stood on shaky ground. John and Lord Brunor plotted against her while her own father negotiated a betrothal that would surely mark her a traitor, and Percival had made her believe the impossible. Now there was Faulke, determined to marry her regardless of the consequences. If he thought to win her trust with smiles and platitudes, he was in for a rude awakening.

The intervening hours had given her plenty of time to recall all of the things she had said and done over the past few days, things that now made her burn with shame. If nothing else, Percival's betrayal reminded her that she must depend only upon herself. She would trust no one. There seemed little reason to doubt that this truly was Faulke Segrave, and that everything he said was the truth, or the truth as he understood it, but she would not let her guard down again so easily.

"If Richard's search is unsuccessful, we will make camp here for the night," he said. "There will be a fire to warm you."

She rubbed the tips of her fingers with her thumbs. Her skin was so wrinkled from being wet for so long that she could scarce feel her hands. "A fire would be welcome."

Faulke nodded, then clasped his hands behind his

back and stared down at her. "We have not had an auspicious beginning, you and I, but I would have you know that I will not hold this . . . situation against you. He played upon your womanly weaknesses to gain your trust, and your aunt did not help the situation with her plotting. You should never have been left alone with any man for any reason, or been allowed to ride out of the keep without an escort." He took a deep breath and released it very slowly, as if he wanted to say much more on the subject but thought better of it. "The damage is done and we shall eventually put this incident behind us. Once we are wed and I am certain your children will be mine, we shall not speak of him again. Do you understand?"

"Aye," she said carefully. His crude words made her hands clench into fists, but she supposed she should feel lucky that another man was so eager to have her as his wife. There was no doubt in Faulke's mind that they would be wed. However rude his declarations, he would soon be her husband and he deserved to hear the truth. Still, she could not look him in the eye as she said it. "I can set your mind at ease on one matter. He did not bed me. You will still have a virgin bride."

He studied her face for a time and she felt her cheeks grow warm, but then he slowly shook his head. "'Tis better if there is no question in anyone's mind. I would not have our first child born for at least a year after the ceremony, which will leave no doubt about the parentage even if the child should arrive early. My people must be certain that any child you bear will be mine. Indeed, all of Wales must be certain that your children are mine."

"I understand," she said in a quiet voice. Indeed, she understood exactly what he was saying. What she had suspected all along was true; he intended to breed the next Prince of Wales with her.

The plain truth did not insult or disappoint her. She certainly did not expect him to say he intended to marry her for some sort of noble or romantic reasons. Such luxuries were reserved for peasants and errant knights who . . .

She forced her thoughts away from that dangerous path. That brief moment of her life was over. The small humiliations she had suffered over the years at John's hands were hardly a comparison, but she found herself almost thankful for his callous treatment. John's spitefulness had hardened her, unwittingly given her the strength to withstand this much crueler blow. She would survive this betrayal. Duty and family were all that mattered now. They were all that had ever really mattered.

When news of the negotiations with the Segraves came to Coleway, she had been pleased that her father had managed to find her such a high-ranking husband. Now the only feelings that penetrated the walls around her heart were pain and dull resignation. Perhaps someday she would once again feel some measure of appreciation that she was getting exactly what she had always thought she wanted.

"Have you recalled anything that might prove helpful?" Faulke asked, bringing her out of her reverie. "Perchance did you overhear one of his men call him a name other than Sir Percival?"

She shook her head and answered in a toneless voice. "He was Sir Percival to them. His men are Oliver and Armand. They also claimed to be English, but all three men spoke fluent Italian. And the boy spoke nothing but Arabic and Italian."

He was still "Sir Percival" to her and always would be. Perhaps that would change when she learned his real name, although she was beginning to doubt that would ever happen. With each hour that passed, it was becoming less likely that he would be returning to the camp with Richard. Even knowing of Percival's betrayal, she could not bear to think of what was likely happening to him and his men. Were they still alive? Were they prisoners?

"Will we be wed at Hawksforth?" she asked, desperate to take her mind off Percival and his fate. Hawksforth was the seat of the Segrave family, a massive castle supposedly twice the size of her father's. She made a conscious effort to keep her gaze focused on Faulke rather than on the road where Richard should have reappeared hours ago. "Is that where we will live?"

"We will wed when we reach Wales, as soon as a priest can be found," he said. "Then we will journey to Hawksforth where you will reside. I travel constantly between my family's holdings, so I am rarely at any one fortress for more than a fortnight. However, I suppose I would call Hawksforth my home. My father is in residence there most of the time, along with his advisers."

Now that she had him talking, she decided it was time to pose the question that concerned her most. She struggled to find words that would not sound insulting or treasonous. "Under these circumstances, do you think Edward will withdraw his consent for our marriage and demand an annulment?"

There was a long silence before he answered and she found herself studying his mouth, trying to imagine his lips upon hers. No matter how pleasant Faulke was to look upon, the shudder that ran through her at the thought of kissing him was not in the least pleasant.

"King Edward cannot deny that a hasty marriage was in your best interest to ensure your safety from unscrupulous rogues," he said. "Even if Edward insists upon an annulment, it would take the Church years to dissolve the marriage and I fully intend to have an heir by

then, which means the Church would be even less likely
to grant an annulment. There will be a fine levied, since
I am required by law to obtain my liege lord's consent to
wed, but that will be the end of the matter."

A boldness she had not known she possessed seemed
to take hold of her. "Since you have no intention of con-
summating our marriage for several months, perhaps it
would be best if I stayed at Weston Castle with my father until—"

"After the trouble I went through to . . . rescue you, I
am not about to give you up for such a paltry reason."
He reached down and tilted her chin upward until she
met his gaze. His eyes held no warmth; the lines of his
face were harsh and forbidding. "Your father understands the benefits of this marriage, and the consequences should he oppose it. Do you understand the
consequences, Avalene?"

"Consequences?" she echoed. "What consequences?"

He gave her an intense look as though trying to decide
if her question was serious. "Your father's holdings
are vulnerable to the de Clare and Mortimer families.
His land sits between the lands owned by those powerful earls and the Segraves. If a civil war were to break
out, he would need an equally powerful ally to hold
the de Clare and Mortimer armies at bay. He needs the
Segraves."

"You think the de Clares and Mortimers would remain loyal to the king?" she asked, before realizing her
words implied that he would turn traitor.

"I know they will be loyal to themselves and use a war
as an excuse to expand their holdings," he answered.
"Weston Castle is a ripe plum they will both wish to
pluck. If the Segraves pledge an alliance with your father, none of the Marcher lords would dare challenge
him. Without an alliance, I would consider laying siege

to Weston Castle myself to ensure it did not fall into the hands of the Mortimers or de Clares. Those are the consequences. Do you understand what I am telling you?"

"I do." Her hands twisted nervously in her lap. He had blackmailed her father into the betrothal. She would be this man's wife within a matter of mere days. A week ago she would have felt like dancing with happiness, knowing that her wedding day was at long last upon her. Now the thought of marriage to Faulke Segrave filled her with dread. So much for the idea of a reprieve at her father's castle. What would her father expect her to do in this situation? What *could* she do? "I would—"

Faulke held up one hand for silence and cocked his head to one side. A moment later he called out, "To arms!"

Instantly all of the men were mounted with their swords drawn while Faulke turned his back to her and drew his own sword. Avalene heard the sounds of approaching riders and held her breath, straining to see into the gathering darkness that shrouded the road. Her breath caught in her throat and her heart pounded as she waited to see if the road would reveal Percival and his men, or just their bodies.

At last she heard Richard call out to his cousin to identify his party in the fading light. A few moments later she scanned the faces of each of the incoming riders, and then she pressed her palms to her forehead and let out a sigh of relief. She did not take time to wonder how Percival and his men had escaped Richard's hunting party. Instead she wondered why she was so relieved they had escaped. She would never see them again. They were criminals who had abducted her from her family. They deserved to be caught and punished.

She shook her head. Despite her wounded feelings, despite *everything*, Percival and his men had taken good care of her. If she had stayed another night at Coleway, her aunt likely would have forced a scandal. Marriage to Coleway's steward would have been the result. There was no sin in being grateful to Percival for rescuing her from that fate, even though he had done so for his own reasons. Not that it mattered anymore. She would soon be trapped in another marriage that could prove even more disastrous.

She watched Richard dismount, his features set in a hard mask. He and Faulke moved aside to speak in quiet tones, even though it was obvious the search party had failed to capture their quarry. She used that time to study the two men and discovered that Faulke looked much more like his cousin than she had initially realized. It was an unfortunate realization, as she had taken a rather strong and immediate dislike to Richard. One side of Richard's lip curled upward more often than was seemly and she had never cared for men who sneered at anything. Sure enough, Faulke's lip curved into the same expression as he listened to Richard's report and another shudder of foreboding went through her.

What if she could not bring herself to like her husband even a little? What if she could not submit to him, as was her duty? She felt an alarming gagging sensation at the back of her throat just thinking about it. Oh, good Lord, what if Faulke came to realize that he repulsed her?

Some measure of fear must have shown on her face because he held up his hands with the palms facing outward as he walked toward her, a gesture men often used when they approached a skittish horse.

"Do not worry, the coward has fled," he told her. "He must know by now that we have you, and there is nothing he can do against so large a force to steal you away again. You are safe, my lady."

She was surrounded by soldiers who were loyal to the man who would soon be her husband. They had chased off the man who had supposedly wanted to imprison her. She should feel safe. At the very least, she should feel gratitude. All she could think about was the growing revulsion she felt at the thought of kissing Faulke Segrave.

"Lady Avalene?" His brows drew together as he tilted his head to one side. "Is something wrong?"

Everything is wrong! She shook her head, even as she looked away from him. Even as the memory of the kisses she had shared with Percival tormented her with the certain knowledge that they would always be a measure of comparison that this man would never meet. Her gaze moved over Faulke's men and she vaguely realized they were making camp. She seized upon the activity as a way to occupy her mind with something other than lewd thoughts, thankful that her voice sounded almost normal. "Do your men need any assistance with the meal? I could help look for dry wood."

"Nay, we carry dry tinder and kindling, and the men will have to range out to find wood that is not soaked through." He pointed to the furs. "I would rather you stay here where we can keep an eye on you. In fact, I must insist upon it."

She supposed it was considerate of him to explain his reasoning, but it did not change the fact that the lean-to had just become her prison. Percival had not made her feel like a prisoner. She bowed her head and remained silent, wishing she could silence the voice in her head. At last Faulke turned and walked away.

She wasn't certain how much time had passed but the camp was mostly set up when an odd sensation came over her, a feeling of being watched. She tried to examine what she could still see of the darkening forest without being too obvious about what she was doing, but she saw nothing.

The odds that Percival would come back for her were almost nonexistent, but she could not seem to shake the feeling that she was being watched by someone other than Faulke's men. It was a warm, shivering feeling she had every so often that felt familiar, as if she would turn around and find Percival walking up to greet her.

It was a foolish notion, of course, likely born of fear coupled with long hours of sitting in wet, clammy clothing. She was starting to hallucinate, seeing movements out of the corners of her eyes then turning to find nothing. She didn't want to find anything . . . or did she?

She tried again to imagine what she would say to Percival if she should ever see him again. One question in particular plagued her. "Why am I still alive?"

The murmured words startled her, having come forth without conscious thought. And yet that was the question her mind returned to over and over again. Why had the king sent an assassin to Coleway, only to abduct her? He could have killed her that first night when he came to her chamber. Why didn't he?

Only two answers came to mind. Either the king had ordered her to be taken alive to be imprisoned in the Tower, just as Faulke suspected, or Percival had become immediately enamored of her and found that he couldn't bring himself to carry out her murder. The latter possibility was so fantastical that the notion would have been laughable, were it not a matter of her own life or death. Her ego was not so inflated as to think she had unwittingly captured the fancy of the most cold-blooded assassin in England. Percival had been playing a part, nothing more. And that was assuming Faulke had told her the truth, which raised yet another prospect. Perhaps the man she knew as Sir Percival really *was* Sir

Percival. What if Faulke had lied to her, just as he said Sir Percival had lied? Faulke could be trying to trick her into going willingly into a forced marriage. What if there was no betrothal?

The possibilities fair made her head spin. She lifted her wrinkled hands to rub away the ache in her temples, but her troubled thoughts of Faulke and Percival retreated when a spark of orange fire caught her eye. Soon the flames began to lick away at the black night, a feeble, fluttering dance at first, but eventually the flames rose higher and stronger with the promise of bone-deep heat. The smell of wood smoke and the sight of the fire drew her as easily as they would a moth. The unspoken order to stay in the lean-to was forgotten as she made her way to stand near the flames. The men who were tending the fire glanced up at her, exchanged a look, and then said nothing. She supposed the sound of her chattering teeth decided the matter.

By the time her hands were warmed there were three sizable fires spaced across the clearing, with cook pots hung on spits and the smell of porridge in the air. One of the soldiers offered her a cup filled with a hot gruel made of barley and dried beef. It was a simple meal but warm and nourishing. She thought it odd that Faulke had not shown her the courtesy of bringing her meal or offering his company while she ate, but mostly she was grateful that he left her alone.

When she finished the meal she handed her empty cup to one of the soldiers but remained standing by the fire ring. The heat from the flames continued to seep through her and she all but hugged the fire in an attempt to dry her clothing.

The flames were like snowflakes, she decided. No two were alike and their unending motion soon held her enthralled. The night was quiet with only the sounds of the crackling fires and she stared into the one before her, mesmerized. She caught herself just as she swayed forward and decided it would be a good idea to sit down.

Oddly enough, the soldiers nearest her looked just as captivated by the flames, and then she glanced toward Richard and Faulke and realized they were seated as well. The day had been exhausting for everyone, it seemed. One by one the soldiers lay down to sleep, even though most did not bother to spread out their bedrolls beforehand, and many simply seemed to slowly fall over. Her own eyelids felt weighted with lead. She thought about the lean-to and the furs that would make a soft if not entirely dry bed, but the fire was warmer. It was a little strange that she didn't recall when she had lain down, but the damp, mossy ground made a surprisingly soft pillow against her cheek.

Her last thought before she fell asleep was that something was wrong. She was just too tired to puzzle out what the problem might be.

14

"All of them are still alive," Armand said in Italian. He dragged another soldier across the campsite by his collar and propped the man into a seated position against a tree. The soldier roused a little and put his hands up as if to push Armand away. Armand simply slipped the loop of a leather ribbon around one of the man's wrists. The ribbon was actually part of a set of reins, one of many sets they had dismantled to use as bindings to tie up Faulke's men. Armand wrapped the rein around the tree, and then tied the end to the man's other wrist. The soldier's head slumped forward onto his chest. "Shall we take their horses with us?"

"Aye," Dante answered. He looked toward Avalene, where she lay sprawled on the ground near one of the campfires. Rami held her head in his lap and stroked her forehead, his movements gentle, as if he were tending to an injury. Dante had not allowed himself to touch her yet, but he knew she was not injured. The knowledge did little to calm his fury. "Rami, go cut the girth on each saddle where it cannot be easily repaired. After you are done, help Oliver string their horses on lunge lines."

"Aye, my lord." Rami gently laid Avalene's head on one of the furs he had dragged over from the lean-to, then rose and skipped off to carry out Dante's order.

"I will need you to take charge of some of their horses," he told Rami. "Can you handle six or eight on a line?"

Rami grinned, clearly delighted to be given a man's job. "Aye, my lord!"

Dante surveyed the campsite. Most of the soldiers had been hog-tied with their own reins, their arms bound behind their backs and their legs bent at the knee so their ankles could be tied to their wrists, rendering them completely helpless. A few others, Faulke and his cousin included, had been tied to trees. Fewer still had roused too easily from the effects of the poison so they had been gagged as well as tied to ensure their comrades stayed unconscious as long as possible.

Everything went so smoothly that he was almost disappointed. A good fight would have been preferable. He was ready to spill a little blood.

He walked over to the tree where they had tied Faulke Segrave and stared down at his enemy. Only long years of mental discipline had kept him in the shadows at Segrave's camp. A good hunter did not rush into a den of lions unprepared, and Dante was a very good hunter. There was little question that Segrave would be a formidable opponent in a fair fight, but Dante had never played fair and Segrave was now at his feet, at his mercy.

Here was the blood he would most like to spill, especially after he had watched Faulke put his hands on Avalene. His reactions to Segrave's impersonal touches were worrisome, to say the least. Strong emotions were never good for a man in his position, and what Segrave had made him feel went far beyond jealousy. Rage would be a more apt description, but even that word sounded too tame, too harmless for the fury that had burned through him when Segrave had lifted Avalene into his arms, when he dared speak to her of bearing his children. His blood was far from cooled, but seeing Segrave bound and helpless appeased his temper and allowed him to once again view his rival through somewhat dispassionate eyes.

Segrave's head had fallen forward, his breathing cluttered occasionally by a soft snore. Instinct told Dante the most obvious solution to this problem was to slit the throat of every man wearing Segrave colors. Unfortunately, he had sworn that he would not harm Faulke. That meant his men enjoyed the same immunity. Besides which, murdering his men was not the way to gain Faulke's cooperation concerning Avalene. Given all he had learned that day, it would take a miracle to talk Segrave out of his determination to marry her.

He had been hiding close enough to the lean-to that he had been able to overhear almost all of the conversations between Faulke and Avalene. It always amazed him how close he could get to his enemy undetected when they thought themselves safe because of sheer numbers, or because they were within their own walls, or within their own camp. Oh, they would rouse to a full-on attack quickly enough, but it never seemed to occur to anyone that a lone man with a talent for stealth could get almost as close as he wished, especially after he liberated a Segrave surcoat and cloak from one of the men sent to hunt for firewood.

He had overheard enough to know that Faulke was dead set on the marriage, and although the very idea turned his stomach, Dante couldn't find fault with his reasons. For a man in Segrave's position, a child with

Avalene would ensure the loyalty of every Welshman in his territory. Still, Avalene did not sound as pleased about the marriage as she had just a few days ago. Was it because Segrave had all but announced that she would be marrying a traitor, which meant she would be branded a traitor as well?

There was also Faulke's belief that the king intended to imprison Avalene in the Tower. The theory was plausible, close enough to the truth that Avalene probably believed it as well. Perhaps she would appreciate the opportunity to make a life for herself in a convent. Or would she see it as another form of imprisonment? Either way, her opinions didn't really matter. The convent was the only choice left to her, since there was no longer any possibility that she would become his mistress.

His fists moved reflexively as he looked down upon the man responsible for taking away that last prospect, still frustrated that the only thing he could do to punish Segrave was take Avalene away from him and make sure he would never again touch her. Now the only question was would she be grateful for her latest rescue?

At the very least, she should be happy that he had saved her from marriage to a traitor, as well as a man so clearly unsuited for her. He had noticed the way she flinched each time Segrave touched her. Aye, she would be much happier in a convent.

Why her happiness should matter to him, he didn't know. He was simply doing what he had pledged to do, although he no longer had a pleasurable reward to look forward to. Her distaste for Segrave would look paltry next to her terror when she realized he had recaptured her. Likely she would scream whenever he tried to touch her in the most innocent of ways. All because of one man's interference.

Faulke Segrave should consider himself the luckiest man in England to still be alive.

He knelt down next to Segrave, grabbed a fistful of hair and pulled his rival's head back. Faulke's eyes opened but it was obvious he had trouble bringing anything into focus.

"Can you hear me, Segrave?"

Faulke made a lunge against his restraints with a sudden speed and ferocity that surprised Dante. "I'll kill you!"

"You can try, but first you must find me," Dante said. Faulke's eyes closed, so he slapped the man's face to bring him around again. He wasn't gentle. "Listen to what I have to say, Segrave. You know that we are bound for London. Do you intend to follow us all the way to the city?"

"Kill you. London," Faulke muttered.

"Aye, London," Dante said agreeably. "We are bound for London, and that is where you and I will finish our business. There is a place in Southwark called the Ox Head Inn. Have you heard of it?"

Faulke's struggles to comprehend Dante's words were readily apparent. His head bobbed and weaved, but he carefully watched Dante's mouth. "London."

"Southwark," Dante clarified. "The Ox Head Inn. Now, repeat what I have just told you."

"Kill you!" Faulke said with more feeling. "London!"

"Meet me at the Ox Head Inn at Southwark," Dante repeated, without any real conviction that Faulke would remember this conversation. He was even more skeptical as Faulke showed no reaction when Dante drew his dagger.

Rather than threaten Faulke, he began to scratch a pattern into one of the leather bracers that covered Faulke's forearms, a crude but recognizable symbol for an ox. Unfortunately, Faulke's arms were bound behind him so he couldn't point out the markings and it would only antagonize the man if he carved the symbol someplace more noticeable, such as his thigh. It was a tempting thought, but when he had finished the pattern on the bracer, he carved the same symbol deep into the dirt next to him and made certain Faulke saw it. "The Ox Head Inn. Southwark. The day after you reach London, I will be there at midday. Do you understand?"

Faulke looked from the symbol to Dante's face, but the movement seemed to once again throw his focus off balance. "Aye."

"You can go to sleep now," Dante told him. His spies would let him know when Faulke entered the city. He would send a street urchin to deliver the same message to Faulke, just to be certain. "I will be waiting for you at the Ox Head Inn. There is nothing else for you to do now but sleep."

Faulke wanted to argue with him, that much was apparent. In the end, his chin eventually returned to his chest and his eyes drifted closed.

"Everything is ready, my lord."

Dante looked up to see Rami peering over his shoulder at Segrave.

"All of the men are tied and those who are alert are gagged," the boy said. "The girths are cut and their horses are on three lunge lines. Are we really going to leave them in the wilderness without horses?"

"We will leave their horses tethered on the road a day's walk from here," Dante said. "The men will likely free themselves by morning. Between searching for their horses and repairing their saddles, 'tis doubtful they will cause us any additional trouble on our journey. Now, go mount up and take your line of horses from Oliver."

"Aye, my lord."

Dante returned to Avalene, eyeing his own men as he walked. They would have their hands full until they rid themselves of Segrave's horses. Already the animals were jostling each other, unaccustomed to being herded so tightly together. He could tell it was a challenge for Oliver and Armand to control their own mounts as well as their lunge lines, but Rami seemed to have no problem with his line of animals. Still, they needed to move quickly.

He spared a quick glance at Avalene's pale face before he hefted her over one shoulder like a sack of grain. It was a challenge, but he managed to mount his own horse with his burden and then he settled her more comfortably in his arms. He turned his horse away from Segrave's camp and finally let himself enjoy the familiar feel of her. He pressed his nose against her temple and took a deep breath, inhaling her scent. His body reacted predictably, but this would be the last time he felt the yielding warmth and softness of her body in his arms. When she awoke, she would no longer look at him with wonderment shining in her eyes. Segrave's words made certain she was lost to him. The loss was inevitable. Hadn't he always known that this innocent creature was never truly meant for a monster like him?

Even his imagined future with her had been a short-lived one, a future that would have lasted only as long as it took her to see the darkness in his soul and realize he was not the honorable, chivalrous Sir Percival who would take her to her family in Wales. Instead she would see a liar and thief who would use her trust and abuse her innocence.

On the other hand, he could not imagine forcing her from his life in just a few short weeks. She was everything he wanted, and everything he would never have. He knew with a certainty that defied logic that even if he lived to a very old age, he would never find another woman like her.

He studied her face in the fading light from the campfires, memorizing her peaceful features. His heart had been a cold stone for longer than he could remember. There had been no room in his life for tender emotions, yet somehow she had reached past his barriers, brought light into the darkest corners of his soul. Just yesterday morn he had counted the long weeks until they reached Venice the way a miser counted his gold. Now they stretched out before him as a trial of endurance, the penance he must pay for daring to dream that she would be his, even for a little while.

Mordecai's last words in the Tower came to him unbidden. *Marriage or murder, mistress or nun, the girl is yours to do with as you wish once Segrave is convinced his marriage prospects lie elsewhere.* Marriage and mistress were off the table. What if he was unable to convince Segrave to relinquish his claim to her? Would the convent also become an impossible future for her? That left only one other possibility. If Mordecai gave the order, could he end her life?

The answer should be obvious and immediate. He had never hesitated in his duty, no matter his opinion of a situation. His faith in Mordecai's strange abilities was absolute; he had seen the proof of it too many times to have any doubts. It was Mordecai's abilities that had shaped Dante's life in England and guaranteed his success in his quest for vengeance. In every sense of the word, he owed Mordecai his life. His willingness to destroy one innocent girl should not even be a question in his mind and yet it echoed there incessantly. *Can you kill her?*

He knew the answer. Something inside him had changed when he met her, every goal and objective in his life revised to include her. He would kill anyone who tried to harm her. Given Mordecai's prediction, his own death might be counted among that number.

. . . it is imperative she remain alive until you convince Faulke Segrave to choose the English bride. Your own fate does not change until that time. Only then will you have a choice of what to do with the girl.

Who was the English bride?

He was suddenly anxious to be back in London, to meet with Mordecai again and get answers to the questions he should have asked in the first place. Somehow Segrave must be convinced. He would not think of Avalene's future again or torture himself with doubts until Mordecai shed more light on the situation. If he could not have her, he would make certain a convent would.

He turned his thoughts to the immediate task of putting more miles behind them. He would not risk another meeting with Segrave until he could be certain Avalene was safe. And that led back to thoughts of her constant presence in his life until they reached Italy. His arms ached already with emptiness and she was still in them. It would be torture to see her every day and yet know she was forever beyond his reach.

The beast inside him whispered sinister suggestions in his ear, ever selfish, ever plotting. Where would be the harm in drugging her again if the yearning to hold her this way became too unbearable over the weeks ahead? She would never remember if he stole a few kisses. He could kiss her now and she wouldn't remember. He could—

She began to stir in his arms and her eyes fluttered open, as if she had heard his dark thoughts. "Sir Percival?"

Her words were slurred from the effects of the poison and he knew that she was no more alert than Faulke and

his men. She would remember nothing of this conversation, but it was time to own up to the truth. Let her see
him for what he was.

"Nay, my lady." He gave her a grim look. "Faulke
Segrave guessed correctly. I am the King's Assassin."

It was the sunlight that awakened Avalene, the light so
bright behind her eyelids that she lifted her hands to
shade her face . . . at least, she tried to lift her hands but
for some reason they wouldn't cooperate. Strangely
enough, that did not alarm her. She felt as if she were
floating along the edges of a dream. There were voices
nearby, familiar voices, those of a boy and a man. Rami
and Sir Percival. She couldn't understand the words, and
then realized they were speaking in Italian. She turned
her head and tried to drift deeper into the dream, but
something kept pushing against her shoulder.

"Lady. Lady." The insistent nudging continued. "*E 'ora
di svegliarsi.*"

She opened her eyes to the blinding sunlight, then
quickly closed them again and groaned. "Rami?"

"*Sì, signora.*"

The sunlight felt warm on her face, stirred by a breeze
that also set leaves to rustling, and she could smell
crushed grass as well as the damp earth. It was the
middle of the day and she was lying on the ground, but
why? Her mind felt as sluggish as her body. She wanted
nothing more than to roll over and continue to sleep,
but then fragments of memories came back to her in a
sudden rush. Faulke Segrave. Sir Percival. Assassin.

Her eyes flew open and her hands worked this time as
she cupped them over her forehead to shield her eyes
from the sunlight. "What . . . where am I?"

"*Mi dispiace, non capisco.*"

She tried to think of the right Italian words but failed. Given the trouble she was having speaking her own language, translations into Italian were beyond her at the moment. Instead she concentrated on taking deep, cleansing breaths. Something was wrong with her. Her limbs felt weighted with lead and her thoughts refused to take focus. Rami made matters worse by tugging on her arms in an obvious attempt to make her sit up.

She finally gave in to his prodding and managed to get herself upright with his assistance, although a wave of dizziness made her thankful she had not tried to stand. At the same time, a shooting pain took up residence between her temples.

"Good. You are awake."

That voice she would know anywhere, the way its deep timbre set her pulse to racing. And yet her pulse no longer fluttered with giddy desire, but a healthy dose of fear. Bits and pieces of the day she had spent with Faulke Segrave were coming back to her. Sir Percival was *not* Sir Percival. She struggled to gather her scattered wits. "W-what happened?"

"You were poisoned."

"W-what?" She tried to look up at him, but the sun sat directly over his shoulder. The blinding rays were more than her head could tolerate and she swiftly lowered her gaze again. Aside from a splitting headache, her stomach protested each abrupt movement and she put one hand over her mouth, hoping that would quell the feeling.

"You were poisoned," he repeated. "I put a potion in the cook pots."

She recalled all the men who had also eaten from those poisoned pots. Were they dead? Why was she still alive? She rubbed her temple with her free hand and tried to make sense of the news.

"*Rami, occuparsi di cavalli,*" he said. After the boy moved away from them, he asked, "Do you feel sick?"

She nodded and then he, too, walked away.

So much for his consideration, she thought, although she should have known there would be no more kindness from him. He was no longer her knight to command, or her lover to seduce. He was a man feared throughout England for his ability to murder anyone, anywhere, at any time. And she was his prisoner to do with as he pleased.

That thought should terrify her. Instead she felt strangely calm. Aye, there was a good measure of fear, but not panic. It was as if she were watching all of this happen to someone else. She supposed it was the poison that had dulled her senses. For now she was still alive and that was all that mattered.

She tried again to look around her. The sunlight was not quite so painful now that her eyes had adjusted to the light, but her vision was still a little blurry. She rested on a small hillock above a wide, grassy meadow. Rami was a few dozen paces away, tending to their saddled horses, while Oliver and Armand were busy tying more than a score of unsaddled horses to a long picket line that stretched beneath a stand of poplar trees. She wondered who the horses belonged to and then realized they were likely the Segraves' mounts. The absence of Faulke and his men spoke volumes.

He returned and held out a water bag. "Here, drink some of this."

She eyed it warily. Her hands began to tremble, whether from the poison or from fear, she could not say. "Do you . . . do you intend to kill me now?"

"If I had wanted you dead, you would be dead long ago." His voice was toneless.

She believed him. Although she heard Sir Percival's

voice when he spoke, this man was a stranger. "Then why—"

"Drink this," he repeated, as he dropped the bag into her lap. "'Tis some of the willow bark tea you brewed for Rami. It will help calm your stomach."

"Th-there is no poison in it?" she asked, as she picked up the bag. And then she remembered Faulke's theory about why she was still alive. It was beginning to make the most sense.

He folded his arms across his chest and remained silent.

"Why did you take me away from Coleway?"

"If I recall correctly, you left Coleway with me quite willingly. Indeed, our escape from the fortress was entirely your idea."

It was the truth, and yet it was wrong. Everything about him was wrong. Two days ago she had thought everything about him was just right. Today she knew better. There would be no magical explanations that would make everything right. Her perfect knight had deceived her. How he must have laughed at her willingness to help in her own abduction. He was no better than John. Indeed, he was much, much worse.

"You must have thought me a fool," she said in a soft voice. She removed the stopper from the water bag but still could not bring herself to drink before she knew the full, damning truth. "Faulke told me that you are not my father's knight. Faulke said you were sent by the king to murder or abduct me so that Faulke could not marry me. He claims you are an assassin. The King's Assassin."

He remained silent.

"You do not deny his charges?"

"Does it matter?" he asked. "You have already decided that I am the enemy. I can see the fear in your eyes."

She had no answer for that bit of truth. The man who stood before her was not Sir Percival. He was not the kind, chivalrous knight she had thought him to be. In addition to her pain and anger, this man frightened her. "Is Faulke dead?"

He said nothing for a long moment. "Why do you care? He blackmailed your father into a betrothal and intended to force you into marriage within the next few days, willing or not. You were his prisoner as much as you are mine."

There was only one way he could know all of that, and she recalled the feeling of being watched while she was in Segrave's camp. How had he managed it? "You heard everything Segrave said to me?"

"Do you care for him?" he countered.

What an odd question. She lowered her head and stared down at the water bag, unwilling to let him study her face as she considered her answer. "How could I care for a man I just met?"

His next remark cut more effectively than a knife. "You developed an affection for me rather quickly."

"That was different!" She regretted the words before they were out of her mouth. There was no way she could explain the difference without sounding pathetic. "Everything Faulke told me came as . . . quite a shock. Still, I do not want to be the cause of his death. I do not want to be responsible for anyone's death!"

"You should have thought of that before we left Coleway," he said. "What did you think I would do if Lord Brunor and his men had caught up with us?"

"There would have been too many of them." She realized even as she spoke that she was being hopelessly naïve. His surrender would have meant his death. He never would have handed her over without a fight if they had been caught. She would have been responsible for unleashing this weapon upon her own family.

"Drink the tea," he said again, in a voice that brooked no argument.

She followed the order in a daze and began to take small sips.

"Segrave and his men are alive," he went on. He sounded as if he spoke of something that disgusted him. "I did not use enough poison to cause any lasting damage. You will all recover within a few hours."

Her head and stomach didn't think so. Still, there was a sense of relief that he intended to keep her alive. For now.

"Your face is the color of parchment," he said, as she swallowed the tea. "You will be of no use to me if you are too sick to ride."

And that would likely be the extent of his concern for her welfare; whether or not she was healthy enough to aid in her own abduction. She took several more sips of tea, relieved that it did, indeed, have a calming effect on her stomach. Even her head felt clearer. Still, nothing made sense.

"Where are they?"

"Who, the Segraves?"

Her gaze went to Oliver and Armand, who were still tending the horses. "Aye."

"They are more than a half day's ride from here, probably feeling much as you do right now."

She had only his word that they were alive. He had lied to her from the moment they met. Nothing he said could be trusted. On the other hand, if the Segraves were already dead, why would he take their horses only to leave them on the road? Surely he would only go to this much trouble if he needed to delay their pursuit.

The tracks from the horses would be easy enough to follow. When and if the Segraves recovered, they would probably send a search party to retrieve the horses, and then return to the camp for their gear and saddles. A half day's lead had just turned into a lead of at least two days. If they really were still alive, and unless something else drastic happened, the Segraves would never catch them before they reached London.

"We have already lost too much time," he said. "You will need to ride your own horse for the rest of the day."

The thought of sitting on a horse made her stomach give an alarming lurch. The thought of riding with Sir . . . Liar or one of his men was equally distasteful. Now that her vision had finally returned to normal, she braced herself, locked down every ounce of weakness, and forced herself to look up at him.

It helped that he had moved to one side, out of the direct line of the sun, but she still had to shade her eyes to see his face. The pain was not as bad as she had feared it would be.

He looked the same; his head held at an aloof angle, his green eyes pierced with intelligence, his face devastatingly handsome. Whatever she had expected to see, evil, or avarice, or anger, she did not find it. No enemy should look so . . . appealing, although his lingering appeal almost made her feel better about being so easily deceived. Surely his virtuous manner had deceived countless people. Perhaps she was not quite so stupidly gullible as she had first thought. He was most definitely the proverbial wolf in sheep's clothing. Her traitorous heart skipped a few beats and she wondered if the sudden heat in her face revealed a telltale blush.

She lowered her gaze before he could see the unexpected wave of longing that washed over her. What was the matter with her? She *knew* that he was her enemy.

She knew that he was . . . Good lord, she did not even know his name.

"Who *are* you?" she asked. "That is, what is your real name?"

He remained silent for so long that she began to think he had no intention of revealing a secret that many in England would likely kill to learn.

"My name is Dante Chiavari," he said at last. "Segrave made another correct guess; I am a foreigner, an Italian by birth."

"That much I had already guessed," she said, mostly because it helped explain his effect on her. She recalled the way the Italian merchants treated the women at Coleway, the way they made each woman feel as if she were the most beautiful and fascinating creature they had ever encountered, and she had watched the women melt into simpering puddles at their feet. Their intense and seemingly genuine appreciation of women was a common trait among the Italians, not a crafted skill, but a mannerism they were all seemingly born with. Dante had simply used the brand of charm on her that had been bred into him. "You speak Italian, Rami speaks Italian, both of your men speak Italian. I realized quickly enough that you were all Italians masquerading as Englishmen."

Her boldness amazed her. She could still speak with him as easily as she had when she thought him to be Sir Percival. In her defense, he looked and sounded the same as her knight, even down to his mannerisms. She watched one eyebrow rise.

"Actually, Oliver and Armand are Englishmen, and Rami is Circassian." His lips curved upward, as if he found humor in her ignorance. "I am the only Italian."

His smiles had always been her downfall, and it was an unpleasant realization that she was no more immune

from them now than she had been before. It should be a
crime, how handsome that grin made him. It drew her
eye to the masculine lines of his face and the rough stubble that spoke of his days away from a shaving blade.
Was that small smile designed to lull her back into his
deceptions? Or was she simply a weak-willed idiot
where he was concerned? Oh, he was good at his craft.

When her mind wandered to the sinful ways he had
touched and kissed her, she looked pointedly away from
him. There was most definitely something wrong with
her. The problem became clearer the longer she refused
to look at him.

It would take time for her heart to accept what her
mind already knew. None of the attraction she felt for
him had been real. It was simply another part of his deception. He would deceive her again, if she allowed it.
She had to push aside the curtain of infatuation and see
the truth. He was not charming her with a smile. He was
laughing at her.

She focused her gaze on a point just past his shoulder.
"Did you murder the real Sir Percival?"

He shook his head. "I have never met the man."

Well, that was a point in his favor, she supposed. "But
you are the King's Assassin?"

"Aye."

The answer was expected, and yet to hear it aloud was
more crushing than she had anticipated. It was the final
nail in the small coffin of hope that this had all been
some sort of terrible misunderstanding. "So, you have
no intention of taking me to my father?"

"None," he confirmed.

"Are we still bound for London?"

"Aye."

It was another expected answer that sank her hopes to
even greater depths. Faulke had been right about every-

thing. There was no marriage in her future. The King's Assassin had done her no favors by allowing her to live. She would be imprisoned in the Tower for the remainder of her life.

"'Tis time to leave." He reached down and took the water bag before she knew what he was about, and then he turned and walked toward the horses. He spoke to her without turning around. "Be on your horse anon, or you will ride with me until you can manage a horse on your own."

It was an effective threat. She struggled to her feet and staggered after him.

15

She still wasn't sure how she had managed it. Her
stomach lurched constantly during her first few hours in
the saddle. *Poisoned, powerless, prey.*

All afternoon she had kept her mind busy by thinking
up words that started with the same letter to keep her
thoughts from even darker places. *Bruised, battered, betrayed.*

The exercise had not been much of a success.

They kept up a hard pace throughout the day until
they reached the outskirts of a small village late in the
afternoon. A signal from Sir Percival . . . *Dante* . . . sent
Armand along a fork in the road that led into the town
while the rest of them slowed their horses to an ambling
gait and continued toward London.

Not that she had much control of her horse's gait.
Rami had removed her reins and a long tether now
stretched from Bodkin's halter to Dante's saddle. Her
horse simply followed the lead of Dante's horse. She supposed they were worried that she would try to escape.

Enemy, evil, escape.

The notion of escape had crossed her mind several hours ago but she quickly dismissed it. There was nowhere to run. Her family had no idea how to find her. Sir Brunor and his men would never guess that she was headed toward London. Faulke Segrave and his soldiers were too far behind them. She would never break free of Dante Chiavari and his men long enough to reach either the Segraves or Coleway Castle. Definitely not long enough to reach her father at Weston. She needed a miracle, and they were in very short supply for her these days.

If Dante Chiavari had his way, she would never be allowed to marry Faulke Segrave. She would not even be allowed to marry a man as odious as Coleway's steward. She would be locked away in some dark, dank cell of a prison.

The thought of living in a small, windowless room for the remainder of her life was as intolerable as it was unimaginable. Such could not be her fate. Of course, every other unjustly imprisoned person before her had likely thought the same thing.

Marriage to a traitorous and possibly murderous Marcher baron was no longer the worst fate that could befall her. More likely, Faulke had been her only hope for any sort of freedom. Now that hope was gone, too. She glanced over her shoulder as she had done many times throughout the day, certain she would see nothing unusual, but still searching the road behind them just the same.

"They will not catch up with us before we reach London," Dante said. "You might as well stop watching for them."

She turned around in the saddle and stared at a point between her horse's ears, refusing to look at him, although she was uncertain if he even cared. He had ignored her all day, riding a few paces ahead of her even when the road was wide enough to ride abreast. His actions made it clear that he wanted nothing more from her than cooperation and silence. She had provided both.

Another ripple of pain reminded her that her heart was still being stubborn. The pain would fade eventually, as it had after her mother's death, and then again when her father had sent her to Coleway. It was foolish to compare this pain to the loss of a parent, but the years had obviously dulled her memory, for this felt much the same as that remembered misery. Possibly worse.

Or perhaps it was the addition of humiliation that made the wound feel deeper. She had played the part of the fool. Her mind had been trying to warn her of a bad outcome the entire time Dante had been lying to her. Instead her heart had blithely ignored the warnings and taken up residence on her sleeve, bared for his ridicule and abuse. Now that the charade had ended he seemed content to ignore her, to pretend that nothing had ever happened between them. It had taken her most of the day to realize that this was the greatest kindness he could show her.

"My lord," Oliver called out from in front of them. He reined in his horse near the side of the road. As they rode closer, she noticed a narrow path that wound its way up the side of the hill to their left. "Do you want me to wait here for Armand?"

Dante shook his head. "Rami can stay behind and then brush over our tracks. I will need your help getting camp set up for the night."

Oh, *joy, jubilation,* and . . . *justice.* She had survived the longest day of her life. Her reward would be an entire night to rest her weary bones. A roof over her head and a warm, dry bed would be true justice, but she would settle for any bed that did not move. Why had she ever thought horseback riding was a pleasurable pursuit? Still, she could hardly complain when the thought of what awaited her at the end of this journey made her throat close up with fear. She was no longer in any hurry to reach London.

They followed the path upward and a few minutes later they were in a small meadow, well hidden from anyone who might pass by on the road below. The grass was so tall that it brushed against her boots and fluttered against the edges of her cloak, a sea of green. They finally halted in a wide expanse where flattened grass marked what she recognized as a deer lay, the place where a herd of deer had recently bedded down. It was an ideal spot to make camp for the night.

Oliver set about hobbling the horses while Dante hauled his saddle and gear along a path that led out from the main deer lay to a smaller, more isolated area of flattened grass. She dismounted and clung to her saddle for a few moments until she was certain her legs would hold her, and then she made her way to the growing pile of supplies that Oliver had removed from the packhorses for the night. She found a seat on an overturned cook pot and refused to offer her captors any assistance as she watched the men set up camp. Her thoughts wandered back to escape.

They were far enough from the village that she would have a long trek if she thought to go there for help, and the surrounding woods and thickets meant she would have to stay on the road where she would be easy to overtake. Still, she wondered what lord held the small manor house near the village, and if there was any possibility of help from that quarter.

Thoughts of the village were pushed aside when Rami and Armand rejoined them. Armand dismounted and placed a bucket on the ground, and then he took a folded cloth from the top of the bucket and spread it out on the ground. Next he began to unpack the contents onto the cloth. The delicious aromas of hot food filled the air and she found herself standing in front of the spread before she was even aware of her feet moving her forward.

"Meat pies and fresh bread," he announced unnecessarily, and then he motioned toward a stoneware jug that Rami placed next to the feast. "Orrick had fresh cider as well."

Orrick? She wondered if that was the name of the village, or someone they knew in the village, or even the local lord. She supposed the only relevant fact was that they knew someone there well enough to have a meal prepared for them in short order, which meant their word would be believed more readily than her own. Her fleeting thoughts of escape were extinguished. Orrick would offer no safe haven for her.

Still, the prospect of hot food took the sting from her disappointment. She had eaten gruel and porridge for so many days that she had almost forgotten the scents of fresh baked pastry and bread. It smelled like heaven.

Armand took a dagger from his belt and sliced one of the small loaves of bread in half, and then placed a meat pie on each slab. Rami carefully cradled one of the slabs and then carried it over to her. He tilted his head to one side when she simply stared at the food. *"Avete fame, la mia signora?"*

"Si." She was indeed hungry, but she eyed the food with the same suspicion that she had when Dante offered her the willow tea. Would they poison her again to keep her quiet for the night?

"Take the food," Dante said from beside her. "There is no poison in it."

It annoyed her that he could still read her thoughts so easily.

Rami gestured toward the cooking pot she had recently vacated. "*Si prega di essere seduti.*"

Something about taking a seat. She complied and Rami settled onto the ground next to her. Dante joined them a few minutes later, and then tilted his head toward Oliver and Armand. Rami took the hint and left to join the two men on the other side of camp.

They did not speak while they ate their meal, but she was well aware of his presence beside her. No matter how much logic her head applied to the situation, her heart needed more time to recover. It caused a physical pain to be this close to him and know that he would never again touch her as he once had, to recall his false words and gentleness as he drew his fingertips down the line of her cheek, or nuzzled his lips against her neck. She let herself catalog a few more remembered touches before she reined in her imagination, disgusted with herself.

The obsession that drew a moth to its death in a flame must feel very much the same, she decided. And just like a moth that had already scorched its wings, she couldn't seem to stop herself from turning toward the fire. But she was not a mindless insect. She could resist destruction. She had to, if she wanted to survive this torture.

Eventually she began to relax a little and even found herself captivated by the sounds of delight and exaggerated faces of rapture that Rami made as he polished off his food. She had never met a child who took such delight in his meals. She managed to catch his eye and held up the remainder of her dinner in offering. The boy glanced at Dante, obviously received some silent sign of consent, and then he practically skipped over to her.

"I have had my fill," she told Rami, as she placed the food in his hands.

"*Grazie, la mia signora.*"

She brushed the crumbs off her hands as she watched the boy all but dance back to his seat. Oh, to be so innocent, so easily satisfied.

"I assumed you would have more questions," Dante said, breaking into her thoughts. "Have you decided not to speak to me, or is there some other reason for your silence?"

She felt like a deer startled in the field by a hunter, frozen in place by the unexpected question. Fight or flight. Retort or silence. She could not decide.

"Not that I am complaining," he continued, as she silently debated. "Most women cannot hold a thought private when they feel wronged. I have actually enjoyed the peace and quiet all day. In fact, forget I made mention of the matter. The silence is most pleasing."

She tried to ignore the ripple of pain his words caused. The way he jested with her was another trait she had once found absurdly appealing. What an even crueler jest that he was now her enemy, making jests at her expense. Oh, why couldn't he simply be Sir Percival?

He gave an impatient sigh. "If you have no questions for me, then will you answer one of mine?"

She finally allowed herself to look at him, to meet his gaze. His face was expressionless and yet there was an intensity in his eyes that she found unsettling. "What is your question?"

"I know you were afraid of me when you first awoke from the poison," he began. "What happened to your fear?"

"I beg your pardon?"

"'Tis obvious you are angry," he said, "and yet 'tis just as obvious that you are no longer afraid of me. Why?"

He was right. She wasn't afraid of him. Angry and mortified by his deceit, fearful and desperately worried about her future, absolutely. Afraid of him? That was probably the only emotion he left mostly untouched in her.

She thought about lying but could see no real harm in telling the truth. "You said yourself that I would already be dead if that was your intent. What else is there to fear?"

His eyes darkened. "Me."

"Why should I fear you?" she asked, genuinely curious. Did he intend to harm her after all?

A flicker of surprise crossed his features. "You know who I am. *What* I am. An assassin. The King's Assassin."

"I know all too well who and what you are." Was he trying to impress her with his reputation? She had not thought him so vain. "You are the man who tricked me to steal me away from Coleway, who fed me poison to take me away from the man I am likely betrothed to marry, and now you intend to take me to London where I will be locked away for the rest of my life in the Tower. If you are wondering, those would be the reasons I am . . . angry with you."

She folded her arms across her chest, secretly pleased and surprised that she was managing this conversation so well. It required less effort than she had anticipated to hide her crushed heart. The years of practice with John and Lady Margaret had definitely helped. She sounded almost like her usual calm, collected self.

"But you are not afraid of me?"

What was his obsession with her lack of fear? "I am not afraid of you."

A small knife appeared in his hand and he turned it over several times in maneuvers that rolled the knife end to end over the back of his hand and then his palm, the movements smooth and practiced. There was something almost inhuman about his reflexes and coordination. What he was doing looked impossible, yet he performed the task seemingly without conscious thought, the way some people drummed their fingers on a table without realizing what they were doing. She glanced up at his face to find him watching her. "You really do not fear me."

She gave an exasperated sigh. "Why is this so surprising?"

"You do not realize how rare you are."

"Oh, not so rare, I think." She looked pointedly toward Rami and his men. "They do not seem to fear you."

"Oliver and Armand are among the few exceptions," he admitted. "However, I terrified them when we first met and they learned my true identity. It took them many months to realize their lives were safe as long as I had their loyalty. Rami still jumps whenever I say a harsh word."

"Well, there is your answer," she said. "I know that I am safe with you."

"Safe," he echoed. The word rolled off his tongue as if he were tasting a new flavor. He opened his mouth to say something more, then changed his mind and closed it again. He remained silent for a long time. "You do not care that murder is my profession?"

Her brows drew together as she realized that he was not bragging about his fearsome reputation. He seemed almost embarrassed by it. How strange.

"I have had plenty of time today to think about your profession," she mused. "Given the ferocity of the tales, you are not at all what I expected."

His gaze held hers captive, the intensity in his unusual green eyes deepening, as if he were silently willing her to tell him her secrets. She had trouble remembering how to breathe. "What did you expect?"

She wasn't exactly sure of that answer herself and said the first things that came to mind. "I expected you to be a good man who wanted to help me. Instead I discovered that you are a *very* bad man who intends to ruin my life. Likely you are one of the most notorious men in England. Most would call you 'evil.' I cannot even imagine how many people you have murdered. There must be—"

He held up one hand to stop her. "I have done what was necessary and I will not apologize."

"I was not asking for an apology," she said. "I was simply remarking upon the fact that my judgment of men leaves much to be desired. In the time I knew you as Sir Percival, I did not see anything in you that was evil. I still cannot reconcile the fact that you are the man in the tales I have heard about the King's Assassin. I thought evilness would somehow mark a man and make him ugly. You are so— That is to say, there is nothing in your appearance that would give the impression that you are so ill-favored."

"I assure you that I am the man you have heard tales about, and I am, indeed, a man with much blood on my hands." His head tilted slightly to one side. "Is that the reason you are not afraid of me? Because you have some misguided belief that I am not an assassin?"

She shook her head. "Even though you deceived me with the charade as Sir Percival, I believe you are who you now claim to be. I just cannot believe you are *what* you claim to be."

"Who and what I am are one and the same." His voice was sure, but his expression reflected his bewilderment.

She knew she was speaking in riddles, but she could not think of an explanation that would make sense to anyone but her. Why was she even trying? "I cannot explain it other than to say that you are not what you are supposed to be."

"Just what do you think I am, other than a man who has killed countless traitors?"

She had intended to change the subject, or to retreat

again into silence, but his words made something in her mind click into place. "That is the answer. You just said it yourself. You have killed countless *traitors*."

She nodded to herself and then stared up at the sky as she mulled over the revelation. All day it had been a minor annoyance in the back of her mind; the inexplicable reasons why it didn't particularly bother her that she was the captive of the notorious King's Assassin. Now she realized why his identity did not matter.

"Some would call it murder," she began, "but I think your profession must be little different than that of the executioner. The king has the authority to order the execution of any man or woman in his realm who breaks his laws or turns traitor. You carry out his warrants. 'Tis not entirely different from a knight riding into battle against the king's enemies, except the violence is focused upon one person rather than an entire army. I do not fear knights who have killed in battle, just as I see no reason to fear you."

He studied his hands as he used the tip of the knife to scrape under his fingernails. "And you are not the least bit afraid to be my prisoner?"

"Whatever reasons you have for my abduction, murder does not seem to be a part of them. And if you truly are an agent of the king . . ." She lifted her shoulders. "'Tis my duty to obey my sovereign's wishes, and yet at the same time I must wonder at the manner of my summons. It does not bode well for my future."

"Hence your anger."

"Aye, hence my anger," she agreed, unable to keep the bitterness from her voice.

He looked away from her and seemed suddenly intent on something across the campsite. "You are a strange woman, Avalene."

He was only just realizing this fact? She was cursed

with a bloodline that made her dangerous to her own king, her father had abandoned her, her aunt and uncle had betrayed her, and she had no friends to speak of. These were hardly the hallmarks of a normal, likable person. He had deceived her into thinking he viewed her differently, into thinking he liked and understood her. She should have known better. Men like Sir Percival truly did not exist. She released a deep, heartfelt sigh and then immediately tried to cover the sound with a small cough.

"Are you really so disappointed that you will not marry Segrave?"

"Aye."

His eyes immediately took on a hard, shuttered look. "You realize that he will never touch you again." It was not a question.

"He was preferable to the Tower," she muttered.

He made a sound that might have been agreement, and then he seemed to relax a little. "Is that really all he is to you, a means of escaping a different fate?"

"Of course." She could see that he didn't understand and wondered why the explanation mattered to him, or, for that matter, why she bothered to provide it. On the other hand, she had nothing better to do and what did it really matter? "He would not be my choice if I had any other. However, I would do almost anything to protect my family and avoid becoming a prisoner for the rest of my life. Who wouldn't?"

"Who indeed," he murmured. "So, you do not feel the same sort of attraction toward Segrave that you felt toward me?"

Her jaw locked shut. She lifted her chin and looked pointedly away from him. The pain was no longer a ripple but now came in crushing waves. Her gaze went to Rami who lay on the ground, rubbing his swollen stomach with all the satisfaction of a well-fed cat. She kept her gaze focused on the boy and tried to keep her mind focused there as well—anything to keep her thoughts away from Dante, away from the pain in her chest and the burning sensation in her eyes. She would never give him the satisfaction of seeing her cry.

"Avalene?"

Leave me alone! "What?"

"Do you care for Segrave?"

Anger burned through her. She spoke in a low, tight voice, her gaze still fastened on Rami. "As you said, he blackmailed my father into the betrothal and it seems likely he intends to incite a rebellion in Wales. I am nothing more to him than a means to secure the support of the Welsh natives. He is nothing more to me than a means to protect my father's lands and avoid imprisonment. So, no, I do not care for him in the way that you mean."

She breathed a sigh of relief that she had made it through that speech without her voice breaking. She refused to add that she despised Segrave for what he wanted from her and what he had done to get his way. However, she would marry a three-headed goat if it meant she could avoid the fate that Segrave threatened for her father or the fate that the king threatened for her.

"Forgive me," he said in a much gentler voice. "I misunderstood."

"Why do you even care?" she demanded, turning to face him again. "You have already assured me that I will never see Faulke Segrave again, much less marry him. What is the point of knowing my feelings about him? Why ask all of these questions?"

"I am curious about you." His expression looked almost apologetic. "The way your mind works intrigues me."

She pressed her lips together and returned her attention to Rami. "How nice that you find my predicament so entertaining."

"Not entertaining," he countered. "Never that. 'Tis you I find fascinating. You said that I am not what you expected. Well, I find you to be just as unexpected. No fear. No hysterics. No pleading or complaints. I am at a loss as to what to make of you."

Wonderful. He found her fascinating. Only because she was not a cowering, sobbing female. He did not know that she never cried, never pleaded, never showed her fears, at least, never where anyone could see or hear her. Lady Margaret had cured her of those weaknesses long ago. *'Stop that bawling or I will give you something to cry about'* was a phrase she had heard often during her first few months at Coleway, usually followed by actions that made her realize the words were not an idle threat but a solid promise. Her aunt could not abide anyone moping about over problems that did not concern her.

And then there was John, of course. The steward was always quick to exploit any vulnerability. She had been careful to keep her emotions firmly in check no matter how mercilessly he provoked her. He delighted in the confrontation when anyone rose to his bait. Her cool disdain had always infuriated him. So she had learned to keep her true thoughts carefully hidden and eventually became so adept at the practice that it had become second nature. Had all the years of hiding her feelings somehow changed her? Dante certainly seemed to think she was abnormal.

Ah, the irony. He was the only person with whom she had ever felt comfortable enough to show her weaknesses, to hold out her heart to him like some silly cow-eyed maiden. She deserved to have it handed back to her in pieces for behaving like such an idiot in the first place.

"Come," he said. He bent down to pick up something from the grass, and then he was on his feet in one fluid movement. He held out his hand to her. "There is a spring near the horses where you can get a drink of fresh water and rinse your hands."

She blinked once at the sudden change of subject. "Aye, that would be welcome."

She followed him past the horses toward a line of trees that marked the path to the spring. He gave her a few moments of privacy, and then seemed in no hurry when she took her time. The water was cold and bracing enough to wash away the melancholy brought on by their conversation. Why had she spoken to him so candidly? There was no harm done that she could imagine, but she should not be sharing any of her private thoughts with him. They were no longer . . . friends, and yet he had effortlessly drawn her out, somehow lulled her into that same deceptive sense of being safe in his company, all while she babbled away about her innermost feelings. Oh, he was good. She pressed her lips together, determined anew to treat him to silence.

After they performed their ablutions, he took her back to the camp and then down the path she had watched him follow earlier where she found their saddles and saddlebags, and a makeshift bed. One bed.

"Where are you going to sleep?" she blurted out. So much for her resolve on the silence issue. But how could she let this go unchallenged? It had to be a mistake. There was no possible way she could sleep with him.

"I am not going to let you out of my sight again," he said. "The only question is whether you will sleep next to me voluntarily, or if I need to tie you to me."

I would rather be tied to a tree. She almost suggested it.

"I did not sleep at all last night," he said, "and very

little the night before. I have no intention of ravishing
you in your sleep."

"I know that," she snapped. She knew very well that
ravishing was the last thing on his mind. There was no
longer any need for that pretense; she was simply his
prisoner and he wanted to make certain she stayed put.
It was her own actions she worried about, especially
after she fell asleep. She would have to do something to
make certain she did not curl up next to him during the
night, unconsciously seeking his heat and the myth of
his protection. That horrid scenario was much more
likely if she were tied to him, and the thought of having
her hands and feet bound alarmed her more than the
thought of sleeping next to him. She gritted her teeth. "I
do not need to be trussed up like a lamb for market."

"Good. I do not want to do anything that would
hurt you."

Their gazes met in an instant exchange of understanding that he had already done things that hurt her much
more deeply than any rope could. He looked away first
and busied himself by straightening the furs that formed
the base of their bed. She bit her lip and tried to decide
how best to handle this uncomfortable situation.

This was nothing new, she reminded herself. She had
slept next to him before, and she was so tired that she
would likely be asleep within moments. Perhaps this would
not be so bad if she could put a few saddlebags between
them. "Why are we so far away from the others?"

"When have you seen my men and me sleep in the
same place at the same time?" he asked, even as he
shook his head. "We spread out in case anyone should
attack us during the night. Distance offers more time
for a warning."

That explanation made sense. She knelt down on the
furs and the grass rose far above her, offering them as

much privacy as if they were within the walls of a chamber. It made her uneasy to be alone with him. "Maybe I should go sleep with Rami."

"He and the men will take turns standing guard tonight." He picked up the saddlebags that she had lined up in the middle of the bed and returned them to their place behind the saddles. "You will stay with me."

She gave the saddlebags a wistful look, even though she knew why he had stowed them away. They had taken up half the space on the bed. She sat down on the furs, and then carefully tucked her skirts and cloak around her legs, hoping that would restrict her movements. She made sure she was on the very edge of the furs, giving Dante as much room as possible, and then she lay back and rested her head on her saddle and closed her eyes.

The bed was surprisingly comfortable. The long grass provided a soft cushion beneath her. They had enough blankets and cloaks to ensure they stayed warm throughout the night, but those comforts were not enough to instantly lull her into sleep. Not until Dante was in his place and she could be certain that nothing untoward would happen. What if his claim that he wouldn't ravish her was another lie? He was a man, she was a woman, and everyone knew that most men were not all that particular about the women they slept with. She opened her eyes again.

The sun had sunk below the trees but there was still plenty of light to watch him prepare for bed. He unbuckled his sword belt, and then began to remove an astonishing number of weapons from an astonishing number of places: inside his sleeves, from straps around his arms, more on his legs and inside his boots, around his neck. He was a veritable fortress. At last he stacked the entire cache a good distance away from the bed.

"Are you not worried that your weapons will be too far away, should we come under an attack?"

He sat down and pulled his boots off. "I am more concerned about your proximity to my weapons."

Her eyes widened. "Do you really think I am a threat to you?"

"Anyone with a weapon is a threat," he said, as he settled next to her. He spread his cloak over both of them and then lay down. "I did not live to a ripe old age by taking chances."

He was hardly ancient, but there was no reason to challenge his opinion. Instead she tried to picture herself holding a knife to him, demanding he set her free. The idea was preposterous. He would have the weapon away from her before she could draw a breath. Then it occurred to her that he was deliberately making it more difficult for her to steal one of his weapons while he slept. Could she attack a sleeping, defenseless man if it meant a chance at freedom?

"I did not intend to give you ideas," he said, once again reading her thoughts. "However, should you ever manage to turn a weapon against me, you had best be prepared to use it without hesitation. You will never get a second chance."

She swallowed audibly and wished she had never asked about his weapons. Perhaps her life was not as safe in his hands as she had imagined. There was fear in her after all. "My father will pay a handsome reward if you take me to him in Wales."

The thought had come from nowhere, but she latched on to it like a lifeline. It was a lie, of course, one he pretended not to hear. At this point she had no idea if her father would even welcome her return, much less reward it. Baron Weston had done many things over the years to ensure her welfare, but she suffered no illusions that he would risk his position to protect her from the king, and probably not from the Segraves, either. Unless he wanted to betray his king, she was unmarriageable, which also meant she was worthless to him. A liability rather than an asset. A very dangerous liability. Baron Weston was a fair and just lord, but he would sacrifice her without hesitation for the greater good of his people.

"I am more valuable than you realize," she said, trying a different tack, pleased when that announcement got his attention.

He turned onto his side and angled his arm to prop up his head. His face was devoid of emotion, but one brow rose slightly. "Pray enlighten me, my lady."

"Do you know why Faulke Segrave wants to marry me?" she asked.

"Aye."

"An alliance with my father was only part of the reason," she said, certain he was unaware of Segrave's real reasons, yet hesitant to reveal them. Both her parents had warned against revealing her mother's heritage to anyone, but what would they expect her to do if it was no longer a secret? Segrave knew. It seemed obvious the king knew as well. Did Dante? "A marriage to me means much more than an alliance with my father."

"I know of your ties to the Welsh crown, if that is what you are trying to tell me."

"Oh." She had not expected the king to be so free with the information. "Then you know I am worth a large ransom to the Segraves or any number of Marcher barons. You could become a wealthy man."

"I am already a wealthy man."

"I did not realize assassins were paid so well that the promise of a rich reward would not prove tempting."

She also did not realize how insulting the words sounded until she heard them aloud.

His brows simply rose a little higher. "I eliminate traitors to the crown. Do you truly think I would become what I hunt?"

She had not thought of him that way, as a hunter, a predator. Yet that was his role and he was extremely good at his profession, if any of the stories about him were to be believed. Still, he hardly fit the tales that said he killed only for gold and his own bloodlust.

It was just her luck to be held hostage by a man reputed to be a greedy villain with no conscience, and yet he had no interest in wealth or rewards if it meant betraying his loyalty to the king. She supposed that made him an honorable man, in his own way. "You could say I escaped."

"You are grasping at straws."

He was right. She pressed her lips together and lowered her gaze.

"The king will never allow you to marry Segrave or any other man who could pose a threat to him in Wales, now or in the future," he said. "There is nowhere in Edward's kingdom that you can run to escape who you are, Avalene."

He was right, but that did not make the truth less painful. If only—

She cut that thought off before it could form. Wishes and dreams were now beyond her grasp. What she must concentrate on was what she needed to do to get through each day, hopefully no worse off than she was the day before. She forced herself to ask the question whose answer she dreaded most. "Am I to be imprisoned in the Tower?"

He was silent for a moment, and then he said, "I do not yet know your ultimate fate, but I have endured a great deal of trouble to bring you to London alive. If you are to be . . . confined, I doubt you will be mistreated."

The answer was both a relief and a disappointment. She had already pieced together that much on her own. "What will happen when we reach London?"

"You will stay with me until I have a chance to meet with Mordecai, one of Edward's advisers, the one who sent me on this mission." His mouth became a hard line as he studied her face, his eyes dark with intensity. "Once your fate is decided I intend to set sail for Italy, likely within a few weeks of our arrival in London. I have no plans to return to England, and the King's Assassin will cease to exist."

"I—I see," she murmured. Her battered heart plummeted. Here was the proof that she was nothing more to him than an assignment. He intended to abandon her to an unknown fate. He would sail away and leave her behind, probably in some damp, dark cell where she would rot her life away. She would never see him again. She would never see anyone again, save her jailers. Meanwhile, he would go on with his life and forget all about her. Just as her father had done.

The sound of her heartbeats was smothered by a cold sense of calm that started at her core and spread outward until every part of her felt numb. "Thank you for telling me."

She turned onto her side to face away from him and closed her eyes, feigning sleep until it finally overtook her.

16

❧

Revelations

In the midst of difficulties the truth will unveil itself in silence. When one world collapses, The Star will shine the light of Promise onto the next. The vision of hope survives all odds.

The numbness lingered the next day. She awoke wrapped in Dante's arms, just as she feared she would, but the cold calm in her veins insulated her from any embarrassment. She simply rolled away and rose from the bed without looking at him. It didn't take long to gather her cloak and walk to the main part of camp where her seat on the cook pot awaited.

No one spoke to her, although Rami watched her with a worried expression and twice seemed about to say something before he changed his mind. His silent offering of food to break her fast was rejected. The men ignored her completely until her horse was saddled and ready. Dante knelt next to the horse on one knee so she could use his other knee as a step to reach her saddle. She did so without her usual word of thanks.

The only thing that gave her pause was when he handed her the reins without explanation. Did they think she no longer contemplated escape? If so, they were sadly mistaken.

The countryside flowed past her in a blur of lush landscapes that left no more than faint impressions of greens and blues. Her thoughts were focused on entirely different scenery, the image of a chamber that looked remarkably like one of the cells in Coleway's dungeons, roughly hewn from the castle's stone foundations, cold, damp, windowless darkness. If a chamber such as this was her future, she wouldn't last the year.

She knew she should put more thought into an actual plan for escape, but there was still nowhere to run. Aside from being easy prey on the open road, where would she go?

She thought of the fairs at Coleway when people crowded into the castle from every corner of Lord Brunor's lands, the crush of crowds near the gates and in the streets of the village. Surely London would be that crowded all of the time. If she slipped off her horse and ran, it would not be so hard to become separated from her captors and be lost in the sea of humanity. She had to believe it was a possibility. Only she could not see what would happen beyond her initial escape. Where would she run to in the city? No one would give her sanctuary against the king, not even the Church.

A solution to that problem came to her midmorning, a solution so obvious, so simple, so *perfect* that she wondered why it hadn't occurred to her earlier. Avalene de Forshay could not seek sanctuary, but a woman unknown to anyone could do as she pleased. She would use a false name and concoct a plausible story that would explain why she was at loose ends in London.

She would be a poor knight's widow who had been turned out of her home by a cruel lord. Aye, she would tell this fantastical tale to the first kindly-looking person she came upon and beg them to help her.

Her skill with a needle and thread was exceptional. If

she could find someone who could direct her to the tailors' guilds, surely she could find a kindhearted seamstress willing to accept her as an apprentice. Surely someone would recognize her talent and take her in?

The firmer the plan became in her head, the lighter her mood turned. The future was not so bleak after all. It might not offer the comforts she had once assumed would always be hers, but compared to dying in prison, meager poverty would be a large step up in the world. It was not the life she was meant for, but she would make the best of whatever her new life offered her. She always did.

"Are you hungry?"

Dante now rode next to her whenever the road allowed, but this was the first time he had spoken to her since last night. She shook her head without looking at him.

They rode awhile longer in silence. Agnes was a nice name, very common, very competent sounding. Her dead husband would be Sir Percival, of course, but she could not decide if she would paint him as the most wonderful of men or the worst. The lord who turned her out would be the worst, she decided, while Sir Percival would wear the title of "wonderful" in her tragic tale. He would live on in her memory in all his chivalrous glory. Live on figuratively, that is, since he had so recently died a tragic death. A *painful,* tragic death. A *lingering,* painful, tragic death. Oh, how her poor beloved had suffered!

Her flights of fancy actually made her smile. Who knew she had such an entertaining imagination?

"Is there something wrong with you?"

She turned to look at Dante and her humor fled. The heat of the day had melted away some of her numbness. A tentative flash of pain rippled through her chest, testing the waters. She drew a deep breath and pushed it away. "Nay."

"Have you been in the sun too long?" he asked. There was a concerned look in his eyes. He must have orders to deliver his prisoner in good health. "Do you want a drink of water?"

"Nay."

"Why were you smiling?"

Because I was thinking of ways to describe your death to others. Come to think of it, you might have some good suggestions on the subject. Would you mind sharing the details of a few lingering, painful deaths? Her smile returned. "I was just thinking pleasant thoughts."

He looked dumbfounded. "About what?"

Apparently captives on their way to a lifetime of imprisonment were not expected to make the journey looking quite so cheerful. The last thing she needed was for him to suspect she was plotting an escape. She tried to think of something that would distract him from her odd behavior. "Are you going home to Venice, or are you from some other part of Italy?"

He continued to stare at her in silence, his suspicion clearly aroused.

She lowered her gaze and pretended great interest in untying the knot in her reins. It was a stupid question. None of her business. Why should he—

"I am going home."

Relief washed through her, but he still watched her with a wary eye. Keep him talking. "Why?"

"Do you remember the story I told you about my uncle," he asked, "the uncle who seized everything that my father owned when my parents died?"

"Aye." She remembered the tale, one she had dismissed as another of his lies.

"The story was not far from the truth, except that it was one of the king's advisers who took in my brother and me when we reached England, rather than your father. I also left out the fact that my uncle ordered my parents' deaths and I was never able to prove him guilty of the crimes. He died recently and I am returning to Venice to reclaim everything that he stole from us while he was alive."

Ah, so it was not to be the pleasant journey that she had imagined. She glanced over to find him gazing at some point on the horizon, his profile the same as the one she had so recently sighed over and admired, his expression suddenly unreadable. Why was he telling her about his family? More to the point, why did she want to know more? The need to keep him distracted was as good an excuse as any to keep him talking. "What were your parents like?"

Surprisingly, he told her. He spoke hesitantly at first, but soon the words began to flow freely. His father was a wealthy merchant who met his mother on one of his journeys to England. She was the youngest daughter of an English baron who was more interested in the rich dower Dante's father provided than the fact that his daughter would be wed to a dreaded foreigner. However, his mother had loved Venice and never felt any desire to return to England.

He made mention of his mother's preference for Venice several more times in slightly different ways, as if this were an important part of his stories. She could not understand its relevance and dismissed the oddity. She found herself drawn in to his childhood world as he told her things that made her feel as if she knew his parents personally.

And then he began to tell her about Venice. He painted such vivid pictures with his words that she could almost hear the water rippling through the canals and feel the Adriatic breezes that cooled the city. She found herself reluctantly fascinated by the tales of a land so vastly different from her own, yearning to hear more about a city she would never see.

The more he talked, the harder it was to remember that they would soon be parted, that he intended to abandon her in London. He even spoke as if they would see the sights of Venice together, a mistake that eventually ended the tales of Venice. It happened while he described one of the more exotic foods of his homeland, one made of *moscardino*, a sea creature that sounded truly gruesome. When she made a face, he laughed and said she would have to try the dish before she decided it was not to her liking.

Their gazes met as they had the previous night and she saw the same wariness in his eyes, as if he were waiting for her to correct his mistake. She would never eat *moscardino*, never see his city, never marvel over its riches. The look he gave her made her think he might be starting to feel guilty about his role in her undeserved fate. And that led her thoughts right back to what awaited her in London. The Tower, or a dangerous escape to an uncertain life.

As if he had guessed the direction of her thoughts, he abruptly changed the subject. He declared that he was tired of monopolizing the conversation and started asking questions about her family. He wanted to know more about her life at Coleway and the people who had been a part of it, who and what she liked and disliked, how she spent her days. She tried to answer his questions with as few words as possible. The source of his interest remained a mystery and she distrusted his motives for being so friendly, so . . . so much like Sir Percival.

However, there was nothing better to do with her time and it was easier to answer his questions than listen to him pester her until she provided the details. Soon she would never be able to talk this freely with anyone about her life, whether she was in prison or living under a false name as the widow Agnes. He seemed especially interested in stories about Coleway's steward, and she quickly warmed to the tales of John's manipulations and deceits. What surprised her most was whenever he laughed at one of her stories or made some jest. One did not expect a sense of humor in an assassin. She had certainly never expected to be laughing *with* him again.

Her friendly behavior toward him was a ploy, of course, a deception to keep him from suspecting she had a plan to escape. At least, that's what she told herself. Their conversations also kept her mind occupied with far less bleak thoughts. By unspoken agreement they both avoided any subject that might lead toward talk of his time at Coleway, or Faulke Segrave, or her fate once he abandoned her. Surprisingly, she had little trouble finding subject matter. Their conversations were interesting yet cautious, a careful dance marked by frequent glances to gauge their partner's reactions.

Her prayer that she would begin to find him repulsive went unanswered. Instead she caught herself marveling that she was chatting so effortlessly with her enemy, the man who had hurt her, a man rumored to have murdered scores of people. She really *should* fear him, but it was becoming pathetically obvious that she enjoyed his company. He was not some crazed killer. He was simply a man. An excessively handsome man who could be every bit as charming as Sir Percival, when he put his mind to it.

She was a little surprised when they made camp for the night in yet another deer-trampled meadow. It didn't seem possible that the day was already spent and yet the lengthening shadows told a different story. Their conversation continued to flow easily enough from the time they ate their meal until they were ready for bed, but there was a new note to the underlying strain, as if they both realized their false camaraderie must soon end.

Again she settled onto the very edge of the furs and turned away from him as he went through the ritual of removing his weapons. Eventually she heard him lie down next to her and she closed her eyes, wishing fervently for sleep to claim her. Her breath caught in her throat when she felt his hand on her shoulder, and then he insistently pulled on her arm until she rolled onto her back.

Looming above her, his eyes were intense. "Tell me about your plan to escape."

"W-what?"

He waited.

She tried to inject just the right tone of affronted innocence into her voice. "I have no plan to escape."

He shook his head. "Last night you were full of suggestions and bribes to avoid your fate in London, and I explained why they were impossible. Then when I suggested the most logical alternative, you turned your back on me and went to sleep.

"This morning you were wrapped again in your anger, but then you smiled and asked me about Venice. It finally occurred to me that my suggestion last night might have been too subtle, that you had only just realized what I meant. So today I cast the bait in more obvious ways and still it remains untouched." He scowled down at her. "And that means I was wrong about your smile. The only other explanation is that you have come up with some plan for escape that you think can work."

Oh, good Lord, his mind was devious. And he was exactly right. But she only understood half of what he said. "What bait?"

"Venice, of course," he said dismissively. "Now, tell

me your plan. I do not want you to get hurt, and whatever escape plan you have come up with will only put yourself in danger. It definitely will not succeed, but you could be injured in the course of its failure."

"Venice is bait for what?"

A crease appeared between his brows. "It was just a suggestion, one that is apparently of no interest."

She gritted her teeth. "I would have to be aware of a suggestion before it would lack interest."

"Are you truly unaware of what I offered?"

"I am truly unaware." She carefully enunciated each word. "What are you talking about?"

"Venice," he said again, now looking bewildered. "I thought you understood. Edward will never allow you to marry anyone who will be a threat to him in Wales. He does not want you anywhere near England or Wales. Soon I will cease to have any interest in Edward's politics. I will be half a world away in Venice, and I have no plans to return to England."

"Aye, you told me that last night." Her voice sounded like it was coming from very far away. She was beginning to suspect what he was going to tell her. It made no sense. She was mistaken. This was another—

"Would you like to come with me?"

"What?" She all but screeched the word. She clapped a hand over her mouth as she sat up, and then managed to ask in a much quieter voice, "What are you talking about?"

"Venice is a very long way from England," he said, speaking in slow, measured tones. It sounded as if he were trying to explain a very simple concept to a child. "As long as no one knows where to find you, exile to Venice would accomplish the same goal as imprisonment in the Tower. 'Tis possible you would be allowed to sail with me."

Her breath caught in her throat and her heartbeat became erratic. Speech was beyond her. She was as stunned as when the lightning bolt had almost killed her. *This* was the bait he had been casting all day? How had she missed it?

"Of course, I would have to swear that you would disappear as completely as if you had been imprisoned in the Tower, provide assurances that you would never again be a threat to the king." His eyes were fathomless pools of green, as compelling and hypnotic as any predator's. He was her enemy, and yet he was offering her an escape. "No one would know you in Venice. You could begin a new life there."

He expected some sort of response; that much was obvious in his expression, but she couldn't trust anything she might say. She stared at his mouth, certain she had heard him wrong. His offer sounded too much like her plan to start a new life in London. How had he known? This was some new deceit, some new lie. Was he hoping to trick her into revealing her plan?

His gaze narrowed. "You don't believe me?"

"Of course not." How could that even be a question in his mind?

"If I *were* telling the truth, would you go with me to Venice?" He watched her carefully, as if her answer were of vital importance.

Surely there was a trap awaiting her, but would it spring forth with the lie or the truth? *Yes* was the only sensible answer. Who in their right mind would say *no*? However, *yes* could confirm his suspicion that she was planning an escape of the same nature. *No* could just as easily confirm the same suspicion. Why would she want to stay in England to rot in prison?

"Is the choice really so difficult?" he asked in a soft voice, his eyes fierce.

"I am trying to decide why you would even ask the question." She shook her head and struggled to sound casual. "You obviously have some purpose in mind. Does it have something to do with your notion that I have a grand plan to escape? Or, do you think I will be more malleable on the journey to prison if you make me believe there is some hope of a reprieve?"

"I deserve that," he murmured, as a crease formed between his brows. "Is it really so hard to believe that I would want to keep you with me?"

"Aye." She made an unladylike sound. Did he really think her so gullible?

"My feelings for you have not changed."

She wasn't certain what his feelings for her were in the first place. Guilt? He had to know that she would not survive long in a dungeon, just as he knew she had done nothing to earn such a punishment. Did he intend to right that wrong, defend her from whatever false charges Edward would use to imprison her? What if he were serious about taking her to Italy? "The king would never agree to such a plan."

"'Tis possible I can make Edward's adviser see the logic of the idea." He rolled onto his back and stacked his hands behind his head to look up at her. "I can be persuasive, when I wish to be."

Oh, she knew that fact all too well. Indeed, she could provide her own testament to his skills at persuasion. Or was this another of his jests? Would his lips suddenly curve into a smile as he laughed at her gullibility? He had never struck her as an intentionally cruel man, but there was still much she did not know about him. She could not allow herself to hope until she was certain this was not another lie.

"Why?" she whispered. "Why would you do such a thing for me?"

"I should think the reasons are obvious."

She gave him a skeptical look. She refused to believe he had any feelings for her in particular that any woman in general could not bestir in equal measure. "You do not have the sort of reputation that lends itself to gallantry toward women."

"My reasons have nothing to do with gallantry," he agreed. "Indeed, they are entirely selfish."

She bit her lower lip and tried to think what other obvious reasons there might be. Nothing obvious or even obscure came to mind. Why was he staring at her mouth?

"You think me strange," she pointed out, deciding it was time for brutal honesty. "And I know you only pretended to . . . like me as part of your deception."

"I think you are unusual," he corrected. "Indeed, you are unlike anyone I have ever known, and I know my fair share of unusual people." He reached out to smooth a loose tendril of hair near her temple, and then his fingers slowly, purposely, trailed along her cheek until her lashes lowered involuntarily and she shivered. "You never react to anything as I think you will or as I know you should. I am a dangerous man, Avalene. Never forget that."

"As if I could," she muttered. One casual touch and her soft, silly heart had fluttered to life again. Anger over his betrayal was her last defense, the last solid wall around her battered heart. That wall would never survive if he turned his charm loose upon her again in full force, if he actually meant to rescue her from the Tower. She spoke as much to herself as to him. "I would bargain with the Devil himself to avoid spending the rest of my life in a prison."

"Hm. Now I am akin to the Devil," he mused. "And I

cannot decide if I am flattered or insulted that you might find my company preferable to prison."

His casual dismissal of her emotions hurt. She was tired of him finding humor in her humiliation, tired of pretending she felt nothing. "You know well enough that I found your company preferable to any other. Just because your feelings for me were not real does not mean that mine were false. I made no mystery of how I felt about you."

He went very still. "Your preference was for a man who does not exist."

"He is before me now," she said, waving her hand toward him. "When I look at you, I still see Sir Percival. When you speak, I hear his voice. I cannot separate Dante Chiavari from Sir Percival in my mind. You are not Sir Percival, and yet you are. Every time I look at you I see the man that I—"

Oh, she would not say those words. They were not true. She had fallen in love with Sir Percival. In that regard, he was absolutely right; *that* man did not exist. *This* man had used her, and felt no regret at all over his actions.

On the other hand, he had also saved her from the steward, and then saved her from a treasonous marriage to Faulke Segrave, and now he was offering to save her from the Tower. He was her champion, and then he was her enemy, and now he offered to be her champion again. Little wonder he had her so confused. Her thoughts were spinning tangled webs faster than her mind could sort through them.

"I am not the sort of man you seem to think I am," he said in a quiet voice. "I am no chivalrous, high-minded knight. I am not even an honorable one."

She studied his face in the fading light and wondered if she only imagined the regret in his voice, even a trace

285

of wistfulness. That was silly. He was the most self-assured man she had ever met, even when he was wrong.

"No matter what you call yourself, no matter what you have done, you are an honorable man in your own way. Why else would you make me such an offer?" That had to be what this was all about. He felt guilty because he was helping imprison an innocent woman. Perhaps his code of honor was not so different from Sir Percival's as she had imagined. Or perhaps this was still some bizarre part of his deception. "No matter your reasons, you cannot expect me to forgive you for deceiving me and making light of my feelings."

He sat up and leaned closer until his warm breath fanned across her face and brought with it his intoxicating scent. She began to feel light-headed. "I would never purposely make light of your feelings, Avalene. If I have done so inadvertently, you have my apology."

"I was not asking for an apology." She sat up straighter and tried to lean away from him without being obvious about it, holding herself stiff. She felt exposed and foolish for having brought up her traitorous feelings in the first place. What was she thinking?

"There is one other thing you are wrong about," he said, his face still so close to hers that she had trouble concentrating on his words rather than the enticing shape of his mouth as he made them. "My attraction to you was not part of the deception. That was the one thing I never lied to you about."

Oh, no. No, no, no. She shook her head, even as she felt the first cracks forming in the last wall. This was not good. "You lied to me from the moment we met. About everything."

"I *wanted* you from the moment we met," he said, "but my ardor cooled each time you called me 'Percival.' I wanted to hear *my* name on your lips. Can you imagine your feelings if I kissed you, and then called you . . . Jane?"

She shook her head, only because it seemed to be the expected thing to do. This was some fevered imagining on her part. Perhaps he had drugged her again.

"I was certain you would be horrified once you learned my true identity." He rubbed his thumb across her lower lip, sending a fresh set of shivers through her. How did he *do* that? "Is it possible you would still come to me willingly, knowing who I really am, knowing I lied to you? How can I still be someone honorable in your eyes?"

"Stop this," she whispered. She rolled her lower lip between her teeth to stop the tingling sensation his touch had ignited, but she did not turn away. "I cannot think straight when you make me feel this way."

"What way?" he asked, as his thumb stroked her chin.

Safe, secure . . . seduced. The words popped into her head unbidden, but they were the truth. She had a formidable reputation for being the most clearheaded, sensible woman among all those she knew. Suddenly she was the most gullible girl ever born. All he had to do was touch her and every rational thought left her head. Well, not every rational thought. "Is this another of your deceptions?"

He shook his head even as his eyes burned with sincerity. "There are endless reasons why I should leave you alone and let you believe my desire was an act, but I know the thought that I deceived you in that way hurts you." He lifted his hand and stroked the backs of his fingers across her cheek. "I do not like to hurt you, Avalene."

Some shred of self-preservation kicked in and she leaned farther away from him. "Why should you leave me alone?"

"Because you are an innocent," he said, "and I am not. Just knowing me will corrupt you, damage your soul in ways you cannot imagine. If I were a truly honorable, compassionate man, I would walk away from you." He placed his fingers over her lips before she could argue. "But I am a selfish man, and I want you too much to let you go. I am yours, if you want me."

Before she could think of anything to say to that astonishing announcement, he lowered his head and kissed her, gently at first, and then with more insistence.

She had almost forgotten how good he tasted until his mouth touched hers, just as she had forgotten about the strange melting sensation. His tongue glided over the seam of her lips and her heart turned traitor. He effortlessly opened her to his seduction, using all of his skill to make her forget everything but his kisses as her body both yielded and strained toward him at the same time. The fabric of his tunic felt soft against her palms, but his chest was the familiar wall of warm stone, the only solid thing to cling to, the only thing that kept her from falling under a wave of desire so strong it made her heart ache.

This is what she had missed, what she had mourned when she had learned of his betrayal; this sense of rightness, the feeling that everything was perfect so long as she remained in his arms. She wanted to lose herself in the heady emotions. However, this time her sensible side refused to be silenced. Reality intruded all too quickly.

He was not safe, and this was madness. She forced herself to turn her head away and then shivered when he trailed a line of kisses down her neck. "This is not right."

"I know." He placed his lips over a pulse point on her neck and gently suckled.

She had trouble maintaining her train of thought. "I—I do not want this."

"Aye, you do."

"Nay, stop. Please." She pushed against his shoulders until he stopped kissing her. He lifted his head and looked down at her, his eyes watchful as she spoke. "I cannot do this again. I know you are lying to me."

His smile was sad. "You have little reason to trust me, but in this I am telling the truth. I want you, and I know you want me, too. Will you deny it?"

She wished she could. "You know I cannot."

He studied her face. "Is that really such a bad thing?"

"Aye." She could be sucked under by his spell again to drown in all the emotions he stirred inside her. How easy it would be to pretend that he felt something special for her. But she could not survive it if he made her believe his lies again, if she allowed herself to hope and it all turned out to be another deception.

"Will you make me one promise? A promise that you will not break, no matter what?" The words sounded foolish even to her own ears. She was asking an accomplished liar not to lie. Her heart rate accelerated. *Stupid, stupid, stupid.*

His expression turned wary. "That depends upon the promise."

She drew an unsteady breath. "Promise that you will not give me false hope."

"What do you mean?"

Ah, the explanation. This should be roundly humiliating. She reached out and placed her fingertips on his lips, as much to enjoy the sensation of touching him as to prevent him from interrupting her. "When you kiss me, I forget what is right and wrong. You make me forget what a good liar you are. 'Tis obvious you can still seduce me. I have little will to resist you. And yet you claim that you do not want to hurt me. If that is true, then do not tell me lies about your feelings for me. Do not make me hope for a future that can never be. Swear that you will not make me any promises that you cannot keep."

He took her hand from his lips and turned it over to press a kiss into her palm. "*Gesù*, I do not deserve you, but you have my word. I will not make any false promises."

She tried to smile. "I am not so grand a prize, but you will not have to put up with me for long."

"What do you mean?"

"I mean that you do not have to lie about taking me to Italy." It was hard to keep her voice steady. "I understand that you must do your duty and turn me over to the king. Perhaps Segrave is wrong about the Tower. Who knows? Rather than prison, I may be allowed to live at court with all the fine lords and ladies." *When hell freezes over.*

He took her face between his hands and then tilted her head back, forcing her to look up at him. Above him the sky was a luminescent shade of indigo blue, casting him into silhouette against a blanket of emerging stars. "You have my promise that I will never allow anyone to imprison you."

She tried to shake her head but he would not allow it.

"You have my promise that you do not have to barter your honor for your freedom to leave England with me. You have my promise that no matter what does or does not happen between us, I will take you to Italy and I will take care of you."

She tried to find the lie in his eyes, but saw only fierce determination. Was it possible he was telling the truth? Could she actually trust him?

Impossible.

She struggled to make her voice sound skeptical rather than breathless. "You would still take me to Italy if I refused you?"

"Aye," he said, without a moment's hesitation. The sureness of his response stunned her.

"Why?" she asked again. "Why would you go to so much trouble, so much risk for me?"

He needed time to think that over. At last he said, "Fate has taken away much in my life. You are a gift I did not expect but one I will selfishly take, even if there is a price I must eventually pay for my greed. You are worth the consequences, Avalene."

He thought she was a gift?

"I intend to court you," he warned, "in ways that are far beyond the bounds of what is proper. I will leave you chaste if that is your wish, but I will also take advantage of every opportunity to seduce you, now that I know you still want me."

"I cannot trust you again so easily," she warned, while her heart raced. She would never be able to resist such a courtship. She pulled away from him a little. "I have not forgotten your . . . deception."

"I had my orders," he said simply. "If I had not arrived when I did, if the real Sir Percival had entered Coleway while you were still there, you would likely be wed to the steward by now. Even if the real Percival managed to take you away from Coleway, he intended all along to turn you over to the Segraves and you would have found yourself wed to a traitor."

"Segrave told me the same story," she said, with a defeated sigh. "But surely you can understand my . . . anger over the complete success of your deception. You fooled me so easily, how can I ever again trust you without question? I never doubted you for an instant as Sir Percival. I can never trust you for an instant as Dante Chiavari."

"I lied to you about my identity," he admitted, "but I did not betray your trust in my intentions nor did I deceive you in the ways that matter most. From the start I have protected you, kept you safe from your enemies and the enemies of the king. The only pretense about my feelings for you is that I have done my best to disguise their depths. When Segrave captured you—"

His mouth became a hard line and he had to take a deep breath before he continued. "You were right about me last night, when you compared what I do to the job of an executioner. I had never viewed it in quite that light before, but it is an appropriate analogy. I do not kill for sport or bloodlust, but when Segrave touched you, when he spoke so crudely of his plans to bed you, I wanted to kill him where he stood."

"*Did* you kill him?" she whispered. Despite his claims otherwise, he'd had the perfect opportunity when they were all disabled by the poison.

He shook his head. "Segrave has not yet committed outright treason, and the king wishes him to live. I gave my word that he would not die by my hand, although it is a promise I have already come to regret. Just the thought of you as his wife, that he has any rights where you are concerned . . . Segrave is luckier than he knows to still be alive."

She took a moment to absorb the possibility that he was jealous.

"I will not let him have you," he vowed. "I will do everything within my power to make you mine. If time is what it will take to regain your trust, you will have it. What else will it take to restore your faith in me?"

What else, indeed? Was it even possible to turn back time, to return her heart to a place where her trust in him was absolute? Was anything he said true, or was all of it true?

The voice of reason laughed at her yearnings. This was how he had deceived her in the first place, by playing upon her own weakness for him. He made her fall in love with a lie. She couldn't risk making the same mistakes all over again, but, oh, how she wanted to.

"I do not know what to say." She gave a mirthless laugh. "I do not even know what to feel. My whole world is turned backward."

"You do not have to say anything for now." There was a trace of disappointment in his voice, but he cupped his hand behind her head and pressed a gentle kiss to her forehead. "We are nearly two days from London, and then we have at least a fortnight before my ship sets sail. You have time to think through my offer. You have even more time to decide if I am worthy of your forgiveness and what I must do to regain your trust."

She had no idea how to answer, and wisely remained silent.

"We will be on the road early again tomorrow morning. We should both try to get some sleep."

All she could do was nod, suddenly exhausted, overwhelmed by all he had told her. She did not resist when he urged her to lie down again, or when he tucked their cloaks around them, or even when he drew her closer. She lay in his arms without protest, his embrace inescapable and yet somehow comforting.

After a long time, she felt the tension in his arms begin to ease and her own body began to relax as well. Finally she drifted into a restless slumber, not truly asleep, but never fully awake. She was certain the nightmares would revisit her. They always did when she was particularly upset about something. This certainly qualified as "something." Instead she dreamed of Sir Percival, and then she dreamed of Dante, and then he became Sir Percival again.

Sometime during the night the two men became one. She wasn't entirely certain what that meant.

17

Choices

Marriage or murder, mistress or nun, the choices lie before you. The Lovers must choose the sacred or profane, and all choices have consequences.

The weather gave Avalene plenty of time to think the next day. The rain started again before dawn, an unpleasant but effective way to ensure they had an early start to the day. They quickly packed up the camp and then rode single file along the muddy road, which gave her little opportunity to speak with anyone. That suited her for a time. The tightness in her chest began to ease as the hours passed, and yet the unwelcome voice of reason refused to be swayed.

Dante's amazing declarations of the night before were too good to be true. She knew that. And yet she could not think of any reasons why he would tell such monstrous lies. Her thoughts grew more and more tangled, to the point that she would have preferred the distraction of conversation.

By midafternoon both the weather and Dante obliged her wishes when the sun reappeared and the road dried enough for them to ride side by side. At first she was apprehensive, almost shy in his company, but mostly they spoke of inconsequential things.

"Will you miss Coleway?"

She pursed her lips as she considered her answer. "I am not sorry to be away from John, but I will miss some of the people."

They had already talked about her childhood and his, and events that had occurred in their lives before they met. They also spoke about things that took place in the immediate present, such as speculation about a fortress they passed where the fieldstones were laid out on a hillside to form a gigantic cross, and then there was a thorough discussion of the weather. She could tell that he was deliberately avoiding anything that might lead to talk of his deception or speculation about their future. It was midafternoon and she was tired of avoiding the subjects.

"I'm not sorry to be away from the Segraves, either," she said, "but I am worried they will lay siege to my father's fortress. Faulke threatened as much, if I tried to cause trouble. I suppose he was hoping to ensure that I would be agreeable when we stood before a priest, but I do not think it is an idle threat. If he and I do not marry—"

"You will not marry him," Dante said in a clipped voice. "As for a siege, the Segraves would be fools to deplete their ranks when they may soon face the king's armies. Faulke Segrave does not strike me as a fool. 'Tis an unlikely outcome."

She wished she could be as certain.

"What are you thinking?"

She looked up at him, startled. "Pardon me?"

"I know that look." His gaze narrowed as he studied her face and she had to admit the effect was forbidding. "Do not ever think that marriage to Segrave would help your father in any way. Do not think that staying with me will be a betrayal to your family. The king placed you in my care, and your father and Segrave are both the king's vassals. You are exactly where you are supposed to be."

She blinked very slowly as his words struck home. He was right. Faulke Segrave's wishes no longer mattered, nor did those of her father. The king's word was law. She *was* exactly where she was supposed to be. If she were entirely honest with herself, she was exactly where she *wanted* to be.

"What now?" Dante asked. His stern expression had faded to a mixture of concern and exasperation.

She couldn't tell him. She wasn't certain how to put it into words. Instead she smiled and said, "Tell me more about Venice."

He looked at her for a long time, and then the corners of his mouth curved into an answering smile and he did as she asked.

He did not ask her to declare herself outright, but they both knew that she had decided to go with him to Italy, just as they both knew it had never really been much of a choice. She could not stay in England. No matter his reasons, he was offering her freedom; the sunlit delights of Venice versus the dark eternity of the Tower. The decision was a simple one.

This time she listened closely to his descriptions of Venice. There was a difference to hearing tales of a city when there was the possibility that you might actually see it someday soon. She asked endless questions about the city that suddenly loomed in her future. He patiently answered each one.

Eventually she suspected his endless stories were told to keep her mind from wandering toward other worries. Indeed, she found plenty of reasons to fret during their infrequent silences. Despite her decision, so much was still in turmoil: her life, her heart, her future. She had been raised to obey the wishes of her family without question, to expect marriage and a family of her own. Everything she contemplated with Dante went against those edicts. Could she really live in sin with a man for the rest of her life? What would happen when he tired of her?

Those were the questions that had occupied the majority of her thoughts until late afternoon when they rode single file up a steep embankment where rain had washed deep ruts into the hillside. He had told her to wait at the base of the hill until he made certain the footing was solid and she watched until he reined in his horse at the top of the rise. Eventually he turned to look down at her and flashed a smile that made her heart skip a beat, and then he beckoned her toward him with a crook of his finger.

The gesture shouldn't have been anything momentous. He was simply signaling to her that the footing was safe. But that was the moment she cut the last of her ties to her old life, the ties to all of the old rules that kept her from moving forward. He was calling her to a new life with new rules. She was ready to join him.

A life with Dante might last a day, or a month, or many years, but there was no longer any doubt that her future included him, no matter the circumstances, no matter the consequences. For the first time in her life she was going to do exactly as she pleased, consequences be damned. Even if they rode through the gates of London and he took her straight to the Tower, she would not regret the decision to let herself hope. He could be standing at the gates of Hell and beckoning her toward him, and she would willingly follow. She no longer had a choice. She had fallen in love with Sir Percival. She was still in love with Dante Chiavari.

Rather than dwell on all the things that could go wrong with her decision, she allowed herself to consider, just for a few moments, what their future together might be like if everything went right. London would be but one adventure. She could not imagine this experience with anyone else at her side. Once they reached Venice, he spoke as if he intended to live with her. She would stay by his side for as long as he wanted her.

She studied each individual feature of his face as he told her something about the docks in London, her gaze lingering, memorizing the arch of his brows, the straight line of his nose, the square line of his jaw. The way he smiled at her every so often made her certain her cow-eyed expression must look silly to him. She didn't care. She had this time with him, and, for the time being, he was hers.

"You will not see those parts of London."

What was that? She had missed something. "What parts?"

"The docks and the stews. They are not safe places for gentlewomen." He pushed a lock of hair off his forehead and looked toward the horizon. "Unfortunately, I can say the same about most of London, where you are concerned. The fewer who know of your presence there, the better."

"Surely you will have to tell the king," she pointed out. It was a sobering thought. "Edward may well deny your request, and you will be obliged to surrender me to his custody. As my father's liege lord, he has the right to appoint himself my guardian."

"I will not surrender you to anyone."

The things he said never ceased to astonish her. She shook her head. "You would defy the king of England?"

"Aye." He easily read the disbelief on her face. "I will never again allow anyone to take you from me."

The look in his eyes was intense. He meant what he said. She smiled and attempted to lighten the mood. "If I should ever again be in need of rescue, I would request that you not use poison. My head and stomach ached all the next day."

"And I would request that you not do anything that would purposely put yourself in need of rescue." He searched her face for something, but there was nothing to find but agreement. She had no intention of doing anything stupid, but his next words managed to startle her yet again. "I will not always be . . . rational where your safety is concerned. I cannot guarantee that I will remain levelheaded if I discover you are in danger. When I found you with the Segraves, I very nearly made mistakes that would have gotten us both killed. My life now depends upon yours."

It took her a moment to realize what he was really saying, and even less time to dismiss it.

"I wish there were some way to *make* you believe me, to make you trust me again." Apparently he was becoming an expert at reading her expressions.

"I do believe you," she said. "I trust you to keep me safe."

"Aye," he agreed, "but you do not believe that I am in love with you."

Shock and astonishment were too tame. No, the things he said left her speechless.

"Surely you guessed," he said. His wry smile belied the careful look in his eyes. "Or are all men so besotted in your presence that you no longer recognize the ailment?"

"Men are never besotted in my presence," she muttered, retreating into disbelief while that fickle fellow,

Hope, fluttered around her heart without permission, searching for a way in.

"*Gesù*, Avalene, you are dangerously unaware of your appeal to men. Has *no one* ever told you how beautiful you are?"

She rolled her eyes. Aside from her parents, who were expected to say such things, no one else had ever called her beautiful.

Still, there seemed to be little reason for him to lie at this point. She had admitted that he could seduce her, that he would not have to force her to his bed, and yet he continued to make these fantastical statements. What if he really was in love with her?

Once again he seemed to read her mind and provided the answer. "I have fallen under your spell, my lady. I cannot imagine living my life without you. Those would be the most obvious reasons why I want to take you with me to Venice."

Hope began to pound its fist against her chest. "What are the other reasons?"

"Will you believe me if I tell you?"

"I—" She decided on honesty. "I do not know."

"Fair enough," he reluctantly conceded, although he did not immediately continue. His hand swept out to indicate the hillsides that surrounded them. "This is not the setting I envisioned for this conversation. I had hoped for a candlelit chamber with a few goblets of wine at hand to fortify my courage."

He did not look particularly fearful. The lock of hair had fallen across his forehead again, framing his handsome face. A slight smile emphasized the strong line of his jaw and his expression would have reeked of self-confidence at any other time, but the smile did not warm his eyes; they were a piercing shade of green, alert and watchful. "I cannot imagine you afraid of anything."

He gave a mirthless laugh. "I have spent the whole of my life controlling my emotions and desires. They are potent weapons against a man in my profession. Now I must hand you these weapons and lay bare my neck, so to speak. I would rather face all of the Segraves unarmed. At least then I would know what I was about."

Her back stiffened. "You do not have to tell me anything against your will, but whatever you confide I will not repeat."

"I doubt anyone would believe you if you did," he murmured. "Which is yet another reason why I want you with me. I never speak this freely with anyone else. You have some mysterious power that puts me at ease."

"Is that why you were being so . . . talkative the past few days? Telling me about Venice and London?"

"Partly," he said, seeming to consider his words. "I wanted to tell you about my homeland, make it a real place to you. A place you would want to go. I also wanted to hear more about your life before I met you. My curiosity about you is insatiable, it seems."

"I feel the same," she admitted. She didn't know if it was the ease with which she had spoken to him all day, or the fact that her heart was once again ready to take up residence on her sleeve, but she actually *wanted* to reveal more of her feelings to him.

No, she just wanted to gauge his reactions, to find the lie. Didn't she?

She decided to tell him a little more of the truth to see where it led to. "I never spend this much time in idle conversation with anyone else. Not willingly. Definitely, I never tell them as much as I have already shared with you. Most people bore or annoy me with their chatter. I can never imagine being bored by you."

"You see how well matched we are?" He smiled at

her, the smile that made her bones melt. "You are the only person I know who finds me so interesting."

He was beginning to make her believe and that frightened her almost as much as the Tower. "I wonder how you can find *me* interesting. Until you came into my life, my days were so normal they were dull. My whole existence was dull. No one found me the least bit out of the ordinary."

"I doubt that," he said. "I would have found you just as remarkable then as I do now. You will always be a source of fascination for me."

Always? She wondered if that word held the same meaning for him as it did for her. How could they be together "always"? "You realize that the king has most likely approved my betrothal to Faulke Segrave by this time?"

"Where did that come from?" he asked with a sudden scowl.

"You said 'always' as if you plan to . . . be with me for quite a while." She lowered her gaze and brushed at a spot of dirt on her skirts. Good-bye, hope. "Segrave is convinced the king will approve the betrothal, in part as a means to keep me from marrying anyone else. I could never be more to you than . . . than . . ."

His grip on the reins tightened enough that his horse tossed its head. "You can be everything to me, Avalene. I do not need a priest's blessing to know that you are mine. I have never felt this way about another woman, and I know that I never will again. You are all that I need. Am I enough for you?"

She could not help but smile. "What a foolish question."

The intensity in his eyes did not lighten. "I have declared my love for you, declared my fondest hope that you will let me care for you for the rest of your life. All you have said is that you doubt the truth of my words. Where do I stand, Avalene? Am I like Segrave, simply a means to escape a less pleasant fate?"

"You are not," she retorted. Was it possible that he doubted her feelings as much as she doubted his? Didn't he understand the impossibility of what he was asking her to believe? She stared at the perfect lines of his face, bewildered that he could look at her and find something even a fraction as desirable. "You are the fate that I am afraid to let myself hope will be mine."

The stiff set of his shoulders relaxed. "When I heard Segrave reveal my deception and saw that you believed him, I was certain you would never again look at me the way you are looking at me right now. I should have known your reaction would be the exact opposite of what I expected." He reached out to brush the backs of his fingers across her cheek. "There really is something wrong with you, *cara*. Whatever it is, I pray that you are never cured."

"You truly do not care that I am legally bound to another man?"

"Words on paper mean nothing," he told her. "You will be mine in every other way."

Whatever he saw in her face made him release a sigh of resignation.

"I cannot promise that Segrave will break your betrothal," he said, "but I will do everything in my power to ensure he renounces you before we leave England. I want you for my wife, Avalene."

Hope and happiness bloomed inside her, even though the doubts were still there. She had never met another man who appealed to her in so many ways. Was it truly possible that he viewed her the same way? She bit her lower lip and tried to imagine a lifetime with Dante.

"Oh, you should not have done that."

Before she could think to ask what he meant, before she could think at all, he reached over and plucked her from her saddle. When she was settled on his lap, he turned her face to his and kissed her, not a gentle kiss this time, but one that spoke of possession. She gave herself over to the moment and this time her thoughts were silenced. There was nothing inside her that said this was wrong. Some elemental part of her knew it was right, that he was the right man for her. The only man for her.

She drew back just enough to look into his eyes. "Do you really think I will be allowed to go to Italy?"

"No matter what happens, I am not leaving England without you." Something dark flickered in his gaze. Determination. "This I promise."

He was telling her the truth. The longer she looked into his eyes, the more she could feel it in her very soul. No matter what else he had lied to her about in the past, this much was true. This amazing man loved her.

She leaned forward and touched her lips to his, surrendering at last without hesitation. His mouth slanted over hers with a fierceness that sent heat racing through her and she looped her arms around his neck to hold him closer. The kiss never seemed to end, but the edge of hunger gradually eased and his hold on her gentled. She didn't think it possible, but his slow, deep kisses turned more erotic. He did things to her mouth that made her whole body tremble.

Just when she began to wonder how far he intended to take their kisses, she felt his body go suddenly rigid and he lifted his head. She smiled up at him but the smile faded as she heard the sound of approaching hoofbeats. The haze of lust disappeared entirely as Armand rode alongside them and then paced his horse to theirs.

"There is a rider on the ridge to our right, my lord. He has followed us for most of an hour."

She started to look toward the ridge but Dante placed his hand along the side of her face in what probably looked like a casual caress. He made certain she could not turn her head and neither man looked toward the potential danger.

"There were no reports of bandits in this area," Dante said to Armand, although his gaze remained on Avalene.

"He carries a shield with no markings and looks well armed." Armand shook his head. "'Tis near impossible the Segraves could have caught up with us this quickly. My guess is mercenaries, likely between postings and looking for opportunity. The valley narrows ahead and we will be forced to ride single file. The passage would be an ideal place for a larger force to lie in wait."

Tension radiated from Dante's body but he said nothing more. Armand continued to ride alongside them, also silent. She could almost hear the men thinking through plans and strategies.

"We will set camp beneath the trees ahead," Dante said at last. "Make certain Rami knows he must act as if nothing is amiss."

Armand spurred his horse forward to where Rami rode point and then slowed again to talk to the boy. She realized with a jolt of surprise that Rami led her horse by the reins and wondered when that had happened. She had been so lost in Dante's kisses that she'd forgotten all about her horse, and hadn't given a thought to the spectacle she made of herself. In different circumstances she would have been mortified. Now her embarrassment seemed irrelevant. Her gaze moved past Armand to the only trees of any size in the grassy valley, a clump of a half-dozen elm trees surrounded by smaller saplings. Rami was already turning his horse toward the elms.

"It appears my levelheadedness where your safety is concerned will be put to the test sooner rather than later." Dante did not sound happy.

She felt helpless. "What can I do?"

"You can do exactly as I tell you," he quipped. He even managed a crooked smile. "Armand could be mistaken about the man's intent. He could be alone, perhaps a knight or soldier from a nearby keep who simply happened upon us and is watching to make sure we pass through his lord's lands without incident."

"You do not really believe that is the case."

"I would rather prepare for the worst possibility and be relieved if it does not come to pass." He glanced at the sun, and then startled her by brushing his mouth across hers in another brief kiss. His lips moved in a purposeful line along her jaw to her ear and he spoke in a quiet tone. "We still have four or five more hours until dark. It will look unusual if we stop this early for no reason. The lie will be made more believable if I appear to be so overcome with lust that I ordered the camp set so I could be with you." His teeth nipped painlessly at her earlobe. "Indeed, it will not be much of a lie."

"How can you—"

"Shhh."

The hushing sound made her teeth clench together as his breath tickled her ear and scattered her thoughts. Oh, good Lord, that felt wicked, almost as if he were somehow inside her head.

"I will make certain you are safe," he murmured. "Their lookout will have to ride ahead to let the others know we have set camp. We will have plenty of time to prepare for them. If they do not appear by nightfall, I will send Armand to find their camp and learn more of their intentions. Now, remember to cling to me."

Before she could think to ask what he meant, he dismounted. She looked around, startled to realize they had reached the stand of elms. Dante put his hands on her waist and gave a small squeeze to remind her of her role, and then he lifted her to the ground. Well, eventually he let her feet touch the ground, but only after he deliberately slid most of her weight down the front of his chest as slowly as possible. He was right. If not for the way her pulse raced from panic, this pretense would not be much of a lie.

He took her hand and walked to where the brush around the trees thinned a little and then he led her to the base of the largest tree. It also happened to have the widest trunk and there were fewer saplings growing in its shade, just sparse grass and wildflowers. The saplings that surrounded them would slow down any attackers, but the horses would never fit within this confined space. That meant some or all of them would have to remain in the open to guard the horses.

"Stay here," Dante murmured, and then he wound his way back out of the saplings.

She could see the men and horses quite clearly through the leafy greenery and suspected her red cloak was just as visible from the road, but probably not from the ridge. The wide trunk sheltered her from that side.

Oliver, Armand, and Rami were already engaged in some of the usual activity associated with setting up camp for the night, unsaddling and hobbling the horses, unloading the packs. They began to haul the gear and saddles to where Avalene stood. Dante knelt down next to one of the packs and pulled out the chain mail he had worn as Sir Percival.

"Take off your cloak," he said, as he draped the chain mail over one arm.

She shed her cloak and then her eyes widened as he held out the chain mail and his intent became obvious. "I cannot wear that."

"You will not have to stand in it," he said, thinking she was worried about the weight of the garment. Thousands of intricate metal links formed the fabric, a sleeveless garment fashioned to cover a man from his neck to his knees. On her it would fall near her ankles. He nodded toward the growing mounds of saddles and packs that surrounded her. "I want you to lie on the ground behind the gear to stay out of sight, but they might have an archer or crossbows. The mail will protect you from any stray arrows or bolts."

"What will protect you?" That was her main concern with taking his armor. He would be left defenseless. Well, less defended. "You should wear the mail."

"I have no need of it." He shook his head at whatever he saw in her face. "Armor is for knightly combat, Avalene. I do not fight fair."

"Good. But I will be safe behind this pile of baggage while you will be an easy target for an arrow or bolt. Surely it could help protect you."

He actually smiled. "The garment would likely prove more hindrance than help, and knowing you wear it will help me stay focused. Now, lean forward so I can get this over your head."

She reluctantly obeyed. After endless days of wearing heavy, rain-drenched clothing the mail was not the burden she feared it would be, but she thought of another worry as Dante adjusted the mail to hang evenly. "Rami will stay here with me?"

"Rami's job is to help tend the horses."

"But he is just a boy!"

"Exactly. They will expect to see him tending the horses." He framed her face between his palms. "Calm down, Avalene. I will not let any harm come to Rami."

She took an unsteady breath, but his touch did calm her a little. "I do not like this."

"Nor do I."

"Perhaps if you gave me a weapon, I could—"

"No."

"What if we are outnumbered? What if—"

This time he silenced her with a kiss. He kept kissing her until she began to relax in his arms and somehow she ended up seated in his lap at the base of the elm. His hands gently rubbed her arms. "I know what I am doing, Avalene."

It took her a moment to gather her wits enough to realize he was talking about the preparations they were making for an attack, although he could have been talking about kissing and she would have agreed on that score as well.

"I will send Rami to you as soon as they begin to move in," he went on. "Oliver and Armand know what to do in this sort of situation. Rami will only be in the way, another distraction we cannot afford. 'Tis your job to make sure the boy stays with you once we send him in. I suspect he will feel as strongly as you do about the need to help us. Without question, you can help us best by making certain you both remain protected behind the baggage. Will you promise to obey me in this matter?"

She bit her lower lip as she considered the request. Once she had promised to obey Sir Percival without question. That seemed a lifetime ago. Could she cower in safety if Dante and his men were threatened, if there were something she might be able to do to swing a fight in their favor?

She couldn't think of anything she could do that

would make a difference. Her experience with weapons came solely from watching Lord Brunor's knights on the practice fields. The odds seemed more favorable that she would distract Dante at a moment that could prove fatal. She looked into his eyes and saw the tension there. He was already distracted by the thought that she might do something foolish. She placed her palms on each side of his face, as he had done earlier to calm her. "I promise."

He breathed a deep sigh of relief. "The wait will be the hardest part. If they did, indeed, intend to attack us in the pass, it will take them time to discuss this change in circumstances and devise a new plan."

She wondered how many men were in the band of mercenaries. If they had a force even half as large as the Segraves, they would be in dire straits. If there even was a band. All of this alarm could be over nothing. "So they are probably discussing their plan as we speak?"

"Aye. Armand is keeping an eye out for their spy. He disappeared soon after it became obvious we were making camp here. He has not reappeared."

So there *was* ample cause for alarm.

"I must make preparations before they return," he said in a quiet voice. "Will you be all right by yourself?"

Translation: Can I trust you to stay put? She could read that worry easily enough in his eyes. "I will be fine. Please, do not worry that I will do something foolish. I trust you to do what is right."

He lifted her hand and pressed a kiss to her wrist. His mouth turned upward in a wry smile. "In this instance, your trust is exceptionally well placed."

Over the next quarter hour she tried to look satisfied with the arrangement as he helped pile more baggage around her until she felt cocooned against the tree. She made a few adjustments to the saddles to make sure there was enough room for Rami in their lair, but that was the extent of the help she could provide. Weighed down by the chain mail, there was no way she could lug saddlebags or gear from the horses. Besides which, she felt ridiculous in the garment. Women did not wear chain mail. She looked down at the gray metal links. Well, most women.

The limited view of the men frustrated her most. She could see them fairly well through the branches, but not when the wind stirred through the saplings. It was at a point when the breeze blew particularly hard that Dante disappeared entirely from the road. Oliver and Armand were still there, now pretending to play a game of dice. She caught an occasional glimpse of Rami as he moved from one horse to the next, brushing down each animal. She would like to be with them, even if it meant pretending to do something. Instead she sat alone in her armor, helpless to contribute anything useful, more of a liability. What had Dante said? Ah, yes, more hindrance than help.

It seemed like a whole day had passed by the time she stretched out on her cloak and stared up at the leaves, watching the play of sunlight and shadows, but the sun had not moved more than an hour or so across the sky. Bored and anxious, it was a strange combination of feelings that made her long to close her eyes for a nap that would make the time pass more quickly. That was out of the question, of course. She was so nervous that she was almost afraid to blink.

"They are coming, my lady," Oliver said, just loud enough for her to hear but not the approaching riders.

She bolted upright amidst the clinking of metal links and scanned the clearing near the road. Oliver and Armand were still playing dice. Rami had finished with the horses and had found a seat near the men. Had she imagined Oliver's warning? No, all three were looking toward the road to the east. Dante was still nowhere in sight.

A moment later she heard the sound of measured hoofbeats and then two of their own horses snorted and blew out their breath, likely in response to the scents of the new animals. At last she saw glimpses of the strangers, her view dappled by dozens of leafy branches. *One, two, three . . . four, five, six . . . Oh, no. Seven, eight.*

They were outnumbered. Badly. Her heart began to thunder inside her chest. Where was Dante?

"Greetings, travelers!" a man called out. He and his men positioned their horses in a semicircle around Oliver and Armand while Avalene studied the strangers from her hiding place. The nondescript clothing the men wore was likely chosen to help them blend in with the soldiers of the next lord who hired them; brown leather pants and vests with linen shirts that all looked in need of a good washing. The man who greeted them was dressed the same as the others, but he was obviously their leader. A breeze shifted the branches for a moment and she glimpsed a gray, grizzled jaw and a thick-lipped mouth drawn back in a smile that revealed rotted teeth. "Is something amiss that you have struck camp so early in the day? Can we be of any help to you, my friends?"

The sound of a thick Italian accent from Armand made her eyes widen. "No, kind men. We are good, thank you."

There was a moment of silence before the mercenary responded. "You are foreigners?"

"Aye, Italians," Armand answered in a friendly tone. She watched him gesture toward Oliver and Rami. "My *compagni* no speak your tongue. My pardon, I no speak so good either."

The accent was so close to those of the Italians she

had encountered at Coleway that she would have sworn it was genuine. The mercenary believed it as well. "What are you doing in England?"

"My master married the English girl," Armand said. "The fathers both merchants, *sì?* We go to the *padrone* in London."

"Dirty outlanders," one of the other mercenaries cut in, with a quiet curse.

"Where is your master and his English girl?" the first mercenary demanded. There was a new, dangerous edge to his voice. "We have business to discuss."

"My master is with his wife," Armand replied, with just the right note of uncertainty in his voice.

A sword appeared in the mercenary's hand and pointed in the general direction where Avalene cowered behind the pile of baggage. "Get them now."

Armand gestured toward her with one hand. *"E 'tempo di andare, Rami."*

She watched Rami pick his way through the saplings, his young face set in hard lines. He scrambled over the pile of baggage to crouch down next to her, and then drew the dagger he wore at his waist, his gaze locked on the mercenaries.

"We want no trouble," Armand said in a placating tone, his hands held up with the palms facing outward toward the mercenaries. "You can be on your way, good sirs."

"We will be on our way when we have what we came for," the mercenary said. "While we are waiting for your master to put his pants back on, start saddling your horses and be sure to load your baggage."

"You want us to go with you?" Armand asked innocently.

"You will not be going anywhere." The mercenary gave an unpleasant laugh. "Cooperate, and we may spare your lives. Definitely we will spare the life of your master's wife. For a while. My scout says she is a fair piece."

The man on the leader's left grunted once, and then slowly slumped forward in his saddle. The leader stared at the man in stunned silence, even as Avalene heard several more grunts and three more men fell from their horses. All of the mercenaries were confused by the sudden and unexpected thinning of their ranks, looking from their comrades to Oliver and Armand who had not moved, and then back to their comrades again. Their bewilderment provided enough distraction for Oliver and Armand to draw their swords. She watched Armand easily block the first blow from the mercenaries' leader.

Rami started forward from their hiding place, determined to join the fight, but Avalene gripped his arm and then shook her head when he turned toward her. Anger flared in his dark eyes, but immediately faded into frustrated acceptance. He moved closer to her, edging her away from the wall of baggage. She finally realized the boy was trying to place himself in front of her, a small, fierce tiger intent on protecting his mistress.

A man's strangled cry and the sounds of swords clanging together took her attention back to the road. The man making the awful sounds held his neck with both hands as blood poured from a wound, and then he fell backward from his horse and she could no longer see him. Oliver's sword slashed out and cut the throat of the horse nearest him, and the animal went down with a scream. Its rider was dead before the horse's head touched the ground.

At the same time, Armand still had his hands full blocking sword blows from the leader of the mercenaries, his own blade ringing out in a steady rhythm against

the enemy's. Avalene had witnessed plenty of sword
fights on the practice fields at Coleway over the years,
and actual sword fights when arguments between soldiers or knights turned deadly. This match looked even
at first, but then Armand did not take advantage of an
opening so obvious that she had to bite her lip to keep
from calling out to him. Was Armand overmatched? She
studied his movements, the way he feinted when he
should attack. It finally dawned on her that Armand
was simply keeping his opponent occupied, wearing him
down, inflicting a few small cuts but nothing that would
prove fatal. Dante must have given orders to keep their
leader alive.

And then she got her first glimpse of Dante just as
another mercenary began to move in on Armand's un-
protected side. He came from the tall grasses on the
other side of the road, moving quickly as he approached
one of the mercenaries on his blind side. Her breath
caught in her throat when he gathered speed and then in
a deft move, he leapt at his prey. Actually, he practically
scaled the side of the man's horse in two agile steps, the
momentum making him level with the mercenary just
long enough to bury his sword in the man's chest, and
then two more steps backward returned him to the
ground, the movement helping pull his blade free of
the mercenary who tumbled from his saddle. She did not
have time to draw a startled breath before Dante was on
the ground again. He made a quick assessment of Armand's fight, and then vaulted onto the leader's horse so
he was seated behind the man. He clamped one arm in a
vise around the leader's sword arm and then placed the
blade of his own sword at the enemy's throat.

Dante's voice was deadly quiet. "I believe we have
business to discuss."

The sword dropped from the leader's hand and fell

harmlessly to the ground, then he lifted his other hand so both were raised in surrender. "We intended no harm!"

Oliver and Armand came to stand in front of the horse and she realized with a start that all of the other mercenaries were dead.

Dante made a sound of impatience. "Who sent you?"

"N-no one," the man stuttered, and then a torrent of words poured from him. "We are in the hire of Lord Althrop, on our way to Wiltshire to fulfill his forty days' service to his liege, the Earl of Hereford. We only stopped to see why you were camped so early in the day. We thought you needed our help."

The story was believable, to a point. Every nobleman and knight owed his liege lord forty days of military service. The wealthy lords who did not relish warfare hired mercenaries to serve in their stead. The higher the rank of the nobleman, the higher the number of mercenaries were owed to take his place. Apparently the earl had agreed that Althrop's service was worth that of eight mounted soldiers. There was nothing unusual about the number. Still, the story did not explain why they had intended to rob them.

"Althrop lacks the coin to send mercenaries to Hereford," Dante said, "and the earl and his army have been in Brecon for close to a year." The mercenary grimaced in pain when Dante wrenched his arm. "Tell me the truth this time."

"Althrop said he would hire us, but when we reached his manor he turned us away. 'Tis the truth!" the mercenary insisted. "The journey to Althrop took all our coin. We *were* making our way to Wiltshire, hoping to hire our swords along the way. We only stopped—"

"Most of these horses and their tack are not those of common soldiers," Dante broke in. "The saddles are trimmed with silver, the horses bred for hunting rather than war. Did you leave their owners alive, or did you murder them as you intended to murder us?"

Answering that question would implicate him in theft and murder, or another denial could further anger his captor. The mercenary wisely remained silent. Dante pushed the man sideways until he fell from his horse and landed in a heap on the ground. Armand's sword replaced Dante's at his throat.

"These saddles do not belong to mercenaries of your caliber, nor do these horses," Dante said. "If they were provided for you to complete this mission, then you were sent here by one of my enemies. If they were stolen, then you and your men simply had the misfortune to choose the wrong victims. Which is it?"

"I . . ." The mercenary's Adam's apple bobbed as he swallowed. "W-we stole the horses from Althrop three days ago. We waited in the forest until Althrop rode to the hunt with his men, and then we robbed them."

"Are they dead?" Dante asked, in a voice that was more curious than judgmental.

The mercenary looked from Dante to Armand, and then back again. He gave a slow nod.

Dante's answering nod was for Armand.

Before the mercenary knew what that signal meant, before he could draw a breath of protest, Armand's sword drew back and then swiftly returned to the mercenary's neck with deadly vengeance. As quickly as the fight had started, it was suddenly over. Avalene turned away from the sight and concentrated on taking deep breaths until she felt Rami stir in front of her.

"Wait," she called out, as she put her hand on his sleeve. "Help me out of this armor."

Rami cocked his head to one side, his brows drawn together.

She plucked at the chain mail, and then pantomimed

pulling it over her head. "I cannot move in this thing. Help me out of it, please."

She doubted Rami understood her words, but he understood the request. He gathered handfuls of the chain mail at the shoulders and began to pull until she was freed. "*Migliore?*"

"*Sì, grazie.*"

Rami nodded, then vaulted over the baggage while Avalene followed at a slower pace. Dante met her before she had worked her way through the saplings. He looped one arm around her waist and turned her back toward the elm.

"Why don't you wait here while we repack the horses," he said. "We shall be gone from here in little time."

"I can help load the horses," she protested. She needed to do something to keep her mind off the massacre she had just witnessed. She leaned down and picked up one of the smaller saddlebags. "We can be gone from here much quicker if I help."

He placed both hands on her shoulders and turned her to face him, then leaned down so they were looking eye to eye. "You do not want to see what is in the road."

"The dead mercenaries?" she asked. "I already saw everything that happened."

Dante turned his head to look toward the road. The gory body of the leader was clearly visible. He sighed. "I had hoped you would not watch."

"I had hoped to be of more help," she quipped, thankful beyond words that none of the mercenary's blood was on Dante. "Let me help now."

He studied her face for a long moment, and then nodded. "Take the bags to Oliver."

She tried not to gawk at the fallen men, but found it was impossible not to look at them. They were everywhere. The smell of blood and gore was nearly overwhelming. Breathing through her mouth helped a little, but her stomach made many frightening turns. Still, she returned for more baggage again and again, determined not to appear weak. Her stomach gave another queasy lurch and she covered her mouth with one hand until the spell passed.

After that close call she kept her eyes on the ground directly in front of her until the horses were ready and she was in her saddle. Rami hobbled the mercenaries' horses that had survived; someone would come along eventually and care for them. The men were left where they fell. It seemed wrong to leave the dead without even covering them or saying a prayer, but she did not bother to ask if they should tend to the bodies. She knew the answer before she asked the question. The Segraves were still in pursuit and they had already lost too much time. She said a silent prayer for the mercenaries' souls, but she could not find it in her heart to forgive them the greed that led to their deaths.

They rode through the pass as the afternoon shadows lengthened and she breathed a little easier when the road widened again. Everyone rode in silence, although she found Dante's brooding gaze upon her whenever she looked at him. She did not want to talk about the mercenaries or what had happened, so she quickly looked away each time their eyes met. He did not question her.

It was almost dark when Armand pointed toward a village nestled in a wooded valley. "Wycombe ahead, my lord."

She could see a mill and its waterwheel along the banks of a river, and could just make out the thatched roofs of the houses in the shadows of dusk. She had heard of this village from merchants and travelers who stopped at Coleway. Wycombe was a market town on the banks of the River Wye, less than a day's ride from

London. The knowledge that they would be in the city by this time tomorrow cheered her considerably. She also knew there would be an inn at Wycombe, but there was no reason to hope they would make use of the inn. Still, her spirits fell when Armand rode past the lane that led to the village and they all continued forward.

About a half mile beyond Wycombe, they turned onto a narrow lane that led away from the road. Eventually a large structure loomed before them, a massive black square against the gray shadows. She felt tears come to her eyes when she realized it was a village tithing barn, likely empty and abandoned at this time of year. They would sleep indoors tonight after all.

Still, a roof over her head was hardly a reason for tears.

"Avalene?" Dante had already dismounted and stood next to her. Rami held both of their horses by the reins, ready to take charge of them for the night. She could barely see Dante's face in the moonlit shadow of the barn, but she heard the worry in his voice. "Do you mind if I help you from your horse?"

Why would she mind? "Of course not."

She let go of her reins as Dante's hands closed around her waist, but he released her as soon as her feet were on the ground, almost as if he were reluctant to touch her longer than was necessary. "Stay here. We have a few candles in one of the packs with the flint. I will return soon."

She nodded and then wondered if he could even see the gesture. "All right."

He hesitated for a moment, and then followed after Rami. She could hear water running in the distance and knew they were close to the river. Oliver was probably watering the horses while Armand and Rami unloaded the packs again for the night. She should be helping, but found herself grateful to be alone for a little while. The inexplicable tears were still clouding her eyes and her breathing felt unsteady. It was just a barn, for goodness' sake. There was no cause to become so emotional, but the tears continued to roll silently down her cheeks.

Dante returned before she could compose herself. She kept her head lowered so the moonlight would not reveal her state.

"There is a doorway on this side," he said, as he motioned her toward the door.

She followed him inside and was immediately swallowed up by the darkness. No dusky shadows or moonlight reached inside the barn. She was completely blind.

"I'll have a candle lit in a moment," he said, his voice very near her. "Just stand still for a few moments."

She heard a rustling sound and then saw the spark of flint and the glint of the dagger he drew along its edge. It occurred to her that there would soon be enough light to see the pesky tears, and she used the sleeve of her gown to wipe them away. The sparks from the flint stopped.

"Are you crying?"

"Of course not." She made a concerted effort to sound firm, in control. "Why should I be crying?"

The scrape of the flint started up again, and then a small flame caught in a kindling pile of hay. Dante lit two candles, and then stamped out the kindling fire with his boot. Candles were dangerous enough in a barn, but a hay fire, even on the earthen floor away from other hay, was madness. The candles would be their only source of light in the cavernous building. Dante handed her one of the candles, and then lifted his higher to explore their surroundings.

The tithing barn was similar to Coleway's; buttressed stone walls with a high pitched roof. At the far edges of the circle of light thrown from the candles she could see a ladder that led to lofts that were built into the rafters to store straw. There were wooden slatted walls on the ground floor, seemingly constructed at random places and in random sizes to hold sacks of grain or sheaves of wheat, each stall standing empty now. The whole place smelled of dried hay, old dust, and cats.

Dante drew his sword and ventured forward into one of the stalls. She followed in time to see him wedge his sword between the slats in one corner of the stall, and then he turned the candle sideways until a small puddle of wax accumulated on the blade. He then placed the bottom of the candle in the puddle and held it steady until the wax cooled enough to hold the candle upright.

"I have to check on the men and horses," he said. He motioned toward a pile of empty grain sacks that were neatly stacked along one side of the stall. "Why don't you make a bed for us from these sacks while I am gone."

She eyed the empty sacks. "What about a bed for Rami and the men?"

"They will sleep outside near the horses and take turns at watch," he said. "I do not want all of us trapped in here, should someone from the village stumble across us. 'Tis the same reason we will not have a fire tonight; we are too close to Wycombe."

She nodded. "I will prepare our bed."

A crease formed between Dante's brows as he studied her. "I will be back very soon."

She nodded again, and then watched him turn and melt into the darkness. The dark, musty air around her felt suddenly empty and she knew he was gone. She went to the sword and placed her candle next to his in its own wax, and then began to peel away the top grain sacks. They were dusty and made her sneeze, but the layers below were still relatively clean. She laid the sacks in neat piles at the center of the stall, away from the walls where spiders lurked, and kept stacking until she had created a pallet several inches thick.

She spread her cloak over the bed, removed her surcoat, and then folded it into a square to use as a pillow. Next she sat on the edge of the pallet and removed her boots. Dante still hadn't returned so she decided to stretch out on the bed for just a few minutes. She couldn't recall ever being so tired on this trip, even on the days when they had covered many more miles in much worse weather. The pace today was almost leisurely by comparison, but she was so exhausted that she could no longer keep her eyes open.

The first things she saw when she closed her eyes were the blood-soaked bodies of the mercenaries. Her eyes popped open again and she stared up at the darkness above her, trying to imagine the stars that were on the other side of the roof, anything to erase the images of the bodies.

The imagined stars were not much of a distraction, so she thought about a tapestry she had worked on before she left Coleway, the intricacies of the design, all of the frustrations she had endured to get the pattern just right before she even picked up a needle. Who would complete the tapestry in her absence? None of Lady Margaret's ladies had enough skill with a needle. It would likely remain unfinished. Perhaps she would redraw the design when they reached Italy. She concentrated on cataloging the colors of thread she would need for the tapestry and the dyes they would require, and closed her eyes again.

The bodies were still waiting for her.

She squeezed her eyes more tightly shut and started naming off the colors of thread and their dyes, picturing the strands in her mind. "Blue woad. Yellow weld. Brown walnut. Red madder—"

"What are you doing?"

Her eyes popped open and she found Dante standing over her, a saddlebag and a linen sack in his hands. She sat up and pretended to busy herself by brushing the wrinkles from her skirt. "I was thinking about a tapestry project I would like to start when this journey ends. 'Tis a depiction of a unicorn hunt. The piece is—" She suddenly ran out of breath and had to take a quick gasp of air before she could continue. "The piece is quite—" And then another gasp. "The piece is quite complex!"

Dante dropped the sack and saddlebag to the ground, and then took a seat next to her. A moment later she was seated in his lap, cradled in his arms. He pressed her head to his shoulder.

"Go ahead and cry," he encouraged. "I have been waiting all afternoon for this dam to break."

Her spine stiffened but she did not lift her head from his shoulder. It felt too heavy to lift, her position far too comfortable to move. "I am per-perfectly fine!"

"Of course you are," he murmured, as he rubbed her back in small, soothing circles. "You are very brave, very fierce. I am so proud of how you handled yourself. Amazed, actually. But you do not have to hide what you are feeling from me."

"I am n-not huh-hiding anything," she insisted. Her arms tightened around him and it was the first she became aware that she was clinging to him as if she would take a great fall if she let go. Why were her teeth chattering? She wasn't cold. "I am s-simply tired, but I d-do not know why."

"I do." He laid her down on the pallet, still wrapped in his arms but with hers pinned against his chest now. His leg curved over her hips, wrapping his big body around hers, as if to protect her from herself. "We are alone now, *cara*. You do not have to hide from me. Tell me what you are feeling."

She kept her head buried against his chest, mortified to realize the dampness there was from her tears. "I see them. Whenever I close my eyes, I see them in the road."

"They cannot hurt you now." He pressed a kiss to the top of her head. "Look at me, Avalene."

She lifted her head reluctantly, and then sniffed once when he used his thumb to brush the tears from her cheeks.

"They were brutal murderers and thieves," he told her. "'Tis the end they deserved, and the fate they intended for us and who knows how many others?"

"I have told myself much the same," she murmured. "You did what was fair and just, and y-yet they haunt me still. I do not know why. This is not the first time I have w-witnessed bloodshed. I have watched men die by the sword; I have tended serious injuries. There was just s-so much . . . blood."

He brushed a strand of hair from her temple and then cupped the side of her face with his hand. "I should have made certain you could not see any of what happened. I will never forgive myself for causing you this pain."

"I am *not* in any pain," she hastened to reassure him. She had been so caught up in her own weepy emotions that she had never considered how her reaction would affect him. Tears, of all things. She had long thought herself immune to them and did not care for their consequences. "Truly, I am just being childish. Everything you said about those men is true. Granted, their . . . executions were more violent than the hangings I have witnessed, but I have seen blood and gore before." She pushed against his shoulder to emphasize her point. "You will *not* feel guilty."

The corner of his mouth kicked up at one side. "Your wish is my command, my lady."

"I am serious," she insisted. "You saved my life. Again. I never intended to make you feel guilty about it."

"I never imagined that a woman could watch me kill so many men, and then calmly offer to help saddle my horses." He brushed his thumb across her bottom lip. "And yet your mouth was set in a hard line from the moment we left the mercenaries. You looked upset."

"I did?"

He nodded. "At first I thought you were angry with me for killing them, rather than just taking them prisoner and letting the local sheriff handle the matter. And then I began to imagine the other reasons you would be upset."

"I was not mad at you."

"I figured that out eventually, but I could have saved myself a great deal of worry if I had simply asked what you were thinking." He pressed his lips to her forehead. "I cannot take away the images of what you witnessed, but the memories will fade in time."

There was little doubt that he spoke from experience. She placed her hand on the side of his face, and then rubbed her palm against the sandy roughness of his cheek. "Help me to forget them."

He took her face between his hands and she watched his eyes darken. As he spoke, one hand curved around the nape of her neck, pulling her closer. "Your wish is my command."

He captured her lips in a demanding, scalding kiss that scattered her senses. Soon all she could think about was the way his mouth moved against hers with hungry yearning. His kisses were as powerful as his poison, drugging her with their potency, and yet imparting a

power of her own when her tongue darted out to taste
him and she heard him moan.

Liquid heat raced through her as his hands moved
over her body, at once soothing and inflaming. The laces
of her gown were soon undone and then he pushed her
chemise off her shoulders and laid her gently on their
bed, his lips never leaving hers. She gasped when he
cupped one breast in his hand. His thumb stroked over
her nipple and the gasp turned into a low moan. His
kisses burned a path down her neck and soon his mouth
replaced his hand, his tongue inflicting painless torture,
then his lips closed over her breast and he began to
suckle. Her back arched and she cried out in astonished
pleasure. His hand moved lower as he continued the
erotic onslaught on her senses, pushing up her skirts, his
fingers trailing a ticklish path along the inside of her
thigh. He pressed his palm to her mound and her cries
turned into mindless whimpers. She quit breathing altogether when his finger slipped inside her.

He lifted his head to look down at her, his eyes blazing
green fire, his breathing labored, and then he began to
move his finger in a slow rhythmic motion while the
palm of his hand pressed against a sensitive spot she
hadn't known existed. The moment was intimate beyond anything she had ever experienced. His gaze held
hers captive while he held her body open and vulnerable, his hand working a dark, sensual magic upon her.

"Put your hand next to mine," he ordered, in a voice
roughened with desire.

She hesitated for a moment, and then did as he asked.

"Do you feel how slick and wet you are, how ready
your body is for mine?" His hips pressed against hers,
and then he shifted his hand over hers to make certain
she knew exactly what he was talking about. "Now
touch your fingers to my lips."

Her eyes widened and she could feel the fire ignite in her cheeks. She couldn't trust her voice, so she gave a small shake of her head.

"Offer yourself to me," he commanded. "Let me taste your desire. Give me the most secret part of yourself."

His hand stroked her with more pressure, encouraging her to do as he asked. Her hand trembled, but she pressed her fingers to his lips. He drew a deep breath through his nose, and then his tongue darted out to thoroughly lick each finger. Once that was done, he drew the tip of each finger into his mouth to gently suckle away all trace of her essence. At the same time, his hips began to move against her in the same rhythm as his hand.

His mouth returned to hers in an abrupt move and there was no longer any trace of gentleness in his kisses. His tongue thrust into her mouth in movements that matched those of his hand and hips, and her body answered his with the same rhythm and demand. And then his thumb began to rub against the sensitive spot between her legs and all sense of shyness fell away. Her body was his to do with as he pleased, her mind driven only by desire.

She cried out in protest against his mouth when his hand left her and she felt him turn slightly away, and then she felt him working at the laces at the front of his pants. A moment later she felt his hot, hard staff press against her bare hip and then his hand resumed the sweet torture. The fire continued to build inside her, centered where he impaled her over and over again with his fingers. Her head began to turn from side to side of its own accord and he dragged his lips down the column of her throat until his mouth closed over her breast again. The moment he drew her into his mouth there was an explosion inside of her. She fisted her hands in his hair, desperate to hold on to him as she fell apart. As the waves of passion crashed over her, she was dimly aware of him pressing his hips harder against hers and then a hot dampness between their skin as he threw his head back and spilled his seed with a growled shout of both frustration and completion.

She could feel the tremors in his body mix with her own, and then he collapsed next to her, his leg thrown over hers and his arm wrapped around her waist to hold her close, his face buried in the crook of her neck. The harsh sounds of his breathing and hers intermingled as she stared up at the inky darkness of the ceiling, stunned by the experience, her muscles trembling in new and previously unknown places. She'd had no idea that such pleasure was possible, although she knew there was more to the act of lovemaking than what they had done, and was intimately aware that their bodies had not joined. If this was the result of love play, she wondered how she would survive when the play turned serious. Her whole body felt contented beyond belief, and yet there was a lingering ache. No, more a sense of emptiness, her body's innate knowledge that what she experienced was very pleasurable, but not entirely fulfilling. She was ready to learn all of the mysteries of what happened between a man and woman. Well, perhaps she would be ready when her body recovered from that first, very satisfying taste.

Eventually their breathing returned to normal and he stirred from her side. He used one of the grain sacks to wipe away the evidence of their tryst, readjusted his clothing, and then gently rearranged her own until she was modestly covered.

"Are you all right?" he asked. He stretched out beside her again, but propped himself up on one elbow and studied her face. There was a worried look in his eyes as he tenderly brushed his hand over her cheek. "Tell me what you are thinking."

She looked up at his shadowed face and said the first thing that came into her mind. "I am in love with you."

He blinked once, and then continued to stare down at her as the silence stretched out between them. It was not the reaction she had expected. She pressed her lips together and turned her head to one side as rejection washed through her.

"Look at me, Avalene."

He had to take her chin in his hand before she reluctantly complied with the order. His severe expression had not changed.

She tried to dismiss her words. "I did not mean to—"

His fingers covered her lips and he made a hushing sound. "Let me savor this moment."

Her brows drew together in confusion.

"Tell me again," he commanded.

A wave of relief washed over her. He was not rejecting her declaration. He was amazed by it. This time the words came hesitantly and she felt suddenly shy. "I love you."

His eyes closed and his expression became almost reverent. When they opened again, raw emotion blazed in his eyes. His voice was hoarse and raw. "Thank you."

It was an odd thing to say, but she did not have long to think about it. His lips covered hers again, but this time his kisses were tender, gentle, no longer driven by physical needs, but the emotions behind them were just as powerful.

At least, the kisses started out short and sweet as they innocently explored each other with their lips. Then the kisses began to linger on places like the pulse point of a wrist, then the corner of a mouth, the curve of an ear, and the need gradually returned, rekindled in the embers of desire. Soon she felt the familiar yearning as her body strained toward the man who could fulfill her desires.

This time she wanted to explore his body as thoroughly as he had explored her own and she slipped her hands beneath his shirt to touch the warm stone wall of his chest. She soon discovered that she could make his breath catch when she pressed her hips against his, and drawing his tongue into her mouth produced a sound like a low growl in the back of his throat. She breathed his name into his ear and felt him shudder. He tilted his head back and she dragged her lips down the strong column of his throat. He shuddered again as her tongue darted out to take small tastes of his skin, and then he firmly but gently pushed her away from her feast.

"We must stop."

She looked up to see if he jested. There was a fierce look of determination in his eyes. "I do not want to stop."

"Nor do I," he admitted, "but you have no idea how tempting you are and my willpower is especially low right now. I do not want to do something I will regret."

Her eyes widened and uncertainty returned. "Do you regret what is already done?"

"How can you even ask?" He gave a frustrated, exasperated sigh, and then pressed a kiss to her forehead. "Avalene, I want you more than anything I have ever wanted in my life, even more so, now that I have sampled your delights. I do not regret our love play, but I would have it go no further."

"Then why—"

"We are only a day's ride from London where an exceedingly comfortable bed awaits us, where we need not worry about a villager stumbling across us, or an attack by mercenaries, or being captured by the Segraves. I want to devote my full attention to you. I want to pamper you with silk sheets and soft pillows." He released a deep sigh and kept a firm hold on her shoulders when she tried to move closer to him. "You need to lie down and go to sleep now. I will keep the candles burning until you are asleep."

She stared at him and tried to decipher his suddenly incomprehensible language. Lie down? Go to sleep? Her pulse still raced and her breath came in small, uneven puffs. "Uhm, sleep?"

"I know you have heard of the word." The trace of a smile curved his lips and he brushed his knuckles across her cheekbone. "You deserve more comforts than a bed of old grain sacks in a musty barn the first time we . . ." His eyes seemed to lose focus for a moment, and then his jaw tightened. "'Tis time to stop this love play while I still can."

"Just a few more kisses," she whispered. "Please?"

He groaned and lowered his mouth to hers again. Soon her thoughts focused entirely on the feel of their bodies where they touched and the way his mouth moved against hers. He was so much larger than she, but somehow he made her feel as if she could control all of the raw, male power beneath her hands. She smoothed her palms over his shoulders, then looped her arms around his neck and pressed her body against his.

In one skillful motion he turned her in his arms and pressed her down onto their bed. His hands kneaded her back as he pulled her closer, pressing her hips against his in a way that left no doubt that he wanted her. She made a small sound that was rewarded with the sharp bite of his teeth at the base of her neck, followed by the soft stroke of his tongue. She felt her heart turn over in her chest. His lips moved to her ear and she felt his words vibrate through her.

"This is not the right time or place," he murmured. "You deserve a proper bed for what I have in mind. I can wait until we reach London."

She stroked his hair, sifting her hands through the soft strands. She wanted to be his in every possible way. "I only want a few small tastes of the feast to come."

His answer was another kiss. He kissed her neck and she remembered the way her skin had tingled just before the lightning had struck the tree above her. His mouth found hers again and she heard herself moan, startled that the sound had come from her, yet unable to make it stop. He deepened the kiss and hooked his leg over the back of hers to pull her even closer, fitting the soft curves of her body against the rigid planes of his own. She twined her arms around his neck and gradually realized that he had shifted her to lie on top of him. He held her so tightly that she could scarce breathe. Finally she had to lift her head to catch her breath.

"That look makes me nervous." His eyes narrowed as he studied her face. "What are you thinking?"

"I am thinking that I could make you forget about a warm bed." She wriggled a little within his hold to better balance her weight and felt him shudder. She did it again just to see if the response would be the same. Interesting.

"You can make me forget almost everything," he admitted. "And I do not think this bed could get any warmer unless we lit it on fire. Still, you are upset by what you witnessed today. I do not want those men to taint our first time together in any way. If you still feel this way tomorrow, I will be more than happy to comply, but there is no need to rush. I said I would court you. You deserve to be courted."

The reminder of the mercenaries made her hesitate, but only for a moment. He had banished the ghosts of the mercenaries from her mind and she would not allow them back in. Now when she closed her eyes, all she saw was Dante. How had she even for a moment thought him coldhearted? Instead, she almost smiled at his look of stubborn belligerence. He was still upset that she had never experienced a courtship and seemed determined to provide one for her, even if it meant his courting took place while he was bedding her. "Does anyone else realize what a kind and considerate man you are?"

"Oh, aye, 'kind' and 'considerate' are my middle names," he said, with a bark of laughter. Their bodies rubbed against each other in new and interesting ways, and his eyes turned serious. "If you could read my thoughts now, you would have to devise a whole new list of words to call me."

He wriggled his brows in a parody of a seductive glance and she gave him a delighted laugh.

"Ah, that every woman would find humor in my lovemaking." He rolled his eyes, still mocking himself. "You have pierced me to the quick, my lady."

The peculiar melting sensation rushed through her again. He was smiling. She had made him laugh. Not only on the outside, but inside, where she knew his spirits were lightened. For a man such as Dante, she felt she had accomplished something momentous.

He loosened his hold, then put his arms over his head and stretched his big body out. She clutched at his chest, but his arms went around her again before she could lose her balance. "This would be a good time to think again about sleep. I do not want you to make me forgetful to the point that I take you in a field like a common—"

She placed her fingers over his lips. "There is nothing

common about what you do to me, or what you make
me feel."

He released another long sigh, and then patted the
pallet next to him. "Please, Avalene. Lie down and go to
sleep. I have had little rest the last few nights, and we
still have another day's ride ahead of us before we reach
London."

She pressed her lips together to keep from arguing. He
was annoyingly determined. She rolled into his side and
nestled in the crook of his arm while he readjusted his
cloak to cover them. The covers were of no concern to
her. The heat coming from his body warmed her in a
way that blankets never could. His tunic smelled of
leather and wool, but it was his own indefinable scent
that had the power to lull her mind. Still, her body was
humming with dozens of emotions. After a few moments, she gave up.

"I cannot sleep."

"Neither can I."

She had expected a sigh of impatience and an argument, rather than ready agreement. "Now what do
we do?"

"I brought us some food," he ventured. "Are you
hungry?"

She shook her head. "What else could we do?"

"Tell me how you intended to escape from me." His
suggestion made her frown, for it was definitely not
what she had in mind. "I have tried to think of every
possible scenario, but I can think of nothing that would
have any possibility of being successful. What plan did
you think would work?"

She bit her lower lip and debated what to tell him.

"The truth would be nice to hear."

How did he do that? She frowned at his chest. "I was
going to slip away into the crowds when we reached

London. I know, I know, it was a foolish plan," she hurried to add, when his arms tightened around her. His body was suddenly rigid with stress.

"Do you have any idea what would have happened to you on the streets?"

From the tone of his voice, apparently it was something very bad. "Rather than speak of what will not happen, I would rather hear about something that will. I would rather hear you tell me more about Venice."

He was silent for a time, and then he began to tell her about the rituals and celebrations of a carnival that took place in Venice, a fascinating tale that she wanted to hear, yet his low, soothing tones were hypnotic. His hand trailed a slow, soothing path up and down her spine that lulled her further toward sleep. The day had been long and trying, and soon she could no longer keep her eyes open.

Falling asleep in the arms of the man you loved was almost as enjoyable as waking up still cradled within his embrace. There was something sinfully delicious about the intimacy of shared warmth and being nestled together as tightly as stacked spoons. She rubbed her cheek against his shoulder and burrowed deeper under the cloak that covered them even as his arms tightened around her. Awareness came in slow degrees.

She really was in Dante's arms. The pleasures they shared the night before were real. All of the things he had said to her the past few nights . . . that was real, too. Amazing. Her lips curved into a secretive smile.

It already seemed a lifetime ago when she worried that he would hold her this close at night only to make certain she didn't try to escape while he slept. Instead he had declared his love for her. At least, he thought he was in love with her. She didn't know how it was possible.

What did he see in her to love that everyone else had overlooked?

How many times over the years had she questioned what was wrong with her and tried to figure out the reasons why no one could love her as much as she loved them? Well, mostly she had wondered that about her father and her aunt. Now she was filled with doubts when someone said he did love her.

He has lied to you before and you believed him. These are more lies.

And there was the sour voice of reason, the voice that demanded to be heard after being silenced for so long. Actually, she had heard it loud and clear from the moment he declared himself but had chosen to ignore the warnings. No matter what happened when they reached London, did she want to live out her life without knowing what it would be like to be loved by this man? Or, at least, knowing a very believable pretense of love?

Last night she had given herself to him without hesitation and with little inhibition. She was not so naïve as to think that was all he wanted from her, and yet it was the thought of her comfort and safety that made him deny them both. Everything he told her was so sincere that it was almost impossible *not* to believe him. And yet, she knew firsthand that he was an accomplished liar. Doubtless his life often depended upon his ability to make others believe his lies.

If she were being sensible, which seemed impossible at the moment, she would not allow herself to truly hope until they were on a ship bound for Italy. Until then she could live for the moment, just as he had once suggested. He was all she had, and he was all she wanted. As much as she had tried to deny what was happening, it was obvious now that her heart belonged to him. It was his to break.

She was still staring up at the rafters when she realized there actually were windows in the barn, narrow slits cut into the walls that allowed in enough light to know it would be dawn soon. They would be on the road again within an hour, perhaps two at the most. That meant they would soon leave their cozy lair for another day of hard riding. She almost groaned at the thought of getting back on her horse. Her makeshift bed felt like heaven in comparison.

For the moment her life and the morning itself remained locked in misty grays, still cloaked in the lingering night. The daytime creatures had yet to rise while the nighttime predators had found their burrows and roosts to hide away from the coming sun. She could hear distant whickers of their horses from beyond the barn doors, but the walls that surrounded them made her feel completely isolated from the others. This was the quietest and most peaceful time of day.

She snuggled closer to Dante's warmth and closed her eyes again, but sleep eluded her. There was no ignoring the fact that today everything would change. Today they would reach London and their journey would end. There was unease over the uncertainties ahead, but no longer dread. Whether it was truth or illusion, Dante made her feel safe. He would show her all of the wonders of London, and then he would take her far across the sea where she would no longer be in danger from anyone. He just had to convince the king that she would never again be a threat to him.

She released a small sigh.

"Are you pretending you are still asleep?" he murmured in her ear.

"I *am* still asleep," she lied. The fact that he was awake didn't surprise her. He was a light sleeper and always seemed to awaken when she did.

"I could be persuaded to rub your back," he said. "A kiss would seem a small payment."

"Let me sleep a little longer," she murmured, not trusting herself anywhere near his lips. Last night her dreams had been filled with hazy images of kissing him, of touching him, of his hands upon her body. There would be no more of that until they reached London. Why start something they would not finish?

As if he could read her thoughts, he shifted closer to her, adjusting the way she fit against him, back to front, holding her hips as he pressed his own against hers in a sensual movement. He made a low sound in the back of his throat. Her eyes widened. She could feel the stiff proof of his erection against her hips and her loins tightened in response.

"Do not worry," he said, mistaking her reaction. His warm breath fanned across her neck and she felt goose bumps raise along her arms. "I will not ravish you. 'Tis normal for a man's body to be aroused in the morning, especially when he awakens to find such a desirable woman in his arms."

"And if I wanted to be ravished?" she wondered aloud.

"London," he murmured. She felt his lips travel along the column of her neck, not really kissing her, but almost tasting her, breathing her in. His mouth opened and she felt his teeth nip painlessly at her neck, then his tongue laved the nonexistent damage he'd done. She shifted her weight to hide the way her body responded with a small shudder. "W-will we reach London today?"

"Aye, by midday," he replied, his voice just as quiet as hers. His hand skimmed a slow path along her side from her waist to her knee, and then back again. "We will have every comfort imaginable at our fingertips. My thoughts have been lewdly dwelling on one in particular. Would you like to share a bath with me?"

She glanced over her shoulder, certain he was teasing, but reassured by his grin all the same. "Are you so bold with all of the ladies you know?"

"You are the only lady I know, aside from my sister. So, as far as my lewd suggestions to ladies are concerned, you are the sole recipient." He rubbed his thumb across her lower lip and his touch sent a familiar shiver of sensual awareness coursing through her.

She bit her lip as his thumb moved across her face to stroke her cheek. "Surely you know some of the ladies at court."

"Some are acquaintances," he admitted, sounding distracted. His gaze was still focused on her mouth. "You are the only woman I would speak with about anything . . . personal. Anything of importance. You and my sister are the only two women who know my true identity, and only a handful of men can make the same claim. I have already shared more of myself with you than I have with any other woman."

She turned onto her back so she could better study his face without craning her neck, trying to decide if he was telling her the truth. It was those sorts of odd comments that kept her off balance and made it nearly impossible to doubt him. He held her gaze for a long moment, and then he lowered his head to kiss her. She unconsciously lifted her chin and closed her eyes, but she felt his lips touch her temple rather than her lips.

"You must ask me to kiss you," he reminded her. He dipped his head again to nuzzle her neck, sending fresh shivers down her spine. "My lips will not touch yours until I hear the words."

"Are you not worried that I will make you forget

yourself?" she asked. "Last night you all but insisted that I *stop* kissing you."

"Last night I was more susceptible," he said. "Today my resolve is stronger. I fully intend to finish what we started, but not this morn. When I take you to my bed in London it will not be for a hurried coupling." His gaze moved lower and then slowly returned to her face. "I intend to linger over you for hours. Perhaps days."

Now it was her turn to feel uncertain over the sensual look in his eyes. He was very good at seducing her, good at kissing and caressing her. He had said she was also a good kisser, but this was all new to her. She had little doubt that he had plenty of practice, likely with some of his beautiful "acquaintances" at court. "What if I do not please you?"

"Impossible."

His immediate answer reassured her that *he* had no doubts. She suddenly had plenty. She worried at her lower lip with her teeth.

The expression in Dante's eyes was serious. "Are you certain this is what you want? That *I* am what you want?"

"Have I not said as much?" Her brows drew together. "Am I not willingly in your bed?"

He shook his head. "What I want to know is if you will come to my bed knowing it will go against your family's wishes, knowing I can never offer you the type of life that you were destined for in England. Will you give up your dreams of marriage to an Englishman to give yourself to me?"

"I am yours already," she answered simply.

She blinked at the speed with which he shifted her to lie beneath him, his gaze never leaving hers. He seemed to be waiting to hear what she would say next, somehow daring her to say or do . . . She was not sure what that look dared her to do or say. And then it finally dawned on her.

"Kiss me."

She had not intended her words to sound like an order, but they did and he obeyed. In one skillful motion he lowered his head and kissed her. This time his mouth was hard and demanding, opening over hers the same way he had just kissed and tasted the sensitive skin on her neck, but driven now with an urgency that was altogether new. Her eyes widened and then fluttered shut as she gave herself over to her feelings, the melting, the falling away of everything except the feel of his mouth over hers, the weight of his body, the restless longing that began to fill her body.

She sighed against his mouth and surrendered to her destiny. Something about this man had called to her soul from the moment she first laid eyes upon him, and now, at last, she was free to answer, to take what he offered and give back as much as she took. The fabric of his shirt felt smooth and warm beneath her hands, but she pulled handfuls of the fabric upward until she could reach beneath the shirt to touch his bare back. His skin felt hot and his muscles moved in constant waves.

The kiss became almost a battle, a contest to see who would dominate. In the end she lost when he dragged his mouth away from hers to press more violent kisses along the column of her neck, biting, sucking, and then once again tracing the damage with his tongue. This time he would leave marks, she was sure of it. They would be the same type of bruises she had noticed on some of the serving wenches' throats in the past. Those women had blushed over the bruises and dismissed them as love bites. At the time she had thought the women foolish. Now she understood. There was something primitive and erotic about being marked by a man, for her, being marked by this man in particular. She tilted her head back to bare more of her neck and heard herself moan.

"Shhh." His fingers covered her mouth, his voice little more than a whisper near her ear. "I will not share any part of you with another, not even the sounds of your pleasure."

Before she could think what he meant, his lips replaced his fingers and she was lost again in the heat of passion. Her hands found their way to his chest, learning and memorizing the contours beneath his shirt, pushing against him one moment, clinging to him the next. His hands were just as busy, touching and caressing her in ways that both soothed and excited her. Her back arched as she pressed herself into him and she heard his sound of pleasure.

It gave her a heady feeling to know she could affect him so easily and she rose up again to test her power. He pressed her back down and then her hips answered the movement until their bodies established a rhythm that felt as natural as breathing. She had always thought of herself as somewhat modest, but now her gown felt like a barrier, as did his clothing. She began to tug on his shirt, driven by some unknown demon to feel his bare skin next to hers.

"*Gesù*," he whispered. "Tell me to stop."

Oh, that would never happen. Before she could say anything he dragged his mouth back to her lips for another searing kiss. The kiss ended abruptly when he rolled onto his back. She tried to follow him, but he laid his arm across her chest and pressed her shoulders to the ground, forcing her to lie still next to him. For a long time all she could hear was the labored sound of their breathing.

Gradually she became aware of her surroundings.

Hints of red and gold colored the sky through the windows. Outside the horses sounded restless, doubtless in anticipation of the ration of oats they would soon receive. The woodland birds had arisen as well and were becoming noisier by the moment as they set off from their nests for the day. And then she heard someone cough.

Was it Oliver or Armand or Rami? The sound traveled clearly. Her eyes widened and her face began to feel hot with a blush. How much had the others heard of their trysts?

"We cannot do that again until we reach London," he said at last. His arm still lay across her chest and she felt his fingertips begin to trace a random pattern on her arm that stopped in midstroke. A moment later, he had his hands clasped behind his head as he stared up at the rafters. "Give me a few moments to calm down."

"All right," she said, still unsteady herself. She stared up at the rafters as well and listened as her breathing and heartbeat began to slow down. "Will you have many duties to attend to when we arrive in London?"

"A few," he said. "Why do you ask?"

She tried to keep her voice casual. "I am just wondering how much time we will have to spend . . . alone together." That sounded needy. She frowned at a cobweb that was still barely visible in the rapidly lightening barn. Would he think she was too clingy? Would he tire of—

He suddenly rolled onto his side and propped himself up on one arm, then leaned down to press a gentle kiss to her forehead. "Avalene, for you, I have all the time in the world."

18
❦

There were some sights that words could not adequately describe. None of the stories Dante told her had prepared her for the sight of the city itself.

They were still miles from the gates, still too far away to reveal many of the city's particulars beyond its size and shape. However, there in the distance, the entirety of London was visible from the crest of the hill where they had reined in their horses.

The city was spread out across the river valley like a rough, spotted blanket made up of mostly browns and grays, laid amongst the greenery of woodlands and rolling green hillsides. The city was split on its south end by a wide ribbon of bluish-green water that had to be the river Thames. Dozens of specks seemed to float motionless on the water, barges and boats with billowing white sails, so far away from their vantage point that it took a few moments of studying the sailboats before she realized most of the boats were actually moving.

The outlines of buildings and towers and church

steeples sprouted up everywhere in thick spikes that reminded her of a cave her mother had taken her to when she was a child, where dark crystals covered the floor and sprouted upward in haphazard yet very sharply defined lines and distinctly squared crystal shapes. London's "crystal" steeples and towers were so numerous that she kept losing count of them and quickly gave up trying.

There were windmills as well, and she was startled to realize that she hadn't even noticed them at first. They were dwarfed and made insignificant by the city itself; the size and scale of the wall that surrounded the city as well as the number of buildings within the walls were beyond anyone's imagination to describe.

"Avalene?"

The sound of Dante's voice finally penetrated her dazed senses and she realized that it was not the first time he had tried to gain her attention. She answered without looking away from the sights before her. "Aye?"

"What think you of London?" he asked, with a gentleness to his voice that she found soothing.

"There are no words for it," she breathed. "That is to say, there are words, but I do not know if I have enough of them. How can all of these people survive in one place? How does the lord mayor of London provide food for so many? How does he hear their complaints and judge those with disputes? How do they all keep warm in so many houses? How can he—"

"Come," he interrupted, with an indulgent laugh. "I will tell you more about the marvels of London on our way. There are more clouds on the horizon and I want to be under a roof the next time it rains. Before you know it, we will be inside the city."

There were still a half-dozen small villages between them and the city, the first no more than a cluster of thatch-covered houses crowded around the road. Each village grew successively larger until there was no longer a gap between the towns and it felt as if they were already in the midst of the city. Dante explained that London had long ago outgrown its walls and the outlying villages were often near the manor houses of nobles and church leaders who preferred living in the countryside along the river, but still needed to be close to London to attend the king at court and accomplish their business.

It was while they were in the last village that he signaled Rami to take Bodkin's reins. He maneuvered his horse next to hers, reached over and slid his arm around her waist, and then plucked her from the saddle and settled her onto his lap. It was a familiar, comforting place to be. Still, she wondered at his actions.

"You will be safer with me," he said, in answer to her silent question. "You have never been to a city of this size and are already so busy gawking that I would not have you plucked away from me in a moment of distraction."

"You think someone is waiting to abduct me in London?" she asked. "How will they know who I am?"

"You are not quite that well known," he said with a chuckle. "There are always ruffians on the streets looking to pluck a pretty dove. A gang could drag you from a horse and disappear with you into the warren of alleys in the space of a heartbeat." He studied her expression and gave her a reassuring squeeze. "I would hunt them down, of course, but you might be injured in the process and I am anxious to reach home and hearth in good time."

She recalled her plan to flee from the men who would keep her safe, the ill-thought idea that she could find a kindly stranger to take her in. He had been right. Her plan for escape would likely have ended in disaster. Still, she wasn't about to admit her misjudgment so she sniffed once over his arrogance in thinking her so helpless . . . and then gave another sniff to test the air. "What is that *smell*?"

"Ah, 'tis the smell of the beast that is London," he said. "Best prepare yourself, my lady. On a warm day such as this, the odor does not improve."

His words were unfortunately prophetic. Still, the smell was not as overwhelming as she had feared it might become and not all of the elements that made up the smell were bad. Most prominent was the smell of fire. A smoky haze covered most of the city from fires that burned wood and charcoal, Dante told her, and other more noxious burning materials that she could not identify. There was also the definite smell of sewage, although it was more pronounced when they were closer to the river and hardly noticeable at other times. Sometimes she could smell livestock, other times the scents of food. She became almost accustomed to the odors by the time they reached the old Roman walls that surrounded the city.

Even having seen the whole of the city from a distance, the reality of the place up close was altogether different. Oliver and Rami became separated from them as they passed through the gates, proving that much of her plan would have worked. Dante pulled up in a wide courtyard to regroup and she realized that was the only part of her plan that was workable.

The hustle and bustle of the city bewildered her, with people coming and going in every direction, the streets a haze of hot dust, and seemingly every person in the city felt a need to shout. Men, women, and children carried baskets filled with goods, or they held wide boards with a rope looped behind their necks and attached to the ends of the boards to balance all sorts of wares. Many hawked hot meat pies and baked ribs, foods that could be eaten with fingers rather than off a trencher. Fruit peddlers shouted out the quality of their fresh strawberries and cherries. Pints of wine were praised in a booming baritone. Still others sold hot sheep's feet and mackerel. The scents of so many dishes set her stomach to rumbling.

Dante signaled to a group of about a dozen men who loitered near the wall, milling about empty handcarts that all appeared to have held unpleasant burdens in the recent past. A pair of men took wooden shovels from a cart and eyed their horses as they walked toward them. Both men wore battered straw hats that might have been yellow in an earlier lifetime and their homespun clothing was just as filthy. The younger-looking one spoke first. "Where to, m'lord?"

"Tower Street near Saint Olave's," Dante answered. "Half now, and half when we reach our destination."

There was a quick back-and-forth discussion about the amount and form of payment, and then they set off again with the two men and their cart trailing behind them.

"Gong farmers," Dante told her, as his horse fell in line behind Armand's. "There is a harsh fine to take a string of horses through town and not clean up after them. Londoners are particular about their streets and want only their own sewage in their trenches." He pointed to a long, narrow building near the wall. "The lord mayors have made themselves popular over the years by sponsoring privy houses and paying for their upkeep. There are two score seats in that particular privy house, half on each side and divided by a wall to separate the men's side from the women's. 'Tis rare to see anyone relieve themselves on the streets."

"London men actually use privies?" she asked, marveling at the concept. "I did not know any man could be trained to be so civil when out of doors."

He rolled his eyes but she found something else to be distracted by before he could respond.

Like most things to do with the city, London's dwellings were like nothing she had seen before. Almost all of the upper stories of the houses projected outward over the streets, which turned the streets into long, narrow tunnels just tall enough for a man on horseback to pass through. She could no longer get any sense of London's vast size and the city shrank to encompass only the small, closed-in areas in their immediate path as they moved through town. All the while the din of the streets never ceased with merchants and peddlers competing with each other to sell their goods.

The goods themselves changed as they passed through different parts of the city where different guilds were based. Sometimes she could tell what guild area they were in from the smells; bakers, fishmongers, dyers, and leatherworkers were easy to identify. There were cloths of every variety for sale near the mercers' guild streets, and then they went through curriers' streets, and then cheeses, chandlers, cutlers, and many more who were clustered together in their own districts.

If the merchants and peddlers weren't enough to deafen a person, there were bands of musicians who roamed the streets or played near inns or alehouses, some of them popular enough to have the crowds singing along and stomping their feet. Then there were the signs; hundreds of them, it seemed, with brightly painted pictures to represent the name of the establishment or public house. She wondered how anyone could hold a thought in their head with all this noise and so many things to hear and see and smell.

What astounded her most of all was the complete lack

of greenery. Dante assured her there were parks scattered around the city, set well away from the roads they traveled, and that some of the houses contained courtyards large enough for small wooded areas. Still, it was strange to ride for so long a time through so many streets and never see so much as a blade of grass. London was a land more foreign to her than any wilderness of Wales.

"Are we almost to your house?" she asked, as a half-dozen tough-looking boys swarmed around them in a ragged circle. All of the boys begged for handouts, first one calling out to distract them while the others rushed forward, and then another called out, almost as if they were volleying their voices back and forth.

She was ready to be off the streets and away from this madness, and realized with a start that she was all but clinging to Dante. She made a conscious effort to shift her weight farther away. Had she really thought to negotiate these streets on her own? He took one of her hands and guided it behind his back until her arm was wrapped securely around his waist, and then he glanced down for just a moment and winked at her.

Just like that her mind turned to mush. London was forgotten. She was in his arms, safe. Everything would be all right.

"My town house is just ahead," he told her with a nod to indicate the direction. "'Tis the row ahead and on the right, where the street opens up again. Look there, past my house, and you can see the Tower of London."

Her heart skipped a beat even as her gaze moved up the street. She could indeed see the gray stone walls that must be part of the Tower. Closer to them she saw a row of what appeared to be seven identical half-timbered houses that rose five stories above the street, capped with slate roofs.

"Which of the houses is yours?" she asked. She had

assumed that a man so well known would be wealthy, and he had claimed as much, but this surpassed her expectations.

He hesitated before answering. "My quarters are in a wing behind this row. These look like separate houses but they are part of the same structure. Do you see the big wooden doors below the middle section? That gateway leads to the courtyard. All of these houses are actually the front of one large palace, once owned by the Earl of Ashland."

She gasped as she realized the enormity of the place. "One man owned all of this?"

"Aye," he said. "There are dozens of palaces scattered across the city, most owned by powerful earls and dukes but a goodly number owned by wealthy barons and merchants. This is one of the larger palaces and it could accommodate four hundred people. You will find the courtyard is much larger than what most Londoners enjoy. The street front is leased to merchants, but most of the palace is empty aside from the score of servants required to keep up the place and another score of soldiers to stand guard. My sister and brother-in-law lodge here when they are in town with their retinue, but they are rarely in London so I have the place mostly to myself."

Her brain could scarce conceive of the notion. All of this was his. He lived in a palace. One of the largest palaces in London.

And she had once thought herself above his station in life?

"The Earl of Ashland," she mused. "He was stripped of his lands and titles years ago."

Dante pressed his lips together and said nothing.

She also recalled that the earl was now dead, although she could not remember the circumstances of his death.

It seemed Dante recalled the circumstances quite clearly. "Oh."

He studied her face for a moment. "This does not upset you."

It wasn't a question, but she answered anyway. "I am sure there is a reasonable explanation."

"You are not curious about the explanation?"

She shook her head. "I would rather not know the details."

A look of relief flickered in his eyes, and then his gaze moved away from her. Armand had dismounted while they spoke and she watched him tug on a bell pull next to a door that was cut into the palace gates. She breathed her own sigh of relief that they were not bound for the Tower. A few minutes later a small, square section of the door opened as a guard apparently checked to see who was on the other side, and then the gates themselves opened. Armand remounted his horse and rode inside. She craned her neck as they followed, her eye drawn by glimpses of greenery. She blinked once as they entered a different world.

Dante had not exaggerated about the size of the courtyard. A long, straight path paved with crushed shells split the wide expanse in two. Lush gardens lined either side of the path in neatly tended squares. Here, at last, was the grass she had missed along with more than a dozen apple and pear trees. Smaller shell paths led away from the main roadway and she noticed a group of perhaps a dozen soldiers milling about beneath some of the trees, almost hidden from view by the greenery. Once the gates were closed the riotous sounds of the streets were little more than a distant buzz, no more annoying than the sound of a bee.

"'Tis amazingly quiet!" she said.

"Aye, the sounds travel up the outer sides of the walls.

You will find everything is louder on the upper stories along the street, but all is fairly peaceful near the gardens. The hall is directly in front of us, along with the kitchen and butteries. There is a solar and suites of rooms in the west wing where we will stay. The stables and river are on the other side, behind the hall, so that lends some quiet as well. There is a—"

She turned to look up at him when he fell silent. "What is wrong?"

He slowly shook his head, but that movement did not seem to be in response to her question. She followed the direction of his gaze to a pair of men who were walking toward them along the pathway. Both wore rich garments made of brocades and silks, accented by finely tooled leather boots and belts. The tall one on the left with blond hair and blue eyes looked like he belonged in a tale of Vikings, although the colors of his tunic were a bit startling. It was a credit to his masculinity that he did not look foolish in the feminine shades of yellow, white, and pink. The second man was older, not as dangerous-looking as the first, and dressed in more somber shades of gray. As she made those brief observations, she felt everything in Dante go still and stiff. Whoever these men were, he was not pleased to see them. He did not bother to dismount when they were close enough to stop and extend a greeting.

"Greetings, my lord," the older man said, as he bowed low to Dante. The look he gave his master was filled with uncertainty. "I was unable to send word to inform you of our visitors. The king commandeered the east wing and much of the main hall for his daughter and her retinue. This is the captain of her guard, Sir Gerhardt. He requested to speak with you immediately upon your arrival."

Dante remained rudely silent, as if his servant had not

spoken at all and deserved no response. She could feel the tension in him, but did not take her eyes off the two men to take a further inventory of his reaction. Instead she folded her hands in her lap and remained silent.

The blond-haired man, Sir Gerhardt, also bowed to Dante, although not as low as the servant. When he spoke, a foreign, guttural-sounding accent made his words hard to understand, but it helped that he had a firm grasp of the language. "I beg your pardon for any inconvenience, Lord Dante. My lady, Isabel of Ascalon, is recently arrived in London and needed quarters for herself and her retinue. Her father suggested your residence would be ideal and, indeed, we have found your hospitality exceptional."

"Why is she here?" Dante asked, his voice hard. "I thought Isabel was wed to some Bavarian noble."

"My lady became a widow when my prince succumbed to a fever last year," Gerhardt said. "The mourning period has ended and her father wishes her to remarry. He bid her return to England to await his choice of husband. My lady was called to court just yesterday to speak with her father about the matter."

"How long will she be here?"

Gerhardt's shoulders lifted in a shrug. If he was offended by the blunt question, he hid it well. "My lady has not made me privy to that knowledge. A few days, a few months, I know not."

"Wonderful," Dante muttered. He released a deep sigh. "Your lady is welcome to my hospitality as long as she wishes, of course. We will be in the west wing and I see no reason for our presence to interrupt you in any way. Let Reginald know if you need anything."

Gerhardt pressed his lips together over the obvious dismissal, but did not move aside. "My lady begs the favor of your company at the evening meal, Lord Dante. May I tell her that you have agreed?"

Dante's horse shifted its weight and pawed the ground with one hoof while Gerhardt awaited his answer. The animal was impatient to be on its way. Avalene guessed that Dante felt the same way. "We have just returned from a long journey and will not be fit company for anyone but ourselves until we have had a chance to rest and refresh ourselves. We look forward to meeting your lady at the midday meal tomorrow."

The corners of Gerhardt's eyes tightened. "Lady Isabel will be greatly disappointed if she does not meet her host this eve."

There was a hostile undercurrent in Gerhardt's tone. Dante's reply formed icicles in that current. "I am certain she will understand."

"As you wish, Lord Dante." Gerhardt gave him another bow that was just short of insolent. "I will inform my lady that she must be patient another day before she can make your acquaintance."

Dante waited until Gerhardt walked away before he addressed his servant, whom Avalene guessed was also his steward. "Are my quarters unoccupied, Reginald?"

Reginald's eyes widened. "Of course, my lord! I would never disobey your orders and let any guest trespass into your private apartments, no matter their rank. Lady Isabel is in the chamber your sister and her husband use when they are in residence. Her retinue fair fills the east wing; her soldiers and the king's soldiers are quartered in the hall and the barracks above the stables. I have moved our soldiers and servants to the west wing."

"There are royal soldiers in residence?" Dante asked, clearly surprised.

"They are to accompany Isabel on her journey to her new husband's castle," Reginald explained. "There are a score of her personal guard from the prince's household, and one hundred of King Edward's soldiers." He gave

Gerhardt's retreating figure a cryptic look. "The king worries for his daughter's safety."

"Apparently," Dante agreed. "We will take the horses to the stables ourselves and take the walkway to my quarters. Have a meal brought to us immediately as well as a tirewoman for my lady and hot water for her bath."

"This shall be done, my lord."

"You will join us for the meal and tell me all you know of this situation."

"Aye, my lord." Reginald gave one more low bow and then stepped aside to let their horses pass.

Dante's body remained so rigid as they rode forward that it dampened much of the awe and enjoyment she felt at seeing his home. Still, she took silent inventory of everything she could see without being conspicuous in her curiosity, including the huge set of steps at the end of the lane that led up to a wide set of double doors; obviously the great hall.

Dante turned onto a path that ran along the front of the hall to an archway cut into the building itself. They emerged on the other side into the stable yard where Dante dismounted first, and then gently set her down before him. She was glad to have his arms to hold on to. He held firmly to her waist until she steadied herself.

She felt a surge of relief that she would not be required to mount a horse again in the immediate future. Her journey had ended, and yet, strangely, she felt as if it had just begun. She spoke to him under her breath. "I cannot believe you referred to this place as a house!"

The corners of his lips quirked upward, the first sign of humor she had seen since they rode through the gates. "I thought it would be easier to show you rather than try to explain." His humor faded. "Although you will not be able to see as much of the place as I would like while Isabel and her people are in residence. This was . . . unexpected."

"You promised me time," she reminded him. "Perhaps we will not see much of your guests at all."

The smile was back, wolfish now. He turned her toward a stairway that led to a door above the arch. "Come, I will show you to our quarters. A hot bath will arrive soon enough." He stopped before a dark wooden door. "Here we are." And then she heard him murmur under his breath in Italian, *"Infine."*

At last.

19

❦

The Palace

The Three Wands rest upon hard work, sacrifice, and new plans that bear fruit. Here is the realization of the spiritual and mystical adventure. Walk toward the future without fear.

Dante never thought much about the palace; it was simply a place to stay when he was in London. His steward made certain of its upkeep and the captain of the guard made certain of its defenses, but he did not consider this his home. That title would always belong to the palazzo in Venice. Still, he had accumulated the usual types of rewards for a man in his position, meaning they were not at all usual since the king rarely paid in coin. There were jewel-encrusted weapons, goblets and plates made of solid gold, exotic silks and spices, along with even more unusual items. Most were stored in the treasury, but some of the best pieces had found their way to his apartments. He appreciated beautiful things.

Now he tried to view his quarters through Avalene's eyes as he led her from the hallway into the large solar, wondering if the comforts he had acquired and the trinkets that were scattered about would please her. His apartments encompassed half a dozen spacious rooms.

There were doors that led to the other chambers from the solar, but only the solar had access to the main hallway. He explained that Oliver and Armand would stay in two of the chambers, and then passed through an antechamber on the opposite side of the solar where a small bed was made up and Rami-sized clothing hung from pegs on one wall, and then he showed her into his bedchamber.

All the while Avalene wandered silently in his wake, her hand tracing over the surfaces of tables and the objects placed there, her slender fingers touching the brocade of cushions and window hangings, her wide gaze taking in an intricately wrought set of silver candlesticks. His eyes lost their focus when she trailed her hand up one of the smooth wooden posters of his bed and then back down again.

Something about the innocent movement was so erotic that his body turned instantly hard. How often had he pictured her here, in his bedchamber? He wanted to take her right then and there. Instead he closed his eyes and took a deep, cleansing breath. Later. For now, she would want time to settle into her new quarters and refresh herself. Tonight he wanted everything to be perfect. Throwing her onto the bed and then tossing up her skirts would hardly be considered perfect. Well, not in her mind.

He smiled to himself at the thought. She would probably surprise him on that score as well. He had never been with a virgin before, but he was fairly certain most were not as . . . enthusiastic as Avalene had been last night. She kept her emotions buried very deep, but drawing them to the surface was like opening Pandora's box; once opened, there was no stopping what poured forth. And yet she worried that she wouldn't please him. She seemed oblivious to the fact that she was as close to perfection as he could imagine, while he was far from it. Fate was, indeed, a kind mistress.

However, her silence since they reached the palace was beginning to bother him. Was it just his imagination, or was she unusually quiet? Her eyes were thoughtful as she examined his bedchamber and then followed him back to the solar, but there were no more questions. He wanted to ask what she was thinking but decided to wait until they were alone. Rami had followed them as far as the solar, and soon the servants arrived with a large wooden tub and then countless buckets of hot water. He directed them to place the tub in his bedchamber, and then motioned for Avalene to go with the tirewoman.

"There is a bathhouse near the river where my men and I will clean up while you are taking your bath," he told her. The look of apprehension on her face made him hesitate. She just needed time to get settled. He pressed a kiss to her forehead. "You are safe here. No one will bother you while we are away."

She lifted her chin in that regal way of hers and gave him a stiff nod. "Of course, my lord. Thank you for arranging a private bath for me. I am sure we will all feel better once we have bathed."

He managed to give her a reassuring smile that lasted until she disappeared into his bedchamber, and then unease unfurled in his belly. Her words seemed to imply that she was not feeling better now, but what was she feeling worse about? He stared stupidly at the closed door to his chamber and wondered if it was significant that this was the first time she had addressed him as "my lord."

The lack of sleep was catching up with him, he decided. He was reading too much into a few polite words. He tucked a bundle of clean clothing under his arm and gave Rami a curt order to guard the door. The look in Avalene's eyes when he told her he was leaving the solar hastened his steps, and he completed his bath in record time.

It worried him, this growing power she held over him, but he no longer had the will or wish to see it ended. The initial attraction that had built from the moment they met had crystallized into something else entirely when she had blithely told him, *I am in love with you.* His whole world had shifted in that moment. Those words still shook something deep inside him. He had never dreamed she would say them, and couldn't help but wonder when she would come to her senses and realize they were a mistake. She still seemed completely un-aware that he was the single most dangerous thing she had ever encountered in her life. And yet somehow she had known that she was completely and utterly safe with him before he knew it himself.

She was right, of course. He would never be able to harm her now, no matter the cost to himself. He would do whatever was necessary to keep her safe. She trusted him. She knew who and what he was, and still she looked at him with that same intoxicating mixture of innocence and desire. How could he not love her?

It was as if Fate had fashioned her just for him. Her breathtaking beauty had been the first thing to catch his eye, but he had known other beautiful women and that alone was not enough to hold his interest. Her true beauty lay within, in her courage and bravery, in the ways she took care of everyone in Lady Margaret's household without even realizing she was doing the job of her incompetent aunt and doing it without complaint, in the ways she cared for her family even when they had abandoned and betrayed her. Then, of course, there was the way she treated *him*. He had never before been the subject of such unabashed adoration.

From the start he had told himself that none of it was real, that she would run from him screaming when she learned the truth. But her soft gazes and the wonderment in her eyes had been impossible to resist. She made him want to be perfectly normal, to cleanse himself of his sins, to become a man worthy of her affections. He had quickly developed an obsession, a *need* to be the focus of her attention, to be connected to her through as many of his senses as possible; his gaze upon her face, his touch upon any part of her body, the sound of her voice, her scent, the taste of her upon his lips. All of these things were required, and yet never enough.

It helped that she felt the same irresistible pull that had initially attracted him to her, its strength such that she seemed to have forgiven him for the charade as Sir Percival. For that, she *should* forgive him, unless she truly had some sadistic wish to be wed to Coleway's steward. Still, there were times when he caught doubt in her eyes and knew that she still had trouble trusting him. Or times, like today, when he would give almost anything to know the truth behind her thoughtful silences.

The food had arrived in his absence and Rami had already descended upon the table like a horde of locusts, albeit a tidy horde. The boy was always careful to leave every dish arranged as carefully as when it had arrived without a crumb out of place, even if crumbs were all that remained of certain dishes. He had expected Rami's obsession with food to fade as the passing weeks proved the certainty of a full belly each day, but it was obviously going to take more time before the boy stopped stockpiling for the next famine. He sent Rami to the bathhouse with a few words and then settled down to wait for Avalene.

Oliver and Armand entered the solar not long behind him, clean-shaven and neatly groomed, and Reginald soon after. Wrapped in thoughts of the woman in his bedchamber, he had almost forgotten his order to meet here. He bid them partake of the food, although he also instructed them to join Isabel and her company for the evening meal to find out what more they could about their guests. Reginald's spies had been busy already. He listened with interest to the tale of Isabel's unexpected arrival and all Reginald had learned in the days since then.

It was as Reginald and Gerhardt had informed him earlier; Edward had a husband in mind for Isabel and she had returned to England to await the wedding. Unwed royals were rarely free of a spouse for long; most were betrothed in the cradle, or, as in Isabel's case, re-married at the close of their mourning period to form a new alliance for the king with another royal family, or as a special reward for one of his higher-ranking nobles. Royal daughters came entailed with riches and titles for their husbands and the children of such unions. Envoys from impoverished princes probably began to land on Edward's doorstep within a month of Isabel's widowhood.

No one yet knew the identity of her future husband, but the more Dante learned of the situation, the more his suspicions were aroused. Isabel's retinue was part of her dowry: a score of her dead husband's royal guards who were completely loyal to her, three score of servants who were also from her husband's household and also loyal only to their mistress, and one hundred of King Edward's royal guard who were loyal to the king. In other words, a good part of Isabel's dowry consisted of an army. And it was an army that would reside within her husband's walls, but one her husband would not control. Interesting.

Reginald struggled to find the politest words possible to call Isabel a spoiled brat. Again, not so unusual for Edward's daughters. They were richer and more powerful than most men, and virtually above the law. He supposed there would be trouble if one of them outright murdered someone in front of witnesses, but even then he would not bet on them suffering many consequences. They were part of the royal family. The rules that most of society followed did not apply to them. Power and wealth on that scale tended to breed arrogance and conceit. He did not envy Isabel's hapless new husband.

As Reginald continued his report, Dante suddenly recalled another act of arrogance, this one on his own part. He had been in a foul mood before he left for Coleway, resentful of the girl who had delayed his retirement from a craft he abhorred. He had known she would need garments upon her arrival in London. In a moment of pique, he had ordered the clothing made up in cheap fabrics and common materials. The gowns that awaited Avalene in his chamber were not fit to touch her skin. Even his servants wore finer garments.

He gave a mental groan and wondered how quickly new gowns could be made. The situation would be bad enough without Isabel's presence. To present Avalene to royalty in peasant garb? He would be lucky if she ever spoke to him again.

His gaze went to the bedchamber door. Matilda was a competent seamstress. Not capable of what he had in mind, but surely she would have Avalene's measure by this time to alter the offensive garments he had provided. Fortunately, he was in a city where anything could be made possible with the right amount of money and influence. He had both.

He gave his orders concerning the clothing to Reginald, certain they would be carried out. He also ordered a messenger sent to the Tower to request an audience with Mordecai on the morrow. He was equally certain Mordecai was already aware of his return to London, but he knew better than to show up on his doorstep uninvited and unannounced. There were a few other matters that needed his decisions and orders, and then he dismissed Reginald. Before he sent Oliver and Armand to the hall, he made certain there would be two guards posted outside the solar who would bar anyone from entering without his permission, and to accompany Avalene if she should leave his quarters without him. He didn't plan to have her out of his sight very often or for very long.

Once the others left he angled his chair toward the chamber door and settled in to wait, plotting, planning all the ways he would coax the words he most wanted to hear from her again. These niggling doubts that her silence meant she had reconsidered her feelings for him would go away as soon as he could hold her again, as soon as he could look into her eyes and see the light that shined there just for him. Once Segrave and his annoying betrothal contract were out of the way, he would ask her to marry him. He wondered how she would react to the question. Mostly he wondered what the hell was taking her so long.

The bathwater was ice cold and still Avalene lingered in the tub, trying to hide her shivers from the tirewoman, Matilda, who had helped wash her hair and scrub her back. Matilda had also poured oil into the water that filled the chamber with the scents of sandalwood and flowers. It felt wonderful to be clean again, to be free of her filthy clothing, but she was not quite ready to leave the sanctuary of her bath to face Dante and his men. Oliver and Armand probably knew she and Dante had done more than just sleep together while they were on the road, but tonight they would know for certain that she intended to share Dante's bed for illicit reasons. Tonight she would become a fallen woman. Would they look at her differently? Treat her differently?

Having Matilda in the room helped calm her nerves for some reason, even though she was a silent presence as she sat on a stool near the tub, busily hemming one of the too-long new gowns while she waited for Avalene to emerge from the tub. She was perhaps a dozen years older than Avalene, her hair covered with a linen snood, her manner all brisk efficiency. She had laid out the pieces of Avalene's new wardrobe on the bed, three gowns in all, along with chemises and stockings, veils, and a pair of suede slippers. Avalene didn't know how Dante managed to purchase clothing for her but she was grateful for it. Her own belt and girdle were barely damaged by their extended wear and once cleaned they would work well enough with the new gowns, along with the circlet that would hold her new veils in place.

She did her best to keep her mind on the garments rather than on the large bed and what would eventually take place there. *Tonight.*

Did Matilda know that tonight was the night? Did everyone in the palace know? She forced her gaze back to the garments still spread out on the bed and decided that while the clothing would suffice for her immediate needs, the sturdy, serviceable gowns made of plain linen were hardly what she would have chosen to meet royalty. In all her imaginings, she never would have guessed

that she would be sleeping under the same roof as one of
the king's daughters. Tonight, of all nights.

The words *tonight is the night* kept growing louder in
her head until she marveled that Matilda did not seem
to hear them. There was nothing to fear, no reason to
feel afraid, and yet her pulse raced each time she looked
at the bed. She knew it would hurt the first time, it
would hurt enough that she would bleed, but she also
knew that Dante would be gentle with her. Indeed, after
last night, she looked forward to this one. At least, she
wanted to look forward to tonight. Why was she so nervous?

She made herself think of Isabel, to speculate about
what the princess would look like, whether or not she
would be friendly. Would she look at Avalene's plain,
ill-fitting clothing and laugh? Of course, Dante might
not have any intention of taking her to the midday meal
tomorrow to meet the illustrious Isabel of Ascalon. Or
perhaps she could delay the meeting until the seamstresses had a chance to work up a gown presentable to
Isabel's company. She could also make great improve-
ments to the current gowns if she could just find some
embroidery thread and trims. Mayhap some of the fur
from her ruined cloak could be salvaged.

Was it just her imagination, or did the bed really grow
larger the longer she stared at it? *Tonight is the night.*

Nay, she was to think about Isabel, how she would
look a great cow next to the dazzling royal daughter and
her court. Then her conscience reminded her of another
reason she would never be allowed to meet Isabel. She
was a fallen woman now, or, soon would be. *Tonight.*
She wasn't sure what the rules were regarding this predicament, having never imagined she would ever be in
the situation, but she was fairly certain kings' daughters
did not consort with harlots.

Ah. Problem solved. What a relief that all of her worries about the garments were unnecessary. Isabel would never see her gowns. She would never even be presented to the princess.

And that freed her mind to decide if she should be pleased or piqued over Dante's obvious influence over one aspect of her new clothing. Everything was red.

Pleased, she decided, although she intended to ask how he knew that red was the only color she wore before he had even met her. She would have to wait to ask that question until they were alone . . . *tonight*.

She sighed and then signaled to Matilda that she was ready to dress. She needed more of a distraction than a bath could provide. It was time to face Dante and the others. Sooner than seemed possible, she was back in the solar.

Dante rose to greet her almost before she entered the room, as if he could sense her approach. He stood at one end of the long trestle table that stood in the center of the room. She had meant to say something trite about feeling refreshed by the bath, but the words froze in her throat when she took a good look at him.

She hadn't realized how unkempt they had all become on their travels until the evidence of their journey was washed and shaved and combed away. He had taken clothes from his chamber before he left for the bathhouse, and he was now dressed completely in black. He was transformed, but not into the chivalrous knight who had first entered the hall at Coleway. The man who stood before her was a handsome, powerful nobleman who took her breath away.

To be fair, he always took her breath away, but this change from knight to nobleman was unexpected. It ignited new worries that had festered all afternoon in a quiet corner of her mind. Now she wondered how they had remained silent all this time.

It must be the garments, she decided, their quality far beyond anything a knight would own. His surcoat was quilted in a diamond pattern and shot through with silver thread, his leather braces and boots dyed an exact shade of black and studded with silver rivets. His belt was also studded with silver, the metal worked into the same diamond pattern as his tunic. It was the type of understated elegance that only the very wealthy could afford.

She looked down at her adequate yet simple clothing and felt like the proverbial ugly duckling. An extremely ungrateful duckling. If not for his thoughtfulness and foresight she would have only her own tattered, filthy clothing to don. Aye, she was an ungrateful wretch, but did he have to look so devastatingly handsome? She tried again to feel grateful. Ah, yes. At least she would not have to face the king's daughter in her plain gowns.

"What is wrong?" His brows were now drawn together in a frown and his smile had vanished.

"Nothing," she assured him, plastering an overly bright smile on her face that also faded before it fully formed. "Where is everyone?"

He looked puzzled for a moment, and then understanding dawned. "Rami is taking his bath. Oliver and Armand are meeting with the soldiers they left in charge during our absence. They will have their meal in the hall with the others."

She glanced behind her, looking for Matilda.

"She just left," he said, guessing her thoughts easily enough. "We are alone."

"Oh." She swallowed once, and then forced her feet to move forward so she could take the seat he offered next to his. A puzzled line appeared between his brows.

She turned her attention to the table, which held an abundance of food that should look enticing to her empty stomach but did not. Even the smell of fresh baked bread did not tempt her. "I did not realize our meal had arrived. Will Reginald be here soon to meet with you?"

"Reginald has been here and gone." His mouth quirked upward at one corner. "You were at your bath a very long time. I began to wonder if Matilda had allowed you to drown."

"Nay, I did not drown." For an instant she wished she had. She sounded like an idiot. Perhaps she should just keep her mouth closed. She folded her hands in her lap and lowered her gaze, trying to look calm and serene, but the lengthening silence began to feel awkward. She looked up and found him already watching her with an enigmatic expression. She blurted out the first thing that came to mind. "You look very handsome."

"You outshine me." He lifted her hand and pressed a light kiss to her fingertips. His words were swift and low. *"Tu siete la donna che più bella ho visto mai."*

She felt herself blush over the blatant lie, the part that she understood about outshining him, and lowered her gaze again. "'Tis obvious I need to expand my grasp of your language. I understood few of those words, but they sound very pretty."

"Mm. You will have time during our journey to Venice to learn more."

Hope lifted its head at the mention of Venice. They were not on the deck of a ship about to set sail, so she ruthlessly pushed it back down. She would live for the moment and let the morrow take care of itself. They were together today, and that was enough for now.

He handed her a goblet filled with wine and she took a few nervous sips. Here they were, warm and dry, and

a soft, comfortable bed awaited. *Tonight is the night.*
She would give herself completely to the man she loved.
She *wanted* to give herself to him. Would he think her
too bold if she excused herself and climbed into bed to
wait for him? All of this waiting around was shredding
her nerves. She did not want to eat or drink. She wanted
him to kiss her, to hold her, to caress her as he had last
night.

Her thoughts strayed once again as she recalled some
of the more intimate moments. Soon her face felt as if it
were on fire and her hands began to tremble. She carefully set the goblet back on the table, thankful she had
not spilled the wine all over herself.

"Would you like something to eat?" he asked, waving
his hand toward the bounty before them. "Ham? Bread
pudding? Fruit? I finally gave up waiting for you and fed
myself, so the rest is yours. Have whatever you like."

There was no way she would be able to swallow any
of it. She shook her head. "Uhm, I am not as hungry as
I thought."

Her stomach chose that moment to make her a liar.
The rumbling sound made one of his brows rise. "You
have hardly eaten today. I think you should eat *something.*"

"Perhaps a piece of bread," she conceded.

He ignored her request and piled her trencher with a
sampling of almost everything on the table, then pushed
it toward her. "Eat what you can. Humor me. Please."

She bowed her head and tried, and then realized it was
not as much of a chore as she had feared. Soon the trencher was almost empty. She made herself eat slowly because it was impolite to wolf down her food, and not
because she was trying to delay anything. She wanted an
end to this awkwardness. Dante studied her over his
steepled fingers, his attention unwavering.

"Are you nervous?" he asked in a gentle voice.

She looked up at him as she swallowed the last bite of an apple. "I think 'terrified' is a more accurate description."

He laughed aloud. Before she knew what he intended, he lifted her effortlessly and settled her onto his lap. She held her back stiff, resisting the urge to lean into his solid chest. "*Cara*, do you remember last night and this morn?"

Did reliving every moment in minute detail count? In that case, she remembered all too clearly. "Aye."

"I have thought of little else all day," he admitted. He drew his fingertip down her cheek and got the expected reaction. She closed her eyes and shivered. "There is nothing to fear. I am the same man you turn to in your sleep, the same man you kissed so passionately. Where is the greedy girl who wanted more than just kisses?"

That thoughtless girl had abandoned them somewhere on the road to London. *This* girl knew exactly what she was about to do, and with whom. She also knew he would not be pleased with her latest epiphany. She bit her lower lip. "You are not the man I thought you were this morning."

His body stiffened and all humor fled from his expression. "What do you mean?"

She waved her hand to indicate their surroundings. "You are *rich*! You live in a palace, you consort with kings and their daughters."

She could almost feel the tension flow out of him.

"You say this as if they were bad things," he teased. He lifted her hand and turned it over to expose her wrist. Rather than kiss the sensitive skin, he rubbed the tip of his nose over the line of delicate veins and inhaled, as if her skin held some addictive scent. Her breathing stopped entirely. "I told you I was a wealthy man. But I only consort with one king, and I have not yet met his daughter."

"I thought you were a landless knight," she managed, as she tugged her hand away to return it to her lap. "And then I thought you were simply an assassin, a foreigner plucked from obscurity to do the king's bidding. Now I discover that you are richer than my father, likely richer than Faulke Segrave and possibly more powerful. You are at least a baron, are you not?"

"Titles and ranking are somewhat different in Venice than they are here," he said, "but you are correct; I am among the nobility. An English earl would be the most likely equivalent."

Her heart beat harder. Ah, there was the familiar pain. She had been almost certain he was a nobleman, but hearing her fear confirmed made it real. And it was worse than she thought. An earl.

Ever observant, he pointed out the obvious. "You are not pleased."

"I thought my rank was above yours." She would never admit that she had viewed her rank as a meager sort of consolation prize for him; a noblewoman for the commoner. "Earls are expected to marry. 'Tis their duty to produce heirs. Someday you will want a wife. Even if you were so inclined, I will never be allowed to marry so long as I am betrothed to Faulke Segrave." Her voice dropped to a whisper. "You will leave me."

"I will not leave you," he said, as if this were an obvious fact. His arms tightened around her and he cradled her to his chest. "How many times must I tell you? I am yours."

"I am pledged to another."

He pressed a kiss to her forehead. "You are meant for no other man but me."

She waited for him to admit that he must eventually

take a wife, that the day would come when he would be forced to cast her aside, but he remained silent as she listened to the steady beat of his heart. Surely he had thought of this already? Not knowing his thoughts was worse than hearing the truth. "What are you thinking?"

"I am thinking that Faulke Segrave is more of a nuisance than I ever dreamed he would be." He released a slow sigh and she tried to look up at him, but his grip on her tightened again and held her immobile. His voice turned thoughtful. "The man who sent me on this mission is named Mordecai. He told me about you, tried to warn me, I suppose, that you would be . . . not what I expected. In my arrogance, I did not hear what he was telling me."

She wondered why this Mordecai person had felt it necessary to *warn* Dante about her. Was she really so bad? How would he even know? She had never met him. "I do not care to meet this person."

His laugh was humorless. "Mordecai is not only one of Edward's advisers, he is a magician. Indeed, that would be the reason Edward keeps him close. One of Mordecai's more useful talents is his ability to see into the future, to see dangers to the king and the results of different decisions he might make, as well as the decisions of others. He saw several possible futures for us, and where our paths would lead depending upon the choices that were made."

She waited for him to laugh. Surely this was another one of his jests? He did not even believe in the Witches' Sabbath, and yet he believed this charlatan magician could see into the future? His expression remained deadly serious.

"Do not tell me you believe him?" She smiled indulgently. "Many magicians attended the fairs at Coleway over the years. Some of them could perform amazing tricks, but their fortune-telling abilities proved remark-ably similar. Every young man had a pretty woman about to enter his life, every old woman could expect the coming year to be one of good health. And everyone was about to experience a turn of good luck or a wind-fall of some sort. Health and happiness all around, but couched in vague warnings that could be interpreted to mean almost anything or serve as an excuse as to why last year's prediction went unfulfilled. I am surprised the king was duped by such a charlatan, and I am even more surprised that you were taken in as well."

He did not return her smile. "Mordecai is an entirely different creature from the magicians you have encoun-tered at fairs."

She made a sound of skepticism.

"I have known Mordecai since I was a boy and I have seen too much over the years to doubt his skills. He is no charlatan."

The look in his eyes convinced her that he believed what he said.

"If you should ever meet him, promise me that you will not voice any doubts of his abilities. 'Tis unlikely he would harm you, knowing what you mean to me, but I have stood witness when he has corrected other people's mistaken beliefs or doubts about him. He has little pa-tience for those who demand explanations and proof." His grip on her arms was almost painful. "Do not pro-voke Mordecai. Ever. Promise me."

"I promise," she said slowly. The look of relief in his eyes was unmistakable, but it faded into wariness at her next question. "What did he see in our future that has you worried?"

"I know that your trust in me is fragile, but I must ask you to trust me again without question, to trust that I will make certain everything will work out for us as it is meant to."

"What do—"

He pressed his fingers against her lips. "All I can tell you is that there are things I must do in the next few days and weeks, decisions I must influence, but, ultimately, they are decisions others must make that will affect our future."

Of course. He had to obtain the king's permission to take her to Italy, but what other plan was he talking about that needed to be kept secret? Whatever it was, he sounded very sure of himself, but then again, confidence was never something he lacked.

"For now," he continued, "know that we have a future. We will be together, no matter what happens."

The words were comforting and worrisome at the same time. "What do you mean, 'no matter what happens'? What else could change our circumstances?"

"I cannot answer your questions," he said quietly.

The answer fueled her frustration. "Cannot, or *will* not?"

"Cannot."

And, just like that, her anger deflated. "Oh."

"I have already told you more than I should," he admitted. "I just wanted to put your mind at ease, but it would seem I have only added to your fears. Is it still so impossible for you to trust me?"

That was a good question. He had already broken her trust, told her lies that she had readily believed. Did he really think she could trust him again so soon, so blindly, without question? He studied her face and found the obvious answer in her expression.

"What you cannot forget is that I lied to you about my identity," he surmised. "I could not tell you the truth when we first met, but I never lied about the way I felt about you and I will always do whatever is necessary to protect you. Can you believe that much at least?"

"Aye." She trusted him to keep her safe. What she still had trouble trusting in was his claim that he loved her, that he felt even a fraction of the love she felt for him.

She had started falling in love the first moment she laid eyes on him, the first time she heard his voice, the first time she looked into his eyes. The more time she spent with him, the deeper she fell. Even after she had learned of his deception her heart had refused to give up its claim. He could break her heart, but he could never return it. It belonged to him now.

Trust, especially blind trust, was the last small part of her heart that she held back, the part she had not already handed over to him. Once he had that piece there would be no way to recover if he deceived her again.

Don't do it, Reason warned. *He will leave you defenseless and broken.*

Your life does not matter without him, Hope countered. *This is what you were born for, who you were born for. He loves you. He wants to spend his life with you. Trust him.*

She thought about the reasons he had lied to her in the first place and came to a sudden, startling conclusion. All this time she had it backward. She had believed him as Sir Percival, and constantly doubted him as Dante Chiavari. In reality, Sir Percival was the liar while Dante had always told her the truth.

The last string of doubt drifted from her grasp and her heart felt suddenly lighter. "You can trust me, too, you know."

"I do trust you," he said.

"What I meant is that you can tell me your secrets and I will not repeat them."

"I trust you to keep *my* secrets," he said, "but I am bound by my oath to keep the secrets of others."

She could not ask him to forsake his oath in favor of her curiosity. She could wait a few days or weeks until the decisions were made that he must influence.

"At least you do not appear 'terrified' anymore," he observed, trying to lighten her mood.

"Terror holds hands with uncertainty." She placed her hand on the side of his face and looked deep into his eyes. "I am no longer uncertain. I trust you."

She wasn't sure he understood what she was telling him until he closed his eyes, his expression one of silent thanks.

"This time I will hold close your trust," he pledged. "I do not intend to lose it again."

And he claimed to have no honor? He had assumed the disguise of the King's Assassin as completely as he had assumed the disguise of Sir Percival. Beneath both cloaks was the most honorable man she had ever known. Did anyone ever see this side of him? Did *he* even see this side of himself?

She wound her arms around his neck and pressed her lips to his, sealing both their vows. He returned the kiss gently at first, rediscovering her lips as if it had been days rather than hours since they last kissed, and then she molded her body to his and the kisses began to burn with an urgency that went beyond physical need. He kissed her as he never had before, fierce, demanding, without hesitation or restraint. Tonight there was nothing to stop him.

"Whatever my future holds, you are a part of it," she murmured, as his lips trailed down her neck. Even if he left her someday to take a wife and all that was left was a heartbreaking memory, the pain would be worth this happiness. She could probably live without him, but without him there would be nothing to live for. The ledge beckoned. She had to make this leap of faith.

"Come to bed with me," he whispered, and then she was on her feet. He took her hand and led her into the bedchamber.

She had expected more kisses once the door closed behind them, more urgency that would drive them toward the massive bed. Instead he moved methodically around the room, finding a flint and then lighting a brace of candles that was placed on a table near the bed. As there was still enough light coming through the window to see by, she assumed he meant to still be awake when it would be too dark to easily find the flint. Her muddled mind never would have thought that far ahead.

Next he went past her cold bath to put more charcoal in the brazier, and then he sat down on the bench at the end of the bed and calmly removed his boots. The braces and belt came off next. She watched in dumbfounded silence as, slowly and surely, his tunic and shirt followed.

"Oh, thank goodness." She breathed a sigh of relief that he had stopped undressing, although it turned into a series of long sighs when her gaze lingered on his chest. The beautiful lines of his body never failed to fascinate her. If she didn't stop breathing so fast, she was going to faint.

"What makes you say that?" he asked, his expression amused.

She had to think a moment to remember what she had said and why, and then she blurted out the answer. "For a moment there I thought you intended to take off *all* of your clothes."

"I do intend exactly that." He studied her face and then added, "Eventually."

Her eyes widened. "Why?"

"Why?" he echoed, clearly baffled.

"You are going to be . . . naked?"

"Of course," he said, with a note of gentleness in his voice that she found out of place.

Oh, she was definitely going to faint.

"Avalene?" He was at her side in an instant.

"People do this *naked*?!"

"It would appear you are not as knowledgeable as I thought," he muttered. He made it sound as if her lack of knowledge was a disappointment.

"I am plenty knowledgeable," she argued. "I just did not realize that people removed all their clothing to . . . I am sure that no one mentioned it. Is this some strange Italian custom?"

"Nay." Now he was smiling. "Actually, I suppose it is an Italian custom, although the custom is just as common throughout the world."

She looked at the brace of candles, and then at the bed. Her breathing sounded as if she had just run up a very long flight of stairs.

She knew the answer to her next question before she asked it. "Do I have to be naked, too?"

Now he was wary, realizing this was all unexpected news to her. "How did you think people could make love when they were fully clothed?" He shook his head. "Never mind. I suppose that question was answered last night."

She gave him a distracted nod. The thought of standing naked next to all of his perfection made her heart do strange things in her chest. "I do not think we need the candles."

His gaze followed hers to the candles and then back to her face. The tenderness of his expression melted the edges of her fear. "Tonight is not for darkness. Avalene, do you not yet realize that you are the most beautiful thing ever to exist in my world?" His fingers slid down the curve of her neck, his touch feather-light, almost as if he were tasting her skin with his fingertips. "I do not want anything more to stand between us, not even clothing. Will you rob me of that pleasure?"

Well, put that way . . . She shook her head.

He leaned down and slowly kissed her ear. "I want to undress you myself, to see you reveal yourself to me one layer of clothing at a time. Will you let me?"

Never. He did something to her ear that made her knees weak. She whispered, "A-Aye."

His lips moved to her mouth while he untied the laces of her gown. His kisses had the curious effect of both soothing and exciting her, and more of the fear melted away. This was not so very different from the other times they were alone together. She knew how to fit her mouth to his, how to return the pleasure he gave her. At first she was hesitant to touch his bare chest, but soon her hands were skimming over every inch of bare skin she could reach. He was so different from her, so much larger, so much harder. His whole body was made of warm stone.

She vaguely realized that her gown had fallen away and she stood only in her chemise. He caught both her wrists in one hand and took a step away from her. His eyes locked with hers and she realized that he was breathing hard, panting between his parted lips as they stared at each other. He had already unlaced her chemise and now he reached out to brush the slender straps from her shoulders. His gaze lowered at the same moment she felt the fabric pool around her feet and she saw a tremor move through his body.

He stared so long that she began to feel self-conscious, and then he shook his head, as if physical movement was necessary to clear his thoughts. "I want to make you understand how beautiful you are to me, but I have no words."

He used his lips and hands instead, starting at her neck, moving down to her shoulders, steadily moving lower as he touched and kissed every part of her. She could hardly stand. He seemed to realize she was becoming unbalanced and he lifted her effortlessly into his arms. The feel of so much bare skin touching sent a shock of awareness through her and she knew he felt it, too, heard it in the catch of his breath. He laid her gently on top of the bed and covered her with his body, most of his weight braced above her on his arms.

"I—" Her voice broke and she had to clear her throat before she could continue. "I thought you were going to be naked, too."

"I will be." He smiled down at her. "I have waited all my life for this moment. Indulge me while I linger over it."

The things he said seemed to be plucked right from her head. "That is what I thought when I saw you enter the great hall at Coleway. I stayed at the railing because I wanted to see your face, hear your voice, but somehow even then I knew that I had been waiting for you. Was it . . . was it anything like that for you when we first met?"

"Not quite," he admitted, and her marvel faded a little. "I was appalled at my reaction to you. It was like nothing I had ever experienced. Long ago I learned to control my emotions, to never give away anything that might be used against me, and to always be aware of my surroundings. When I looked at you, a herd of belled cattle could have stampeded by me and I never would have known they were there. John and even Brunor knew immediately that I was besotted. It was embarrassing."

She smothered a giggle. Ah, marvel again. He felt the same.

He made a face. "I think Brunor felt sorry for me."

"Poor thing," she murmured. She stroked his cheek, and realized she was no longer self-conscious about her nudity. This was Dante. She had nothing to hide from him.

His expression was suddenly serious as the tip of his finger traced her lips. "I never understood why history is filled with stories of men who waged wars over a woman they loved. There are many women in the world, and it was beyond my grasp what made one woman special enough to go to such extremes." He pressed a kiss to her forehead. "Now I understand."

His lips found hers again and he kissed her with a passion that left her breathless, his body a welcome weight upon hers. He settled his hips between her legs and she could feel the hard proof of his arousal. His hand slid down the length of her back and then lower, pulling her closer even as he pushed against her. She arched toward him, helping his impossible quest to press her closer to his body.

He made a sound low in his chest and then moved lower, his hips no longer joined to hers, the weight of his body now pinning her down as his hands and mouth cherished her, kissing, stroking, caressing everywhere he could reach. It was shocking. It was pleasurable beyond bearing. She began to make small sounds of pleasure and impatience. And then suddenly his weight was gone.

She blinked once and saw him standing next to the bed, untying the laces on his pants. His eyes burned as he looked down at her.

"You cannot know how many times I imagined you in my bed at just this moment." The knotted laces suddenly snapped in his hands and then he pushed the leather pants to the floor and stepped away from them. She had little more than a glimpse of his stiff sex before he rejoined her on the bed. "My meager imagination did not do you justice."

Again he had plucked the thoughts from her head. He found his place again between her legs, the cradle where he fit so perfectly. Her arms welcomed him as well, wrapping around his neck, pulling him closer. His hand moved lower until his palm pressed against her. She closed her eyes and let her head fall back as she gave herself over to the primitive emotions that raged inside her body, a body that no longer seemed her own but one that knew exactly how to respond to him, how to please him.

She arched her back, which thrust her chest toward him, and he accepted the offering. He leaned down to kiss first one breast and then the other, and then he started to do more amazing and shocking things with his tongue and mouth. The last shreds of her virtue fell away and her hands tangled in his hair, at times tugging hard enough to cause him pain when he tried to move on to a new torment before she had her fill of the last one. She urged him to do whatever he wanted, as long as he did not stop.

"Put your legs around my waist," he said, his voice barely recognizable. He pressed a hard line of kisses from her shoulder to her lips. There was nothing gentle about the way his mouth slanted over hers, opening her lips, and then stroking her mouth with his tongue in a blatant echo of what he planned to do to her body.

He positioned himself so the length of his sex pressed against her slick, heated flesh. She could hear his labored breathing, the small catches in his breath when he moved against her. Her hips lifted of their own accord and he returned the pressure, not penetrating, but letting her feel the length of him between her legs, his hips pressed tightly to hers. There was a sudden lack of air in the room. A tremor went through his body and the muscles in his arms and chest became even harder beneath her hands. The muscles in his neck stood out in stark relief as he began to move against her, the friction against her most sensitive skin a near unbearable pleasure.

There was a fire building inside her. Each movement of his hips seemed to move her closer to the heat. She wanted to tell him how he was making her feel but words were beyond her. Small moans were the only sounds she seemed capable of making. She had thought her body incapable of handling any more sensation until his hand cupped her breast and he roughly flicked his thumb across her nipple. She was on fire.

"Something is . . ." Her breath came in small gasps. "I cannot . . ."

"Let it happen." His voice was a dark presence against her ear, his breath scorching. "Let yourself fall. I will keep you safe, Avalene. Trust me."

He knew what was happening to her. She knew he would keep her safe. She let go of her last hold on sanity and let the flames consume her. She felt as if she were flying, soaring upward, and then floating motionless, stunned joy and a tempest's fury all at once. She barely had time for the emotions to register when she felt his teeth sink painlessly into her shoulder. He shifted his weight, then with one long, powerful thrust, he was inside her. "Oh!"

"Forgive me, *cara*." The words were torn from his chest. He buried his face against her neck and thrust himself even deeper.

"Oh!" Her nails dug into his shoulders, deep and hard.

He let out a hiss of pain, but only gathered her closer. One arm wrapped around her waist, the other above her shoulders so his hand could cradle her head. He held himself still for one long, breathless moment, then he drew back ever so slowly.

The sensations were invasive, foreign and raw, and yet she felt a strange sense of alarm that he was leaving her. A small sound of distress came from her unbidden.

"Shh, *cara,* I cannot stop." There was distress in his voice, but he entered her again with a smooth stroke that made her gasp again at the renewed shock of his invasion. "Not yet. Soon. Soon."

Instinctively she knew that he was trying to be gentle. His body was beyond his control now, just as hers had been only moments before. She clung to his arms, to muscles that had turned to marble. He was deep within her, his warm skin slick with his efforts to be gentle, his musk a lush blanket over her senses. He moved slowly, sometimes almost imperceptibly.

The pain was beginning to fade when he began to thrust harder, burying himself even deeper until she felt his sex swell within her body. Suddenly he stopped, a statue frozen in a moment of time, a moment of such intense pleasure that it might be pain. A low, primitive sound came from inside him and his muscles convulsed as he held her impaled. He was looking down at her with those hypnotic, intense green eyes, as if words failed him.

In that moment she discovered her whole reason for being, the entire point of being alive. She was awed, speechless with wonder. The shudder that wracked his body vibrated through her, powerful beyond anything she had ever felt, as if he were imparting some measure of his strength to her. His eyes closed and small tremors began to run along the muscles of his arms, and then he crushed her to his chest, trembling and winded.

She listened to the sound of their heartbeats, uncertain

whether it was hers or his or some combination of the two. Even their labored breathing shared the same pattern, inhaling at the same time, exhaling at the same time. Nothing that she had ever heard or seen or been told could have prepared her for this . . . this feeling of completion, that they were two parts of the same whole, separate, and yet only truly complete when they were joined together. She had thought her feelings for him were as deep as she was capable, certain of her love for him, certain what she felt for him could not grow any stronger. Now she realized there were not any words to encompass her feelings. It went beyond her ability to describe. Words were not enough, and yet she could no longer contain the paltriest of them.

"I love you."

20

The Princess

The Page of Wands is a bearer of tidings and a teller of stories. A new stirring of potential manifests itself as restlessness and dissatisfaction. Nurture the harbingers of inspiration, even if initial strategies prove impractical or impossible. Justice is at hand.

"*Mi sei mancato molto!*"

Avalene dutifully repeated Rami's words, albeit not as effortlessly.

"*Abbastanza bene,*" Rami said, with a small shrug. "*Hai bisogno di più pratica.*"

"Aye, I need much more practice," she agreed. She watched him push a lock of dark hair from his eyes and realized it needed the attention of a good pair of shears. The words for such a request in Italian weren't within her grasp but she would ask Dante about it later. "*Ho bisogno di fare pratica con il mio italiano.*"

"*Sì.*" Rami was growing bored with the Italian lessons. He made a show of turning his attention toward the end of the table and gave their empty trenchers a wistful look, punctuated by a pitiful sigh. "*Ho fame.*"

"Impossible. There is no way you can be hungry again," she admonished. "We just ate."

He turned a sad gaze upon her and his big, brown eyes seemed to swallow up his face. "*Ho fame.*"

"You are shameless." She watched his lower lip tremble. "Oh, very well! When the servants come to clear this away, I will ask them to bring a few nuncheons. *Cicchetti, sì?*"

His smile was beatific. He turned over the whetstone he held in one hand and continued to hone the blade of his dagger. The metal made a soft *whisp, whisp, whisp* sound against the stone. He began to sing a jaunty little tune in rhythm to the strokes. It was a song about pastries and pies.

She rolled her eyes and then turned her attention back to the hem she was sewing on one of her new gowns. She murmured again the phrase he had just taught her, this time under her breath. *"Mi sei mancato molto."* I missed you so much.

Dante had departed a few hours ago, as reluctant to leave as she was reluctant to see him go, but he had received a message that Mordecai wished to meet with him immediately. And just like that, the most magical night of her life was over . . . even though the sun had already been high in the sky when it ended. Her lips curved into a secretive smile. There was always tonight.

She pretended to stretch again as if she were yawning, just to take inventory of her new body once more. Last night had changed her in many ways, but physically, that was the most surprising change of all. He made her shockingly aware of every part of her that could be touched and kissed and caressed, awakened responses that she wasn't even aware she possessed.

"Possessed" was actually a good word for what he made her feel. Naked, pressed against the length of him, his hands on her and hers on him, she felt as if she were an entirely different creature, lean, sensual, lithe, all smooth flow and warm movement. He all but made her purr. Today there was still some lingering stiffness and soreness to remind her of the transformation.

She used some of the fabric spread across her lap to fan her face. It was suddenly very warm in the solar.

A sharp knock on the door to the hallway cut off Rami's song in mid-verse. Armand entered the solar without waiting for her to bid him enter.

"Forgive the interruption, my lady." He gave a low, quick bow of apology, even as Oliver and three servants crowded into the room behind him. They were followed by four more soldiers. "Isabel was displeased when Lord Dante did not present himself at the midday meal to greet her. She has determined to come here to await his return."

Even as he spoke, the servants placed large trays on the table that held pitchers and goblets, and then cleared away the remnants of Avalene's and Rami's meal. Oliver and the soldiers took up a position along the wall behind her. Armand remained by the door. She felt Oliver's hand touch her shoulder.

"I am sorry, my lady. We cannot deny her entrance."

"Of course not," she said, finally finding her voice. The servants departed but they left the door open. She saw that two more soldiers still stood guard outside the door. She looked behind her, then again toward the doorway. Eight soldiers, counting Oliver and Armand. Were they expecting a siege?

Already she could hear several women's voices in the hallway, but they were still too far away for her to understand any of the words. She stood up and the forgotten gown slid to the floor. Just as she bent down to retrieve the garment, she heard a woman's voice quite clearly.

"What a cozy solar! Gerhardt, do you think it larger than my own?"

Her words were marked with a trace of the same accent that Avalene had heard in Gerhardt's voice the day before. How odd. She had not expected an English princess to sound foreign. She straightened in time to hear Gerhardt's answer.

"I do not think so, my lady. One assumes the rooms in each wing are the same dimensions."

The lady in question gave a delicate sniff. "How unimaginative."

Avalene felt her jaw unhinge at the sight before her. Isabel was more than a head taller than she, the same height as most of the men in the room. She wore a pink bliaut made of a shimmering fabric she had never seen before. The fabric was covered with hundreds of delicate flowers and vines and birds stitched in gold thread. Gold braid trimmed the waist, neckline, and sleeves, and a snow-white surcoat lined with the same pink fabric covered her bliaut. The profile of a fierce-looking bird with widespread wings was stitched onto each shoulder of the surcoat, fashioned of gold beads with their beaks and talons made of hundreds of tiny pink beads.

Gold, pink, and white ribbons encased her long, dark plait that ended in a gold tassel that nearly touched the floor. On her head was an enormously tall, flared barbette covered with more of the shiny pink fabric. The crenellated crown was encrusted with seed pearls and the whole of it topped with a profusion of long white feathers that looked like weightless strings that bowed and swayed with the slightest movement of her head. More pearls decorated her earrings and necklace, much larger than those on her barbette, yet still delicate-looking against skin that was nearly the same color. Her lips were the exact shade as her bliaut, but her eyes were a piercing blue, shrewd and intelligent as she examined the solar as thoroughly as Avalene examined Isabel. A small frown creased between her dark brows as her gaze moved over Avalene and then dismissed her.

Isabel gave a delicate wave of her hand and two more ladies stepped forward, their heads bowed. At first Avalene thought they were twins. Blue-eyed and blond-haired, they wore identical white bliauts with pink surcoats, the fabrics and jewels not as lavish as that of their mistress, but still far richer than anything Avalene owned. She looked down at her own sorry gown and amended that thought with, anything that she *used* to own. Between the three women, they wore more jewels than she had ever seen in one place at one time.

One of the two blond-haired girls carried a stack of pink cushions that she held while the other took a stool from the table and placed it to one side of the room. A cushion was placed on the stool and then the two remaining cushions were placed on the floor on either side of the stool. The two girls sank gracefully onto the floor cushions to take their seats, their skirts spread out around them like puddled flowers that left the scent of sandalwood in their wake. Isabel took her seat on the stool, and then three soldiers, also dressed in their mistress's colors, took up position behind the women. The room was suddenly quite crowded.

Avalene continued to stare at the tableau in dumbfounded silence. *All* of Isabel's people were blond-haired and blue-eyed, all dressed in the outrageously feminine colors of pink, gold, and white, and the picture they presented was as something from a religious painting. The room fairly glowed with their radiance. She had lost track of Gerhardt, who still stood near Armand at the door, but she realized he had taken a step forward when Isabel held up one hand to halt his progress.

"She is English, Gerhardt. The customs are different here." Isabel turned her head slightly to address Armand. "In my land . . . that is, in my husband's land, a lady's head must never be raised higher than my own."

Avalene abruptly took her seat.

"This is no lady," Gerhardt growled, as he jerked his head in Avalene's direction. He spoke to Armand. "Remove your lord's whore from my lady's presence."

Several things happened at once, but one thing happened first. A long misericorde appeared in Armand's hand with the deadly tip resting at Gerhardt's throat. Every other soldier present drew his sword and all the ladies gasped. Even Rami leapt to his feet and positioned himself in front of Avalene, his small dagger clutched in one hand and pointed toward the German soldiers.

"Apologize," Armand said in a mild tone, as if Gerhardt had made some flippant remark that was hardly worth mention. But a drop of blood began to trickle down Gerhardt's neck, changing direction slightly when Gerhardt swallowed and his Adam's apple bobbed beneath the blade.

Avalene wanted to run from the solar but she could not make herself move a muscle. This was her fault. She had disregarded the rules she had lived by all her life and allowed herself to be swept into a world that contained only Dante. There were consequences to every decision and it was time she faced the truth of her new life. Gerhardt had merely called her the name she refused to acknowledge to herself. He was about to die for simply speaking the truth.

She could see that Gerhardt had no intention of apologizing, and she could see just as clearly that Armand would cut his throat for the imagined insult. And then Isabel's soldiers would kill Armand and God knew who else. Their blood would be on her hands, all because she was a fallen woman, because she had selfishly taken the pleasure Dante offered her. She had to do or say something. She couldn't speak a word.

"This . . . peasant cannot be in my lady's presence," Gerhardt insisted.

Isabel rose to her feet but Avalene remained frozen in her seat, her eyes wide with horror. Of course she was an affront to Isabel, an insult not to be borne by so high a lady. She must make herself rise, make some excuse that Armand would find acceptable, remove herself to the bedchamber where she belonged. She should not be in the solar. Whores did not loiter in places where the daughter of the king could happen upon her.

"He is my favorite," Isabel said in a low voice to Armand. "I will be seriously displeased if you kill him."

Armand answered without taking his eyes from Gerhardt. "He would be dead already were my lord, Dante, present."

"Your lord *is* present," Dante said from the doorway. His gaze swept over the room as he moved forward. He kept an eye on Armand and Gerhardt when he walked past them but continued straight to Avalene. He wore the same black garments as the night before and now held a small wooden chest beneath one arm. The wooden chest was placed on the table, and then he lifted her cold hand and gently kissed her fingertips as if he had all the time in the world and nothing were amiss behind him. As if a man's life did not now rest upon the end of a blade. "My apologies for my late arrival, my lady. I was unavoidably delayed by this lady's father. Will you forgive me?"

He cocked his head in Isabel's direction but rudely kept his back to her. It took Avalene a moment to realize he had been in an audience with the king. Speech was beyond her at the moment, so she merely inclined her head.

Dante drew her to her feet and then turned to face their audience with Avalene fitted close to his side. One arm rested around her waist. His other hand reached over to hold hers and his thumb rubbed in a soothing motion over her fingers. She had to concentrate just to breathe, but she did notice that Isabel's gaze moved to their joined hands.

"Apparently I missed an insult to my lady," Dante said. He seemed unconcerned by the deadly blades that bristled all around them. "'Tis probably best if it remains unspoken in my presence. However, my men do not act without provocation and I am certain my lady is due an apology that I have not yet heard."

Isabel's eyes tightened at the corners and she spoke to Gerhardt in a swift volley of words, the guttural language one Avalene had never heard.

Gerhardt cleared his throat, his head now tilted back at an awkward angle in a useless effort to avoid the sharp point of the misericorde. "I apologize. No offense was intended."

Avalene didn't think that was strictly true, but kept her opinion to herself.

Dante inclined his head toward her, his voice still no more forceful than if they spoke of the weather, but it was hard to miss the undercurrent of steel. "Do you accept this miserable cur's apology?"

"Aye, my lord. No offense was intended." She had a very good idea of what would happen if she declined.

Armand waited for Dante's slight nod, and then the blade came away from Gerhardt's throat. She could hear many sighs of relief as Dante's soldiers lowered their weapons. Isabel gave a small wave of her hand and her soldiers' swords returned to their scabbards as well. Gerhardt produced a handkerchief from his sleeve and blotted away the blood on his neck.

"You must be Dante Chiavari," Isabel said, her hauteur fully recovered. "You will forgive my captain. The customs here are much different from those in our homeland. Indeed, they seem to be different from those I recall from my childhood. Your . . . friend is welcome to remain, of course."

"Of course," Dante echoed. He loosened his hold on Avalene just enough to give Isabel a curt bow. "If you will permit me, I would like to introduce you to Lady Avalene de Forshay, daughter of Baron Weston, one of your father's loyal Marcher barons in Wales."

Isabel's eyes widened slightly as Avalene dropped into a curtsey that was made awkward since Dante kept hold of her hand and did not let go of her waist. "My lady, I am most honored to make your acquaintance."

A furrow appeared between Isabel's brows. "What are you doing here, Lady Avalene, in the company of a foreigner, dressed in servant garb?"

I fell madly in love with a handsome Italian and have happily made myself his harlot. Uncertain how to answer that question aloud, she looked to Dante.

"Lady Avalene was forced to flee her home unexpectedly," Dante answered smoothly. "She was unable to take any of her belongings on the journey and her clothing was damaged beyond repair on the trip to London. Her new garments will begin arriving this afternoon."

"Did you steal her away from her husband?" Isabel asked.

"Nay, my lady. She is here on your father's orders."

"*Natürlich.*" Isabel looked disappointed, and then her face brightened again as she looked at Avalene. "You will join us in my solar in the afternoons, Lady Avalene. I have been away from England for much of my life. So much has changed! You will help reacquaint me with all

I have forgotten and entertain us with stories of your journey to London. How wonderful and frightening to be accompanied by only a boy and three men. Our journey to England was quite a trial, what with so large a baggage train and so many mouths to feed and so many to bed down each night."

It took Avalene a moment to absorb this complete change in Isabel's demeanor toward her. Did she now expect them to be fast friends? The princess and the harlot? Amazing.

"I would be pleased to join you in the afternoons," Avalene said. Gerhardt had obviously described their small party to Isabel after their arrival yesterday. She had no intention of telling Isabel anything about her reasons for being in London and the details of her journey would be quite sketchy. Still, she could hardly refuse a royal summons.

"Please be seated again, ladies," Dante told them. "I am actually glad to find you here, Princess. Your father bid me give you a message; he would like to meet with you tomorrow morning to discuss the particulars of your upcoming marriage."

The feathers on Isabel's barbette danced as though they were living things when she turned her head sharply to look toward the windows. "I was not aware that a betrothal had been contracted."

"The negotiations are completed," Dante said.

Isabel's mouth tightened, and then she released a small sigh and took her seat again. Avalene quickly followed suit, although that earned her a puzzled look from Dante, who had missed the explanation about raised heads. She gave him a barely perceptible shake of her head and a look that she hoped conveyed, *Later*.

"Actually," Dante said slowly, still looking at Avalene, "I brought the contracts with me for your advisers to review before your meeting with Edward." His gaze went to Isabel. "The king gave me leave to relay the particulars, should you care to hear them."

"The details must be dire, indeed, if my father cannot relay them to me himself." She fingered one of the braided tassels that hung from her girdle and seemed almost to speak to herself. "I suppose he thinks I will be in better spirits tomorrow if he gives me the night to mull over whatever bad news you bear."

"The situation *is* somewhat complicated," Dante admitted. He reached down for Avalene's hand and gave it a reassuring squeeze. "I had hoped to speak with Lady Avalene privately before I met with you. This news affects her, too."

Avalene's head shot up. "Me?"

"You would be the only Lady Avalene in the chamber," Dante teased, but the humor did not quite reach his eyes. He turned again to Isabel. "The man your father chose for you is presently betrothed to Lady Avalene."

Every gaze in the room turned to Avalene. She looked at Dante and blinked once. "The king intends to give his *daughter* to Faulke Segrave?"

"Aye," Dante nodded. "Faulke's father came to the king with the betrothal contracts that Faulke and your father signed to get Edward's approval. The king proposed a betrothal to Isabel instead. The contracts are drawn up and all the details have been agreed to by Faulke's father and Isabel's. However, your father and Faulke both signed *your* betrothal contracts. Your betrothal still stands until Faulke and your father renounce it, and Faulke signs Isabel's contracts."

It took her a moment to digest all of that information, and then she smiled up at him. It took a concentrated effort to remain seated. She wanted to wrap her arms around his neck, throw her head back and laugh aloud. "He will renounce me! How could he not? Princess Isabel will bring much more to a marriage than I ever could."

Dante did not return her smile. "What she would bring to the marriage is most of the problem."

"What do you mean?" Isabel demanded. "Who is this Faulke Segrave?"

Dante gave such a brief description of Faulke that Avalene wondered how he could think it sufficient for the woman who would hopefully marry him.

She half listened as Isabel began to pepper Dante with questions that he patiently answered, questions about Segrave's family, their importance in Wales, their holdings and fortresses, and then more about Faulke himself, his previous wives, his daughters, their ages, his age. More than an hour passed before her initial curiosity was satisfied.

"And what does this baron's daughter have that he would find preferable to a royal daughter's dowry?" Isabel asked at last.

Avalene supposed the question was not meant to sound insulting. Isabel certainly hadn't called her a whore or harlot, but simply wanted to know Faulke's motivations in the whole matter. Indeed, she was curious about the answer herself. Why did Dante have any doubts that Segrave would refuse Isabel? No sane man would refuse such a match.

"Avalene represents an opportunity for the Segraves to set themselves up as the next princes of Wales," Dante explained. "Rebellion is always a worry for Edward in the Marches, and Avalene is a direct descendant of the last prince. If Segrave had a son with her, every native in Wales would rally to their cause.

"On the other hand, marriage to you means an English earldom, a few more minor titles, and extensive properties in England along with their incomes. Segrave's father is anxious to acquire all of it, but Faulke has his mind turned toward rebellion and freedom from English rule." Dante gestured toward Gerhardt. "Edward insists that your personal guard and one hundred of his own soldiers reside with you in your husband's household, within Segrave's fortress. Segrave will have a hard time leading a rebellion when the enemy is already within his walls."

Clever, Avalene thought. And little wonder Faulke would not be keen on such a marriage when the conditions meant openly living with the king's spies and soldiers. His own wife would be his jailer.

Isabel studied Dante's face. "There is more."

"Aye," he said, his mouth turning downward. "All titles and claims already conveyed to the Segraves by the Crown will be forfeited and then given back in your name to be held for the children of your marriage. Segrave will hold his lands and titles through you during your lifetime. If you die before Segrave and have an heir, Segrave will hold his heir's claims and titles through his lifetime. If you were to die without issue or if you and your heirs die before Segrave, everything will revert to the king. The Segraves would lose all rights to the titles and lands they now hold in addition to all the titles and lands that are part of your dowry."

Avalene felt her joy fade. No wonder Dante looked so resigned. Faulke would never agree to those terms unless he could be absolutely certain Isabel would provide him with heirs who would outlive him, and who could know such a thing? The only thing that could possibly sway his decision was the fact that Dante had no intention of letting Faulke have her, while Isabel was Faulke's for the taking.

Isabel pursed her lips, her expression thoughtful. The room was so quiet that every small noise seemed magnified: the rustle of fabric as one of the German women smoothed her skirts, a quiet cough from one of the soldiers, the sound of fingernails against skin as someone scratched an itch. Gradually the corners of Isabel's mouth curved upward into a smile, and then she laughed aloud.

"Ah! I see my father's plan." The feathers on her barbette danced a merry dance as she tilted her head back and laughed as Avalene had wanted to laugh earlier. "'Tis a brilliant strategy! Not that I would expect any less from a Plantagenet. I wonder what excuse he gave?"

Avalene looked at Dante, but his expression remained impassive. He had no more idea of what Isabel meant than she did.

Isabel's voice was still touched with laughter when she spoke to Gerhardt, a torrent of words in his strange language. The only word Avalene recognized was "Segrave." Isabel laughed again at the end of her small speech, but Gerhardt did not smile with her. He looked . . . worried.

Avalene's gaze went to the other members of Isabel's entourage who also understood what their mistress had just told Gerhardt. The two women kept their gazes carefully lowered, but both were blushing. All three soldiers wore frowns. Why wasn't anyone but Isabel smiling?

She looked again at Dante and noticed his lips were pressed together ever so slightly. Her eyes widened as she realized he understood their language. Her curiosity was aroused even more.

"So," Isabel said to Dante, as she dabbed the corner of her eye with her sleeve, "how do we convince the hapless Faulke Segrave to relinquish his Welsh maiden in favor of an English earldom?" Before Dante could answer, she turned again to Gerhardt and this time spoke in English. "Did you ever imagine a man would need such incentives to marry a Plantagenet?"

"Nay, my lady," Gerhardt murmured. His frown looked permanent.

"We encountered Segrave on our journey to London," Dante told her. "He also journeys to the city and I have sent out a search party to watch for his approach. My spies will let me know when he is near the walls. He will then be brought here to be presented with the new contracts. Your father hopes you will allow Segrave to be introduced to you at that time. Once he renounces Avalene and signs the betrothal contract, arrangements can be made for your journey to Wales."

"Wales," Isabel repeated, tapping her chin as she gazed across the room at no point in particular. "It would seem we are to live amongst the savages, Gerhardt."

"Aye, my lady." Gerhardt looked glum at the prospect.

Isabel rose gracefully and inclined her head toward Dante. "I will meet with my father tomorrow, and then I will likely have more questions for you. Lady Avalene, I will see you in my solar tomorrow afternoon."

Avalene kept a polite smile on her face. Dante seemed distracted by the parade of Isabel's retinue trailing from the solar. Her timing for an escape to the bedchamber was perfect. "If you do not mind, I would like to excuse myself now. My head aches, but I am certain I will feel better if I can just lie down for a little while."

"Of course," Dante murmured. "I will come with you."

Her eyes widened. Everyone in the solar would make lewd assumptions if they both retired to the bed-

chamber. She looked around at all of Dante's soldiers
and felt herself blush. She spoke to him in a low whisper.
"Could you at least dismiss some of your men before we
both excuse ourselves?"

He gave her a puzzled look, and then she watched
understanding dawn. Men could be so obtuse at times.
He gave her a wry smile. "Go on to our chamber. I will
join you after I have dismissed everyone."

Avalene was seated on the edge of his bed and looking
toward the window when he entered the chamber an
hour later. A soft smile curved her lips when she saw
him, but her eyes looked sad. He had known she would
not react well to the news about Isabel and Segrave. He
could not blame her. He had been just as elated when
Mordecai had told him the identity of Faulke's English
bride, initially just as certain as Avalene that Faulke
would be eager to renounce her in favor of such a prize.
He should have known it would not be easy.

"I thought you wanted to lie down," he said as he
loosened the laces to his tunic. She might appear composed to anyone else, but he could sense the stress in her,
and could see it in the tightness around her eyes and the
stiff set of her shoulders. It had been a stressful day for
them both. He slipped off his tunic and boots, and then
stretched out on the bed behind her with a stack of pillows at his back. "Is your head feeling better?"

"A little."

She had her back to him so he picked up the end of her
braid and rubbed the soft tassel against his hand. The
tickling sensation reminded him of another time he had
felt the same touch in a very different place. His body
hardened in anticipation and his breathing quickened.
No. He shut that part of himself down, forced it from

his consciousness. He was here to comfort her, to calm her fears. After everything that had been said and done today in the solar, she was likely in shock. He had promised to take care of her, and that did not always mean his own selfish needs would be taken care of in the process.

A distraction occurred to him, one that was sure to please her. "I have a surprise for you in the solar."

She looked over her shoulder and lifted her brows.

"Reginald tells me a few of your new gowns have arrived. Would you like to see them?"

"What color are they?" she asked suspiciously.

He smiled. "Red, of course."

She made a face, not disappointment or disgust, nor was it elation. He wondered at the thoughtful expression even as she gave a small shrug. "I can wait until our evening meal to see them."

His smile faded. During their journey she had mentioned Brunor's odd edicts about the clothing colors at Coleway. Red was the only color she had worn for years. What if she now loathed the shade? "Would you rather have gowns made up in different colors?"

"Perhaps," she mused. This time she seemed shy as she looked at him over her shoulder at him. "Why did you choose red?"

"That is your color," he said simply. "Aside from chemises and nothing at all, that is the only color I can imagine you wearing." He reached out to stroke her cheek. "You even wear red in your cheeks."

He liked the way she turned her face toward his hand to prolong his touch, the way her lips curved into a sweet smile.

"There is also the fact that red and gold are *my* colors," he went on. "They are the colors on my family's banners and devices, worn by all Chiavari males when they ride into battle, and worn by their ladies at tournaments or other important occasions. You can imagine my surprise when a lady wearing Chiavari colors fell into my arms inside a drafty castle in England."

"I doubt the color of my gown was the first thing you noticed," she teased.

"No, that was not the first thing I noticed." His voice had gone soft with the memory. The first thing he had noticed was how right she had felt in his arms, the realization that his arms had been empty until that moment when he found what belonged there, *who* belonged there. He held out his arms to her now. "Come, lean back and I will rub your temples."

She settled against his chest, all warmth and softness. He rested his chin upon her head and inhaled the sweet scent of her, glad he had angled his body so she wouldn't be aware of what her nearness did to him. The thought of what she would feel like pressed against him even more intimately made him shift his legs a little farther away from her. Comfort. Need. The two requirements were becoming tangled in his mind. He placed his fingertips on her temples and started a gentle massage using just enough pressure to ease the tight muscles. She made a sound of contentment and sighed. Comfort was enough for now.

"I must have scared you witless, a big, red bundle, hurtling at you from the sky," she said, still recalling their first meeting.

"I knew you were behind the tapestry," he said. "I also knew the railing was about to give way. I was waiting for you, waiting for your fall."

Waiting all my life for you, he added silently, *waiting all my life for you to fall in love with me.* Last night and the night before she had said that she loved him, spoken the words quite clearly, but on both occasions the words had been uttered in the aftermath of passion. Could he make her say the words now?

And there was that selfishness again. He mentally shook his head. Comfort now. Need later.

"What did Isabel say to Gerhardt?" she asked suddenly. "Just after she started laughing over her father's strategy?"

He stopped rubbing her temples, filtering through his memories of the afternoon for the moment she was asking about. Ah, yes. "What makes you think I could understand what they were saying?"

"I could tell you understood." She reached up to nudge his hands, working his fingers back into motion on her temples. "Your mouth tightened a little, and I could tell you were just as displeased. It made me curious."

Her curious mind missed little. No one else had ever been able to read his expressions as effortlessly as she did. She always seemed to know his mind, her assessments so accurate that sometimes he wondered if she could read his thoughts or somehow gauge his emotions in ways that were outside the normal way of things. If she were his enemy, he would be in trouble. Because it was Avalene, he liked the talent, liked knowing she was so attuned to him, connected in a way that no one else could be.

"Isabel is barren."

"What?" She stiffened against him. "How can anyone know that for certain?"

"She was married for many years," he said. "She has no children, not even a stillborn. And yet, her dead husband has many bastards to prove his virility. Edward told her to keep the information about her husband's bastards to herself. He had his spies spread a story that her husband contracted mumps as a young man and was incapable of producing children to explain away her lack of them and to make her more marriageable. Few Englishmen travel to that part of the world and it's unlikely that anyone here will contradict the story before she is wed."

"The Segraves do not know," she said slowly. "Faulke has proven that he can sire children, so his father must assume it will be only a matter of time before Faulke will sire heirs on Isabel to secure the riches of her dowry as well as reestablish the rights to their own lands and titles." Her voice took on an affronted edge. "Edward is tricking them!"

"Aye."

"That is . . . that is not fair!" she sputtered.

"Was it fair, what Faulke intended for you?" he countered. "When kings and nobles are involved, life and fairness bear little relation. There is always the chance that Isabel and her husband were simply not suited and she will produce a dozen heirs with Faulke. No matter, you must keep the secret. It will be hard enough for me to convince him to marry her without that hanging over his head as well."

"Why must *you* convince him?" she asked.

"Because he has something I want."

She became still, and then she sat up enough that his hands fell to her sides as she turned to look at him.

There was a puzzled line between her brows. Did she not yet understand?

"He has a betrothal contract that says he has the right to wed you. I intend to marry you, Avalene. I assumed that was what you wanted, too. If I am wrong—"

She pressed her fingers to his lips and smiled, the quiet smile that made her look like a serene Madonna. "You are not wrong. Until today, it seemed unlikely there would even be that possibility."

His temper flared over her doubt, but he tamped it down. She would be his wife. No matter what obstacles stood in his way, he would surmount them. Just one word had put that steel in his conviction. He *had* heard the name Gerhardt called her.

It had taken every ounce of his self-control to remain in the hallway where the sound of Gerhardt's angry words had frozen him in his tracks. Somehow his instincts prevailed over the haze of fury. He had a few moments to think through his response and act rationally. Gerhardt was Isabel's favorite. She would be displeased if the man were murdered before her eyes. She might not cooperate with his scheme to convince Segrave to marry her, which meant he could not wed Avalene.

That realization had decided his course, but he had also vowed that no one would ever have cause to make such an assumption about Avalene ever again in her lifetime. He was ashamed that he was the cause of the mistake being made in the first place. It was his selfish refusal to provide a suitable chaperone and separate quarters for her the moment they reached the palace, as well as the tawdry gowns he *had* provided. He had treated her like a whore. He could not blame Gerhardt for mistaking what appeared obvious. Luckily for him it did not seem to occur to her to blame him for the incident. God, he loved her.

She began to move her fingertips back and forth over his lips and he caught her hand before she could distract him any further.

"Mordecai chose me for this mission because he knew I would be the only one with sufficient motivation to convince Faulke that his future lies with Isabel. However, until my meeting with Mordecai and Edward, I did not know that Isabel was his intended bride. Now that we know all of the particulars, I will be able to form an effective means of persuasion. I will make certain he signs the betrothal contracts within a day of setting foot in London. Once I deliver the contracts to Edward, he will give his permission for us to wed. We can be married before we sail for Venice."

Her smile turned to one of joy and something he could not quite define. "You really do love me."

"I do." He couldn't help but smile back at her, at the note of wonder in her voice as if she were the lucky one. His finger traced the small dimple in her cheek. "But I doubt you will ever be able to understand how much. My world was a very dark place before you came into it. I am at home in the darkness, and you will likely see traces of it still lingering in the years to come. Intrigues abound in Venice, and I will be vigilant about protecting you. There will likely be times when you see a side of me that is . . . unpleasant, although hopefully not as unpleasant as the day we encountered the mercenaries."

She looked at him with blank surprise. "How could I find fault with anything you might do to keep me safe?"

"How, indeed?" he murmured. He playfully tapped the tip of her nose with his finger and earned a smile. Being able to make her look this happy justified his existence. She was *happy* that he wanted to marry her, not because of the wealth or power she would enjoy as his wife, and despite knowing the sort of monster he had been for most of his life. She was happy because she loved him. He could see it shining in her eyes.

"I learned a new phrase today while you were away." She turned in his arms and then placed her hand on his chest. Her gaze lowered, suddenly shy. "*Mi sei mancato molto.*"

Sometimes it was acceptable for comfort and need to collide. He leaned down and kissed her, a kiss to seal his promises, a kiss that meant they were going to miss their evening meal.

21

❦

It took Faulke Segrave four more days to reach London. Dante spent much of that time keeping his promise to linger over Avalene, but each afternoon he released her from their self-imposed exile in his apartments to join Isabel and her ladies in the great hall. He wondered if she knew what it cost him to pretend he did not worry each moment she was out of his sight, to manufacture important matters to occupy his time while she was away so he would not constantly check on her, matters that were not at all important in his mind. Nothing was more important to him than Avalene.

Caring this much for someone was dangerous. Not only dangerous for himself, but equally dangerous for Avalene. He had never before been foolish enough to hand his enemies such a potent weapon. Hopefully they would be far away from England before her importance to him became common knowledge. Once they arrived in Venice there would be time to worry about the new enemies he would acquire. He was already making plans for the steps he would take to keep her safe in Italy. He would not repeat his father's mistakes.

For the time being, he had to keep faith in the measures he had already taken to ensure her safety at the palace when he could not be with her. He did not quite trust Isabel or her guards, and yet Avalene seemed to enjoy Isabel's company and therefore he could not forbid what brought her pleasure. Still, he made certain she was always guarded by men who knew their lives depended upon her safety.

The group of women had moved their gatherings to the great hall out of necessity, since Gerhardt insisted on having four of his soldiers on hand to protect Isabel, and Dante insisted upon an equal number to protect Avalene. Apparently there had been much eye-rolling amongst the ladies about that level of security, but they did not much complain. Avalene spent most of her time telling Isabel everything she knew of the Segraves, both the good and the bad. She felt certain the information would be put to good use by the king's daughter.

It was midafternoon when Dante returned to the palace. The women and their retainers would all be gathered in the great hall at this time of day, which was perfect for his plan. He wanted plenty of people who could swear to the fact that they witnessed Faulke renounce Avalene. Those inside the hall would also know of their arrival by now. Hell, half of London knew of their arrival. It was hard to miss Faulke and his score of men, Dante and a handful of his own soldiers, along with forty of the king's guard and an edict from the king to persuade Faulke to come quietly. It made Londoners nervous when so many armed soldiers rode through their streets. But the small army was now safely within the courtyard with the curious citizenry on the other side of the gates. That left only the curious on this side of the gate to deal with.

All of the Segraves had been bound with their hands tied behind their backs well before they reached London, their horses placed on tethers, and then they were marched into the city on foot. Now they were herded into a group in the roadway where the king's soldiers could keep an eye on them. Faulke and his men were dirty and dusty, and looked like they had been on the road for weeks in foul weather, which they had been. Dante wondered if he and his men had looked as grisly when they arrived at the palace. If so, it was a testament to the strength of their bond that Avalene had found something appealing in a face that looked anything like the ones before him.

At a signal from Dante, Faulke and Richard were brought forward, a soldier on either side of them. Another soldier cut their bonds and then both men began to rub their hands and wrists to get the blood moving again. Faulke looked livid, Richard merely looked surly.

He had told them very little, as of yet, only that the king had ordered them brought to this palace to receive his message and documents related to the message.

"Lady Avalene will be in our company this afternoon," Dante told Faulke and Richard, recalling the incident with Gerhardt. If either man said or did something to insult Avalene, his temper was likely beyond the control he had exercised in the solar. He would give them fair warning. "You will speak to her with the utmost courtesy or I will cut out the tongue that offends her. If either of you manages to touch her, I will cut the skin from the hand that has soiled her and then I will fillet the flesh from the bones. Do you understand me?"

"Aye," Faulke said in a curt tone. He still looked furious. Richard looked wary. Apparently Richard was more adept at hearing the truth than Faulke, who seemed to dismiss the promises as empty threats. "When do you intend to tell us why we were brought here? We were to meet at the Ox Head Inn."

"As I said earlier, you will listen to the king's message and read the documents he has sent for your signature. There is also someone here who wishes to meet you. At the conclusion of our business, you and your men will be free to leave."

He did not add that they might not be breathing when they left, if Faulke failed to make the correct decisions. He would keep his promise to Mordecai for as long as possible, but this man was all that prevented him from making Avalene his wife. His death was a price he was willing to pay.

He turned on his heel and made his way into the great hall.

Avalene was nowhere in sight, nor were Oliver and Armand, whom he'd left to guard her. A ribbon of unease unfurled in his belly. She must be in their apartments with his men, or occupied in some other part of the palace for whatever reasons. There was no need to worry, but he could not ignore the chill that ran through him. Isabel and her people were missing as well, but two strangers were seated at one end of the head table. Both were finely dressed, one mostly in shades of blue that accentuated his white hair and blue eyes. The older of the two men had steel-gray hair and wore black and red; Segrave colors. The older man's dark eyes were fixed on Faulke as they walked forward and Dante knew without being told that this was Faulke's father, Baron Carreg. His gaze moved to the man in blue and he realized the white hair still bore traces of blond. The blue eyes were the same shade as those he had looked into just this morning when he bid Avalene good-bye. Baron Weston.

Another man stepped out from the shadows of the massive fireplace that dominated the wall behind the head table. His dark robes had made him almost invisible against the blackened stones of the hearth.

Mordecai.

The magician smiled. Dante's steps faltered.

"Ah, at last everyone is present."

"I did not expect to see you here," Dante managed.

"I am here as the king's representative," Mordecai said, his eyes lit with humor. A wooden box that was identical to the one Dante had brought from his audience with the king sat on the table before Mordecai. "Did you really think I would miss this meeting?"

"I suppose I should have known." Dante rubbed the back of his neck. "Where is Avalene?"

His steward, Reginald, who had been standing to one side of the table with his gaze fixed on the flagstones at his feet, took a step forward. His voice trembled noticeably. "Lady Avalene is in your solar, my lord." Reginald's hand swept out to indicate the two barons, while Dante's racing pulse began to calm. "These men demanded she be brought to the hall. One claims to be her father. I informed them that Lady Avalene is not to receive visitors in your absence."

"Actually," Mordecai said, "Baron Weston insisted upon the matter, but your man, Armand, convinced him that it would be healthier for all involved to wait for your arrival. He was most persuasive."

"He threatened us!" Baron Weston broke in. "He refused to admit our soldiers to the hall and had them taken to some stable yard under guard. Now you haul in Carreg's son and his cousin as if they are common criminals. Are we *all* prisoners here? What is the meaning of this, Mordecai?"

"Aye," Dante echoed. "What *is* the meaning of this?"

"Please, everyone, take your seats and I will explain." Mordecai's voice was grave, but Dante saw a spark of humor in his eyes. He was enjoying this little drama. "Perhaps stools could be brought for Lord Faulke and his cousin?"

Dante motioned toward Reginald and the stools soon appeared, and then he walked around the table to take his own seat. Unlike those of his guests, his chair had a backrest and arms. He leaned back and pretended to make himself comfortable, crossing his legs by propping one ankle across his knee and folding his hands across his stomach. Baron Weston's cold glare followed him the entire time, his hands fisted so tightly atop the table that his knuckles were bone white. He was fairly certain Avalene's father wished to strangle him. Not that he blamed the man. If he had a daughter and was forced to sit at the same table with the man who had ruined her . . . Aye, Weston was showing remarkable restraint.

Then again, perhaps Weston did not yet know the role he played in Avalene's abduction or realize that she shared his bed. Thank God, Armand had made certain she remained in the solar. He did not want her to see her father's reaction when he learned the truth, if he did not know already. He returned Weston's furious glare with a cool gaze and watched the man actually bare his teeth at him. Oh, Weston knew, all right.

"King Edward thought it best if all parties involved in these proceedings gathered to make certain there were no misunderstandings," Mordecai said, when everyone had taken their seats. He removed several scrolls from the box that bore massive seals and were bound with elaborate ribbons, and then carefully spread them on the table. "There are three betrothal contracts before me. The first is Faulke's betrothal contract to Avalene. Baron Weston has already struck his name from the contract. Faulke, once you renounce your claim to Avalene and strike your name, the contract will be broken."

"I will not do it," Faulke declared. "The king must approve or deny my betrothal to Avalene de Forshay. Either way, the other Marcher barons will hear of what was done here."

"The king offers you another choice," Carreg said, his voice a deeper, harsher version of his son's. "I have negotiated in your name with the king for a betrothal more advantageous than your betrothal to Avalene de Forshay."

"More advantageous to the Segraves, or to you?" Faulke demanded. "What price have you put upon my honor this time? What could possibly be more advantageous than a marriage to Avalene de Forshay?"

"Watch your tongue," Carreg warned. "You will have an earldom from this, you ungrateful wretch, and more wealth than you know what to do with."

Faulke's eyes widened and his gaze moved to Mordecai.

"'Tis true," Mordecai said, as he pushed one of the scrolls toward Faulke. "Actually, you will gain four titles; the earldom of Malden being the most important, as well as Lord of Helmsford, Sildon, and Thurock. The castles, manors, and lands entailed to the titles are listed in the contract, along with the annual income from the properties. Your father has reviewed the detailed reports of each holding and has pronounced himself satisfied with the settlements. However, you should also read the contract to make certain you agree to the terms."

Faulke looked as if he had swallowed a frog. The whites of his eyes showed all around, and his mouth hung open in an expression that might have been comical in other circumstances.

"We shall be men of great consequence," his father informed him. "We shall have the standing and resources to make life either easy or difficult for the king. The terms of this betrothal are more than you could ever hope to acquire through a marriage to Weston's daughter."

"Who is the bride?" Faulke managed.

"The king's own daughter!" Carreg declared, smiling now. There was a calculating glint of greed in the old man's eyes. "Your wife shall be Isabel of Ascalon, the widow of some Frankish prince, but she is yet young and healthy, well able to provide you with heirs."

Faulke took a moment to digest that astonishing news, then his eyes narrowed. "How many children does she have?"

"None so far." Carreg waved away that detail. "Her husband suffered mumps or measles or some such disease in his youth and could not even sire a bastard. You must look at the number of children her mother bore. Sixteen, in all, near thirty years of fertility! Her married sisters are fruitful as well. You have already proven your virility and I have every confidence that you will have an heir from Isabel within a year."

"You had best read the contract," Mordecai told him. "Or do you need someone to read the documents for you?"

Richard leaned in to whisper something in his cousin's ear. Faulke scowled and then began to read through each parchment. The contract was several pages long and included much more detail than Avalene's betrothal contract. They would all be waiting quite a while before Faulke would finish reading. Dante signaled to Reginald to bring more wine and refreshments, and then settled back to wait.

His gaze went often to the door that led to his apartments. He would give almost anything to leave the hall and go to Avalene, just to reassure himself that she was all right. She had to be worried. However, he had no wish to give Faulke any reason to refuse the betrothal to Isabel. Avalene's beauty was enough to tempt any man. Given the terms of Isabel's betrothal, having Avalene within sight could sway Faulke's decision in the wrong direction. The patience that always came to him so naturally was now forced into place.

He knew the exact moment Faulke came to the thornier terms of the contract. His fist slammed onto the table, making both barons flinch in surprise.

"This is outrageous!" He stood up and swept the pages of the contract to the floor, and then leaned across the table toward Dante. "There is my answer. Our business is concluded. Honor your bargain and allow my men and I to leave, and release my betrothed to me."

Dante took a sip of his wine and watched Faulke flex his fists. "Regardless of your answer, you will leave here without Avalene. You will never see her again. If you refuse the king's daughter, you will have no bride, and you will have no reason to blame Edward for your circumstances. Indeed, I would imagine the insult to his highness will reap its own rewards."

Faulke opened his mouth to argue and then closed it again. His brows smoothed from a scowl to a puzzled frown. "What do you mean?"

"You could not capture Avalene and force a marriage, so you intended to use Edward's refusal to approve your betrothal to Avalene as an excuse to return to Wales and incite rebellion. However, if you refuse the betrothal to Isabel, Edward *will* approve your betrothal to Avalene."

"Fine," he said, with a sharp nod. "She will go with us, as I said."

Dante shook his head and gave him the type of look that a parent would bestow upon a child who had disappointed him. "Did I not make clear what would happen if you touched her?"

Faulke merely folded his arms across his chest and glared. "If Edward tries to keep her from me, the barons will see this injustice just as clearly as the injustice of a refusal."

"Edward will have nothing to do with keeping her from you."

Understanding dawned on Faulke's face. "You cannot keep her." He glanced at Baron Weston, but turned to Mordecai. "He cannot keep her. The king must order him to release her to my care. Despite whatever coercion the king used upon my father and hers, she is still my betrothed!"

Mordecai lifted his shoulders. "I do not think an order or the king's involvement would make much difference. The dispute is between you and Dante."

"He is on English soil, subject to—"

Dante cut him off. "If you refuse to renounce Avalene, all you will have of her is a scrap of parchment that says she is your betrothed. You will never have a bride."

"That is unacceptable!" Faulke was now breathing hard. "I will not allow it."

"*I* will not allow any man to lay claim to what is mine," Dante said. "There is only one course of action that will assure you live long enough to create an heir. Renounce your claim to Avalene and pursue the much more favorable match with Isabel of Ascalon."

"I have known Dante many years," Mordecai added. "He does not make idle threats."

Faulke pursed his lips and lowered his furious gaze to the parchment that lay scattered on the flagstones.

"Think of your people," Richard said to Faulke. "Think what the wealth of an earldom will mean to them."

For the first time all afternoon, Faulke looked thoughtful. He turned again to his father. "Is Isabel sickly? Is she prone to illness?"

Carreg cleared his throat. "I have only seen the lady

from a distance at court, but I have it on the best authority that she is healthy as a horse."

"Have you lost your mind?" Faulke demanded of his father. "You have not even met the woman, and yet you would risk everything, our lands, our titles, *everything*, on the health and fertility of a childless widow?"

"I have every faith that you can manage to keep the woman alive, at least until she gives you a few heirs," his father argued. "Aye, 'tis a gamble, but look what we will gain! Nothing worth having is easy or without risk."

"You realize that you would have to give up your own title upon my marriage," Faulke pointed out. "*All* of our titles are relinquished to the king and then given back in his daughter's name. Even so, I will merely be a caretaker of all this importance and wealth for the miracle heir who must also be as healthy and long-lived as his mother, else we are all made paupers. The risk is too high. Avalene de Forshay is—"

"Avalene is nothing to you," Dante interjected. He studied the beds of his fingernails. "I grow tired of hearing her name upon your lips."

"She is not worth the trouble," Carreg added, before Faulke could argue. He turned to Baron Weston. "No offense, my friend, but what your daughter would bring to a marriage cannot compare to Isabel's dowry."

"Do not claim me as a friend," Weston retorted. He crossed his arms across his chest and glared at Carreg. "I did not *willingly* choose your son for my daughter. Still, I was resigned to make the best of the match. Now that you have what you really wanted, you throw her to the wolves like a meatless bone. Do not think I will soon forget this insult, Carreg."

Dante felt a small bit of relief at no longer being the sole focus of Weston's malice. He was also glad to see some small indication that Weston actually cared what happened to his daughter. Of course, that might not work to his benefit, but he would tell Avalene of her father's concern.

"The king decided his daughter was better suited for my son than yours," Carreg pointed out. "Do you question our king's decision?"

Weston clenched his jaw so tight that Dante could almost hear his teeth grind.

"What do you get from this?" Faulke interrupted, looking at his father. "You agreed to be stripped of your titles, stripped of your lands and much of your income. Unless you somehow benefit more than what is apparent in this contract, you would never willingly step meekly aside while I assume your mantle. Why did you agree to this betrothal?"

"Your new properties are mostly along the coastline far to the east of London," Carreg began, "the opposite side of England from our holdings in Wales. Our Welsh holdings require a lord to be in residence much of the year while Isabel's properties have long been managed by the sheriff of Malden. The sheriff has decided to step down from his position, so I shall serve at the pleasure of the king as Malden's new sheriff and continue to oversee Isabel's properties there."

Dante surmised that Carreg would live as an earl in one of Malden's castles and collect an income from the king, as well as a substantial portion of the income from Isabel's properties. A sheriff was but one rank below a baron, and many wielded considerably more power than the noblemen who outranked them. Most were far richer than the barons since they reaped the rewards of a lordship without the burden of the expenditures. Carreg's vast properties in Wales sustained themselves, but produced little income. He would be made far wealthier as Malden's sheriff.

"The risk is staggering," Faulke finally muttered. "Could you not convince the king to leave your title and lands intact?"

It was Mordecai who answered the question, but he looked at Carreg as he spoke. "Edward is disturbed that you have already buried three wives at such a young age. The dispensation to the heirs of Isabel's body is intended to ensure that the king's daughter and his future grandchildren receive the care and nurturing due royal personages. The clause eases his mind and makes him more certain that Isabel will live a long and happy life as your wife."

In other words, Dante thought, there would be no more killing off one wife when a wealthier one happened along. And if he read Mordecai correctly, it was the baron rather than his son who bore responsibility for Faulke's frequent marriages. He wondered if Faulke was aware that one or more of his wives had died by his father's hand or order, and then decided it was none of his concern. His only concern was—

A sudden flash of inspiration came to mind. He sat up straighter in his chair.

"The terms of Isabel's contract are much the same as those of her sister, Joan," Dante pointed out. "Gilbert de Clare was no coward three years ago when he risked his lands and titles to marry Joan, and already she has presented him with his heir and a daughter, and she will deliver another child to him this fall. Gilbert faced the same decision you must make today, except he was forced to give up his rights to two earldoms and receive them back in his wife's name with the same risk that Joan might die before she bore him heirs. Great men seize the opportunities laid before them. Will you prove yourself less of a man than a de Clare?"

Dante struggled not to smile in the face of Faulke's

outrage. The de Clares were the sworn enemies of the Segraves, both families intent upon expanding their holdings in Wales at the expense of the other. To infer that Faulke was less of a man than a de Clare was akin to calling his mother a whore. He moved in for the kill before Faulke could lose hold of his temper.

"You can be a wifeless rebel who will be stripped of all your lands and titles the moment you raise a sword against England, or you can be an English earl wed to the king's own daughter with wealth and power beyond that of any other Marcher baron." He worked to keep his shrug casual. "Surely even you can see that your people will benefit far more from wealth than they will from war. The choice is yours."

"What are *your* intentions in Wales?" Faulke demanded. "You obviously intend to keep Avalene for yourself. What makes you think Edward will agree to your intent more readily than he agreed to mine?"

Beneath the table, Dante's hand closed reflexively into a fist. He would like nothing more than to smack the affronted insolence from Faulke's face. "My intentions do not concern you. She will be no threat to you *or* to the king. That is all you need to know of the matter."

And all Dante intended to tell him. He wanted Faulke out of Avalene's life, completely. Rather than wait for another of Faulke's arguments, he reached for Avalene's contract and pushed it toward Faulke.

"Before you can accept and sign the betrothal to Isabel, you must renounce your contract with Avalene." He tilted his head toward the end of the table where Mordecai watched Faulke with an unblinking gaze. "Mordecai will act as the king's witness."

"I have not yet agreed to anything." Faulke brushed his hand across the pages of Isabel's contract. "I *will* not agree to anything before I read every word of this contract, and then I will make my decision. What I decide is what will be best for my people, and not what is best for you or the king, or my father."

Carreg made a sound of impatience. "Read the thing already. Once you sign Isabel's contract, we will be granted an audience with the lady and you will see for yourself that she is all you could hope for in a wife."

Faulke's face was an interesting shade of red and growing darker by the moment, but he returned his attention to the contract. At last he came to the end.

"So be it!" Faulke snarled, his attention once again on Dante. "I renounce my betrothal to Avalene de Forshay, you spawn of the Devil! Instead I will wed the spawn of my great and illustrious king."

"'Tis the right decision," his father put in, smiling broadly now. "All will be well. You shall see."

"Oh, I can scarce wait to begin this glorious new life you have made for me." Faulke's voice dripped with sarcasm. "You will grow fat and rich at Malden while I shall become a prisoner in my own fortress. Mark my words well, Father; do not become too comfortable amidst your new wealth. 'Tis likely the daughter is just as capricious as her sire, and unlike you, I will not play lapdog to any Plantagenet."

"Perhaps you should withhold judgment until you meet your bride," Mordecai said. He rose calmly from his seat and then took an inkwell, blotting sand, and a quill from the wooden box, along with several copies of the betrothal contract. He spread the documents across the table and then held the quill out to Faulke. "I would imagine Isabel is growing impatient to make your acquaintance. You should not keep her waiting."

22
※

The Magician

*Here lies the start of the jour-
ney, both a beginning and an
end. The Magician reaches to
the heavens for guidance and
points toward the paths of
greatest potential. From his
hand accept the power to shape
destiny and the will that manifests great change.*

The contracts were already signed by the king and
Baron Carreg. When he signed the last copy of the contract, Dante began to breathe again. He could almost
feel the weight lift from his shoulders. Avalene was free.

"Escort our guests to Isabel's solar," Dante told Reginald, anxious to see all of the Segraves leave the hall.
Mordecai and Baron Weston remained.

Mordecai reached into the wooden box and retrieved
a scroll, bound with the same ribbon and seal as Isabel's
betrothal contracts. He spoke loudly enough for everyone who remained in the hall to hear his words as he
handed Dante the scroll. "Dante Chiavari, you have interfered in the marriage of one of his loyal baron's
daughters to the son of another loyal baron. As you are
a foreigner and a guest in this land, the punishment for
your crimes is banishment from England for no less than
one full year. You are to leave England as soon as suitable passage can be obtained."

Dante's smile turned wry. "This can be arranged."

"Excellent." Mordecai placed his hands in his sleeves. "Having taken her unlawfully from her family and for holding her captive without her family's knowledge or permission, or the king's, a betrothal contract has been drawn up that orders you to wed Avalene de Forshay immediately."

Dante lifted a brow over the blatant lies about "knowledge" and "permission." "I have no argument with the edict. We shall be wed on the morrow."

He was already reaching for the inkwell when Mordecai's answer froze his hand in midair.

"Baron Weston must also agree to the terms." Mordecai's gaze flickered to Avalene's father, who was again staring daggers at Dante. "Weston understands the potential difficulties that might someday arise from any marriage Avalene might make to one of Edward's subjects, but he argued quite convincingly that his daughter should not be punished with banishment and marriage to a foreigner. He feels his daughter should be allowed to take the veil and retire to a convent. The king has no wish to interfere if Avalene has a calling to God, and agreed to leave the decision in her father's hands."

"You said the choice was mine," Dante said between his teeth. "Faulke has made his choice. I have made mine. Avalene will be my wife."

"I have no intention of signing that contract," Weston said. "Avalene will go to a convent."

"No." Dante folded his arms across his chest and leaned back. The matter was settled.

"I will not allow my daughter to marry a hired killer, and a foreigner to boot." Weston emphasized his point by bringing his fist down upon the table. "The king gave his word that she could leave here with me today, and then take her vows and become a nun."

"She will go nowhere with you today or any day,"

Dante warned. "You had years to claim your daughter or commit her to a convent, but instead you let her languish in your sister's questionable care until the Segraves forced you to recall her existence." He turned to Mordecai. "You must make Edward see reason. He does not want to test my loyalty on this issue."

"Edward is determined on the matter," Mordecai said, which most likely meant Mordecai was determined on the matter. "The decision lies with Baron Weston. I would suggest you stop insulting the man you hope to make your father-in-law."

Dante clenched his fists beneath the table and took a slow, deep breath through his nose, doing everything within his power to hold on to his temper. He had done everything asked of him, followed every instruction. Avalene was to be his reward. It was the future Mordecai himself had predicted, and Mordecai was very rarely wrong. He had no doubt about his ability to keep Avalene from her father, but if Mordecai sided with the baron, that was another matter altogether.

He decided to ignore Weston for the moment. In truth, everything depended upon Mordecai's decision. "What has changed? Why is the choice no longer mine?"

"Nothing in the future is ever certain," Mordecai said. "All depends upon choices and decisions made in the present, words that are spoken as well as those that go unsaid. Baron Weston originally intended to leave for Wales after he struck his name from Avalene's betrothal to Segrave, with assurances from the king that no harm would come to his daughter. The baron assumed she would be placed in a convent, but Edward mentioned that a wedding might be a more likely outcome. 'Tis no secret that Baron Weston does not approve of you for his daughter."

Dante briefly closed his eyes. It was not like Edward

to let slip any information that he wanted kept private. The king was not happy that Dante intended to leave his service, and it was entirely like Edward to let his displeasure be known in such a petulant manner. That Mordecai backed the king's interference meant there was more at work here than royal spite. *Gesù.* His future really *did* depend upon Weston's decision. At last he turned his attention to the man who held his fate and Avalene's in his hands.

"My lord, we have not had a good start," he began. "I do not know how much you have been told about me or my family—"

"Oh, I know all about you," Weston cut in. "Mordecai told me everything."

He did not sound impressed.

"Then you must know I can match the settlements the Segraves offered. Indeed, I can double their value. If you need more men to defend your lands, I will provide the wages required to keep a company of soldiers no less than five years." He was starting to sound desperate. Best to stop offering bribes until he knew exactly what Weston wanted in return for his agreement. "I will take good care of your daughter, Baron. She shall not want for anything as my wife."

"My daughter is not for sale," Weston said flatly. "And I will not reward the man who ruined her by bestowing her hand in marriage after you haggle over her like a sack of grain. She will go to a convent."

Dante's first impulse was to again tell him "no," and perhaps shout it this time, but the baron's words revealed something Dante had not expected. Was it possible Weston truly cared for his daughter? "I promised Avalene that I would not allow anyone to imprison her and I will keep that promise, even if the prison is a convent."

"'Tis hardly imprisonment if she goes willingly to God."

"She will not go willingly."

Weston's scowl deepened. "She cannot wish to marry the likes of you, especially when it means she must leave her homeland forever."

"She does so wish."

"Perhaps we should eliminate the conjecture and ask the lady herself?" Mordecai suggested. And then he made another suggestion that Dante recognized as an order. "Dante, why don't you send Reginald to request Avalene's presence in the hall?"

"Aye, I would very much like to see my daughter," Weston said.

It was the older man's expression that made Dante more inclined to cooperate. A signal to Reginald sent him on his way, but Dante kept all of his attention focused on Weston, processing the possibility that Weston might be more concerned with his daughter's best interests than his own. The baron's next words lent weight to his suspicions.

"She must be made to understand that she is free to leave with me today," Weston said to Mordecai. "You must assure her that the king's soldiers will follow your orders on the matter and release her to my care."

Mordecai merely inclined his head in agreement.

Dante narrowed his eyes and began to plot.

Avalene finally entered the hall escorted by his men and Rami, but his eyes were for her alone. She wore the finest of her new gowns; a red brocade shot through with gold thread. Beneath her veil and circlet, she wore her hair the way he liked it best; unbound. No other woman could hold a candle to her beauty, and she belonged to him. His chest tightened with pride.

Their eyes met and a look of relief joined the smile

that curved her lips. However, the smile faltered when her gaze went to her father. He watched her face tighten into the same cool, aloof expression she wore when she spoke with Lady Margaret and Lord Brunor.

He decided not to ruin her careful composure by sweeping her into his arms, as he would like to do. Still, he was on his feet and moving toward her before the conscious thought to do so entered his mind. It was hard to stand so close to her and do nothing more than lift her hand to press a chaste kiss to her fingers as he whispered an apology. "I did not know this audience awaited me, else I never would have left you this morn."

"Do not concern yourself, my lord." She gestured behind her to where Oliver, Armand, Rami, and a half dozen of his soldiers stood guard. "I was well cared for in your absence."

He tucked her hand in the crook of his arm and covered her hand with his. Despite her outward calm, he could feel her trembling and he gently stroked her fingers. Her hands were ice cold.

Baron Weston was on his feet, a curious expression on his face as he watched his daughter walk toward him. Avalene had been nine years old the last time Weston saw her. Obviously the baron had known she would no longer be a child, but still he looked both startled and impressed by the woman before him. Dante let go of Avalene's hand long enough for her to curtsey to her father.

"My lord, I am honored by your presence."

Weston's jaw tightened at the mention of the word "honor." His gaze narrowed and brushed over Dante, and then returned to his daughter. "These are not the circumstances I had hoped to greet you under, but 'tis good to see you, daughter. You have grown into a fine woman."

"Thank you, my lord."

It was the moment that a father should open his arms to properly greet his daughter after so long a separation, but Weston clasped his hands behind his back and rocked backward on his heels. The ensuing silence became awkward.

Dante turned her toward Mordecai. "My lady, may I make known to you the king's adviser, Mordecai. He has news of which your father wishes you to be made aware."

"'Tis good to at last make your acquaintance," Mordecai said, as Avalene curtsied to him. "Please, have a seat. The news is lengthy and you will wish to make yourself comfortable."

"Come, my lady." Dante led Avalene around the table. Reginald had already brought another armchair and placed it next to Dante's. Weston and Mordecai settled again at their places after Avalene was seated. Dante reached out beneath the table to hold her hand.

"First, I believe you will be pleased to learn your betrothal to Faulke Segrave has been broken," Mordecai began. He then told her of the king's edict to banish Dante and his approval of a marriage, should her father agree to the match. Otherwise, she would be allowed to take the veil and retire to a convent. He finished with, "Dante and your father are in disagreement about which choice you would make, if the decision were in your hands."

"I am here to take you home," Weston said baldly. "That is, you will return with me to Wales, and then I will make arrangements for you to enter a convent."

"No."

Weston's eyes widened. "What did you say?"

Avalene's nails dug into Dante's palm but he did not flinch. Indeed, it was all he could do not to grin. He heard her draw an unsteady breath and then she turned to look up at him, her blue eyes clear. "Do you want me to enter a convent?"

"No." He stroked his thumb over the back of her hand. "'Tis a grave sin to steal a nun from a convent. I would rather not be excommunicated."

She rolled her eyes only a little, and then turned toward her father. "I am going to Italy."

Weston's face was almost as red as Avalene's gown. "You will go where I tell you, and you will do what is best for your family."

"This *is* what is best for my family." She gave Dante a shy smile. "What did you offer him for settlements?"

"Double the Segraves' offer," he said. "Plus coin to pay a company of soldiers for five years."

Her eyes widened in an expression that he had seen earlier on her father's face. "That is a most generous settlement, my lord."

"For you, I would—"

She placed her hand over his mouth and gave him a stern look. "You would offer no more than twice the Segraves' settlement plus a company of soldiers."

He couldn't help himself. He stuck out his tongue and licked her palm. She blinked, twice, and then slowly drew her hand away. Her fingers curled around the spot on her palm where he had tasted her. She looked a little dazed.

"I have refused his offer," Weston declared. His arms were once again folded over his chest, but his gaze was speculative as he watched his daughter.

The interruption seemed to recall Avalene to her mission. She folded her hands in her lap and gave her father a prim look. "Aye, rather than collect a rich settlement, the convent will require a handsome dowry that includes my mother's lands. The Church does not provide settlements. You will receive nothing in return. On the other hand, my marriage to a foreigner means you would still control those lands in my absence. Will it not be better for my family to have the bulk of my dowry plus Dante's settlements rather than the expense of a convent?"

"I will not have you wed to a murderous thief!"

"He is not a thief!"

In different circumstances, Dante would find it amusing that Avalene's furious expression mirrored her father's almost exactly.

"He stole *you*," Weston pointed out. "He's a liar as well."

Avalene gave Dante a pleading look, obviously looking for support.

Dante shrugged his shoulders. "'Tis hard to argue with the truth."

"Hah!" Weston crowed. "From his own lips, he admits to his crimes. No father would want his daughter wed to this monster. Once you are away from his vile influence, you will realize that convent life is by far preferable to being tied in marriage to such a fiend."

"You know nothing about him," she argued. "Just as you know nothing about me! I wish you had never—"

"That is enough," Dante interrupted. He put his hands on Avalene's shoulders and turned her to face him. "He is trying to do what he thinks is best for you. Do not say words you will soon regret."

Avalene pressed her lips together.

He leaned toward her father. "'Tis true, I am a murderer, a liar, and a thief. 'Tis equally true that I will use whatever monstrous talents I possess to keep your daughter at my side. You can take Avalene to a convent at the ends of the earth and I will find her and steal her away again. I will lie to God, himself, to free her. I will protect her with my life, and I will murder anyone who threatens her.

"You resigned yourself to a marriage between Faulke and Avalene, yet the Segraves also count murderers, liars, and thieves amongst their numbers. If Avalene had married Faulke and then not proved useful, I have little doubt that a fatal accident or illness would befall her. The woman means nothing to them, while her lineage means everything. To me, Avalene is all that matters. I love her more than my own life. She shall never want for anything as my wife, and as she so delicately pointed out, you will grow far richer. What more will it take to convince you that our marriage is what is best for everyone?"

Weston's piercing gaze moved to his daughter. "Do you love him?"

"More than my life."

Weston slowly nodded as he rolled his lower lip between his teeth. Dante's eyes widened as he realized that Avalene had inherited that particular habit, and then he smiled. He knew Weston's decision before he spoke.

"I will sign the betrothal," Weston said at last. "As you both pointed out, I would be foolish not to and my daughter is lost to me either way."

"She is not lost to you," Dante told him, his voice suddenly thick with emotion. "You are welcome to visit us whenever you wish, albeit the journey is a long one. You are also welcome to visit her while we remain in London. I know she has missed your company."

"I must leave Town by the end of the week," Weston said. "You had best make plans to be wed by then. I intend to witness the ceremony."

"That will not be a problem," Dante said. "I have already spoken with the priest at St. Paul's. The banns will be read before the ceremony and we can be wed on the morrow."

Weston nodded his agreement, and then motioned toward the betrothal contracts. "Send me the inkwell and quill, and let us be done with this matter."

While Weston signed copies of the contract, Avalene looked up at Dante, her lips slightly parted, her beautiful eyes dazed. Slowly, as if she were awaking from slumber, she returned his smile and whispered, "I am *free!* I am *yours.*"

He reached over to cover both her hands with his and continued to stare into her eyes, seeing the future there, knowing she saw the same in his eyes. The happiness that swept through him was like nothing he had known before. She was his. There were no more shadows. He could proclaim to the world that she belonged to him. He wanted to carry her to their chamber that moment to make proclamations that were best made in private. He was probably grinning like an idiot, and he didn't care. She was his.

When it was Dante's turn to sign the documents, Weston rose and clasped his hands behind his back, then began to pace before the table. The hall was silent except for the sounds of Weston's spurs striking the flagstones. Rami, who could doubtless understand no more than the tone of the previous conversations, began to hum in rhythm to the metallic *clink*s of Weston's spurs.

"I had planned to leave London on the morrow," Weston said, when Dante handed the signed documents to Mordecai. "There are arrangements I must make to extend my stay. Release the soldiers who came here with me and our horses, and I will take my leave."

"Reginald will have your men and horses in the courtyard anon," Dante said, even as he motioned the order to his steward.

Before he knew what she intended, Avalene rose and walked around the table to approach her father. Weston took the hands she offered, and then she kissed each of his cheeks. "Thank you, Father. I appreciate all you have done for me, today and every other day of my life."

"Here now," Weston said in a gruff voice when he noticed the tears in Avalene's eyes. His own eyes were suspiciously bright. "I will see you tomorrow at St. Paul's, and I will call upon you here every day until your ship sets sail. This is not the last you will see of me, my girl."

Avalene nodded, and then gave his cheeks another set of kisses before Reginald escorted Weston from the hall. Dante was at her side by the time she turned again toward the table and he drew her into his arms. She bit her lower lip and her gaze slid sideways toward Mordecai.

Dante did not care that they were in the great hall. He did not care that dozens of curious gazes were watching them. He slid his hands up the sides of her throat and cradled her head, and then he fitted her tight up against him and kissed her ruthlessly, his tongue scorching her mouth.

Avalene's arms were wrapped around his neck and his hands were beginning to stray to improper places when he heard someone clear his throat. And then he heard someone cough. Reluctantly recalled to their audience, he lifted his head but was immediately distracted by the sight of Avalene's kiss-swollen lips. His head began to lower again.

"Ahem-ahem-*a-hem*!"

Dante scowled and tilted his head toward the head table.

"I must be on my way as well," Mordecai said. He

began to walk toward the passage that led to Isabel's solar. "I told Edward I would be present during Faulke's first meeting with Isabel."

"Mordecai, wait." Dante took a step away from Avalene to help clear his senses. He lowered his voice so that only she and Mordecai could hear him. "You never involve yourself so closely in these affairs. Any of the king's advisers could have come here today with the contracts. What haven't you told me? What is the real reason I was sent to Coleway?"

"I would have thought you had figured some small part of that out by now." Mordecai looked pointedly toward Avalene.

What did that mean? "Are you telling me that Avalene is my reward? That much I already know."

Mordecai rolled his eyes. "Dante, you are always more aware of your surroundings than any other man, but you can be blind when you so choose to be. Have you never remarked upon our resemblance?"

"We look nothing alike." He said it surely, knowing it was no more than the obvious truth.

Mordecai tilted his head back and looked toward the ceiling, waiting. But for what? For Dante to figure out their resemblance? They were opposites in almost every aspect; dark hair versus blond, green eyes versus blue, tall versus slight, solid versus slim . . . Blond, blue-eyed, slender . . .

Dante's eyes widened and his gaze went to Avalene. Her eyes were already wide open as she stared at Mordecai. "*Gesù!*"

"Do not worry," he assured them, "'tis not as close a connection as you might fear. We are . . . distantly connected, but connected all the same."

"But why—"

"I told you at the beginning that this was about balance," Mordecai said. "The only purpose for my involvement was to make certain the two of you met. The balance that exists between you is the key; two halves of a whole. Together you are the perfect match." The wink he gave Dante was so quick that he might have imagined it, but there was definitely a twinkle in his eye. "Your children will be . . . exceptional."

Dante could only stare at him, dumbfounded.

"Now I must make certain Isabel does not ruin all of my efforts on her behalf." He tucked his hands into his sleeves and gave them a slight bow. "If you will excuse me."

It was not a question, and he did not wait for a reply that was obviously not coming. Both their gazes followed the magician as he left the hall. Avalene was the first to recover.

"Well, of course our children will be exceptional," she muttered. Her voice did not sound quite steady. "Next I suppose he shall tell us that there will be health and happiness all around. I tell you, these magicians are nothing but—"

Dante caught her face in his hands and took only a brief moment to appreciate its beauty before he kissed her, staking a claim that was already his. Her response was just as enthusiastic and they were soon at the point where they left off before Mordecai's rude interruption. Once again, the sounds of someone repeatedly clearing his throat penetrated his senses. Rami, bless him, reminding them that they were making a spectacle of themselves in the midst of the great hall. Dante didn't care, but he supposed Avalene might.

He took a reluctant step backward, but she looked none too steady on her feet. He smiled to himself as he wrapped one arm around her waist to steady her and then turned them toward the passageway to his quarters.

"'Tis time to start working on those exceptional children, my lady."

ACKNOWLEDGMENTS

My mother instilled in me a love of reading, a thirst for learning, and a sense of adventure. Without her influence and encouragement, I never could have become an author. She fostered the dream then helped it come true. I miss you every day, Mom.

1

❧

LONDON, 1293

> ### Isabel
>
> *In the game of chess, a queen
> can be the most valuable piece,
> or she can be the most vulner-
> able. Strategy, planning, and
> patience are her most valuable
> assets.*
>
> —ISABEL PLANTAGENET

"May I present Faulke Segrave, the only son and heir of the Baron of Carreg?" The English knight gestured for the second man to step forward, and then he cleared his throat. "May I also present Lord Faulke's cousin, Sir Richard Segrave of Hawksforth?"

At my nod, Sir Crispin cleared his throat once more, bowed low, and then returned to his station by the door. I eyed the two newcomers.

Everyone who knew Faulke Segrave claimed he was tall and handsome with dark hair and blue eyes, and had a personality most ladies found pleasing. What stood before me was definitely tall and blue-eyed. His brows and beard might be dark beneath the dust and dirt, but a chain mail hood covered most of his hair which made confirmation of its color difficult. The color of his beard was just as mysterious since it was caked with dried mud. As for a pleasing personality, I did not hold out much hope.

Faulke's cousin, Richard, was a near twin in appearance as well as in filth. The men's heights were similar, their eyes the same shade of blue, their scowls equally fierce. Everything they wore from the soles of their boots to mid-thigh was a stiff, dusty brown color, the obvious effects of being thigh-deep in mud at some point, and then there were liberal splatters of dried mud from their thighs to their shoulders. They both looked—and smelled—as if they had recently rolled through a bog.

The two Segrave men did not react to their introductions in any way, but their unwavering scowls made it plain they did not want to be here. Neither did I. Those two facts did not bode well for this meeting.

I lifted two fingers of my right hand no more than an inch and then let them settle again onto the polished wooden arm of my chair. The captain of my guard recognized the signal and stepped forward to introduce me to our visitors in his heavily accented English.

"I present to you Her Royal Highness Isabel of Ascalon, Dowager Crown Princess of Rheinbaden, Princess of England, Countess of Malden, Baroness Helmsford, Baroness Sildon, daughter of King Edward of England, and widow of Crown Prince Hartman of Rheinbaden."

The list of titles was meant to intimidate, to make certain the Segraves understood who held the advantage between us. Gerhardt returned to his place by my side and we all waited as the Segraves stared back at us in a silence that grew more uncomfortable with each passing moment. No one in the room shifted their weight or cleared their throat or coughed. The only sounds were the muffled chirps of songbirds from the gardens beyond the windows of my solar.

It soon became obvious that the Segraves intended to turn this silence into some sort of contest. Men were so foolish. And so predictable. They were about to learn that they would never outlast me in a contest of wills. I had played court politics all my life and knew every trick to maintain a superior bargaining position. I would do nothing to indicate I had any interest in them or in the outcome of this meeting. Instead I continued to stare at the two men just as rudely as they stared back at me, even though it was difficult to show no reaction to their appearance.

The differences between us might be comical under different circumstances. Their garments were covered in mud while mine smelled pleasantly of the sandalwood-lined trunks where I stored my finest clothing. I doubt they had washed their hands or faces in the last week whereas I had taken a long, leisurely bath in rosewater just that morning. I had spent hours preparing for this meeting to make certain there would be no doubt in the Segraves' minds that they were dealing with a very wealthy, very powerful noblewoman. They looked as if someone had just dragged them from a ditch. However, beneath the mud and grime, their armor and clothing looked to be of fine quality. Not as fine as what I wore, of course, but then again, few people could afford garments like mine.

It had taken scores of seamstresses hundreds of hours to stitch delicate flowers, vines, and birds into the pink silk of my bliaut, all in gold thread. A snow white surcoat covered my gown, lined with the same pink silk and trimmed with braid made of more gold threads. Tiny pink glass beads formed the profile of an eagle with spread wings on each of my shoulders, with the eyes, beaks, and talons worked in gold beads. White, gold, and pink silk ribbons wove around the dark plait of my hair and ended with a thick gold tassel that brushed against the floor when I stood up. On my head I wore a crenellated barbette that mimicked the shape of a crown, encrusted with seed pearls and lined with strands of white ostrich feathers that bowed and swayed with the slightest movement of my head. More gold and pearls hung from my earrings, necklace, and girdle, and thousands of seed pearls covered the long, fitted cuffs of the sleeves that encased my arms from wrist to elbow.

The cost of the jewels and clothing I wore could feed a small army for a year, or so my husband had claimed when he presented me with the wardrobe. The entire ensemble probably outweighed the Segraves' armor, but the effect was worth a little discomfort. I had greeted kings in these garments. They were seeing me at my very best. I sincerely hoped I was seeing them at their worst.

Most people consider an audience with royalty an occasion of some importance. At the very least, they don clean clothing and shave. That the Segraves did not care enough to even bathe before we met spoke volumes.

The men continued to study us with derisive sneers, their gazes already moving beyond me to survey my people. They looked at us as if they found our cleanliness somehow ridiculous. I had insisted that everyone wear their finest court clothing, which meant my people wore the royal colors of Rheinbaden. My soldiers wore white shirts and breeches covered by pink surcoats that were emblazoned with the white Rheinbaden eagle upon their chests. My ladies also wore pink surcoats with white bliauts trimmed in pearls. More than a dozen long, colorful pennants hung from the walls. These were the banners we marched beneath during our long journey to England: marks of heraldry that announced to all we encountered that we were from the royal court of Rheinbaden. The entire solar was awash in white, pink, and gold.

Just this morning my one and only friend in England, Avalene de Forshay, had surveyed us with a critical eye and claimed we were so radiant that only a religious painting could inspire greater awe. It was the exact effect I had hoped to create, but the mocking looks from the Segraves gave me pause. And then I recalled that most English considered pink an unmanly color. They did not understand that pink represents the color of blood mixed with snow in the Alps of Rheinbaden.

Richard leaned closer to his cousin, obviously meaning to speak under his breath, but the utter silence in the solar amplified his voice. "We should have insisted—"

Faulke cut him off with a sharp look, and then he turned to glare again at me.

Gerhardt, the captain of my guard, expressed my sentiments exactly. *"Sie sind beleidigend."*

Aye, they were insulting. I had expected no less from them, but I had hoped. Gerhardt, however, was too stoic for foolish notions such as hope. Like most of my people, the captain of my guard bore the obvious marks of his Germanic heritage; blond hair and blue eyes, tall and solidly built, and absolutely no sense of humor. I watched his hand flex on the hilt of his sword as his mouth became a flat line. Sometimes Gerhardt saw insult where none existed, but in this instance I agreed with him.

Regardless of insults, the thought of staring at each other for the remainder of the afternoon held little appeal. I let my mouth curve into what I hoped was a condescending smile, and then I spoke loudly enough for everyone in the solar to hear, confident of the Segraves' inability to understand German. *"Soll das ein Scherz sein? Kommen. Bring uns mal zum Lachen."*

Gerhardt hesitated, and then his mouth turned upward into a painful-looking smile. My two ladies-in-waiting managed to giggle. There were even a few guffaws from the half dozen soldiers who stood behind me. None of it sounded genuine to my ears, but the Segraves did not know us and would probably take the bait. Another political lesson was to never let an insult go unanswered. The Segraves' deepening scowls said they did, indeed, believe they were being laughed at.

Faulke's hands became fists at his sides and his gaze went to Gerhardt. His voice was deeper than I expected, and I found myself momentarily distracted by the sound of it. "Do *any* of you speak English?"

The room again fell silent.

One does not address a servant when their master or mistress is present. Regardless of that fact, Faulke had yet to offer a formal greeting that would acknowledge our introduction. It was insult upon insult, and it would serve him right if we all pretended ignorance. I actually toyed with the idea until Faulke took a threatening step toward Gerhardt. Political posturing was not worth spilled blood. Not yet, anyway.

I rose from my seat and saw Faulke's eyes widen. He was taller than most men, but so am I. The wooden heels I wore allowed me to gaze squarely into his face while the barbette made me appear even taller. The expression I wore was one I practiced often in a mirror; aloof disinterest. "My subjects do not speak to *ausländers* without my permission, Lord Faulke. If you have something to say to me, I can converse in English, French, Latin, or German."

He simply stared at me.

"I believe additional introductions are in order," I went on in a brisk tone. "The man you just addressed is the captain of my guard and my closest advisor. Gerhardt also speaks English. My ladies, Gretchen and Hilda, along with most of my people, speak only a few words of your language, but that should not matter since anything you wish to say to them should be said first to me."

This was the moment I had waited for since the Segraves first entered this chamber, radiating their anger and contempt. They were men and therefore thought themselves above me. I had just corrected their thinking. Now would come the well-deserved apologies.

"Do you speak Welsh?" Faulke asked.

"Of course not," I quipped. "The Welsh are barbarians. Their language is hardly one I would—"

"*Chwerthin yn uchel,*" Faulke said to his cousin.

Richard smiled, and then he laughed out loud. The laughter stopped abruptly when Faulke made a quick cutting motion with his hand, and then Richard's face resettled into a mask of surly anger.

"We can play childish games all day," Faulke said. "I do not particularly care who declares themselves the winner."

I blinked once in astonishment. So much for an apology. And so much for thinking he would not know how to answer *my* insult. Before I could think of an appropriate response, he, too, decided to make a more informative introduction.

"An hour ago I was faced with the prospect of immediate imprisonment or a royal bride. You may be happy to know that I have just signed our betrothal papers. It seems we shall be married within the month." He folded his arms across his chest, which brought my attention to the size of his arms. They were huge. "You might be a princess, but I am the man you will soon call your lord and master."

His arrogance made mine pale in comparison, which was not an easy feat. He also made my father's generosity sound like a punishment, the ungrateful churl.

"Most men would think themselves blessed to gain such prizes," I retorted.

"Most men are not brought to the altar at the point of a sword."

My gaze went to his side and I noticed for the first time that his scabbard was empty. Indeed, both men had been relieved of their weapons. So the rumors were true. The Segraves had been brought to Ashland Palace as prisoners. Little wonder they were so angry. Still, it was their own greed that formed this prison, and they were being amply compensated for their troubles.

Despite my own frustration with the situation, I made an unexpected discovery as I watched Faulke draw in a deep breath and then slowly release it through pursed lips. Despite the wild beard, there was something appealing about the shape of his mouth. That is, if one were attracted to rude, uncivilized sorts of men with intriguing mouths, which I am not. Still, amidst the dirt and anger, I was beginning to understand what other women might find somewhat appealing. He was a man who had Presence, that indefinable air that was part and parcel of all natural leaders. And if pressed I might even admit that his eyes were his most compelling physical feature. They reflected a sharp, piercing intelligence that he directed squarely in my direction. His unwavering gaze made me feel as if he knew full well there were secrets inside my head that affected him, and I suspected he was already developing strategies to pry them loose. I would do well not to underestimate this man.

"Our marriage will provide your family with more wealth and power than you could have ever hoped for from a marriage to Avalene de Forshay," I pointed out. "Gilbert de Clare is the only other Englishman to be so rewarded by our king and he was already a powerful earl before he wed my sister, Joan. Indeed, de Clare petitioned my father for years before he finally won my father's blessing. By all accounts the earl is well pleased with the marriage. You have just been handed a similar marriage on a platter."

His appealing mouth turned downward and the tone of his voice turned darker. "An hour ago I also learned that Avalene de Forshay, the woman I was legally betrothed to marry, has been promised to another and put forever beyond my reach by your father's order." He shook his head. "The day may come when I am pleased with our impending marriage, but today is not that day."

I was not particularly pleased with this day myself. I had hoped for a man who would be the complete opposite of my first husband, Hartman. This would teach me to be careful what I wished for.

Of course I had expected a certain amount of resentment from the Segraves. After all, Faulke just learned that he had been outmaneuvered by my father. Still, I had not anticipated this level of hostility. He had never met Avalene de Forshay until he tried to abduct her a month ago. He had held her prisoner for less than a day, so he could hardly claim loss of affections. The titles he would gain with my dowry included an earldom, several baronies, manors, lands, and all the wealth that went with those lands. Faulke would soon be one of the richest and most powerful men in England. All he had to do was tamp down his ambitions in Wales. Was that really such a sacrifice?

It was a stupid question. I had been surrounded by ambitious men all my life and none of them welcomed the sacrifice of their ambitions with open arms. Why did I think Faulke would be any different? I knew the Segraves' history. "Ruthless Ambition" should be their family motto.

I recalled a conversation I had earlier in the day with Faulke's former betrothed. Avalene had been terrified at the thought of becoming his bride. However, she had

452

made a thorough study of Faulke and his family in anticipation of their marriage. She had proved my best source of information about the Segraves since I was now his betrothed and she was freed to marry another man, one she loved to distraction. She had happily shared her vast stores of Segrave knowledge with me. Indeed, she often seemed downright grateful, as if imparting her information about the Segraves was somehow cleansing. "Lady Avalene warned me that you would not be happy with our betrothal, but I did not fully comprehend just how displeased you would be."

Something dark flickered in his eyes, a spark of interest perhaps, as if I had just said something he wanted to hear. "Gilbert de Clare did not want to wed your sister half as much as I wanted to wed Lady Avalene. She is everything I want in a wife."

Which meant that I was *not* what he wanted. Was he trying to make me jealous of Avalene, or simply taking another opportunity to insult me?

Most women *would* be jealous of Avalene de Forshay. She possessed the variety of fair-haired beauty that turned men's brains to sap. She also had a sweet, sincere demeanor, and naïve honesty that made it impossible not to like her. Even if she were an ugly shrew, it was difficult to be jealous of a woman who was head over heels in love with a notorious assassin. Dante Chiavari, her soon-to-be husband, was not even an Englishman. If my father had told me I must wed a murderer for hire and move to Italy for the remainder of my life, I would think it the harshest of punishments. Avalene was ecstatic. As far as I was concerned, the woman inspired more astonishment than jealousy. And that proved how little Faulke knew Avalene if he thought he could stir my jealousy toward her.

I pretended to adjust the cuff of my sleeve as I considered my response, letting my fingers trail across the smooth bumps of the seed pearls that encased my arm. One sleeve of my gown was worth more than Avalene's entire dowry. The Segraves were driven by greed. There was nothing sentimental about the reasons he wanted Avalene for his wife.

"You are barely acquainted with Lady Avalene," I said, "which means that what she would have brought to your marriage was more important than the lady herself. And yet she has very little in the way of lands or wealth."

He spread his hands and lifted his shoulders, a silent admission of the truth. "Surely you are aware of the reasons I sought her out."

"Aye. Our impending marriage is a direct result of those reasons," I said, and then I repeated the story told to me by the king. "Your father and the other English Marcher barons on the frontier of Wales rule your Welsh lands by your own laws. Many resent the fealty you owe to England and most would like to set themselves up as kings in Wales, but you would have to fight the Welsh as well as my father's armies if you rebel. Avalene is the only English noblewoman with direct blood ties to the last Prince of Wales. If you wed Avalene and then father a son on her, the native Welsh would accept him as their prince even as a newborn babe. They would fight willingly in an army of Englishmen if it meant they would see one of their own once again on the Welsh throne. Other Marcher barons in Wales would be drawn to stand with you to gain independence from England. You could rule all of Wales through such a child."

"Those possibilities existed," he admitted, as he tilted his head in a mockery of a bow. "However, now that your father has interfered, there is no longer any possibility that Avalene will be my wife."

"My father is no fool."

"Nor am I," he warned. "You were married nearly ten

years and yet you have no children. My father is the first baron of Carreg and he has no other male heirs. It appears your father has found an expensive yet certain means of extinguishing my family's line and insuring that all of our lands and titles will revert to the crown."

Ah, here was the true crux of his anger. I had hoped all the Segraves would be so blinded by the wealth and titles my father intended to rain upon them that they would meekly accept the explanations for my childless state and hope for the best. The accusation should not have caught me unaware, but I had to force my reply through stiff lips. "My husband contracted mumps many years ago, just before our first child was stillborn."

That much was true. Hartman and I had both contracted mumps and then I went into labor while I was still ill. Hartman nearly died. I wanted to. According to the physicians, my poor babe never stood a chance.

Everyone knew that mumps was a mild illness in children, but much more severe in adults. Indeed, cases as severe as Hartman's often left a man unable to father children. My child's birth had also been sufficiently difficult to make the physicians question my ability to carry another child. There was crushing disappointment, but no real surprise when I could not get pregnant again.

After I became a widow and once more marriageable, my father made certain everyone at his court knew that I had carried a child before Hartman's illness. Without that explanation, a barren daughter would be impossible to marry off to any nobleman who needed an heir, no matter my wealth or my bloodline. However, my father was not foolish enough to marry me to anyone he intended to keep as an ally. He also had a limited amount of time before the gossip in Rheinbaden followed me to England.

"Mumps is the rumor," Faulke agreed, "but it does not change the fact that your ability to produce a healthy heir is unproven. The betrothal contracts are such that only an heir of your body can inherit the lands and titles your father will bestow upon me, as well as the lands and titles my family already possess."

"Gilbert de Clare agreed to the same terms when he wed Joan," I pointed out. "She was also unproven and yet provided his heir within the first year of their marriage and even now she is pregnant with their third child in three years."

"Aye, the fertility of your mother and sister proved persuasive in getting my father to agree to the terms," he said. "That, and the fact that you carried a child before your husband fell ill."

The look he gave me said he did not share his father's opinion. I could hardly blame him. No one in England knew that Hartman's mistress bore him four children after his illness while I remained childless. At least, the English didn't know about it just yet. Rumors were bound to follow my return to England. One of my own people might let something slip. But in the meantime, the king had, indeed, found a way to extinguish Faulke's line.

I had sworn an oath to my father that I would not reveal the truth before my marriage. Trapping Faulke in this marriage would save hundreds, likely thousands of lives by averting a war and it would remove the Segraves as a threat in Wales. Of greater importance to me, personally, was my father's promise that he would assure the future of my people should anything happen to me. Assuring their future meant insuring they had a future. The unspoken threat was that my people would suffer greatly if I proved difficult. All in all, marriage to this churl was a small price to pay to keep my people safe and prevent a war.

A year ago I never could have envisioned a day when the son of a lowly English baron had to be blackmailed into marrying me. Granted, kings and princes would never again vie for my hand, but I still could scarce believe that my future would be banishment to the wilderness of Wales to live amongst the barbarians with a man who was most likely a traitor and possibly a murderer.

I dismissed the guilt I felt about my part in this deception. It was the Segraves' actions that had led all of us to this place. Faulke was hardly the innocent victim. Indeed, he even looked the part of a villain with his wild beard and fouled clothes. I gazed at him with cool eyes. "The terms of our marriage are due in great part to your own matrimonial history, Lord Faulke. You are extremely young to have buried three wives. My father found it most coincidental that your wives tended to die whenever a more attractive marriage prospect presented itself."

In an instant the anger in his eyes turned to icy fury. His lips barely moved. "I did not murder my wives."

"I do not particularly care," I lied, although I did store away the knowledge that the subject of his unfortunate wives could provoke a reaction. "The terms of our marriage are such that you now have a vested interest in my health and longevity. If I die without an heir, everything reverts to the crown, including your father's titles. If I die with an heir, my child immediately inherits the lands and titles you hold in stewardship, although you may act as regent if the child is younger than twenty."

"I am well aware of the terms," Faulke bit out. "I am a wealthy earl only so long as you live."

"My father feels that is sufficient motivation to insure I do not fall victim to the sorts of unusual accidents and illnesses that befell your previous brides."

Faulke released another long breath, the muscles in his jaw now rigid with anger. "Are you such a dutiful daughter that you would willingly enter into marriage with a man rumored to murder his wives, a man who makes no secret of the fact that he wants another woman as his bride?"

"It is a daughter's duty to obey her father," I said in an even tone. "It is the duty of a princess to serve her country and to obey her king. Do you suggest I commit treason?"

"Refusing a suitor is hardly grounds for treason," he growled. "You are the daughter of a king and the widow of a crown prince. Aside from my unsavory reputation and ambitions, one of my grandfathers was in trade, the other was a lowly knight in service to your great uncle at Pembroke. My grandmothers are even less illustrious. The only reason we hold any title at all is because my father happened to be in the right place to save your grandfather's life on the battlefield. Will you truly be content with a man of such ill-repute with so low a rank, a man with the blood of commoners in his veins?"

His questions gave me pause. He was the first person who expected me to voice an opinion on the matter. I wondered why he cared. My opinion counted for nothing. It certainly wouldn't make a difference in our circumstances.

And then his strategy became suddenly clear. He could not refuse the betrothal without gravely insulting his king. Men had found themselves locked in the Tower for more minor offenses, and it sounded as if he had been promised exactly that outcome. Faulke obviously valued his freedom and thought there was another escape from the trap of our marriage. "Do you think I have some choice in this matter?"

"Daughters hold a special place in the hearts of their fathers," he said with a small shrug. "Surely your father would take your happiness into consideration."

Was he jesting? If my father had a special place in his heart for paternal love and affection, I had never encountered it. But the children of kings are a far different matter than the children of commoners, or, more specifically, the children of a newly made baron. Faulke had three daughters. Did they hold a special place in *his* heart? What a novel concept.

"The king is most assuredly unlike most fathers," I said. "He takes into consideration what is best for England, which also happens to be what is best for him. I suppose he hopes for my happiness, but I am certain it is a sacrifice he is willing to make should he be forced to choose between my happiness and the good of the realm."

Faulke studied my face for a long moment, and then he tilted his head forward to rub his brow. His shoulders dropped and I could almost see the fight seep out of him. "Then it seems we are to be married."